#1 *New York Times* bestselling author Nora Roberts delves into the world of elite firefighters who thrive on danger and adrenaline—men and women who wouldn't know how to live life if it wasn't on the edge.

Little else in life is as dangerous as fire jumping. But there's also little else as thrilling—at least to Rowan Tripp. Being a Missoula smoke jumper is in Rowan's blood: her father is a legend in the field. At this point, returning to the wilds of Montana for the season feels like coming home—even with reminders of the partner she lost last season still lingering in the air.

One of the best of this year's rookie crop, Gulliver Curry is a walking contradiction, a hotshot firefighter with a big vocabulary and a winter job at a kids' arcade. And though Rowan, as a rule, doesn't hook up with other smoke jumpers, Gull is convinced he can change her mind . . .

But everything is thrown off balance when a dark presence lashes out against Rowan, looking to blame someone for last year's tragedy. Rowan knows she can't complicate things with Gull—any distractions in the air or on the ground could be lethal. But if she doesn't find someone she can lean on when the heat gets intense, her life may go down in flames.

CHASING FIRE

"A riveting, five-alarm tale of romantic suspense." —*Booklist*

"A wonderfully written, compelling novel that perfectly blends romance, suspense, and a touch of humor . . . Roberts' writing is exceptional." —*The Newark Star-Ledger*

"Exhilarating." —*Midwest Book Review*

Turn the page for a complete list of titles by Nora Roberts and J. D. Robb from the Berkley Publishing Group.

Nora Roberts

Series

Nora Roberts & J. D. Robb

REMEMBER WHEN

J. D. Robb

Anthologies

FROM THE HEART
A LITTLE MAGIC
A LITTLE FATE

MOON SHADOWS
(with Jill Gregory, Ruth Ryan Langan, and Marianne Willman)

The Once Upon Series
(with Jill Gregory, Ruth Ryan Langan, and Marianne Willman)

ONCE UPON A CASTLE
ONCE UPON A STAR
ONCE UPON A DREAM

ONCE UPON A ROSE
ONCE UPON A KISS
ONCE UPON A MIDNIGHT

SILENT NIGHT
(with Susan Plunkett, Dee Holmes, and Claire Cross)

OUT OF THIS WORLD
(with Laurell K. Hamilton, Susan Krinard, and Maggie Shayne)

BUMP IN THE NIGHT
(with Mary Blayney, Ruth Ryan Langan, and Mary Kay McComas)

DEAD OF NIGHT
(with Mary Blayney, Ruth Ryan Langan, and Mary Kay McComas)

THREE IN DEATH

SUITE 606
(with Mary Blayney, Ruth Ryan Langan, and Mary Kay McComas)

IN DEATH

THE LOST
(with Patricia Gaffney, Mary Blayney, and Ruth Ryan Langan)

THE OTHER SIDE
(with Mary Blayney, Patricia Gaffney, Ruth Ryan Langan, and Mary Kay McComas)

TIME OF DEATH

THE UNQUIET
(with Mary Blayney, Patricia Gaffney, Ruth Ryan Langan, and Mary Kay McComas)

MIRROR, MIRROR
(with Mary Blayney, Elaine Fox, Mary Kay McComas, and R. C. Ryan)

Also available . . .

THE OFFICIAL NORA ROBERTS COMPANION
(edited by Denise Little and Laura Hayden)

CHASING
FIRE

NORA ROBERTS

JOVE BOOKS, NEW YORK

THE BERKLEY PUBLISHING GROUP
Published by the Penguin Group
Penguin Group (USA) LLC.
375 Hudson Street, New York, New York 10014, USA

USA I Canada I UK I Ireland I Australia I New Zealand I India I South Africa I China

Penguin Books Ltd., Registered Offices: 80 Strand, London WC2R 0RL, England
For more information about the Penguin Group, visit penguin.com.

CHASING FIRE

A Jove Book / published by arrangement with the author

Jove Books are published by The Berkley Publishing Group.
JOVE® is a registered trademark of Penguin Group (USA) LLC.
The "J" design is a trademark of Penguin Group (USA) LLC.

For information, address: The Berkley Publishing Group,
a division of Penguin Group (USA) LLC,
375 Hudson Street, New York, New York 10014.

ISBN: 978-0-515-15473-3

PUBLISHING HISTORY
G. P. Putnam's Sons hardcover edition / April 2011
Jove mass-market edition / April 2012
Read Pink mass-market edition / October 2013

PRINTED IN THE UNITED STATES OF AMERICA

10   9   8   7   6   5   4   3   2   1

Cover design by Richard Hasselberger.

To Bruce
For understanding me, and loving me anyway

INITIAL
ATTACK

Soon kindled and soon burnt.

WILLIAM SHAKESPEARE

1

Caught in the crosshairs of wind above the Bitterroots, the jump ship fought to find its stream. Fire boiling over the land jabbed its fists up through towers of smoke as if trying for a knockout punch.

From her seat Rowan Tripp angled to watch a seriously pissed-off Mother Nature's big show. In minutes she'd be inside it, enclosed in the mad world of searing heat, leaping flames, choking smoke. She'd wage war with shovel and saw, grit and guile. A war she didn't intend to lose.

Her stomach bounced along with the plane, a sensation she'd taught herself to ignore. She'd flown all of her life, and had fought wildfires every season since her eighteenth birthday. For the last half of those eight years she'd jumped fire.

She'd studied, trained, bled and burned—outwilled pain and exhaustion to become a Zulie. A Missoula smoke jumper.

She stretched out her long legs as best she could for a moment, rolled her shoulders under her pack to keep them loose.

Beside her, her jump partner watched as she did. His fingers did a fast tap dance on his thighs. "She looks mean."

"We're meaner."

He shot her a fast, toothy grin. "Bet your ass."

Nerves. She could all but feel them riding along his skin.

Near the end of his first season, Rowan thought, and Jim Brayner needed to pump himself up before a jump. Some always would, she decided, while others caught short catnaps to bank sleep against the heavy withdrawals to come.

She was first jump on this load, and Jim would be right behind her. If he needed a little juice, she'd supply it.

"Kick her ass, more like. It's the first real bitch we've jumped in a week." She gave him an easy elbow jab. "Weren't you the one who kept saying the season was done?"

He tapped those busy fingers on his thighs to some inner rhythm. "Nah, that was Matt," he insisted, grin still wide as he deflected the claim onto his brother.

"That's what you get with a couple Nebraska farm boys. Don't you have a hot date tomorrow night?"

"My dates are always hot."

She couldn't argue, as she'd seen Jim snag women like rainbow trout anytime the unit had pulled a night off to kick it up in town. He'd hit on her, she remembered, about two short seconds after he'd arrived on base. Still, he'd been good-natured about her shutdown. She'd implemented a firm policy against dating within the unit.

Otherwise, she might've been tempted. He had that open, innocent face offset by the quick grin, and the gleam in the eye. For fun, she thought, for a careless pop of the cork out of the lust bottle. For serious—even if she'd been looking for serious—he'd never do the trick. Though they were the same age, he was just too young, too fresh off the farm—and maybe just a little too sweet under the thin layer of green that hadn't burned off quite yet.

"Which girl's going to bed sad and lonely if you're still dancing with the dragon?" she asked him.

"Lucille."

"That's the little one—with the giggle."

His fingers tapped, tapped, tapped on his knee. "She does more than giggle."

"You're a dog, Romeo."

He tipped back his head, let out a series of sharp barks that made her laugh.

"Make sure Dolly doesn't find out you're out howling," she commented. She knew—everyone knew—he'd been banging one of the base cooks like a drum all season.

"I can handle Dolly." The tapping picked up pace. "Gonna handle Dolly."

Okay, Rowan thought, something bent out of shape there, which was why smart people didn't bang or get banged by people they worked with.

She gave him a little nudge because those busy fingers concerned her. "Everything okay with you, farm boy?"

His pale blue eyes met hers for an instant, then shifted away while his knees did a bounce under those drumming fingers. "No problems here. It's going to be smooth sailing like always. I just need to get down there."

She put a hand over his to still it. "You need to keep your head in the game, Jim."

"It's there. Right there. Look at her, swishing her tail," he said. "Once us Zulies get down there, she won't be so sassy. We'll put her down, and I'll be making time with Lucille tomorrow night."

Unlikely, Rowan thought to herself. Her aerial view of the fire put her gauge at a solid two days of hard, sweaty work.

And that was if things went their way.

Rowan reached for her helmet, nodded toward their spotter. "Getting ready. Stay chilly, farm boy."

"I'm ice."

Cards—so dubbed as he carried a pack everywhere—wound his way through the load of ten jumpers and equipment to the rear of the plane, attached the tail of his harness to the restraining line.

Even as Cards shouted out the warning to guard their reserves, Rowan hooked her arm over hers. Cards, a tough-bodied vet, pulled the door open to a rush of wind tainted with smoke and fuel. As he reached for the first set of streamers, Rowan set her helmet over her short crown of blond hair, strapped it, adjusted her face mask.

She watched the streamers doing their colorful dance against the smoke-stained sky. Their long strips kicked in the turbulence, spiraled toward the southwest, seemed to roll, to rise, then caught another bounce before whisking into the trees.

Cards called, "Right!" into his headset, and the pilot turned the plane.

The second set of streamers snapped out, spun like a kid's wind-up toy. The strips wrapped together, pulled apart, then dropped onto the tree-flanked patch of the jump site.

"The wind line's running across that creek, down to the trees and across the site," Rowan said to Jim.

Over her, the spotter and pilot made more adjustments, and another set of streamers snapped out into the slipstream.

"It's got a bite to it."

"Yeah. I saw." Jim swiped the back of his hand over his mouth before strapping on his helmet and mask.

"Take her to three thousand," Cards shouted.

Jump altitude. As first man, first stick, Rowan rose to take position. "About three hundred yards of drift," she shouted to Jim, repeating what she'd heard Cards telling the pilot. "But there's that bite. Don't get caught downwind."

"Not my first party."

She saw his grin behind the bars of his face mask—confident, even eager. But something in his eyes, she thought. Just for a flash. She started to speak again, but Cards, already in position to the right of the door, called out, "Are you ready?"

"We're ready," she called back.

"Hook up."

Rowan snapped the static line in place.

"Get in the door!"

She dropped to sitting, legs out in the wicked slipstream, body leaning back. Everything roared. Below her extended legs, fire ran in vibrant red and gold.

There was nothing but the moment, nothing but the wind and fire and the twist of exhilaration and fear that always, always surprised her.

"Did you see the streamers?"

"Yeah."

"You see the spot?"

She nodded, bringing both into her head, following those colorful strips to the target.

Cards repeated what she'd told Jim, almost word for word. She only nodded again, eyes on the horizon, letting her breath come easy, visualizing herself flying, falling, navigating the sky down to the heart of the jump spot.

She went through her four-point check as the plane completed its circle and leveled out.

Cards pulled his head back in. "Get ready."

Ready-steady, her father said in her head. She grabbed both sides of the door, sucked in a breath.

And when the spotter's hand slapped her shoulder, she launched herself into the sky.

Nothing she knew topped that one instant of insanity, hurling herself into the void. She counted off in her mind, a task as automatic as breathing, and rolled in that charged sky to watch the plane fly past. She caught sight of Jim, hurtling after her.

Again, she turned her body, fighting the drag of wind until her feet were down. With a yank and jerk, her canopy burst open. She scouted out Jim again, felt a tiny pop of relief when she saw his chute spread against the empty sky. In that pocket of eerie silence, beyond the roar of the plane, above the voice of the fire, she gripped her steering toggles.

The wind wanted to drag her north, and was pretty insistent about it. Rowan was just as insistent on staying on the course she'd mapped out in her head. She watched the ground as she steered against the frisky crosscurrent that pinched its fingers on her canopy, doing its best to circle her into the tailwind.

The turbulence that had caught the streamers struck her in gusty slaps while the heat pumped up from the burning ground. If the wind had its way, she'd overshoot the jump spot, fly into the verge of trees, risk a hang-up. Or worse, it could shove her west, and into the flames.

She dragged hard on her toggle, glanced over in time to see Jim catch the downwind and go into a spin.

"Pull right! Pull right!"

"I got it! I got it."

But to her horror, he pulled left.

"Right, goddamn it!"

She had to turn for her final, and the pleasure of a near seamless slide into the glide path drowned in sheer panic. Jim soared west, helplessly towed by a horizontal canopy.

Rowan hit the jump site, rolled. She gained her feet, slapped her release. And heard it as she stood in the center of the blaze.

She heard her jump partner's scream.

THE SCREAM followed her as she shot up in bed, echoed in her head as she sat huddled in the dark.

Stop, stop, stop! she ordered herself. And dropped her head on her updrawn knees until she got her breath back.

No point in it, she thought. No point in reliving it, in going over all the details, all the moments, or asking herself, again, if she could've done just one thing differently.

Asking herself why Jim hadn't followed her drop into the jump spot. Why he'd pulled the wrong toggle. Because, *goddamn it,* he'd pulled the wrong toggle.

And had flown straight into the towers and lethal branches of those burning trees.

Months ago now, she reminded herself. She'd had the long winter to get past it. And thought she had.

Being back on base triggered it, she admitted, and rubbed her hands over her face, back over the hair she'd had cut into a short, maintenance-free cap only days before.

Fire season was nearly on them. Refresher training started in a couple short hours. Memories, regrets, grief—they were bound to pay a return visit. But she needed sleep, another hour before she got up, geared up for the punishing three-mile run.

She was damn good at willing herself to sleep, anyplace, anytime. Coyote-ing in a safe zone during a fire, on a shuddering jump plane. She knew how to eat and sleep when the need and opportunity opened.

But when she closed her eyes again, she saw herself back on the plane, turning toward Jim's grin.

Knowing she had to shake it off, she shoved out of bed. She'd grab a shower, some caffeine, stuff in some carbs, then do a light workout to warm up for the physical training test.

It continued to baffle her fellow jumpers that she never drank coffee unless it was her only choice. She liked the cold and sweet. After she'd dressed, Rowan hit her stash of Cokes, grabbed an energy bar. She took both outside where the sky was still shy of first light and the air stayed chill in the early spring of western Montana.

In the vast sky stars blinked out, little candles snuffed. She pulled the dark and quiet around her, found some comfort in it. In an hour, give or take, the base would wake, and testosterone would flood the air.

Since she generally preferred the company of men, for conversation, for companionship, she didn't mind being outnumbered by them. But she prized her quiet time, those little pieces of alone that became rare and precious during the season. Next best thing to sleep before a day filled with pressure and stress, she thought.

She could tell herself not to worry about the run, remind herself she'd been vigilant about her PT all winter, was in the best shape of her life—and it didn't mean a damn.

Anything could happen. A turned ankle, a mental lapse, a sudden, debilitating cramp. Or she could just have a bad run. Others had. Sometimes they came back from it, sometimes they didn't.

And a negative attitude wasn't going to help. She chowed down on the energy bar, gulped caffeine into her system and watched the day eke its first shimmer over the rugged, snow-tipped western peaks.

When she ducked into the gym minutes later, she noted her alone time was over.

"Hey, Trigger." She nodded to the man doing crunches on a mat. "What do you know?"

"I know we're all crazy. What the hell am I doing here, Ro? I'm forty-fucking-three years old."

She unrolled a mat, started her stretches. "If you weren't crazy, weren't here, you'd still be forty-fucking-three."

At six-five, barely making the height restrictions, Trigger Gulch was a lean, mean machine with a west Texas twang and an affection for cowboy boots.

He huffed through a quick series of pulsing crunches. "I could be lying on a beach in Waikiki."

"You could be selling real estate in Amarillo."

"I could do that." He mopped his face, pointed at her. "Nine-to-five the next fifteen years, then retire to that beach in Waikiki."

"Waikiki's full of people, I hear."

"Yeah, that's the damn trouble." He sat up, a good-looking man with gray liberally salted through his brown hair, and a scar snaked on his left knee from a meniscus repair. He smiled at her as she lay on her back, pulled her right leg up and toward her nose. "Looking good, Ro. How was your fat season?"

"Busy." She repeated the stretch on her left leg. "I've been looking forward to coming back, getting me some rest."

He laughed at that. "How's your dad?"

"Good as gold." Rowan sat up, then folded her long, curvy body in two. "Gets a little wistful this time of year." She closed ice-blue eyes and pulled her flexed feet back toward the crown of her head. "He misses the start-up, everybody coming back, but the business doesn't give him time to brood."

"Even people who aren't us like to jump out of planes."

"Pay good money for it, too. Had a good one last week." She spread her legs in a wide vee, grabbed her toes and again bent forward. "Couple celebrated their fiftieth anniversary with a jump. Gave me a bottle of French champagne as a tip."

Trigger sat where he was, watching as she pushed to her feet to begin the first sun salutation. "Are you still teaching that hippie class?"

Rowan flowed from Up Dog to Down Dog, turned her head to shoot Trigger a pitying look. "It's yoga, old man, and yeah, I'm still doing some personal trainer work off-season. Helps keep the lard out of my ass. How about you?"

"I pile the lard on. It gives me more to burn off when the real work starts."

"If this season's as slow as last, we'll all be sitting on fat asses. Have you seen Cards? He doesn't appear to have turned down any second helpings this winter."

"Got a new woman."

"No shit." Looser, she picked up the pace, added lunges.

"He met her in the frozen food section of the grocery store in October, and moved in with her for New Year's. She's got a couple kids. Schoolteacher."

"Schoolteacher, kids? Cards?" Rowan shook her head. "Must be love."

"Must be something. He said the woman and the kids are

coming out maybe late July, maybe spend the rest of the summer."

"That sounds serious." She shifted to a twist, eyeing Trigger as she held the position. "She must be something. Still, he'd better see how she handles a season. It's one thing to hook up with a smoke jumper in the winter, and another to stick through the summer. Families crack like eggs," she added, then wished she hadn't as Matt Brayner stepped in.

She hadn't seen him since Jim's funeral, and though she'd spoken with his mother a few times, hadn't been sure he'd come back.

He looked older, she thought, more worn around the eyes and mouth. And heartbreakingly like his brother with the floppy mop of bleached wheat hair, the pale blue eyes. His gaze tracked from Trigger, met hers. She wondered what the smile cost him.

"How's it going?"

"Pretty good." She straightened, wiped her palms on the thighs of her workout pants. "Just sweating off some nerves before the PT test."

"I thought I'd do the same. Or just screw it and go into town and order a double stack of pancakes."

"We'll get 'em after the run." Trigger walked over, held out a hand. "Good to see you, Hayseed."

"You too."

"I'm going for coffee. They'll be loading us up before too long."

As Trigger went out, Matt walked over, picked up a twenty-pound weight. Put it down again. "I guess it's going to be weird, for a while anyway. Seeing me makes everybody . . . think."

"Nobody's going to forget. I'm glad you're back."

"I don't know if I am, but I couldn't seem to do anything else. Anyway, I wanted to say thanks for keeping in touch with my ma the way you have. It means a lot to her."

"I wish . . . Well, if wishes were horses I'd have a rodeo. I'm glad you're back. See you at the van."

SHE UNDERSTOOD Matt's sentiment, couldn't seem to do anything else. It would sum up the core feelings of the men, and four women including herself, who piled into vans for the ride out to the start of the run for their jobs. She settled in, letting the ragging and bragging flow over her.

A lot of insults about winter weight, and the ever-popular lard-ass remarks. She closed her eyes, tried to let herself drift as the nerves riding under the good-natured bullshit winging around the van wanted to reach inside and shake hands with her own.

Janis Petrie, one of the four females in the unit, dropped down beside her. Her small, compact build had earned her the nickname Elf, and she looked like a perky head cheerleader.

This morning, her nails sported bright pink polish and her shiny brown hair bounced in a tail tied with a circle of butterflies.

She was pretty as a gumdrop, tended to giggle, and could—and did—work a saw line for fourteen hours straight.

"Ready to rock, Swede?"

"And roll. Why would you put on makeup before this bitch of a test?"

Janis fluttered her long, lush lashes. "So these poor guys'll have something pretty to look at when they stumble over the finish line. Seeing as I'll be there first."

"You are pretty damn fast."

"Small but mighty. Did you check out the rookies?"

"Not yet."

"Six of our kind in there. Maybe we'll add enough women for a nice little sewing circle. Or a book club."

Rowan laughed. "And after, we'll have a bake sale."

"Cupcakes. Cupcakes are my weakness. It's such pretty country." Janis leaned forward a little to get a clearer view out the window. "I always miss it when I'm gone, always wonder what I'm doing living in the city doing physical therapy on country club types with tennis elbow."

She blew out a breath. "Then by July I'll be wondering what I'm doing out here, strung out on no sleep, hurting everywhere, when I could be taking my lunch break at the pool."

"It's a long way from Missoula to San Diego."

"Damn right. You don't have that pull-tug. You live here. For most of us, this is coming home. Until we finish the season and go home, then that feels like home. It can cross up the circuits."

She rolled her warm brown eyes toward Rowan as the van stopped. "Here we go again."

Rowan climbed out of the van, drew in the air. It smelled good, fresh and new. Spring, the kind with green and wild-flowers and balmy breezes, wouldn't be far off now. She scouted the flags marking the course as the base manager, Michael Little Bear, laid out requirements.

His long black braid streamed down his bright red jacket. Rowan knew there'd be a roll of Life Savers in the pocket, a substitute for the Marlboros he'd quit over the winter.

L.B. and his family lived a stone's throw from the base, and his wife worked for Rowan's father.

Everyone knew the rules. Run the course, and get it done in under 22:30, or walk away. Try it again in a week. Fail that? Find a new summer job.

Rowan stretched out—hamstrings, quads, calves.

"I hate this shit."

"You'll make it." She gave him an elbow in the belly. "Think of a meat-lover's pizza waiting for you on the other side of the line."

"Kiss my ass."

"The size it is now? That'd take me a while."

He snorted out a laugh as they lined up.

She calmed herself. Got in her head, got in her body, as L.B. walked back to the van. When the van took off, so did the line. Rowan hit the timer button on her watch, merged with the pack. She knew every one of them—had worked with them, sweated with them, risked her life with them. And she wished them—every one—good luck and a good run.

But for the next twenty-two and thirty, it was every man—and woman—for himself.

She dug in, kicked up her pace and ran for, what was in a very large sense, her life. She made her way through the pack and, as others did, called out encouragement or jibes, whatever worked best to kick asses into gear. She knew there would be knees aching, chests hammering, stomachs churning. Spring training would have toned some, added insult to injuries on others.

She couldn't think about it. She focused on mile one, and when she passed the marker, noted her time at 4:12.

Mile two, she ordered herself, and kept her stride smooth, her pace steady—even when Janis passed her with a grim smile. The burn rose up from her toes to her ankles, flowed up her calves. Sweat ran hot down her back, down her chest, over her galloping heart.

She could slow her pace—her time was good—but the stress of imagined stumbles, turned ankles, a lightning strike from beyond, pushed her.

Don't let up.

When she passed mile two she'd moved beyond the burn, the sweat, into the mindless. One more mile. She passed some, was passed by others, while her pulse pounded in her ears. As before a jump, she kept her eyes on the horizon—land and sky. Her love of both whipped her through the final mile.

She blew past the last marker, heard L.B. call out her name and time. *Tripp, fifteen-twenty.* And ran another twenty yards before she could convince her legs it was okay to stop.

Bending from the waist, she caught her breath, squeezed her eyes tightly shut. As always after the PT test she wanted to weep. Not from the effort. She—all of them—faced worse, harder, tougher. But the stress clawing at her mind finally retracted.

She could continue to be what she wanted to be.

She walked off the run, tuning in now as other names and times were called out. She high-fived with Trigger as he crossed three miles.

Everyone who passed stayed on the line. A unit again, all but willing the rest to make it, make that time. She checked her watch, saw the deadline coming up, and four had yet to cross.

Cards, Matt, Yangtree, who'd celebrated—or mourned—his fifty-fourth birthday the month before, and Gibbons, whose bad knee had him nearly hobbling those last yards.

Cards wheezed in with three seconds to spare, with Yangtree right behind him. Gibbons's face was a sweat-drenched study in pain and grit, but Matt? It seemed to Rowan he barely pushed.

His eyes met hers. She pumped her fist, imagined herself dragging him and Gibbons over the last few feet while the seconds counted down. She swore she could see the light come on, could see Matt reaching in, digging down.

He hit at 22:28, with Gibbons stumbling over a half second behind.

The cheer rose then, the triumph of one more season.

"Guess you two wanted to add a little suspense." L.B. lowered his clipboard. "Welcome back. Take a minute to bask, then let's get loaded."

"Hey, Ro!" She glanced over at Cards's shout, in time to see him turn, bend over and drop his pants. "Pucker up!"

And we're back, she thought.

2

Gulliver Curry rolled out of his sleeping bag and took stock. Everything hurt, he decided. But that made a workable balance.

He smelled snow, and a look out of his tent showed him, yes, indeed, a couple fresh inches had fallen overnight. His breath streamed out in clouds as he pulled on pants. The blisters on his blisters made dressing for the day an . . . experience.

Then again, he valued experience.

The day before, he, along with twenty-five other recruits, had dug fire line for fourteen hours, then topped off that little task with a three-mile hike, carrying an eighty-five-pound pack.

They'd felled trees with crosscut saws, hiked, dug, sharpened tools, dug, hiked, scaled the towering pines, then dug some more.

Summer camp for the masochist, he thought. Otherwise known as rookie training for smoke jumpers. Four recruits had already washed out—two of them hadn't gotten past the initial PT test. His seven years' fire experience, the last four on a hotshot crew, gave Gull some advantage.

But that didn't mean he felt fresh as a rosebud.

He rubbed a hand over his face, scratching his palm over bristles from nearly a week without a razor. God, he wanted a hot shower, a shave and an ice-cold beer. Tonight, after a fun-filled hike through the Bitterroots, this time hauling a hundred-and-ten-pound pack, he'd get all three.

And tomorrow, he'd start the next phase. Tomorrow he'd start learning how to fly.

Hotshots trained like maniacs, worked like dogs, primarily on high-priority wilderness fires. But they didn't jump out of planes. That, he thought, added a whole new experience. He shoved a hand through his thick mass of dark hair, then crawled out of the tent into the crystal snowscape of predawn.

His eyes, feline green, tracked up to check the sky, and he stood for a moment in the still, tall and tough in his rough brown pants and bright yellow shirt. He had what he wanted here—or pieces of it—the knowledge that he could do what he'd come to do.

He measured the height of the ponderosa pine to his left. Ninety feet, give or take. He'd walked up that bastard the day before, biting his gaffs into bark. And from that height, hooked with spikes and harness, he'd gazed out over the forest.

An experience.

Through the scent of snow and pine, he headed toward the cook tent as the camp began to stir. And despite the aches, the blisters—maybe because of them—he looked forward to what the day would bring.

Shortly after noon, Gull watched the lodgepole pine topple. He shoved his hard hat back enough to wipe sweat off his forehead and nodded to his partner on the crosscut saw.

"Another one bites the dust."

Dobie Karstain barely made the height requirement at five six. His beard and stream of dung brown hair gave him the look of a pint-sized mountain man, while the safety goggles seemed to emphasize the wild, wide eyes.

Dobie hefted a chain saw. "Let's cut her into bite-sized pieces."

They worked rhythmically. Gull had figured Dobie for a washout, but the native Kentuckian was stronger, and sturdier, than he looked. He liked Dobie well enough—despite the man's distinctly red neck—and was working on reaching a level of trust.

If Dobie made it through, odds were they'd be sawing and digging together again. Not on a bright, clear spring afternoon, but in the center of fire where trust and teamwork were as essential as a sharp Pulaski, the two-headed tool with ax and grub hoe.

"Wouldn't mind tapping that before she folds."

Gull glanced over at one of the female recruits. "What makes you think she'll fold?"

"Women ain't built for this work, son."

Gull drew the blade of the saw through the pine. "Just for baby-making, are they?"

Dobie grinned through his beard. "I didn't design the model. I just like riding 'em."

"You're an asshole, Dobie."

"Some say," Dobie agreed in the same good-natured tone.

Gull studied the woman again. Perky blond, maybe an inch or two shy of Dobie's height. And from his point of view, she'd held up as well as any of them. Ski instructor out of Colorado, he recalled. Libby. He'd seen her retaping her blisters that morning.

"I got twenty says she makes it all the way."

Dobie chuckled as another log rolled. "I'll take your twenty, son."

When they finished their assignment, Gull retaped some of his own blisters. Then, as the instructors were busy, taped Dobie's fresh ones.

They moved through the camp to their waiting packs. Three miles to go, Gull thought, then he'd end this fine day with that shave, shower and cold beer.

He sat, strapped on the pack, then pulled out a pack of gum. He offered a stick to Dobie.

"Don't mind if I do."

Together they rolled over to their hands and knees, then pushed to standing.

"Just imagine you're carrying a pretty little woman," Dobie advised, with a wiggle of eyebrows in Libby's direction.

"A buck-ten's pretty scrawny for my taste."

"She'll feel like more by the time we're done."

No question about it, Gull mused, and the instructor didn't set what you'd call a meandering pace along the rocky, quad-burning trail.

They pushed one another, that's how it was done. Ragged one another, encouraged one another, insulted one another, to get the group another step, another yard. The spurring fact was, in a few weeks it would be real. And on the fire line everyone's life depended on the other.

"What do you do back in Kentucky?" Gull asked Dobie while a hawk screamed overhead and the smell of group sweat competed with pine.

"Some of this, some of that. Last three seasons I doused fires in the national forest. One night after we beat one down, I got a little drunk, took a bet how I'd be a smoke jumper. So I got an application, and here I am."

"You're doing this on a bet?" The idea just appealed to his sense of the ridiculous.

"Hundred dollars on the line, son. And my pride that's worth more. You ever jump out of a plane?"

"Yeah."

"Takes the crazy."

"Some might say." Gull passed Dobie's earlier words back to him.

"What's it feel like? When you're falling?"

"Like hot, screaming sex with a beautiful woman."

"I was hoping." Dobie shifted his pack, winced. "Because this fucking training better be worth it."

"Libby's holding up."

"Who?"

Gull lifted his chin. "Your most recent bet."

Dobie gritted his teeth as they started up yet another incline. "Day's not over."

By the time it was, Gull got his shower, his shave, and managed to grab a brew before falling facedown on his bunk.

MICHAEL LITTLE BEAR snagged Rowan on her way into the gym. "I need you to take rookie training this morning. Cards was on it, but he's puking up his guts in the john."

"Hangover?"

"No. Stomach flu or something. I need you to run them on the playground. Okay?"

"Sure. I'm already on with Yangtree, on the slam-ulator. I can make a day eating rooks. How many do we have?"

"Twenty-five left, and they look pretty damn good. One beat the base record on the mile-and-a-half course. Nailed it in six-thirty-nine."

"Fast feet. We'll see how the rest of him does today."

She knocked thirty minutes off her planned ninety in the gym. Taking the recruits over the obstacle course would make up for it, and meant she'd just skated out of a stint sewing personal gear bags in the manufacturing room.

Damn good deal, Rowan thought as she put on her boots.

She grabbed the paperwork, a clipboard, a water bottle and, fixing a blue ball cap on her head, headed outside.

Clouds had rolled in overnight and tucked the warm in nicely. Activity swarmed the base—runners on the track or the road, trucks off-loaded supplies, men and women crossed from building to building. A plane taxied out taking a group up for a preseason practice jump.

Long before the fire siren screamed, work demanded attention. Sewing, stuffing, disassembling equipment, training, packing chutes.

She started toward the training field, pausing when she crossed paths with Matt.

"What're you on?" he asked her.

"Rook detail. Cards is down with some stomach deal. You?"

"I'm up this afternoon." He glanced skyward as the jump plane rose into the air. "I'm in the loadmaster's room this morning." He smiled. "Want to trade?"

"Hmm, stuck inside loading supplies or out here torturing rookies? No deal."

"Figured."

She continued on, noting the trainees were starting to gather on the field. They'd come in from a week of camping and line work, and if they had any brains would've focused on getting a good night's sleep.

Those who had would probably feel pretty fresh this morning.

She'd soon take care of that.

A few of them wandered the obstacle course, trying to get a gauge. Smart, she judged. Know your enemy. Voices and laughter carried on the air. Pumping themselves up—and that was smart, too.

The obstacle course was a bitch of the first order, and it was only the start of a long, brutal day. She checked her watch as she moved through the wooden platforms, took her place on the field.

She took a swig from her water bottle, then set it aside. And let out a long, shrill whistle. "Line up," she called out. "I'm Rowan Tripp, your instructor on this morning's cakewalk. Each of you will be required to complete this course before moving on to the next exercise. The campfire songs and roasted marshmallows of the last week are over. It's time to get serious."

She got a few moans, a few chuckles, some nervous glances as she sized up the group. Twenty-one men, four women, different sizes, shapes, colors, ages. Her job was to give them one purpose.

Work through the pain.

She consulted her clipboard, did roll call, checked off the names of those who'd made it this far. "I hear one of you rooks beat the base record on the mile-and-a-half. Who's the flash?"

"Go, Gull!" somebody shouted, and she watched the little guy elbow-bump the man next to him.

About six-two, she judged, dark hair clean and shaggy, cocky smile, easy stance. "Gull Curry," he said. "I like to run."

"Good for you. Speed won't get you through the playground. Stretch out, recruits. I don't want anybody crying about pulled muscles."

They'd already formed a unit, she determined, and the smaller connections within it. Friendships, rivalries—both could be useful.

"Fifty push-ups," she ordered, noting them down as they were completed.

"I'm going to lead you over this course, starting here." She gestured at the low platform of horizontal squares, moved on to the steep steel walls they'd need to hurdle, the ropes they'd climb, hand over hand, the trampoline flips, the ramps.

"Every one of these obstacles simulates something you will face during a fire. Get one done, hit the next. Drop out? You're done. Finish it, you might just be good enough to jump fire."

"Not exactly Saint Crispin's Day."

"Who?" Dobie asked at Gull's mutter.

He only shrugged, and figured by the sidelong glance the bombshell blonde sent him, she'd heard the remark.

"You, Fast Feet, take the lead. The rest of you, fall in behind him. Single file. If you fall, get your ass out of the way, pick up the rear for a second shot."

She pulled a stopwatch out of her pocket. "Are you ready?"

The group shouted back, and Rowan hit the timer. "Go!"

Okay, Rowan thought, fast feet and nimble feet.

"Pick up those knees!" she shouted. "Let's see some energy. For Christ's sake, you look like a bunch of girls strolling in the park."

"I am a girl!" a steely-eyed blonde shouted back, and made Rowan grin.

"Then pick up those knees. Pretend you're giving one of these assholes a shot in the balls."

She kept pace with Gull, jogging back as he raced for, charged up, then hurdled the first ramp.

Then the little guy surprised her by all but launching over it like a cannon.

They climbed, hurdled, crawled, clawed. L.B. was right, she decided. They were a damn good group.

She watched Gull execute the required flips and rolls on the tramp, heard the little guy—she needed to check his name—let out a wild yee-haw as he did the same.

Fast feet, she thought again, still in the lead, and damned if he didn't go up the rope like a monkey on a vine.

The blonde had made up ground, but when she hit the rope, she not only stalled, but started to slip.

"Don't you slide!" Rowan shouted it out, put a whiplash

into it. "Don't you slide, Barbie, goddamn it, and embarrass me. Do you want to start this mother over?"

"No. God, no."

"Do you want to jump fire or go back home and shop for shoes?"

"Both!"

"Climb it." Rowan saw the blood on the rope. A slide ripped the skin right off the palms, and the pain was huge. "Climb!"

She climbed, forty torturous feet.

"Get down, move on. Go! Go!"

She climbed down, and when she hurdled the next wall, left a bloodstain on the ramp.

But she did it. They all did, Rowan thought, and gave them a moment to wheeze, to moan, to rub out sore muscles.

"Not bad. Next time you have to climb a rope or scale a wall it might be because the wind shifted and fire just washed over your safe zone. You'll want to do better than not bad. What's your name—I'm a Girl Barbie?"

"Libby." The blonde rested her bloody hands on her knees, palms up. "Libby Rydor."

"Anybody who can climb up a rope when her hands are bleeding did better than not bad." Rowan opened the first-aid kit. "Let's fix them up. If anybody else got any boo-boos, tend to them, then head in, get your gear. Full gear," she added, "for practice landings. You got thirty."

Gull watched her apply salve to Libby's palms, competently bandage them. She said something that made Libby— and those hands had to hurt—laugh.

She'd pushed the group through the course, hitting the right combination of callous insult and nagging. And she'd zeroed in on a few as they'd had trouble, found the right thing to say at the right time.

That was an impressive skill, one he admired.

He could add it to his admiration of the rest of her.

That blonde was built, all maybe five feet ten inches of her. His uncle would have dubbed her statuesque, Gull mused. Himself? He just had to say that body was a killer. Add big, heavy-lidded blue eyes and a face that made a man want to look twice, then maybe linger a little longer for a third time, and you had a hell of a package.

A package with attitude. And God, he had a hard time resisting attitude. So he stalled until she crossed the field, then fell into step beside her.

"How are Libby's hands?"

"She'll be okay. Everybody loses a little skin on the playground."

"Did you?"

"If you don't bleed, how do they know you've been there?" She angled her head, studied him with eyes that made him think of stunning arctic ice. "Where are you out of, Shakespeare? I've read *Henry the Fifth*."

"Monterey, mostly."

"They've got a fine smoke-jumper unit in Northern California."

"They do. I know most of them. I worked Redding IHC, five years."

"I figured you for a hotshot. So, you're wanted in California so you headed to Missoula?"

"The charges were dropped," he said, and made her smile. "I'm in Missoula because of Iron Man Tripp." He stopped when she did. "I'm figuring he must be your father."

"That's right. Do you know him?"

"Of course. Lucas 'Iron Man' Tripp's a legend. You had a bad one out here in 2000."

"Yeah."

"I was in college. It was all over the news, and I caught this interview with Iron Man, right here on base, after he and his unit got back from four days in the mouth of it."

Gull thought back, brought it into the now in his head. "His face is covered with soot, his hair's layered with ash, his eyes are red. He looks like he's been to war, which is accurate enough. The reporter's asking the usual idiot questions. 'How did it feel in there? Were you afraid?' And he's being patient. You can tell he's exhausted, but he's answering. And finally he says to the guy, 'Boy, the simplest way to put it is the bitch tried to eat us, and we kicked her ass.' And he walks away."

She remembered it as clearly as he did—and remembered a lot more. "And that's why you're in Missoula looking to jump fire?"

"Consider it a springboard. I could give you the rest of it over a beer."

"You're going to be too busy for beer and life stories. Better get your gear on. You've got a long way to go yet."

"Offer of beer's always open. Life story optional."

She gave him that look again, the slight angle of the head, the little smirk on the mouth that he found sexily bottom-heavy. "You don't want to hit on me, hotshot. I don't hook up with rookies, snookies or other smoke jumpers. When I've got the time and inclination for . . . entertainment, I look for a civilian. One I can play with when I'm in the mood over the long winter nights and forget about during the season."

Oh, yeah, he did like attitude. "You might be due for a change of pace."

"You're wasting your time, rook."

When she strolled off with her clipboard, he let himself grin. He figured it was his time to waste. And she struck him as a truly unique experience.

GULL SURVIVED being dragged up in the air by a cable, then dropped down to earth again. The not-altogether-fondly-dubbed slam-ulator did a damn good job of simulating the body-jarring, ankle-and-knee-shocking slam of a parachute landing.

He slapped, tucked, dropped and rolled, and he took his lumps, bumps and bruises. He learned how to protect his head, how to use his body to preserve his body. And how to *think* when the ground was hurtling up toward him at a fast clip.

He faced the tower, climbing its fifty feet of murderous red with his jump partner for the drill.

"How ya doing?" he asked Libby.

"I feel like I fell off a mountain, so not too bad. You?"

"I'm not sure if I fell off the mountain or on it." When he reached the platform, he grinned at Rowan. "Is this as much fun as it looks?"

"Oh, more." Sarcasm dripped as she hooked him to the pully. "There's your jump spot." She gestured to a hill of saw-dust across the training field. "There's going to be some speed on the swing over, so you're going to feel it when you hit. Tuck, protect your head, roll."

He studied the view of the hill. It looked damn small from where he was standing, through the bars of his face mask.

"Got it."

"Are you ready?" she asked them both.

Libby took a deep breath. "We're ready."

"Get in the door."

Yeah, it had some speed, Gull thought as he flew across the training field. He barely had time to go through his landing list when the sawdust hill filled his vision. He slammed into it, thought *fuck!*, then tucked and rolled with his hands on either side of his helmet.

Willing his breath back into his lungs, he looked over at Libby. "Okay?"

"Definitely on the mountain that time. But you know what? That was *fun*. I've got to do it again."

"Day's young." He shoved to his feet, held out a hand to pull her to hers.

After the tower came the classroom. His years on a hot-shot crew meant most of the books, charts, lectures were refreshers on what he already knew. But there was always more to learn.

After the classroom there was time, at last, to nurse the bumps and bruises, to find a hot meal, to hang out a bit with the other recruits. Down to twenty-two, Gull noted. They'd lost three between the simulator and the tower.

More than half of those still in training turned in for the night, and Gull thought of doing so himself. The poker game currently under way tempted him so he made a bargain with himself. He'd get some air, then if the urge still tickled, he'd sit in on a few hands.

"Pull up a chair, son," Dobie invited as Gull walked by the table. "I'm looking to add to my retirement account."

"Land on your head a few more times, you'll be retiring early."

Gull kept walking. Outside, the rain that had threatened all day fell cool and steady. Shoving his hands into his pockets, he walked into the wet. He turned toward the distant hangar. Maybe he'd wander over, take a look at the plane he'd soon be jumping of.

He'd jumped three times before he'd applied for the program, just to make sure he had the stomach for it. Now he was anxious, eager to revisit that sensation, to defy his own instincts and shove himself into the high open air.

He'd studied the planes—the Twin Otter, the DC-9—the most commonly used for smoke jumping. He toyed with the idea of taking flying lessons in the off-season, maybe going for his pilot's license. It never hurt to know you could take control if control needed to be taken.

Then he saw her striding toward him through the rain. Dark and gloom didn't blur that body. He slowed his pace. Maybe he didn't need to play poker for this to be his lucky night.

"Nice night," he said.

"For otters." Rain dripped off the bill of Rowan's cap as she studied him. "Making a run for it?"

"Just taking a walk. But I've got a car if there's somewhere you want to go."

"I've got my own ride, thanks, but I'm not going anywhere. You did okay today."

"Thanks."

"It's too bad about Doggett. Bad landing, and a hairline fracture takes him out of the program. I'm figuring he'll come back next year."

"He wants it," Gull agreed.

"It takes more than want, but you've got to want it to get it."

"I was just thinking the same thing."

On a half laugh, Rowan shook her head. "Do women ever say no to you?"

"Sadly, yes. Then again, a man who just gives up never wins the prize."

"Believe me, I'm no prize."

"You've got hair like a Roman centurion, the body of a goddess and the face of a Nordic queen. That's a hell of a package."

"The package isn't the prize."

"No, it's not. But it sure makes me want to open it up and see what's in there."

"A mean temper, a low bullshit threshold and a passion for catching fire. Do yourself a favor, hotshot, and pull somebody else's shiny ribbon."

"I've got this thing, this . . . focus. Once I focus on something, I just can't seem to quit until I figure it all the way out."

She gave a careless shrug, but she watched him, he noted, with care. "Nothing to figure."

"Oh, I don't know," he said when she started into the dorm. "I got you to take a walk in the rain with me."

With one hand on the door, she turned, gave him a pitying smile. "Don't tell me there's a romantic in there."

"Might be."

"Better be careful then. I might use you just because you're handy, then crush that romantic heart."

"My place or yours?"

She laughed—a steamy brothel laugh that shot straight to his loins—then shut the door, metaphorically at least, in his face.

Damned if he hadn't given her a little itch, she admitted. She liked confident men—men who had the balls, the brains and the skills to back it up. That, and the cat-at-the-mousehole way he looked at her—desire and bottomless patience—brought on a low sexual hum.

And picking up that tune would be a mistake, she reminded herself, then tapped lightly on Cards's door. She took his grunt as permission to poke her head in.

He looked, to her eye, a little pale, a lot bored and fairly grungy. "How're you feeling?"

"Shit, I'm okay. Got some bug in my gut this morning. Puked it, and a few internal organs, up." He sat on his bed, cards spread in front of him. "Managed some time in manufacturing, kept dinner down okay. Just taking it easy till tomorrow. Appreciate you covering for me."

"No problem. We're down to twenty-two. One of them's out with an injury. I think we'll see him back. See you in the morning then."

"Hey, want to see a card trick? It's a good one," he said before she could retreat.

Tired of his own company, she decided, and gave in to friendship and sat across from him on the bed.

Besides, watching a few lame card tricks was a better segue into sleep than thinking about walking in the rain with Gulliver Curry.

3

Gull lined up in front of the ready room with the other recruits. Across the asphalt the plane that would take them up for their first jump roared, while along the line nerves jangled.

Instructors worked their way down, doing buddy checks. Gull figured his luck was in when Rowan stepped to him. "Have you been checked?"

"No."

She knelt down so he studied the way her sunflower hair sculpted her head. She checked his boots, his stirrups, worked her way up—leg pockets, leg straps—checked his reserve chute's expiration date, its retainer pins.

"You smell like peaches." Her eyes flicked to his. "It's nice."

"Lower left reserve strap attached," she said, continuing her buddy check without comment. "Lower right reserve strap attached. Head in the game, Fast Feet," she added, then moved on up the list. "If either of us misses a detail, you could be a smear on the ground. Helmet, gloves. You got your letdown rope?"

"Check."

"You're good to go."

"How about you?"

"I've been checked, thanks. You're clear to board." She moved down to the next recruit.

Gull climbed onto the plane, took a seat on the floor beside Dobie.

"You looking to tap that blonde?" Dobie asked. "The one they call Swede?"

"A man has to have his dreams. You're getting closer to owing me twenty," Gull added when Libby ducked through the door.

"Shit. She ain't jumped yet. I got ten right now says she balks."

"I can use ten."

"Welcome aboard," Rowan announced. "Please bring your seats to their full upright position. Our flying time today will depend on how many of you cry like babies once you're in the door. Gibbons will be your spotter. Pay attention. Stay in your heads. Are you ready to jump?"

The answer was a resounding cheer.

"Let's do it."

The plane taxied, gained speed, lifted its nose. Gull felt the little dip in the gut as they left the ground. He watched Rowan, flat-out sexy to his mind in her jumpsuit, raise her voice over the engines and—once again—go over every step of the upcoming jump.

Gibbons passed her a note from the cockpit.

"There's your jump site," she told them, and every recruit angled for a window.

Gull studied the roll of the meadow—pretty as a picture— the rise of Douglas firs, lodgepole pines, the glint of a stream. The job—once he took the sky—would be to hit the meadow, avoid the trees, the water. He'd be the dart, he thought, and he wanted a bull's-eye.

When Gibbons pigged in, Rowan shouted for everyone to guard their reserves. Gibbons grabbed the door handles, yanked, and air, cool and sweet with spring, rushed in.

"Holy shit." Dobie whistled between his teeth. "We're doing it. Real deal. Accept no substitutes."

Gibbons stuck his head out into that rush of air, consulted

with the cockpit through his headset. The plane banked right, bumped, steadied.

"Watch the streamers," Rowan called out. "They're you."

They snapped and spun, circled out into miles of tender blue sky. And sucked into the dense tree line.

Gull adjusted his own jump in his head, mentally pulling on his toggles, considering the drift. Adjusted again as he studied the fall of a second set of streamers.

"Take her up!" Gibbons called out.

Dobie stuffed a stick of gum in his mouth before he put on his helmet, offered one to Gull. Behind his face mask, Dobie's eyes were big as planets. "Feel a little sick."

"Wait till you get down to puke," Gull advised.

"Libby, you're second jump." Rowan put on her helmet. "You just follow me down. Got it?"

"I got it."

At Gibbons's signal, Rowan sat in the door, braced. The plane erupted into shouts of Libby's name, gloved hands slammed together in encouragement as she took her position behind Rowan.

Then Gibbons's hand slapped down on Rowan's shoulder, and she was gone.

Gull watched her flight; couldn't take his eyes off her. The blue-and-white canopy shot up, spilled open. A thing of beauty in that soft blue sky, over the greens and browns and glint of water.

The cheer brought him back. He'd missed Libby's jump, but he saw her chute deploy, shifted to try to keep both chutes in his eye line as the plane flew beyond.

"Looks like you owe me ten."

A smile winked into Dobie's eyes. "Add a six-pack on it that I do better than her. Better than you."

After the plane circled, Gibbons looked in Gull's eyes, held them for a beat. "Are you ready?"

"We're ready."

"Hook up."

Gull moved forward, attached his line.

"Get in the door."

Gull leveled his breathing, and got in the door.

He listened to the spotter's instructions, the drift, the wind, while the air battered his legs. He did his check while the plane circled to its final lineup, and kept his eyes on the horizon.

"Get ready," Gibbons told him.

Oh, he was ready. Every bump, bruise, blister of the past weeks had led to this moment. When the slap came down on his right shoulder, he jumped into that moment.

Wind and sky, and the hard, breathless thrill of daring both. The speed like a drug blowing through the blood. All he could think was, Yes, Christ yes, he'd been born for this, even as he counted off, as he rolled his body until he could look through his feet at the ground below.

The chute billowed open, snapped him up. He looked right, then left and found Dobie, heard his jump partner's wild, reckless laughter.

"Now *that's* what I'm talking about!"

Gull grinned, scanned the view. How many saw this, he wondered, this stunning spread of forest and mountain, this endless, open sky? He swept his gaze over the lacings of snow in the higher elevations, the green just beginning to haze the valley. He thought, though he knew it unlikely, he could smell both, the winter and the spring, as he floated down between them.

He worked his toggles, using instinct, training, the caprice of the wind. He could see Rowan now, the way the sun shone on her bright cap of hair, even the way she stood—legs spread and planted, hands on her hips. Watching him as he watched her.

He put himself beside her, judging the lineup, and felt the instant he caught it. The smoke jumpers called it on the wire, so he glided in on it, kept his breathing steady as he prepared for impact.

He glanced toward Dobie again, noted his partner would overshoot the spot. Then he hit, tucked, rolled. He dropped his gear, started gathering his chute.

He heard Rowan shouting, saw her running for the trees. Everything froze, then melted again when he heard Dobie's shouted stream of curses.

Above, the plane tipped its wings and started its circle to

deploy the next jumpers. He hauled up his gear, grinning as he walked over to where Dobie dragged his own out of the trees.

"I had it, then the wind bitched me into the trees. Hell of a ride, though." The thrill, the triumph lit up his face. "Hell of a goddamn ride. 'Cept I swallowed my gum."

"You're on the ground," Rowan told them. "Nothing's broken. So, not bad." She opened her personal gear bag, took out candy bars. "Congratulations."

"There's nothing like it." Libby's face glowed as she looked skyward. "Nothing else comes close."

"You haven't jumped fire yet." Rowan sat, then stretched out in the meadow grass. "That's a whole new world." She watched the sky, waiting for the plane to come back, then glanced at Gull as he dropped down beside her. "You had a smooth one."

"I targeted on you. The sun in your hair," he added when she frowned at him.

"Jesus, Gull, you *are* a romantic. God help you."

He'd flustered her, he realized, and gave himself a point on his personal scoreboard. Since he hadn't swallowed his gum, he tucked the chocolate away for later. "What do you do when you're not doing this?"

"For work? I put in some time in my dad's business, jumping with tourists who want a thrill, teaching people who think they want, or decide they want, to jump as a hobby. Do some personal training." She flexed her biceps.

"Bet you're good at it."

"Logging in time as a PT means I get paid to keep fit for this over the winter. What about you?"

"I get to play for a living. Fun World. It's like a big arcade—video games, bowling, bumper cars, Skee-Ball."

"You work at an arcade?"

He folded his arms behind his head. "It's not work if it's fun."

"You don't strike me as the kind of guy to deal with kids and machines all day."

"I like kids. They're largely fearless and open to possibilities. Adults tend to forget how to be either." He shrugged. "You spend yours trying to get couch potatoes to break a sweat."

"Not all of my clients are couch potatoes. None are when I'm done with them." She shoved up to sit. "Here comes the next group."

With the first practice jump complete, they packed out, carrying their gear back to base. After another stint of physical training, classwork, they were up again for the second jump of the day.

They practiced letdown in full gear, outlined fire suppression strategies, studied maps, executed countless sit-ups, pull-ups, push-ups, ran miles and threw themselves out of planes. At the end of a brutal four weeks, the numbers had whittled down to sixteen. Those still standing ranged outside Operations answering their final roll call as recruits.

When Libby answered her name, Dobie slapped a twenty into Gull's hand. "Smoke jumper Barbie. You gotta give it to her. Skinny woman like that toughs it through, and a big hoss like McGinty washes."

"We didn't," Gull reminded him.

"Fucking tooting we didn't."

Even as they slapped hands a flood of ice water drenched them.

"Just washing off some of the rookie stink," somebody called out. And with hoots and shouts, the men and woman on the roof tossed another wave of water from buckets.

"You're now one of us." From his position out of water range, L.B. shouted over the laughter and curses. "The best there is. Get cleaned up, then pack it in the vans. We're heading into town, boys and girls. You've got one night to celebrate and drink yourself stupid. Tomorrow, you start your day as smoke jumpers—as Zulies."

When Gull made a show out of wringing out his wet twenty, Dobie laughed so hard, he had to sit on the ground. "I'll buy the first round. You're in there, Libby."

"Thanks."

He smiled, stuffed the wet bill in his wet pocket. "I owe it all to you."

Inside, Gull stripped off his dripping clothes. He took stock of his bruises—not too bad—and for the first time in a week took time to shave. Once he'd hunted up a clean shirt and pants, he spent a few minutes sending a quick e-mail home to let his family know he'd made it.

He expected that news to generate mixed reactions, though they'd all pretend to be as happy as he was. He slid a celebratory cigar into his breast pocket, then wandered outside.

The e-mail had cost him some time, so he loaded into the last of the vans and found a seat among the scatter of rookies and vets.

"Ready to party, rook?" Trigger asked him.

"I've been ready."

"Just remember, nobody gets babysat. The vans leave and you're not in one, you find your own way back to base. If you end up with a woman tonight, the smart thing is to end up with one who has a car."

"I'll keep that in mind."

"You dance?"

"You asking?"

Trigger hooted out a laugh. "You're almost pretty enough for me. The place we're going has a dance floor. You do it right, dancing with a woman's the same as foreplay."

"Is that the case, in your experience?"

"It is, young Jedi. It surely is."

"Interesting. So . . . does Rowan like to dance?"

Trigger raised his eyebrows. "That's what we call barking up the wrong tree."

"It's the only tree that's caught my interest and attention."

"Then you're going to have a long, dry summer." He gave Gull a pat on the shoulder. "And let me tell you something else from my vast experience. When you've got calluses on your calluses and blisters on top of that, jerking off isn't as pleasant as it's meant to be."

"Five years as a hotshot," Gull reminded him. "If the summer proves long and dry, my hands'll hold up."

"Maybe so. But a woman's better."

"Indeed they are, Master Jedi. Indeed they are."

"Have you got one back home?"

"No. Do you?"

"Had one. Twice. Married one of them. Just didn't take. Matt's got one. You got a woman back home in Nebraska, don't you, Matt?"

Matt shifted, angled around to look back over his shoulder. "Annie's back in Nebraska."

"High-school sweethearts," Trigger filled in. "Then she went off to college, but they got back together when she came home. Two minds, one heart. So Matt doesn't dance, if you get my drift."

"Got it. It's nice," Gull continued, "having somebody."

"No point in the whole screwed-up world if you don't." Matt shrugged. "No point doing what we do if nobody's waiting for us once we've done it."

"Sweetens the pot," Trigger agreed. "But some of us have to settle for a dance now and again." He rubbed his hands together as the van pulled up in a lot packed with trucks and cars. "And my toes are already tapping."

Gull scanned the long, low log building as he stepped out of the van, contemplated a moment on the flickering neon sign.

"'Get a Rope,'" he read. "Seriously?"

"Cowboy up, partner." Trigger slapped him on the shoulder, then strutted inside on his snakeskin boots.

An experience, Gull reminded himself. You could never have too many of them.

He stepped into the overamplified screech and twang of truly, deeply bad country music performed by a quartet of grungy-looking guys behind the dubious protection of a chicken-wire fence. At the moment the only things being hurled at them were shouted insults, but the night was young.

Still, people crowded the dance floor, kicking up boot heels, wiggling butts. Others ranged along the long bar or squeezed onto rickety chairs at tiny tables where they could scarf up dripping nachos or gnaw on buffalo wings coated with a suspicious substance that turned them cheese-puff orange. Most opted to wash that combo down with beer served in filmy plastic pitchers.

The lights were mercifully dim, and despite the smoking ban dingy blue clouds fogged the air that smelled like a sweat-soaked, deep-fried, overflowing ashtray.

The only reasonable thing to do, as Gull saw it, was to start drinking.

He moved to the bar, elbowed in and ordered a Bitter Root

beer—in a bottle. Dobie squeezed beside him, punched him in the arm. "Why do you wanna drink that foreign shit?"

"Brewed in Montana." He passed the bottle to Dobie, ordered another.

"Pretty good beer," Dobie decided after a pull. "But it ain't no Budweiser."

"You're not wrong." Amused, Gull tapped his bottle to Dobie's, drank. "Beer. The answer to so many questions."

"I'm going to get this one in me, then cut one of these women out of the herd, drive 'em on the dance floor."

Gull sipped again, studied the fat-fingered lead guitar player. "How do you dance to crap like this?"

Dobie's eyes slitted, and his finger drilled into Gull's chest. "You got a problem with country music?"

"You must've busted an eardrum on your last jump if you call this music. I like bluegrass," he added, "when it's done right."

"Don't bullshit me, city boy. You don't know bluegrass from bindweed."

Gull took another swig of beer. "I am a man of constant sorrow," he sang in a strong, smooth tenor. "I've seen trouble all my days."

Now Dobie punched him in the chest, but affectionately. "You're a continual surprise to me, Gulliver. Got a voice in there, too. You oughta get up there and show those shit-kickers how it's done."

"I think I'll just drink my beer."

"Well." Dobie tipped up the bottle, drained it. Let out a casual belch. "I'm going for a female."

"Good luck with that."

"Ain't about luck. It's about style."

Gull watched Dobie bop over to a table of four women, and decided the man had a style all of his own.

Enjoying the moment, Gull leaned an elbow back on the bar, crossed his ankles. Trigger, true to his word, already had a partner on the dance floor, and Matt—true to his Annie—sat with Little Bear, a rookie named Stovic and one of the pilots they called Stetson for his battered and beloved black hat.

Then there was Rowan, chowing down on the orange-coated nachos at a table with Janis Petrie, Gibbons and Yangtree. She'd pulled on a blue T-shirt—snug, scoop-necked—that molded her breasts and torso. For the first time since he'd met her she wore earrings, something that glittered and swung from her ears when she shook her head and laughed.

She'd done something to her eyes, her lips, he noted, made them bolder. And when she let Cards pull her to her feet for a dance, Gull saw her jeans were as snug as her shirt.

She caught his eye when Cards swung her into a spin, then stopped his heart when she shot him a wide, wicked smile. He decided if she was going to kill him, she might as well do it at closer range. He ordered another beer, carried it over to her table.

"Hey, fresh meat." Janis toasted him with a dripping nacho. "Want to dance, rookie?"

"I haven't had enough beer to dance to whatever this is."

"They're so bad, they're good." Janis patted Rowan's empty chair. "A few more drinks, they'll be nearly good enough to be bad."

"Your logic tells me you've walked this path before."

"You're not a Zulie until you've survived a night at Get a Rope." She glanced toward the door as a group of three men swaggered in. "In all its glory."

"Local boys?"

"Don't think so. They're all wearing new boots. High-dollar ones." She topped off her beer from the pitcher on the table. "I'm guessing city, dude-ranch types come to take in some local color."

They headed toward the bar, and the one in the lead shoulder-muscled his way through the line. He slapped a bill on the bar.

"Whiskey and a woman." He punched his voice up, deliberately, Gull imagined, so it carried above the noise. The hoots and laughter from his friends told Gull it wouldn't be their first drink of the night.

A few people at the bar edged over to give the group room while the bartender poured their drinks. The lead guy tossed it back, slapped down the glass, pointed at it.

"We need us some *females*."

More group hilarity ensued. Looking for trouble, Gull concluded, and since he wasn't, he went back to watching Rowan on the dance floor.

Janis leaned toward him as the band launched into a painful cover of "When the Sun Goes Down." "Ro says you work in an arcade."

"She talked to you about me?"

"Sure. We pass notes in study hall every day. I like arcades. You got pinball? I kill at pinball."

"Yeah, new and vintage."

"Vintage?" She aimed a narrow look with big brown eyes. "You don't have High Speed, do you?"

"It's a classic for a reason."

"I love that one!" Her hand slapped the table. "They had this old, beat-up machine in this arcade when I was a kid. I got so good at it, I'd play all day on my first token. I traded this guy five free games on it for my first French kiss." She sighed, sat back. "Good times."

Following her gaze as it shifted to the bar, Gull glanced back in time to see the whiskey-drinker give a waitress passing by with a full tray a frisky slap on the ass. When the woman looked around, he held up both hands, smirked.

"Asshole. You can't go anywhere," Janis said, "without running into assholes."

"Their numbers are legion." He shifted a little more when Rowan stepped off the dance floor.

"That's my seat."

"I'm holding it for you." He patted his knee.

She surprised him by dropping down on his lap, picking up his beer and drinking deep. "Big spender, buying local brew by the bottle. Don't you dance, moneybags?"

"I might, if they ever play something that doesn't make my ears bleed."

"You can still hear them? I can fix that. Time for shots."

"Count me out," Gibbons said immediately. "The last time you talked me into that I couldn't feel my fingers for a week."

"Don't do it, Gull," Yangtree warned him. "The Swede has an iron gut. Got it from her old man."

Rowan turned her face close to Gull's and smirked. "Aw, do you have a tender tummy, hotshot?"

He imagined biting her heavy bottom lip, just one fast, hard nip. "What kind of shots?"

"There's only one shot worth shooting. Te-qui-la," she sang it, slapping her palm on the table with each syllable. "If you've got the balls for it."

"You're sitting on my balls, so you ought to know."

She threw back her head on that sexy saloon girl laugh. "Hold them for a minute. I'll get us set up."

She hopped up, swung around a couple times when Dobie grabbed her hand and gave her a twirl. Titania to Puck, Gull thought.

Then she hooked her thumbs in her front pockets and joined him in some sort of boot-stomping clog thing that had some of the other dancers whistling and clapping.

She shot a finger at Gull—and damn, there went his heart again—then danced over to the bar.

"Hey, Big Nate." Rowan leaned in, hailed the head bartender. "I need a dozen tequila shots, a couple saltshakers and some lime wedges to suck on."

She glanced over, gave the man currently grabbing his crotch a bored look, shifted away again. "I can take them over if Molly's busy."

The crotch-grabber slapped a hundred-dollar bill on the bar in front of her. "I'll buy your shots and ten minutes outside."

Rowan gave the bartender a slight shake of the head before he could speak.

She turned, looked the drunk, insulting bastard in the eye. "I guess since you lack any charm, and the only way you can get a woman is to pay her, you think we're all whores."

"You've been wiggling that ass and those tits out there since I came in. I'm just offering to pay for what you've been advertising. I'll buy you a drink first."

At the table, Gull thought, *shit*, and started to rise. Gibbons put a hand on his arm. "You don't want to get in her way. Trust me on this."

"I don't like drunks hassling women."

He shoved up, noted the noise level had diminished, so he

clearly heard Rowan say in a tone sweet as cotton candy, "Oh, if you'll buy me a drink first. Is that your pitcher?"

She picked it up and, with her height, had no trouble upending it over the man's head. "Suck on that, fuckwit."

The man moved pretty quick for a sputtering drunk. He shoved Rowan back against the bar, grabbed her breasts and squeezed.

And she moved faster. Before Gull was halfway across the room she slammed her boot on the man's instep, her knee into the crotch he'd been so proud of, then knocked him on his ass with an uppercut as fine as Gull had ever seen when the drunk doubled over.

She back-fisted one of his buddies who'd been foolish enough to try to yank her around. She grabbed his arm, dragged him forward, past her. The boot she planted on his ass sent him careening into his friend as the man started to struggle to his feet.

She whipped around to man number three. "You want to try for me?"

"No." This one held up his hands in a don't-shoot-me gesture. "No, ma'am, I don't."

"Maybe you've got half a brain. Use it and get your idiot friends out of here before I get mad. Because when I get mad, I just get *crazy*."

"I guess she didn't need any help," Dobie observed.

"That does it." Gull laid a hand over his heart, beat it there. "I'm in love."

"I don't think I'd want to fall in love with a woman who could wipe the floor with me."

"No risk, no point."

He hung back as a half dozen Zulies moved in to help the three men to the door. And out of it.

Rowan gave her T-shirt a fussy tug. "How about those shots, Big Nate?"

"Coming right out. On the house."

Gull took his seat again, waiting for Rowan to carry the tray over.

"Are you ready?" she asked him.

"Line them up, sweetheart. You want some ice for your knuckles?"

She wiggled her fingers. "They're okay. It was like punching the Pillsbury Doughboy."

"I hear he's a mean drunk, too."

She laughed, then dropped down into the chair Gibbons pulled over for her. "Let's see what kind of drunk you are."

4

Gull watched her eyes as he and Rowan knocked back the first shot, as the tequila hit his tongue, his throat, and took that quick, hot slide to the belly.

That, he realized, was her first appeal for him. Those clear, cool blue eyes held so much *life*. They sparkled now with challenge, with humor, and there was something in the way they leveled on his that made the moment intimate—as much of a hot slide through the system as the tequila.

Matching his pace to hers, he picked up the next shot glass.

Then there was her mouth, just shy of wide, heavy on the bottom—and the way it so naturally, so habitually formed a smirk.

Small wonder he lusted for a good, strong taste of it.

"How ya doing, hotshot?"

"I'm good. How about you, Swede?"

In answer she tapped her third shot glass to his before they tossed back the contents together. She brought the lime wedge to her mouth. "Do you know what I love about tequila?"

"What do you love about tequila?"

"Everything." After a wicked laugh, she drank the fourth

with the same careless gusto as the first three. Together they slapped down the empties.

"What else do you love?" he asked her.

"Hmm." She considered as she downed number five. "Smoke jumping and those who share the insanity." She toasted them to a round of applause and rude comments, then sat back a moment with her full glass. "Fire and the catching of it, my dad, ear-busting rock and roll on a hot summer night and tiny little puppies. How about you?"

Like her, he sat back with his last shot. "I could go along with most of that, except I don't know your dad."

"Haven't jumped fire yet either."

"True, but I'm predisposed to love it. I have a fondness for loud rock and tiny little puppies, but would substitute heart-busting sex on a hot summer night and big, sloppy dogs."

"Interesting." They tossed back that last shot, in unison, to more applause. "I'd've pegged you for a cat man."

"I've got nothing against cats, but a big, sloppy dog will always need his human."

Her earrings swung as she cocked her head. "Like to be needed, do you?"

"I guess I do."

She pointed at him in an *aha* gesture. "There's that romantic streak again."

"Wide and long. Want to go have heart-busting sex in anticipation of a hot summer night?"

She threw back her head and laughed. "That's a generous offer—and no." She slapped a hand on the table. "But I'll go you another six."

God help him. "You're on." He patted his pocket. "I believe I'll take a short cigar break while we get the next setup."

"Ten-minute recess," Rowan announced. "Hey, Big Nate, how about some salsa and chips to soak up some of this tequila? And not the wimpy stuff."

The woman of his dreams, Gull decided as he opted to go out the back for his smoke. A salsa-eating, tequila-downing, smoke-jumping stunner with brains and a wicked uppercut.

Now all he had to do was talk her into bed.

He lit up in the chilly dark, blew smoke up at a sky sizzling with stars. The night struck him as pretty damn perfect. Crappy music in a western dive, cheap tequila, the companionship of like-minded others and a compelling woman who engaged his mind and excited his body.

He thought of home and the winters that engaged and absorbed most of his time. He didn't mind it, in fact enjoyed it. But if the past few years had taught him anything, it was he needed the heat and rush of the summers, the work and, yes, the risk of chasing fires.

Maybe it was just that, the combination of pride and pleasure in what he'd accomplished back home, the thrill and satisfaction of what he knew he could accomplish here that allowed him to stand in a chilly spring night in the middle of almost-nowhere and recognize perfection.

He wandered around the building, enjoying his cigar, thinking of facing Rowan over another six tequila shots. Next time—if there was a next time—he'd make damn sure they had a bottle of Patrón Silver. Then at least he'd feel more secure about the state of his stomach lining.

Amused, he came around the side of the building. He heard the grunts first, then the ugly sound of fist against flesh. He moved forward, toward the sounds, scanning the dark pockets of the parking lot.

Two of the men Rowan had dealt with in the bar held Dobie while the third—the big one—whaled on him.

"Shit," Gull muttered, and, tossing down his cigar, rushed forward.

Over the buzz of rage in his ears, Gull heard one of the men shout. The big man swung around, face full of mean. Gull cocked back his fist, let it fly.

He didn't think; didn't have to. Instinct took over as the other two men dropped Dobie in a heap and came at him. He embraced the madness, the moment, punch, kick, elbow strike, as he scented blood, tasted his own.

He felt something crunch under his fist, heard the whoosh of expelled air as his foot slammed into belly fat. Someone dropped to his knees and gagged after his elbow jabbed an exposed throat. Out of the corner of his eye, Gull saw Dobie had managed to gain his feet and limped over to the retching man to deliver a solid kick in the ribs.

One of the others tried to run. Gull caught him, flung him so he skidded face-first over the gravel.

He didn't clearly remember knocking the big guy down, getting on top of him, but it took three of his fellow jumpers to pull him off.

"He's had enough. He's out." Little Bear's voice penetrated that buzz of rage. "Ease off, Gull."

"Okay. I'm good." Gull held up a hand to signal he was done. As the grips on him loosened, he looked over at Dobie.

His friend sat on the ground surrounded by other jumpers, a few of the local women. His face and shirtfront were both a bloody mess, and his right eye was swollen shut.

"Did a number on you, pal," Gull commented. Then he saw the dark stain on Dobie's right pant leg, and the dripping pool. "Christ! Did they knife you?"

Before Gull reached him, Dobie two-fingered a broken bottle of Tabasco out of his pocket. "Nah. Busted this when I went down. Got a few nicks is all, and a waste of good Tabasco."

L.B. crouched to get a better look at Dobie. "You carry Tabasco in your pocket?"

"Where else would I carry it?"

Shaking his head, Gull sat back on his heels. "He dumps it on everything."

"Damn right." To prove it, Dobie shook out the little left on the ass of one of the semiconscious men. "I came out for a little air, and the three of them jumped me. Laying for me—or any of us, I reckon. You sure came along at the right time," he said to Gull. "You know kung fu or some shit?"

"Something like that. Better go get patched up."

"Oh, I'm okay."

Rowan moved through, crouched in front of Dobie. "They wouldn't have gone after you if they hadn't been pissed at me. Do me a favor, okay? Go get patched up so I don't have to feel guilty." Then she leaned over, kissed his bruised and bloody cheek. "I'll owe you."

"Well . . . if it'll make you feel better."

"Do you want me to call the law?" Big Nate asked him.

Dobie studied the three men, shrugged. "Looks to me more like they need an ambulance." He shrugged again. "I don't care if they go to jail, to fiery hell or back wherever they came from."

"All right then." Big Nate stepped over, toed the man sitting up nursing his face in his hands. "You fit to drive?" When the man managed a nod, Big Nate toed him again a little harder. "You're going to get in your truck with the fuckers you travel with. You're going to drive, and keep on driving. If I see you around my place or any other place I happen to be, you're going to wish to God almighty I had called the law. Now get off my property."

To expedite the matter, several of the men hoisted the barely conscious big guy and his moaning companions into the truck, then stood like a wall until it drove away.

Gull received a number of shoulder and back slaps, countless offers of a drink. He wisely accepted all of them to avoid an argument as he watched Libby, Cards and Gibbons help Dobie into one of the vans.

"Do you want a doc to look you over?" Little Bear asked him.

"No. I've had worse falling out of bed."

Little Bear watched the van as Gull did. "He'll be all right. It takes more than three assholes to down a smoke jumper." He gave Gull a last shoulder slap, then turned back toward the bar when the van pulled out of the lot.

Gull stayed where he was, trying to reach for his calm again. He knew it was in there, somewhere, but at the moment, elusive.

"Is this yours?"

He turned to see Rowan holding his cigar.

"Yeah. I guess I dropped it."

"Butterfingers." She took a few puffs until the tip glowed true again, then helped herself to one long, deep drag. "Prime cigar, too," she added, then offered it back. "Shame to waste it."

Gull took it, studied it. "That's it," he decided.

He flung it down again and, grabbing her, yanked her against him. "That's it," he repeated before his mouth crushed down on hers.

A man could only take so much stimulation before demanding release.

She slapped both hands on his chest, shoved. "Hey."

For a moment he figured he'd experience her excellent uppercut up close and personal. Then she mirrored his initial move and yanked him back.

Her mouth was as he'd imagined. Hot and soft and avid. It met his with equal fervor, as if a switch had been flipped in each of them from stop to go. She pressed that killer body to his without hesitation, without restraint, a gift and a challenge, until the chilly air under the sizzling stars seemed to smoke.

He tasted the sharp tang of tequila on her tongue, a fascinating contrast to the scent of ripe peaches that clung to her skin; felt the hard, steady gallop of her heart that matched the pace of his own.

Then she drew back, looked in his eyes, held there a moment before drawing away.

"You've got skills," she stated.

"Ditto."

She blew out a breath—a long one. "You're a temptation, Gull, I can't deny it. Stupid to deny it, and I'm not stupid."

"Far from it."

She rubbed her lips together as if revisiting his taste. "The thing is, once you mix sex into it, even smart people can get stupid. So . . . better not."

"No's your choice. Mine's to keep trying."

"I can't hold that against you." She smiled at him now, not her usual smirk but something warmer. "You fight like a maniac."

"I tend to get carried away, so I try to avoid it when I can."

"That's a good policy. What do you say we postpone the tequila and get some ice on that jaw of yours."

"That's fine."

As they started back, she glanced over at him. "What was that technique you were using on those bastards?"

"An ancient form called kicking ass."

She laughed, gave him a friendly hip bump. "Impressive."

He returned the hip bump. "Sleep with me and I'll give you lessons."

She laughed again. "You can try harder than that."

"I'm just getting warmed up," he told her, then opened the door to the overheated bar and lousy music.

ROWAN ZIPPED her warm-up jacket as she stepped outside. She'd put in some time in the gym, and checked the jump list on the board in Operations. She was first load, fourth man. Now she wanted a solid run on the track, maybe some chow. She'd already checked and rechecked her gear. If the siren sounded, she'd be ready.

Otherwise . . .

Otherwise, she thought as she shot a wave to one of the mechanics, there was always work, always training. But the fact was she was ready, more than ready, to jump her first fire of the season. She cast a look up at the sky as she walked toward the track. Clear, wide and as pretty a spring blue as anyone could want.

Below it, the base chugged along in early-season morning mode. Jumpers and support staff stayed busy, washing vehicles or tuning them up—or tuning themselves with calisthenics on the training field. After the night's revelry, plenty were getting a slow start, but she wanted air and effort.

And saw as she looked toward the track, she wasn't the only one.

She recognized Gull not only by the body, but the speed. Fast feet, she thought again. Obviously tequila shots and a bar fight hadn't slowed him down.

She had to admire that.

As she jogged closer she noted that despite the cool air he'd worked up a good sweat, one that ran a dark vee down the faded gray tee he wore.

She had to admire that, too. She liked a man who pushed himself, who tested his limits even when he was in his own world.

Though she'd already loosened up, she paused to stretch before peeling off her jacket. And timed her entrance to the track to veer on beside him.

"What're you up to?"

He held up two fingers, saving his breath.

"Going for three?" When he nodded, she wondered if he could keep up that killing pace for another mile. "Me too. Go ahead, Flash, I can't keep up with you."

She fell off his pace, found her own rhythm.

She loved to run, loved it with a pure heart, but imagined if she'd had Gull's speed, she'd have adored it. Then she forgot him, tuned into her own body, the air, the steady slap of her shoes on the track. She let her mind empty so it could fill again with scattered thoughts.

Personal supply list, juggling some time in for sewing some PG bags, Gull's mouth, Dobie. She should give her father a buzz since she was on call and couldn't get over to see him. Why did Janis paint her toenails when nobody saw them anyway? Gull's teeth scraping over her bottom lip. Assholes who ganged up on a little guy.

Gull kicking ass in a dark parking lot.

Gull's ass. Very nice.

Probably better to think of something else, she told herself as she hit the first mile. But hell, nothing else was as appealing. Besides, thinking wasn't doing.

What she needed—what they all needed—was for the siren to blast. Then she'd be too busy to fantasize about, much less consider, getting tangled up with a man she worked with.

Too bad she hadn't met him in the winter, though how she'd have run into him when he lived in California posed a problem. Still, say she'd taken a vacation, dropped into his arcade place. Would she have experienced that sizzle if she'd met him across the lane in the bowling alley, or over a hot game of Mortal Kombat?

Hard to say.

He'd have looked as good, she reminded herself. But would there have been that punch if she'd looked into those green eyes when he sold her some tokens?

Wasn't at least part of the zip because of what they both did here, the training, the sweat, the anticipation, the intense satisfaction of knowing only a select few could make the cut and be what they were?

And, hello, wasn't that the reason she didn't get sexually or romantically involved with other jumpers? How could you trust your feelings when they were pumped through the adrenaline rush? And what did you do with those feelings when and if—and most likely when—things went south? You'd still have to work with, and trust your life to, somebody you'd been sleeping with and weren't sleeping with anymore. And one or both of you had to be fairly pissed about it.

Entirely better to meet somebody, even if he sold you tokens in an arcade, have a nice, uncomplicated short-term relationship. Then go back to doing what you do.

She kicked up her pace to hit the last mile, then eased off to a cool-down jog. Her eyebrows lifted when Gull fell into pace beside her.

"You still here?"

"I did five. Felt good."

"No tequila haze this morning?"

"I don't get hangovers."

"Ever? What's your secret?" When he only smiled, she shook her head. "Yeah, yeah, if I sleep with you, you'll tell me. How's the jaw, et cetera?"

"It's okay." Banging like a drum after the five miles, but he knew that would subside.

"I heard Dobie nixed the overnight for observation. L.B.'s got him off the jump list until he's fit."

Gull nodded. He'd checked the list himself. "It won't take him long. He's a tough little bastard."

She slowed to a walk, then stopped to stretch. "What were you listening to?" she asked, gesturing to the MP3 player strapped to his arm.

"Ear-busting rock," he said with a smile. "You can borrow it the next time you run."

"I don't like music when I run. I like to think."

"The best thing about running is *not* thinking."

As he stretched, she checked out the body she'd been thinking about. "Yeah, you're probably right."

They started the walk back together.

"I didn't come out here because I saw you on the track."

"Well, hell. Now my day's ruined."

"But I did admire your ass when you were whizzing by."

"That's marginally satisfying," he considered, "but I find it doesn't fully massage my ego."

"You're a funny guy, Gull. You tend to use fancy words, and read fancy books—I hear. You're mean as a rattler in a fight, fast as a cheetah and spend your winters with foosball."

He bent to snag her jacket off the ground. "I like a good game of foosball."

As she tied the sleeves around her waist, she gave his face a long study. "You're hard to figure."

"Only if you're looking for one size fits all."

"Maybe, but—" She broke off as she spotted the truck pulling up in front of Operations. "Hey!" she shouted, waved her arms, then ran.

Gull watched the man get out of the truck, tall and solid in a battered leather jacket and scarred boots. Silver hair caught by the wind blew back from a tanned, strong-jawed face. He turned, then opened his arms so Rowan could jump into them. Gull might have experienced a twinge of jealousy, but he recognized Lucas "Iron Man" Tripp.

And it was a pretty thing, in his opinion, to see a man give his grown daughter a quick swing.

"I was just thinking about you," Rowan told her father. "I was going to give you a call later. I'm on the second stick, so I couldn't come by."

"I missed you. I thought I'd check in, grab a minute and see how it's all going." He pulled off his sunglasses, hooked them in his pocket. "So, a strong crop of rooks this year."

"Yeah. In fact . . ." Rowan glanced around, then signaled to Gull so he'd change direction and join them. "Here's the one who broke the base record on the mile-and-a-half. Hotshot out of California." She kept her arm around her father's waist while Gull walked to them.

"Gulliver Curry, Lucas Tripp."

"It's a genuine pleasure, Mr. Tripp," Gull told him as he extended a hand.

"You can drop the mister. Congratulations on the base record, and making the cut."

"Thanks."

She had her father's eyes, Gull noted as they covered the small talk. And his bone structure. But what made more of an impression was the body language of both. It said, simply and unquestionably, they were an unassailable unit.

"There's that son of a bitch." Yangtree let the door of Operations slap behind him, and came forward to exchange one-armed hugs with Lucas.

"Man, it's good to see you. So they let you skate through again this year?"

"Hell. Somebody's got to keep these screwups in line."

"When you're tired of riding herd on the kids, I can always use another instructor."

"Teaching rich boys to jump out of planes."

"And girls," Lucas added. "It's a living."

"No packing in, packing out, no twenty hours on a line. You miss it every day," Yangtree said, and pointed at him.

"And twice on Sunday." Tripp ran a hand down Rowan's back. "But my knees don't."

"I hear that."

"We'll get you a couple rocking chairs," Rowan suggested, "and maybe a nice pot of chamomile tea."

Lucas tugged her earlobe. "Make it a beer and I'm there. Then again, I heard the bunch of you had plenty of those last night, and got into a little ruckus."

"Nothing we couldn't handle," Yangtree claimed, and winked at Gull. "Or you couldn't handle, right, Kick Ass?"

"A momentary distraction."

"Did the momentary distraction give you that bruise on your jaw?" Lucas wondered.

Gull rubbed a hand over it. "I'd say you should see the other guys, but it's hard to be sure how they looked since they ran off with their tails tucked."

"From having them rammed into your fists." Lucas nodded at Gull's scraped and swollen knuckles. "How's the man they ganged up on?"

"Do you know everything?" Rowan demanded.

"Ear to the ground, darling." Lucas kissed her temple. "My ear's always to the ground."

"Dobie's a little guy, but he got some licks in." Yangtree turned his head, spat on the ground. "They beat on him pretty good until Kick Ass here came along. Of course, before all that, your girl put two of them on their asses."

"Yeah, I heard about that, too."

"I didn't start it."

"So I'm told. Starting it's stupid," Lucas stated. "Finishing it's necessary."

Rowan narrowed her eyes. "You didn't come by to check in, you came by to check *on*."

"Maybe. Want to fight about it?"

She gave her father a poke in the chest, grinned.

And the siren went off.

Rowan kissed her father's cheek. "See you later," she said, and took off running. Yangtree slapped Lucas's shoulder and did the same.

"It was good to meet you."

Tripp took the hand Gull offered, studied the knuckles. "You're off the list because of these."

"Today."

"There's tomorrow."

"I'm counting on it."

Gull headed to the ready room. He was off the jump list, but he could lend a hand to those on it. Already jumpers were suiting up, taking their gear out of the tall cabinets, pulling on Kevlar suits over the fire-retardant undergarments. By the time he spotted her, Rowan had dropped into one of the folding chairs to put on her boots.

He helped with gear and equipment until he could work his way to her.

Over the sound of engines and raised voices, he shouted at her, "Where?"

"Got one in the Bitterroots, near Bass Creek."

A short enough flight, he calculated, to warrant a buddy check prior to boarding. He started at her bootstraps, worked his way up. He'd already gotten past the state of his knuckles, and his temporary leave from the jump list.

No point in regrets.

"You're clear." Gull squeezed a hand to her shoulder, met her eyes. "Make it good."

"It's the only way I know."

He watched her go, thought even the waddle enforced by the suit and gear looked strong and sexy on her.

As he walked out to watch the rest of the load, he saw Dobie hobbling over. And in the distance Lucas "Iron Man" Tripp stood, hands in his pockets.

"Fuckers screwed our chances." Puffing a little, his face a

crescendo of bruises, his brutalized eye a vivid mix of purple and red, Dobie stopped beside Gull.

"Others to come."

"Yeah. Shit. Libby's on there. I never thought she'd catch one before me."

Together they stood as the plane taxied, as its nose lifted. Gull glanced down to where Lucas stood, saw him lift his face to the sky. And watch his daughter fly toward the flames.

5

The heart of the wildfire beat hot and hard. Cutting through it loosed a waterfall of sweat that ran down Rowan's back in constant streams. Her chain saw shrieked through bark and wood, spitting out splinters and dust that layered her clothes, gloves, hard hat. The roar and screams of saws, of cracking wood, crashing trees fought to smother that hard, hot beat.

She paused only to chug down water to wet her throat and wash out the dust and smoke or to swipe off her goggles when the sweat running down her face blurred them.

She stepped back when the ponderosa she'd killed to save others whooshed its way to the forest floor.

"Hey, Swede." Gibbons, acting as fire boss, hailed her over the din. Ash blackened his face, and the smoke he'd hiked through reddened his eyes. "I'm taking you, Matt and Yangtree off the saw line. The head's shifted on us. It's moving up the ridge to the south and building. We got spots frigging everywhere. We need to turn her while we can."

He pulled out his map to show her positions. "We got hotshots working here, and Janis, Trigger, two of the rooks, flanking it here. We've got another load coming in, and they'll take the saw line, chase down spots. We've got repellent on the way, should dump on the head in about ten, so make sure you're clear."

"Roger that."

"Take them up. Watch your ass."

She grabbed her gear, pulled in her teammates and began the half-mile climb through smoke and heat.

In her mind she plotted escape routes, the distance and direction to the safe zone. Small, frisky spot fires flashed along the steep route, so they beat them out, smothered them before continuing up.

Along their left flank an orange wall pulsed with heat and light, sucked oxygen out of the air to feed itself as it growled and gobbled through trees. She watched columns of smoke build tall and thick in the sky.

A section of the wall pushed out, skipped and jumped across the rough track in front of them, and began to burn merrily. She leaped forward kicking dirt over it, using her Pulaski to smother it while Yangtree beat at it with a pine bough.

They beat, shoveled and dug their way up the ridge.

Over the din she caught the rumble of the tanker, pulled out her radio to answer its signal. "Take cover!" she shouted to her team. "We're good, Gibbons. Tell them to drop the mud. We're clear."

Through the smoke, she watched the retardant plane swing over the ridge, heard the thunder of its gates opening to make the drop, and the roar as the thick pink rain streaked down from the sky.

Those fighting closer to the head would take cover as well, and still be splattered with gel that burned and stung exposed skin.

"We're clear," she told her team as Yangtree gnawed off a bite of an energy bar. "We're going to jag a little east, circle the head and meet up with Janis and the others. Gibbons says she's moving pretty fast. We need to do the same to keep ahead of her. Let's move! Keep it peeled for spots."

She kept the map in her head, the caprices of the fire in her guts. They continued to chase down spot fires, some no bigger than a dinner platter, others the size of a kid's swimming pool.

And all the while they moved up the ridge.

She heard the head before she saw it. It bellowed and

clapped like thunder, followed that with a sly, pulsing roar. And felt it before she saw it, that rush of heat that washed over her face, pushed into her lungs.

Then everything filled with the flame, a world of vivid orange, gold, mean red spewing choking clouds of smoke. Through the clouds and eerie glimmer she saw the silhouettes, caught glimpses of the yellow shirts and hard hats of the smoke jumpers, waging the war.

Shifting her pack, she pushed her way up the ridge toward the ferocious burn. "Check in with Gibbons," she shouted to Matt. "Let him know we made it. Yo, Elf!" Rowan hailed Janis as she hurried forward, waving her arms. "Cavalry's here."

"We need it. We got scratch lines around the hottest part of the head. The mud knocked her down some, and we've been scratching line down toward the tail. Need to widen it, and down the snags. Jesus."

She took a minute to gulp some water, swipe at the sweat dripping into her eyes. The pink goo of repellent pasted her hat and shirt. "First fire of the season, and this bitch has a punch. Gibbons just told me they're sending in another load of jumpers, and they put Idaho on alert. We gotta cut off her head, Swede."

"We can start on widening the line, downing the snags. Hit a lot of spots on the way up. She keeps trying to jump."

"Tell me. Get started. I got the rooks up there, Libby and Stovic. Keep 'em straight."

"You got it."

Rowan dug, cut, beat, hacked and sweated. Hours flashed by. She sliced down snags, the still-standing dead trees the fire would use for fuel. When she felt her energy flag, she stopped long enough to stuff her mouth with the peanut-butter crackers in her PG bag, wash it down with the prize of the single Coke—nearly hot now—she'd brought with her.

Her clothes sported the pink goo from a second drop of repellent, and under it her back, legs, shoulders burned from the heat and the hours of unrelenting effort.

But she felt it, the minute it started to turn their way.

The massive cloud of smoke thinned—just a little—and through it she saw a single hopeful wink of light from the North Star.

Day had burned into night while they'd battled.

She straightened, arched her back to relieve it, and looked back, into the black—the burned-out swatch of the forest the fire had consumed, the charred logs, stumps, ghostly spikes, dead pools of ash.

Nothing to eat there now, she thought, and they'd cut off the supply of fuel at the head.

Her energy swung back. It wasn't over, but they'd beaten it. The dragon was beginning to lie down.

She downed a dead pine, then used one of its branches to beat out a small, sneaky spot. The cry of shock and pain had her swinging around in time to see Stovic go down. His chain saw bounced out of his hands, rolled, and the blood on its teeth dripped onto the trampled ground.

Rowan let her own drop where she stood, lunged toward him. She reached him as he struggled to sit up and grab at his thigh.

"Hold on! Hold on!" She pushed his hands away, tore at his pants to widen the jagged tear.

"I don't know what happened. I'm cut!" Beneath the soot and ash, his face glowed ghastly white.

She knew. Fatigue had made him sloppy, caused him to lose his grip on the saw or use it carelessly enough, just for a second, to allow it to jerk back.

"How bad?" he demanded as she used a knife from her pack to cut the material back. "Is it bad?"

"It's a scratch. Toughen up, rook." She didn't know either way, not yet. "Get the first-aid kit," Rowan ordered when Libby dropped down beside her. "I'm going to clean this up some, Stovic, get a better look."

A little shocky, she determined as she studied his eyes, but holding.

And his bitter litany of curses—a few of them Russian delivered in his Brooklyn accent—made her optimistic as she cleaned the wound.

"Got a nice gash." She said it cheerfully, and thought, Jesus, Jesus, a little deeper, a little to the left, and bye-bye, Stovic. "The blade mostly got your pants."

She looked him in the eye again. She'd have lied if necessary, and her stomach jittered with relief she didn't need the lie. "You're going to need a couple dozen stitches, but that shouldn't slow you down for long. I'm going to do a field dressing that'll hold you until you get back to base."

He managed a wobbly smile, but she heard the click in his throat as he swallowed. "I didn't cut off anything essential, right?"

"Your junk's intact, Chainsaw."

"Hurts like hell."

"I bet."

He gathered himself, took a couple slow breaths. Rowan felt another wave of relief when a little color eked back into his face. "First time I jump a fire, and look what I do. It won't keep me grounded long, will it?"

"Nah." She dressed the wound quickly, competently. "And you'll have this sexy scar to impress the women." She sat back on her haunches, smiled at him. "Women can't resist a wounded warrior, right, Lib?"

"Damn right. In fact, I'm holding myself back from jumping you right now, Stovic."

He gave her a twisted grin. "We beat it, didn't we, Swede?"

"Yeah, we did." She patted his knee, then got to her feet. Leaving Libby tending him, she walked apart to contact Gibbons and arrange for Stovic to be littered out.

Eighteen hours after jumping the fire, Rowan climbed back onto the plane for the short flight back to base.

Using her pack as a pillow, she stretched out on the floor, shut her eyes. "Steak," she said, "medium rare. A football-size baked potato drowning in butter, a mountain of candied carrots, followed by a slab of chocolate cake the size of Utah smothered in half a gallon of ice cream."

"Meat loaf." Yangtree dropped down beside her while somebody else—or a couple of somebody elses by the stereophonics—snored like buzz saws. "An entire meat loaf, and I'll take my mountain in mashed potatoes with a vat of gravy. Apple pie, and make that a gallon of ice cream."

Rowan slid open her eyes to see Matt watching her with a sleepy smile. "What's your pick, Matt?"

"My ma's chicken and dumplings. Best ever. Just pour it in a five-gallon bucket so I can stick my head in and chow it down. Cherry cobbler and homemade whipped cream."

"Everybody knows whipped cream comes in a can."

"Not at my ma's house. But I'm hungry enough to eat five-day-old pizza, and the box it came in."

"Pizza," Libby moaned, then tried to find a more comfortable curl on her seat. "I never thought I could be this empty and live."

"Eighteen hours on the line'll do it." Rowan yawned, rolled over, and let the voices, the snoring, the engines lull her toward sleep.

"Gonna hit the kitchen when we get back, Ro?" Matt asked her.

"Mmm. Gotta eat. Gotta shower off the stink first."

The next thing she knew they were down. She staggered off the plane through a fog of exhaustion. Once she'd dumped her gear she stumbled to her room, ripped the wrapper off a candy bar. She all but inhaled it while she stripped off her filthy clothes. Barely awake, she aimed for the shower, whimpered a little as the warm water slid over her. Through blurry eyes she watched it run dingy gray into the drain.

She lathered up, hair, body, face, inhaling the scent of peaches that apparently tripped Gull's trigger. Rinse and repeat, she ordered herself. Rinse and repeat. And when, at last, the water ran clear, she made a halfhearted attempt to dry off.

Then fell onto the bed wrapped in the damp towel.

THE DREAM crept up on her in the twilight layer of sleep, as her mind began to float back from the deep pit of exhaustion.

Thundering engines, the whip of wind, the heady leap into the sky. The thrill turning to panic—the pound, pound, pound of heart against ribs as she watched, helplessly, Jim plunge toward the burning ground.

"Hey. Hey. You need to wake up."

The voice cutting through the scream in her head, the rough shake on her shoulder, had her bolting up in bed.

"What? The siren? What?" She stared into Gull's face, rubbing one hand over her own.

"No. You were having a nightmare."

She breathed in, breathed out, slitting her eyes a little. It was morning—or maybe later—she could tell that much. And Gulliver Curry was in her room, without her permission.

"What the hell are you doing in here?"

"Maybe you want to hitch that towel up some? Not that I mind the view. And, in fact, could probably spend the rest of the day admiring it."

She glanced down, saw she was naked to the waist, and the towel that had slipped down wasn't covering much below either. Baring her teeth, she yanked it up and around. "Answer the question before I kick your ass."

"You missed breakfast, and you were heading toward missing lunch."

"We worked the fire for eighteen hours. I didn't get to bed till about three in the morning."

"So I hear, and good job. But somebody mentioned you didn't get to eat, and have a fondness for bacon-and-egg sandwiches, with Jack cheese. So . . ." He jerked his thumb at the bedside table. "I brought you one. I was going to leave it on the nightstand, but you were having a bad one. I woke you up, you flashed me—and just let me insert you have the most magnificent rack it's ever been my privilege to view—and that brings us up to date."

She studied the sandwich, the bottle of soda beside it. This time when she breathed in, the scent nearly made her weep with joy. "You brought me a bacon-and-egg sandwich?"

"With Jack cheese."

"I'd say you earned the flash."

"I can go get you another if that's all it takes."

She laughed, yawned, then secured the towel before grabbing the plate. The first bite had her closing her eyes in ecstasy. Wrapped in pleasure, she didn't order him off the bed when she felt it give under his weight.

"Thanks," she said with her mouth full of bite two. "Sincerely."

"Let me respond, sincerely. It was way worth it."

"I do have exceptional tits." She reached for the drink, twisted the top off. "The fire kept changing direction on us, spitting out spots. We'd get a line down, and she'd say, Oh, you want to play that way? Try this. But in the end, she couldn't beat the Zulies. Have you got any word this morning on Stovic?"

"Now known as Chainsaw. He and his twenty-seven stitches are doing fine."

"I should've kept a closer eye on him."

"He passed the audition, Rowan. Accidents happen. They're part of the job description."

"Can't argue, but he was part of my team, and I was senior member in that sector." She shrugged. "He's okay, so that's okay."

She shifted her gaze. "Your hands look better."

"Good enough." He flexed them. "I'm back on the jump list."

"Dobie?"

"He's coming along, but it'll be a couple more days anyway. Little Bear discovered Dobie can sew like Betsy Ross, so he's been keeping Dobie chained to a machine. I won fifty-six dollars and change at poker last night, and Bicardi—one of the mechanics—got half lit and sang Italian opera. That, I believe, is all the news."

"I appreciate the update, and the sandwich. Now go away so I can get dressed."

"I've already seen you naked."

"It'll take more than a breakfast sandwich for you to see me naked again."

"How about dinner?"

God, he made her laugh. "Out, hotshot. I need to hit the gym, put my time in and work out some of these kinks."

"To show what a classy guy I am, I'll refrain from making any of the obvious comments to that statement." He rose, picked up the empty plate. "You're one gorgeous female, Rowan," he said as he walked out. "It keeps me up at night."

"You're one sexy male, Gulliver," she murmured when he'd gone. "It's messing with my head."

She put in ninety in the gym, but kept it light and slow to avoid overworking her system, then hit the cookhouse.

Feeling human again, she texted the basics to her father.

Killed the fire. Am A-OK. Love you, Ro

She headed to the loft to check the chute she'd hung the night before. She began to check for holes, snags, defects.

She glanced up when Matt and Libby came in.

"Well, don't you look flat-tailed and dull-eyed."

"Remind me never to eat like a pig before crawling into bed." Libby pressed a hand to her belly. "I couldn't settle till after five, then lay there like a beached whale."

"You didn't make it to the cookhouse," Matt commented when he brought his chute over.

"By the time I scraped off the stink, I barely made it from the shower to the bed. Slept like a rock," she added, smiling at Libby. "Had room service, put in my ninety PT, ate more, and here I am ready to do it all again."

"Sweet." Libby spread out her chute. "Room service?"

"Gull brought me a breakfast sandwich."

"Is that what they call it in Missoula?"

Rowan pointed a finger. "Just the sandwich, but he did earn some points. Have either of you seen Chainsaw?"

"Yeah, I poked in before I ran into Matt. He showed me his stitches."

"Is that what they call it in California?"

"Walked right into that one."

"He's lucky," Matt said. "Only hit meat. An inch either way, different story."

"It comes down to inches, doesn't it?" Libby ran her fingers over her chute. "Or seconds. Or one tiny lapse of focus. The difference between having an interesting scar or . . ."

She trailed off, paled a little. "I'm sorry, Matt. I wasn't thinking."

"It's okay. You didn't even know him." He continued his inspection, cleared his throat. "To tell you the truth, I didn't know, not for sure, if I was going to be able to really do it again until yesterday. In the door, looking down at the fire, waiting for the spotter's hand to come down on my shoulder. I didn't know if I could jump fire again."

"But you did," Rowan murmured.

"Yeah. I told myself I did it for Jim, but until I actually did it . . . Because you're right, Libby. It is about inches and seconds. It's about fate. It's why we can't let up. Anyway." He let out a long breath. "Did you know Dolly's back?" he asked Rowan.

"No." Surprised, Rowan stopped what she was doing. "When? I haven't seen her on base."

"She came back yesterday, while we were on the fire. She came by my room this morning after breakfast." He kept his gaze fixed on his chute. "She looks okay. Wanted to apologize for how she was after Jim died."

"That's good." But Rowan felt a twist in her belly as she completed her chute inspection.

"I told her she ought to do the same to you."

"Doesn't matter."

"Yeah, it does."

"Can I ask who Dolly is?" Libby wondered. "Or should I mind my own business?"

"She was one of the cooks," Rowan told her. "She and Jim had a thing. Actually, she tended to have things with a variety, but she'd narrowed it down to Jim most of last season. She took it hard when he died. Understandable."

"She came at you with a kitchen knife," Matt reminded her. "There's nothing understandable about that."

"Well, Jesus."

"She sort of came at me," Rowan corrected as Libby gaped at her.

"Why?"

"I was Jim's jump partner that day. She needed to blame somebody. She went a little crazy, waved the knife at me. But basically she blamed all of us, said we'd all killed him."

Rowan waited a beat to see if Matt would comment, but he kept his silence.

"She took off right after. I don't think anyone expected she'd be back, or get hired back, for that matter."

Matt shifted his feet, looked at her again. "Are you okay with it?"

"I don't know." Rowan rubbed the back of her neck. "I guess if she doesn't wave sharp implements at me or try to poison me, I'm cool with it."

"She's got a baby."

It was Rowan's turn to gape. "Say what?"

"She told me she had a baby, a girl, in April." His eyes watered up a little, so he looked away. "Dolly named her Shiloh. Her ma's looking after her while Dolly's working. She said it's Jim's."

"Well, God, you didn't know before? Your family doesn't know?"

He shook his head. "That's what she apologized for. She asked if I'd tell my mother, my family, and gave me some pictures. She said I could go see it—her—the baby—if I wanted."

"Did Jim know?"

Color came and went in his face. "She said she told him that morning, before the jump. She said he was really excited, that he picked the name. Boy or girl, he told her, he wanted Shiloh. They were going to get married, she said, in the fall."

He drew a wallet-sized photo out of his pocket. "Here she is. This is Shiloh."

Libby took the picture. "She's beautiful, Matt."

His eyes cleared at that, and the smile spread. "Bald as a melon. Jim and I were, too, and my sister. I've got to call my ma," he said as Libby passed the photo to Rowan. "I can't figure out how to tell her."

Rowan studied the chubby-cheeked, sparkle-eyed infant before handing the photo back. "Go take a walk, work it out in your head. Then call your mother. She'll be happy. Maybe a little mad she didn't know sooner, but overall she'll be happy. Go on. I'll take care of your chute."

"I can't get it off my mind, so I guess you're right. I can finish the chute later."

"I'll take care of it."

"Thanks. Thanks," he repeated, and wandered out like a man in a dream.

"It's a lot to deal with," Libby commented.

"Yeah, it's a whole lot."

She let it simmer in the back of her mind while she worked. Others came in, and since word of Dolly Brakeman's return spread, it reigned as the hot topic of the day.

"Have you seen her yet?"

Rowan shook her head at Trigger. Since she'd finished clearing her own chute, she focused on Matt's.

"Word is she came in yesterday afternoon, with her mother and her preacher."

"Her *what*?"

"Yeah." Trigger rolled his eyes. "Some Reverend Latterly.

The word is it's her mother's preacher guy, and Dolly's going to church regular now. And so they closeted up with L.B. for an hour. This morning, she's in the kitchen with Lynn and Marg, frying up the bacon."

"She can cook."

"Yeah, that was never her problem."

She met Trigger's eyes, gave another quick shake of her head. "She's got a kid now." Rowan kept her voice low. "There's no point shaking all that out."

"You think the kid's Jim's, like she says?"

"They were banging like bunnies, so why not?" Because, neither of them said, she had a habit of hopping to lots of male bunnies. "Anyway, it's not our business."

"He was one of ours, so you know that makes it our business."

She couldn't deny it, but she tuned out the gossip and speculation until she had stowed the chutes. Then she hunted out Little Bear.

He straightened from his hunch over his desk, gestured for her to close the door. "I figured you'd be stopping by."

"I just want to know if I need to watch my back. I'd as soon not end up with a bread knife between my shoulder blades."

He rubbed a spot between his eyebrows. "Do you think I'd let her on base if I thought she'd give you any trouble?"

"No. But I wouldn't mind hearing that right out loud."

"She worked here three years before Jim. The only problem we ever had was the wind from how fast she'd throw up her skirts. And nobody much had a problem with that, either."

"I don't care if she gave every rookie, snookie, jumper and mechanic blow jobs in the ready room." Rowan jammed her hands in her pockets, did a little turn around the room. "She's a good cook."

"She is. And from what I heard, a lot of men missed those bj's once she hooked up with Jim. And she's got a kid now. From the timing of it, and from what she says, it's his." L.B. puffed out his cheeks. "She brought her preacher with her. Her mother got her going to church. She needs the work, wants to make amends."

He waved a hand in the air. "I'm not going to deny I felt sorry for her, but I'd've turned her off if I hadn't believed she wanted a fresh start for her and the baby. She knows if she gives you or anybody else any trouble, she's out."

"I don't want that on my head, L.B."

He gave Rowan a long look out of solemn brown eyes. "Then think of it on mine. If you're not all right with this, I'll take care of it."

"Hell."

"She's singing in the choir on Sundays."

"Give me a break." She shoved her hands in her pockets again as L.B. grinned at her. "Fine, fine." But she dropped down in a chair.

"Not fine?"

"Did she tell you she and Jim were going to get married, and he was all happy about the baby?"

"She did."

"The thing is, L.B., I know he was seeing somebody else. We caught that fire last year in St. Joe, and were there three days. Jim hooked up with one of the women on the cook line; he seemed to go for cooks. And I know they met at a motel between here and there a few times when he was off the jump list. Others, too."

"I know it. I had to talk to him about expecting me to cover for him with Dolly."

"And the day of his accident, I told you, he was jittery on the plane. Not excited but nervous, jumpy. If Dolly dropped the pregnancy on him before we got called out, that's probably why. Or part of why."

He tapped a pencil on the desk. "I can't see any reason Dolly has to know any of that. Do you?"

"No. I'm saying maybe she found God, or finds some comfort in singing for Jesus, but she's either lying or delusional about Jim. So it's fine with me if she's back, as long as we understand that."

"I asked Marg to keep an eye on her, let me know how she does."

Satisfied, Rowan stood up again. "That's good enough for me."

"They're getting some lightning strikes up north," L.B. told her as she started out.

"Yeah? Maybe we'll get lucky and jump a fire, then everybody can stop talking about the return of Dolly. Including me."

She might as well clear it up altogether, Rowan decided, and made the cookhouse her next stop.

She found dinner prep under way, as she'd anticipated.

Marg, the queen of the cookhouse, where she'd reigned a dozen years, stood at the counter quartering red-skinned potatoes. She wore her usual bib apron over a T-shirt and jeans, and her mop of brown hair secured under a bright pink do-rag.

Steam puffed from pots on the stove while Lady Gaga belted out "Speechless" from the playlist on the MP3 Marg had on the counter.

Nobody but Marg determined kitchen music.

She sang along in a strong, smoky alto while keeping the beat with her knife.

Her Native American blood—from her mother's grand-mother—showed in her cheekbones, but the Irish dominated in the mild white skin dashed with freckles and the lively hazel eyes.

Those eyes caught Rowan's now, and rolled toward the woman washing greens in the sink.

Rowan lifted her shoulders, let them fall. "Smells good in here." She made sure her voice carried over the music.

At the sink, Dolly froze, then slowly switched off the water and turned.

Her face was a bit fuller, Rowan noted, and her breasts as well. She had her blond hair in a high, jaunty ponytail, and needed a root job.

But that was probably unkind, Rowan thought. A new mother had other priorities. The rose in her cheeks came from emotion rather than blush as she cast her gaze down and dried her hands on a cloth.

"We got pork roasting to go with the rosemary potatoes, butter beans and carrots. Veggies get three-cheese ravioli. Gonna put a big-ass Mediterranean salad together. Pound cake and blueberry crumble for dessert."

"Sign me up."

Rowan opened the refrigerator and took out a soda as Marg went back to her potatoes.

"How are you doing, Dolly?"

"I'm fine, and you?" She said it primly, chin in the air now.

"Good enough. Maybe you could take a quick break, catch a little air with me?"

"We're busy. Lynn—"

"Better get her skinny ass back in here right quick," Marg interrupted. "You go on out, and if you see her, send her in."

"I need to dry these greens," Dolly began, but shrunk—as all did—under Marg's steely stare. "Okay, fine." She tossed aside her cloth, headed for the door.

Rowan exchanged a look with Marg, then followed.

"I saw a picture of your baby," Rowan began. "She's beautiful."

"Jim's baby."

"She's beautiful," Rowan repeated.

"She's a gift from God." Dolly folded her arms as she walked. "I need this job to provide for her. I hope you're Christian enough not to do anything that gets me fired."

"I don't think about it being Christian or otherwise, Dolly. I think about it as being human. I never had a problem with you, and I'm not looking to have one now."

"I'll cook for you just like I cook for the rest. I hope you'll show me the respect of staying clear of me and I'll do the same. Reverend Latterly says I have to forgive you to get right with the Lord, but I don't."

"Forgive me for what?"

"You're the reason my baby's going to grow up without her daddy."

Rowan said nothing for a moment. "Maybe you need to believe that to get through, and I find I don't give a shit either way."

"I expect that from you."

"Then I'm happy not to disappoint you. You can claim to have tripped over God or to've been born again, I don't care about that, either. But you've got a baby, and you need work. You're good at the work. What you're going to have to suck up, Dolly, is to keep the work, you have to deal with me. When I feel like coming into the kitchen, I will, whether you're around or not. I'm not going to live my life around your stipulations or misplaced grudges."

She held up a hand before Dolly could speak. "One more thing. You got away with coming at me once. You won't get away with it again. New baby or not, I'll put you down. Other than that, we won't have a problem."

"You're a heartless whore, and one day you'll pay for all you've done. It should've been you instead of Jim that day. It should've been you, screaming your way to the ground."

She ran back to the kitchen.

"Well," Rowan mumbled, "that went well."

6

Rowan slept poorly, and put the blame squarely on Dolly. She'd checked the radar, the logs, the maps before turning in. Fires sparked near Denali in Alaska and in the Marble Mountains of Northern California. She'd considered—half hoped—she'd be called up and spend part of her night on a transport plane. But no siren sounded, no knock banged on her door.

Instead, she'd dreamed of Jim for the second night in a row. She woke irritated and itchy, and annoyed with her own subconscious for being so easily manipulated.

Done with it, she promised herself, and decided to start her day with a good, hard run to blow the mood away.

As her muscles warmed toward the first quarter mile, Gull fell into step beside her.

She flicked him a glance. "Is this going to be a habit?"

"I was running first yesterday," he reminded her. "I like putting in a few miles first thing. Wakes me up."

He'd gotten a look at her, too, and decided she looked a little pissed off, a little shadowed around the eyes. "Are you going for time or distance?"

"I'm just going for the run."

"We'll call it distance then. I like having an agenda."

"So I've noticed. I think three."

He snorted. "You've got more than that. Five."

"Four," she said just to keep him from getting his way. "And don't talk to me. I like being in my head when I run."

Obligingly he tapped the MP3 playing on his arm and ran to his music.

They kept the pace steady for the first mile. She was aware of him beside her, of the sound of their feet slapping the track in unison. And found she didn't mind it. She could speculate on what music he ran to, what *agenda* he'd laid out for the rest of his day. How that might tumble apart if they caught a fire.

They were both first stick on the jump list.

When they crossed the second mile she heard the sound of an engine above, and saw one of her father's planes glide across the wide blue canvas of sky. Flying lesson, she determined—business was good. She wondered if her father or one of his three pilots sat as instructor, then saw the right wing tip down twice, followed by a single dip on the left.

Her dad.

Face lifted, she shot up her arm, fingers stretched high in her signal back.

The simple contact had the dregs of annoyance that the run and Gull's companionship hadn't quite washed away breaking apart.

Then her running companion picked up the pace. She increased hers to match, knowing he pushed her, tested her. Then again, life without competition was barely living as far as she was concerned. The building burn in her quads and her hamstrings scorched away even those shattered dregs.

Her stride lengthened at mile three. Her arms pumped, her lungs labored. The bold sun the forecasters had promised would spike the temperatures toward eighty by afternoon skinned her in a thin layer of sweat.

She felt alive, challenged, happy.

Then Gull glanced her way, sent her a wink. And left her in his dust.

He had some kind of extra gear, she thought once he kicked in. That's all there was to it. And when he hit it, he was just fucking gone.

She dug for her own kick, found she had a little juice yet. Not enough to catch him—not unless she strapped herself to a rocket—but enough not to embarrass herself.

The last half-mile push left her a little light-headed, had her breath whooping as she simply rolled onto the grass beside the track.

"You'll cramp up. Come on, Ro, you know better than that."

He was winded—not gasping for air as she was, but winded, and she found a little satisfaction in that.

"Minute," she managed, but he grabbed her hands, pulled her to her feet.

"Walk it off, Ro."

She walked her heart rate down to reasonable, squeezed a stream from the water bottle she'd brought out with her into her mouth.

Watching him, she stood on one leg, stretched her quads by lifting the other behind her. He'd worked up a sweat, and it looked damn good on him. "It's like you've got an engine in those Nikes."

"You motor along pretty good yourself. And now you're not pissed off or depressed anymore. Was that your father doing the flyover?"

"Yeah. Why do you say I was pissed off and depressed?"

"It was all over your face. I've been making a study of your face, and that's how I tagged the mood."

"I'm going to hit the gym."

"Better stretch out those hamstrings first."

Irritation crawled up her back like a beetle. "What are you, the track coach?"

"No point getting pissed at me because I noticed you were pissed."

"Maybe not, but you're right here." Still, she dropped down into a hamstring stretch.

"From what I've heard, you've got cause to be."

She lifted her head, aimed that icy blue stare.

"Let me sum up." He opened the kit bag he'd tossed on the edge of the track, took out some water. "Matt's brother and the blond cook spent a good portion of last season tangling the sheets. Historically, said cook tangled many other sheets with dexterity and aplomb."

"Aplomb."

"It's a polite way of saying she banged often, well and without too much discrimination."

"That also sounded polite."

"I was raised well. In addition, Jim also tended to be generous with his attentions."

"Get you."

"However," Gull continued, "during the tangling and banging, the cook decided she was in love with Jim—that I got from Lynn, who got it from the blonde—and the blonde broke the hearts of many by focusing her dexterity exclusively on Jim, and closed her ears and eyes to the fact he didn't exactly reciprocate."

"You could write a book."

"The thought's crossed. Toward the end of this long, hot summer, the cook gets pregnant, which, rumor has it, since she avoided this eventuality previously, may have been on purpose."

"Probably." It was one of the things she'd already considered, and one of the things that depressed her.

"Sad," he said, and left it at that. "The cook claims she told Jim, who greeted the news with joy and exaltation. Though I didn't know him, that strikes me as sketchy. Plans to marry were immediately launched, which strikes sketchier yet. Then more sadly yet, Jim's killed during a jump which the ensuing investigation determines was his error—but the cook blamed his jump partner, which would be you, and tried to stab you with a kitchen knife."

"She didn't exactly try to stab me." The hell of it was, Rowan thought, she couldn't figure out why she kept defending the lunatic Dolly on that score. "Or didn't have time to because Marg yanked the knife away from her almost as soon as she'd picked it up."

"Points for Marg." He watched her face as he spoke, cat eyes steady and patient. "Grief takes a lot of forms, and a lot of those are twisted and ugly. But blaming you, or anyone on that load, for Jim's accident is just stupid. Continuing to is mean and stupid, and self-defeating."

She didn't want to talk about this. Why was she? She couldn't seem to help it, she realized, with him watching her intently, speaking so calmly.

"How do you know she still blames me?"

The sunlight picked out the gold in his brown hair as he drank down more water. "To wind it up, the cook takes off, and finds religion—or so she claims and maybe even believes. Not enough grace and faith to tell the father's grieving family about the baby, until she comes back to base looking for work. So I call bullshit on the God factor."

"Okay." Maybe she couldn't help it because he'd laid it out flat, and in exactly the way she saw it. "Wow."

"Not quite finished. You seek out the cook, engage her in private conversation. Though, of course, privacy is slim pickings around here. During the not-so-private conversation, the cook becomes very steamed, does a lot of snarling and pointing, then storms off. Which leads me to conclude finding religion didn't include finding forgiveness, charity or good sense."

"How did you get all this? And I do mean all."

"I'm a good listener. If you care, the general consensus on base is she had Jim's kid—and Matt's niece—so she should get some support. In fact, Cards is taking donations for a college fund in Jim's name."

"Yeah," Rowan replied. "He'd think of that. He's just built that way."

"The consensus continues that if she gives you grief or talks trash about you, she gets one warning. Second time, we meet with L.B., lay it out and she goes. You've got no say in it."

"I—"

"None." The single syllable remained calm, and absolutely final. "Everybody pretty much wants her to keep her job. And nobody's going to let her keep it if she causes trouble. So if you don't agree with that, you're outvoted. You might as well stop being pissed off and depressed because it's not going to do you any good."

"I guess I don't agree because it's me. If it was somebody else, I'd be right there."

"I get that."

"Leaving out a lot of stuff I'm not in the mood to talk about, my mother died when I was twelve."

"That's hard."

"They weren't together, and . . . that's the lot of stuff I'm not in the mood to talk about. My father raised me, with his

parents taking a lot of the weight during the season when he
was still jumping. What I'm saying is, I know it's not easy to
be a single parent, even with help and support. I'm willing to
cut her some slack."

"She's getting slack already, Rowan. She's working in the
kitchen. It'll be up to her if she stays."

They'd walked back while they talked. Now he gestured
toward the gym. "Feel like lifting?"

"Yeah. Can I use this?" She tapped his MP3 player. "I want
to check out your playlist."

"Working out without the tunes is a sacrifice." He pulled it
off, handed it to her. "Consider that when you're lining up the
reasons to sleep with me."

"I'll put it at the top of the list."

"Nice. So . . . what did it bump down?"

She laughed and walked inside ahead of him.

Once she finished her daily PT, cleaned up, she hiked to the
cookhouse to fuel up on carbs.

In the dining hall, Stovic chowed down on bacon and eggs
and biscuits while Cards ragged on him for being a malingerer
between forkfuls of pancakes. Gull had beaten her there and
was already building a stack of his own from the breakfast
buffet.

Rowan grabbed a plate. She flopped a pancake onto it, laid
two slices of bacon over that, added another pancake, two
more slices of bacon. She covered that with a third pancake
over which she dumped a hefty spoonful of berries.

"What do you call that?" Gull asked her.

"Mine." She carried it to the table, dropped into a chair.
"What's the word, Cards?"

"Plumbago."

"That's a good one. Sounds like a geriatric condition, but
it's a flower, right?"

"Shrub. Half point for you."

"The flower on the shrub, or plant, is also called plumbago," Gull pointed out.

Cards considered. "I guess that's true. Full point."

"Yippee." Rowan dumped syrup over her bacon pancakes.
"How's the leg, Chainsaw?"

"Stitches itch." He glanced over as Dobie wandered in, grinned. "But at least it's not my face."

"At least I didn't do it to myself," Dobie tossed back, and studied the offerings. "If I hadn't lost that bet, I'd've joined up just for the breakfasts." To prove it, he took a sample of everything.

"Your eye looks better," Rowan told him.

He could open both now, and she recognized the symphonic bruising as healing.

"How are the ribs?"

"Colorful, but they don't ache much. L.B.'s got me doing a shitload of sit-down work." He pulled out a bottle of Tabasco, pumped it over his eggs. "I asked if I could have some time today. I figured I'd walk on down, check out your daddy's operation. Watch some of those pay-to-jump types come down."

"You should. A lot of people make a picnic of it. Marg would pack you up something."

"Maybe I'll go with you."

Dobie wagged an impaled sausage at Stovic. "You've got that gimp leg."

"The walk'll take my mind off the itch."

It probably would, Rowan thought, but just in case. "I'll give you the number for the desk. If you can't make it, they'll send somebody to get you."

Marg stepped in, scanned the table as she walked over and set a tall glass of juice in front of Rowan. "Are you all going to be wandering in and out of here all morning, and lingering at my table half the day? What you need is a fire."

"Can't argue with that." Rowan picked up the glass, sampled. "Carrots, because there are always carrots, celery, I think, some oranges—and I'm pretty sure mango."

"Good for you. Now drink it all."

"Marg, you're looking more beautiful than ever this morning."

Marg cast a beady eye on Dobie. "What do you want, rookie?"

"I heard tell you might could put together a bag lunch if me and my fellow inmate here mosey on down to Rowan's daddy's place to watch the show."

"I might could. You tell Lucas, if you see him, it's past time he came in to pay a call on me."

"I'll sure do that."

AS HE HAD a short window before a tandem jump, Lucas made a point of walking out when he got word a couple of the rookies from the base were on the grounds.

A lot of tourists and locals came by to watch the planes and the jumpers, with plenty of them hooking the trip to his place with a tour of the smoke jumpers' base. He figured it was good for business.

He'd started with one plane, a part-time pilot and instructor, with his mother handling the phones. When they rang. His pop ran dispatch, helped with the books. Of course in those days, he'd only been able to give the half-assed business his attention off-season, or when he was off the jump list.

But he'd needed to build something for his daughter, something solid.

And he had. He took pride in that, in his fleet of planes, his full-time staff of twenty-five. He had the satisfaction of knowing one day, when she was ready, Rowan could stand on what he'd built and have that solidity under her.

Still there were days he watched a plane rise into the sky from the base, knew the men and women on it were flying to fire, that he missed it like a limb.

He knew, now, what it was to be on the ground and know someone he loved more than anything in the world and beyond was about to risk her life. He wondered how his parents, his daughter, even the wife he'd had so briefly had ever stood that constant mix of fear and resignation.

But today, so far, the sirens stayed silent.

He stopped a moment to watch one of the students—a sixty-three-year-old banker from town free-fall from the Otter. Applause broke out in the audience of watchers when the chute deployed.

Zeke had been Lucas's banker for close to forty years, so Lucas watched a moment longer, gave a nod of approval at the form, before he walked over to the blanket where the two men from the base stretched out with what he recognized as one of Marg's famous boxed lunches.

"How's it going?" he asked, and crouched down beside them. "Lucas Tripp, and you must be Dobie. I heard you got in a scuffle at Get a Rope the other night."

"Yeah. I'm usually prettier. It's a pleasure meeting you," Dobie added as he held out a hand. "This one's Chainsaw, as he likes to use one to shave his legs."

"Heard about that, too. If you're going to get banged up, it might as well be early in the season, before things heat up."

"It's a real nice operation you got here, Mr. Tripp," Stovic commented.

The polite deference made Lucas feel old as an alp. "You can hang the mister around my father. We're doing pretty well here. See that one." He gestured toward where Zeke touched down and rolled. "He won't see sixty again. Bank manager out of Missoula. Granddaddy of eight with two more coming. Known him longer than either of you have been alive, and up until a couple months ago, he never said a word to me about wanting to jump. *Bucket List*," Lucas told them with a grin. "Since that movie came out, we're getting a lot of clients and students with some age on them coming in.

"I've got a tandem jump coming up. Client's due in about fifteen. Fifty-seven-year-old woman. High-school principal. You never know who's got a secret yen to fly."

"Do you miss it?" Dobie asked him. "Jumping fire."

"Every day." Lucas shrugged as he watched his banker wave to a trio of his grandkids. "But old horses like me have to make room for you young stallions."

"You must have a lot of stories from back in the day."

And older yet, Lucas thought, but grinned at Stovic. "Get a couple beers in me, I'll tell them all, whether you want to hear them or not."

"Anytime," Dobie said. "Anyplace."

"I might take you up on it. I better get on, give the principal the thrill of her life." Lucas pushed to his feet. "Enjoy your day off. You won't get many more of them."

"I don't see how he could come to give it up," Dobie commented. "I don't think I could."

"You haven't jumped fire yet," Stovic pointed out.

"In my head I have." Dobie bit into a drumstick Marg had fried to a crispy turn. "And I didn't try to castrate myself with a chain saw."

Stovic gave him a good-natured punch in the arm. "It got the Swede's hands on my thigh. Worth every stitch."

"You try to move on that, Gull'll give you more than a few stitches. His eyes're homed in that direction."

"I ain't blind. But she's sure got a nice touch." Stovic dug into the potato salad as they watched the next jumper.

LUCAS CHECKED HIS LOGS, the aircraft, had a quick conversation with his mechanic and the pilot for the tandem. Even if the client arrived on time, Marcie—his service rep—would sit her down for an overall explanation, have the client fill out the necessary forms. Since she'd ordered the DVD package, he swung through to make sure his videographer was lined up for the go.

When he walked into the operations building, he spotted Marcie and the client at one of the tables dealing with the paperwork. His first thought was a cliché, but true nonetheless.

They hadn't made principals like that when he'd been in high school.

She had red hair, and a lot of it, that kind of swept around her face, and eyes like forest shadows. Deep and green. When she smiled at something Marcie said, shallow dimples popped out in her cheeks, and her lips turned up in a pretty bow.

He wasn't shy around women—unless he was attracted to one. He felt the wash of embarrassed heat run up the back of his neck as he approached the table.

"And here's your jump master," Marcie announced, "and the owner of Zulie Skydiving. Lucas, I was just telling Mrs. Frazier she's about to experience the thrill of a lifetime, and she's got the top dog to take her through it."

"Well," Lucas managed as the heat spread to the top of his skull.

"If I'm going to be thrilled, I like knowing it's with the top dog." She offered her hand—narrow, slender-fingered. Lucas took it loosely, released it quickly, worried he might crush it.

"Mrs. Frazier's son bought her the package for Christmas," Marcie added.

"Make it Ella, since we'll be jumping out of a plane together. He heard me say I wanted to try skydiving one day, and took me seriously, even though I believe I'd had several glasses of wine at the time." Those lips bowed up again; the dimples popped. "He and his family are out poking around, as are my daughter and hers. They're all excited to watch."

"That's good. That's nice."

"So . . ." Ella waited a beat. "When do we start?"

"We'll get you suited up." Though she beamed smiles, Marcie slid a puzzled look up at Lucas. "While we do, you'll watch a short instructional video. Then the boss will give you a little training, answer any questions. That'll take about thirty minutes, so you'll be familiar with the equipment, feel comfortable and learn how to land."

"Landing would be key. I don't want to traumatize my grandchildren." She said it with a sparkle in her eye.

Married. Lucas's brain caught up with the rest of him. With kids. With grandkids. Knowing she was married eased the shyness. Now he could just admire how pretty she was, seeing as she was off-limits.

"No worries about that." He was able to grin back at her. "They'll remember today as the day they watched their grandmother fly. If you're done with the paperwork, we'll get you your flight suit."

He changed into his own while Marcie got the client outfitted. He generally enjoyed doing tandems with first-timers, soothing their nerves if they had them, answering questions, giving them the best experience possible, and a memory they'd carry for the rest of their lives. He expected this run would be no exception.

The client looked fit, which helped. He glanced at his copy of the form and noted he'd been on the mark on her statistics. Five-five, 123 pounds. No physical problems.

He stepped outside to wait for her.

"I feel official." She laughed and did a little turn in her flight suit and jump boots.

"Looking good. I know Marcie went over the procedure with you, but I can go over it again, answer any questions you've got."

"Marcie was thorough, and the video was great. The harness attaches me to you, start to finish, which is very important from my point of view."

"It's a good way to make a first jump. Low stress."

She bubbled out a laugh. "Easy for you to say. I guess you're used to screamers."

"Don't worry about that. I'm betting you're going to be too happy and too dazzled by the view to scream." He led her to a small training field. "We'll go up to about fourteen thousand feet. When you're ready, I'll take you on a trip into that big sky. The free fall's a rush, exhilarating. It'll last about a minute before the chute deploys. Once it does, you'll float, and listen to the kind of quiet only jumpers know."

"You love it."

"Absolutely."

"I'm doing this for a couple of reasons. First for my son. I just couldn't disappoint him. And second, I realized on the way here, to remind myself I used to be fearless. Tell me, Mr. Tripp—"

"Lucas."

"Lucas, how many people chicken out once they're up there?"

"Oh, there's some, sure. I can usually peg them before we get off the ground." He gave her an easy smile. "You won't be one of them."

"Because?"

"You were fearless once. You don't forget what you are. Sometimes you just put it aside awhile."

The dimples fluttered in her cheeks. "You're right. I've learned that lesson the last few years."

He showed her how to land, how to use him, her own body for a soft touchdown. He strapped the harness so she could get accustomed to the feel of it, and having his body against hers.

The little jump in the belly he felt had him relieved to remind himself she was married.

"Any questions? Concerns?"

"I think I've got it. I'm supposed to relax and enjoy—and hope I don't scream the whole way down so the DVD shows me with my mouth wide open and my eyes squeezed shut."

"Hey, Mom!"

They looked over at the group hovering at the edge of the field.

"The family. Do you have time to meet them before we do this?"

"Sure."

He walked over with her, made some small talk with her son—he looked pale and nervous now that it was zero hour—her daughter, the three children, including the one watching him like an owl from his daddy's hip.

"You're sure about this? Because if—"

"Tyler." Ella rose to the toes of her jump boots, kissed her son's cheek. "I'm revved and ready. Best Christmas present ever."

"Nana's gonna do this." A boy of about five shot the toy parachutist from their gift shop into the air. It floated down on a bright red chute.

"You bet I am. Watch me."

After hugs and kisses, she walked off with Lucas toward the waiting Twin Otter. "I'm not nervous. I'm not going to be nervous. I'm not going to scream. I'm not going to throw up."

"Look at that sky. It doesn't get prettier. Until you're floating in it. Here's Chuck. He'll be videographing your entire experience."

"Chuck." She shook hands. "You'll get my best side, right?"

"Guaranteed. Nobody gives a tandem like Iron Man, ma'am. Smooth as silk."

"Okay." She blew out a breath. "Let's do it, Iron Man."

She turned, waved to her family, then got onboard.

She shook hands with the pilot, and to Lucas's eye stayed steady and attentive through the flight. He expected more questions—about the plane, the equipment, his experience—but she played it up for the camera, obviously determined to give her family a fun memento.

She mugged, pretended to faint and surprised Lucas by crawling into his lap and telling her kids she was flying off to Fiji with her jump master.

"We need to go back for a bigger plane," he told her, and made her laugh.

When they reached jump altitude he winked at her. "Ready to harness up?"

Those lips bowed up with nerves around the edges. "Let's rock and roll."

He went over the procedure again, his voice soothing, easy, as he hooked them together.

"You're going to feel a rush of air, hear more engine noise when we open the door. We're miked, so Chuck will pick up what we say for your DVD."

As he spoke he felt her breathing pick up. When the door opened, he felt her jerk, felt her tremble.

"We don't go until you say go."

"I swam naked in the Gulf of Mexico. I can do this. Let's go."

"We're go." He nodded to Chuck, who jumped first. "Watch the sky, Ella," he murmured, and leaped with her.

She didn't scream, but after a strangled gasp, he heard her clearly shout, "Holy fucking shit!" and wondered if they'd want that edited out for the grandchildren.

Then she laughed, shot her arms out like wings.

"Oh, my God, oh, my God, oh, my *God* ! I did it. Lucas!"

She vibrated against him, and in tune with her he recognized exhilaration rather than fear.

The chute deployed, a rush of wings, and the whippy dive became a graceful float.

"It was too fast, over too fast. But, oh, *oh*, you were right. This is beautiful. This is . . . religious."

"Put your hands on the toggles. You can drive awhile."

"Okay, wow. Look at Nana, Owen! I'm a skydiver. Thank you, Tyler! Hi, Melly, hi, Addy, hi, Sam!" She tipped her head back. "I'm in the sky, and it's blue silk."

She fell silent, then sighed. "You were right about the quiet. You were right about everything. I'll never forget this. Oh, there they are! They're waving. You'd better take over so I can wave back."

"You have a beautiful family."

"I really do. Oh, gosh, oh, wow, here comes the ground."

"Trust me. Trust yourself. Stay relaxed."

He brought her down soft.

With excited screams, wild cheers, her family jumped and waved. When Lucas detached the harness, she dropped into an exaggerated curtsy, blew kisses.

Then she spun around, her face glowing, and stunned him

by throwing her arms around him and kissing him firmly on the mouth.

"I'd have done that in midair if I could have because, my God, that was orgasmic. I don't know how to thank you."

"I think you just did."

She laughed, made him laugh by doing a quick victory dance. "I jumped out of a damn plane. My ex-husband said I'd be crazy to do it, the jerk. But I *feel* crazy, because I'm going to do it again."

Still laughing, she ran over, arms wide, to her family.

"Ex-husband," Lucas managed. And the heat spread up the back of his neck again.

7

With the siren silent, Rowan spent most of her time in the loft checking, clearing or mending chutes. She'd caught up on paperwork, repacked her personal gear bag, checked and rechecked her own chute, readied her jump gear.

She remained first jumper, first stick.

"Going stir-crazy here," Cards said when he got up from the machine.

"Aren't we all. And the word of today is . . ."

"Fastidious. We've been doing dick-all but cleaning and organizing. The ready room's freaking fastidious enough to suit my mother's scary standards."

"It can't last much longer."

"I hope to Christ not. I had to kick my own ass for cheating at solitaire yesterday, and I'm starting to think about crafts. We'll be knitting next."

"I'd like a nice scarf to match my eyes."

"It could happen," he said darkly. "At least I had phone sex with Vicki last night." He pulled the deck of cards from his shirt pocket, shuffling as he paced. "It's fun while it lasts, but it doesn't really do the job."

"And gone are the days you'd hunt up a companion for actual sex?"

"Long gone. She's worth it. I told you she and the kids are coming out next month, right?"

"You mentioned it." One or two thousand times, Rowan thought.

"Gotta get in some time now, so I can take a couple days next month. I need to work, need the pay, need—"

"To resist trolling the aisle of the craft store," Rowan finished.

"I won't be trolling alone if this lull lasts much longer. Have you got anything to read? All Gibbons has are books that give me a headache. I read one of Janis's romance novels, but that doesn't help keep my mind off sex."

"Nothing deep, nothing sexy. Check." She signed and dated the tag on the repaired chute. "What're you after?"

"I want something gory, where people die miserable deaths at the hands of a psycho."

"I could fix you up. Come on. We'll peruse my library."

"Dobie's in the kitchen with Marg," Cards told her, passing a hand over Rowan's head, then flipped out an ace of spades. "He got some recipe of his mother's, and he's in there cooking up some pie or other."

Cooking, knitting—that bake sale could be next. Then struck, Rowan paused. "Is Dobie hitting on Marg?"

Cards only shook his head. "She's got twenty years on him."

"Men routinely hit on women twenty years younger."

"I'm bored, Ro, but not bored enough to get into a tangle on that with you."

"Coward." But when they stepped outside, she paused again. "Look, check out those clouds."

"We got scouts." His face brightened as he studied the clouds over the mountains. "A nice string of them."

"Could mean smoke today. With any luck, we'll have that ready room messed up again before afternoon. Do you still want that book?"

"Might as well. I'll get myself all settled in, good book, good snack. It's like guaranteeing we'll fly today."

"It's the slowest start to a season I remember. Then again,

my father once told me when it starts cool, it ends hot. Maybe we shouldn't be so eager to get going."

"If it doesn't get going, what're we here for?"

"No argument. So . . ." She tried for a casual tone as they crossed to her end of the barracks. "Have you seen Fast Feet this morning?"

"In the Map Room. Studying. At least he was about an hour ago."

"Studying. Huh." She wasn't interested in settling down with a book, but a little byplay with Gull might be just the solution to boredom she needed.

Inside, she led the way to her quarters. "Gruesome murder," she began. "Do you want just violence, or sex and violence? As opposed to romantic sexy."

"I always want sex."

"Again, it's hard to—" She broke off as she opened her door. The slaughterhouse stench punched like a fist in the throat.

A pool of blood spread over the bed. Dark rivers of it ran down hills of clothes heaped on the floor. On the wall in letters wet and gleaming dripped the statement:

BURN IN HELL!

In the center of the ugliness, Dolly whirled to face the door. Some of the blood in the canister she held splattered on her shirt.

"Son of a *bitch*!" Fists up, her mind as red and vicious as the blood, Rowan charged. A war-paint line of pig's blood splatted on her face as Dolly screamed and dropped to the ground—seconds before Cards grabbed Rowan's arms.

"Wait a minute, wait a minute."

"Fuck you." Rowan pushed off her feet, adding to the blood when the back of her head connected sharply with Cards's nose and had it spurting.

He yelped, and through sheer grit managed to hold on for another second or two.

"You're so dead!" Rowan shouted at Dolly, and, blind to anything but payback, jabbed her elbow into Cards's ribs, sprang free.

Shrieking, scrabbling back, Dolly pitched the canister. Globs of blood flew, striking wall, ceiling, furniture, when Rowan batted it away.

"You like blood? Let's see how you like painting with yours, you crazy *cunt*."

Rowan clamped her hands on Dolly's ankles when Dolly tried to crawl under the bed. Even as she hauled Dolly across the blood-smeared floor, men who'd come running at the commotion dived in to grapple Rowan back.

Rowan didn't waste her breath. She punched, kicked, jabbed and kneed, heedless of where blows landed, until she ended up facedown on the floor, pinned.

"Just stay down," Gull said in her ear.

"Get off me. Goddamn you, get off me. Do you see what she did?"

"Everybody sees it. Jesus, somebody get that screaming idiot out of here before *I* punch her."

"I'm going to kick every square inch of her skanky ass. Let me *up*! You hear that, you psycho? First chance I get it won't be pig's blood you're wearing, it'll be your own. Let me the fuck *up*!"

"You're down until you calm down."

"Fine. I'm calm."

"Not even close."

"She's got Jim's blood on her," Dolly wept as Yangtree and Matt pulled her from the room. "You all have his blood on you. I hope you all die. I hope you all burn alive. All of you."

"I think she lost her religion," Gull commented. "Listen to me. Rowan, you listen. She's gone, and if you try to go after her and take a shot at her now, we're just going to put you down again. You already bloodied Cards's nose, and I'm pretty sure Janis is going to be sporting a black eye."

"They shouldn't have gotten in my way."

"If they, and the rest of us, hadn't, you'd have punched a pathetic lunatic, and you'd be off the jump list until it got sorted out."

That, he noted, had her taking the first calming breath. He signaled for Libby and Trigger to let go of her legs and, when she didn't try to kick them, pointed to the door.

Libby shut it quietly behind them.

"I'm letting you up." He eased his grip on her arms, braced to grab them again if necessary. Then, cautiously, he shifted off her, sat on the floor.

Blood covered both of them, but he was pretty sure she had the worst of it. It smeared her face, dripped from her hair, coated her arms, her shirt. She looked as if she'd been whacked with an ax. And it made him sick.

"You know, it's a goddamn pigsty in here."

"That's not funny."

"No, it's not, but it's the best I got." He eyed her coolly as she pushed up to sit, watched her right hand bunch into a fist. "I can take a punch if you need to throw one."

"Just get out."

"No. We're just going to sit here awhile."

Rowan used her shoulder to wipe at her face, smeared it with more blood. "She got that crap all over me. All over my bed, the floor, the walls."

"She's sick and she's stupid. And she deserved to have every square inch of her skanky ass kicked. She'll get fired, and everybody on base and within fifty miles will know why. That might be worse."

"It's not as satisfying." She looked away a moment as, with the wild heat of temper fading, tears wanted to sting. She clamped her hands together; they'd started to shake.

"It smells like a slaughterhouse in here."

"You can sleep in my room tonight." He hitched a bandanna out of his pocket, used it to wipe blood from her face. "But everybody who sleeps in my room has to be naked."

She huffed out a tired breath. "I'll bunk with Janis until I get it cleaned up. She has the naked rule, too."

"Now that was just mean."

She looked at him then, just sat and looked while he ruined his bandanna on a hopeless job. It helped to see he wasn't as calm as he sounded, helped to see the temper and disgust on his face.

Oddly, seeing it calmed her just a little.

"Did I give you that bloody lip?"

"Yeah. Back fist. Not bad."

"I'll probably be sorry for it at some point, but I can't work it up right now."

"It took five of us to take you down."

"That's something. I have to go wash up."

She started to rise when L.B. knocked briskly on the door, opened it. "Give us a minute, will you, Gull?"

"Sure." Before he stood, Gull leaned over, laid a hand on Rowan's knee. "People like her? They never get people like you. It's their loss."

He pushed to his feet, and closed the door on his way out.

L.B. looked around the room, rubbed a hand over his face. "Jesus, Ro. Jesus. I'm sorry. I can't tell you how sorry."

"You didn't do it."

"I shouldn't have hired her on. I shouldn't have taken her back. This is on me."

"It's on her."

"She got the chance to come at you this way because I gave her one." He hunkered down so their faces were on level. "We've got her in my office, with a couple of the guys watching her. She'll be fired, banned from base. I'm going to call the law on this. Do you want to press charges?"

"I do because she earned it." The tears had backed off, thank God. Now she only felt sick, sick and tired. "But the baby didn't. I just want her gone."

"She's gone," he promised. "Come on, you need to get out of here. We'll have some of the cleaning crew deal with it."

"I need to get some air. Apologize to some people. I need to take a shower, wash this off me." She blew out another breath as she looked down at herself. "I probably need the full *Silkwood.*"

"Take as long as you need. And nobody needs you to apologize."

"I need me to. But this shit's all over my stuff. I need to clean some of it up myself."

She got up, opened the door. Looked back. "Did she love him this much? Is this love?"

L.B. stared at the bloody words on the wall. "It's got nothing to do with love."

THE SIREN SOUNDED as she stepped out of the shower.

"Perfect," she muttered. She dragged on underwear without

bothering to dry off, pulled on a shirt, her pants, and zipped them on the run.

The nine other jumpers on the list beat her to the ready room. She listened to the rundown as she suited up. Lightning strikes on Morrell Mountain. She and Cards had judged those morning clouds correctly. The lookout spotted the smoke about eleven, around the time she'd surprised Dolly and her goddamn pig's blood.

Over the next hour or so, the fire manager officer had to consider letting it burn, do its work of clearing out some brush and fallen trees, or call in the smoke jumpers.

A few more lightning strikes and unseasonably dry conditions made the natural burn too big a risk.

"Ready for the real thing, Fast Feet?" She put her let-down rope in her pocket while Gull grabbed gear from the speed rack.

"Jumping the fire, or you and me making some?"

"You'd better keep your mind off impossible dreams. This isn't a practice jump."

"Looking good." Dobie slapped Gull on the back. "Wish I was going with you."

"You'll be off the disabled list soon. Save me some pie," Rowan called out, and shambled over to the waiting plane.

She tucked her helmet in the crook of her elbow. "Okay, boys and girls, I'll be your fire boss today. For a couple of you, this is your first fire jump. Do it by the numbers, don't screw up, and you'll do fine. Remember, if you can't avoid the trees . . ."

"Aim for the small ones," the crew responded.

Once they were airborne she sat next to Cards. "At least the nose didn't ground you."

He pinched it gently to wag it back and forth. "So I don't have to be pissed at you. Like I said, Swede, the girl's batshit."

"Yeah. And it's done." She took the note passed back to her from the cockpit. "We're going to hold off while they drop a load of mud. It was a hard winter in that area, and there's a lot of downed trees fueling this one. It's moving faster than they figured."

"Almost always does."

She pulled out her map, scanned the area. But in moments

she only had to look out the window to see what they were dealing with.

A tower of smoke spewed skyward, gliding along the mountain's ridge. Trees, standing and downed, fueled the wall of fire. She scanned for and found the stream she'd scouted out on the map, calculated the amount of hose they had on board, and judged they'd be able to use the water source.

The plane bucked and trembled in the turbulence while jumpers lined the windows to study the burning ground. And bucking, they circled to wait for the mud drop on the head that shot up flames she estimated at a good thirty feet.

She waddled over to L.B., who'd come on as spotter.

"See that clearing?" he shouted. "That's our jump spot. A little closer to the right flank than I'd like, but it's the best in this terrain."

"Saves us a hike."

"The wind's whipping her up. You want to keep clear of that slash just east of the spot."

"You bet I do."

Together they watched the tanker thunder its load onto the head. The reddened clouds of it made her think of the blood soiling her room.

No time for brooding, she reminded herself.

"That'll knock her down a little." When the tanker veered off, L.B. nodded at her. "Are you good?"

"I'm good."

He gave her arm a squeeze, a tacit acknowledgment. "Guard your reserves," he called out, and went to the door.

From his seat, Gull watched Rowan as the wind and noise rushed in. About an hour earlier she'd been spitting mad with blood on her face and blind vengeance in her fists. Now, as she consulted with their spotter over the flight of the first streamers, the cool was back in those gorgeous, icy eyes. She'd be the first out, taking that ice into fire.

He didn't see how the fire had a chance.

He looked out the window to study the enemy below. In his hotshot days, he'd have gone in, one of twenty handcrew, transported in The Box—the crew truck that became their home away from home every season.

Now he'd get there by jumping out of a plane.

Different methods, same goal. Suppress and control.

Once he was down, he knew his job and he knew how to take orders. He shifted his gaze back to Rowan. No question she knew how to give them.

But right at the moment, it was all about the getting there. He watched the next set of streamers, tried to judge for himself the draft. With the plane bucking and rocking beneath them, he understood the wind wasn't going to be a pal.

The plane bumped its way up to jump altitude at L.B.'s order, and as Rowan fixed on her helmet and face mask, as Cards—her jump partner—got into position behind her, Gull felt his breathing elevate. It climbed just as the plane climbed.

But he kept his face impassive as he worked to control it, as he visualized himself shoving out the door, into the slipstream and past it, hurtling down to do his job.

Rowan glanced over briefly so he caught that flash of blue behind her mask. Then she dropped down into position. Seconds later, she was gone. Gull shifted back to the window, watched her fly, and Cards after her. As the plane circled around, he changed angles, saw her chute open.

She slid into the smoke.

When the next jumpers took positions, he strapped on his helmet and mask, calmed and cleared his mind. He had everything he needed, equipment, training, skill. And a few thousand feet below was what he wanted. The woman and the blaze.

He made his way forward, felt the slap of the wind.

"Do you see the jump spot?"

"Yeah, I see it."

"Wind's going to kick, all the way down, and it's going to want to shove you east. Try to stay out of that slash. See that lightning?"

Gull watched it rip through the sky, strike like an electric bullet.

"Hard not to."

"Don't get in its way."

"Got it."

"Are you ready?"

"We're ready."

"Get in the door."

Gaze on the horizon, Gull dropped down, pushed his legs out into the power of the slipstream. Heat from the fire radiated against his face; the smell of smoke tanged the air he drew into his lungs.

Once again L.B. stuck his head out the door, scanning, studying the hills, the rise of trees, the roiling walls of flame.

"Get ready!"

When the slap came down on his shoulder, Gull propelled himself out. The world tipped and turned, earth, sky, fire, smoke, as he took a ninety-mile-an-hour dive. Greens, blues, red, black tumbled around him in a filmy blur while he counted in his head. The sounds—a roaring growl—amazed. The wind knocked him sideways, clawed him into a spin while he used strength, will, training to revolve until he was head up, feet down, stabilized by the drogue.

Heart knocking—adrenaline, awe, delight, fear—he found Trigger, his jump partner, in the sky.

Wait, he ordered himself. Wait.

Lightning flared, a blue-edged lance, and added a sting of ozone to the air.

Then the tip and tug. He dropped his head back, watched his chute fly up, open in the ripping air like a flower. He let out a shout of triumph, couldn't help it, and heard Trigger answer it with a laugh as Gull gripped his steering toggles.

It was a fight to turn to face the wind, but he reveled in it. Even choking on the smoke that wind blew smugly in his face, hearing the bomb-burst of thunder that followed another crack of lightning, he grinned. And with his chute rocking, his eyes tracking the ugly slash, the line of trees, the angry walls of flames—close enough now to slap heat over his face—he aimed for the jump site.

For a moment he thought the wind would beat him after all, and imagined the discomfort, embarrassment and goddamn inconvenience of hitting those jack-sawed trees. And on his first jump.

He yanked down hard on his toggle, shouted, "No fucking way."

He heard Trigger's wild laugh, and seconds before he hit, Gull pulled west. His feet slapped ground, just on the east end of the jump spot. Momentum nearly tumbled him into the slash, but he flipped himself back in a sloppy somersault into the clearing.

He took a moment—maybe half a moment—to catch his breath, to congratulate himself on getting down in one piece, then rolled up to gather his chute.

"Not bad, rook." Cards gave him a waggling thumbs-up. "Ride's over, and the fun begins. The Swede's setting up a team to dig fire line along the flank there." He pointed toward the wicked, bellowing wall. "And you're elected. Another team's going to set up toward the head, hit it with the hoses. Mud knocked her back some, but the wind's got her feeling sexy, and we're getting lightning strikes out the ass. You're with Trigger, Elf, Gibbons, Southern and me on the line. And shit, there goes one in the slash and the other in the trees. Let's haul them in and get to work."

Gull trooped over to assist Southern, but stopped when his fellow rookie got to his feet among the jagged, jack-sawed trees.

"You hurt?" Gull shouted.

"Nah. Damn it. A little banged, and my chute's ripped up."

"Could've been worse. Could've been me. We're on the fire line."

He maneuvered through the slash to help Southern gather his tattered chute. After stowing his jumpsuit, Gull headed over to where Cards was ragging on Gibbons.

"Now that Tarzan here has finished swinging in the trees, let's do what we get paid for."

With his team, Gull hiked half a mile in full pack to the line Rowan had delegated Cards to dig.

They spread out, and with the fire licking closer, the sounds of pick striking earth, saw and blade slicing tree filled the smoky air. Gull thought of the fire line as an invisible wall or, if they were lucky, a kind of force field that held the flames on the other side.

Heroic grunt work, he thought while sweat ran rivulets through the soot on his face. The term, and the job, satisfied him.

Twice the fire tried to jump the line, skipping testing spots like flat stones over a river. The air filled with sparks that swarmed like murderous fireflies. But they held the flank.

Now and then, through the flying ash and huffing smoke, Gull spotted a quick beam of sunlight.

Little beacons of hope that glowed purple, then vanished.

Word came down the line that the hose crew had to fall back, and with the flank under control, they would move in to assist.

After more than six hours of laying line, they hiked their way up the mountain and across the black where the fire had already had her way.

If the line was the invisible wall, he thought of the black as the decimated kingdom where the battle had been waged and lost. The war continued, but here the enemy laid scourge and left what had been green and golden a smoldering, skeletal ruin.

The thin beams of sun that managed to struggle through the haze only served to amplify the destruction.

Limping a little, Southern fell into step beside him.

"How're you holding up?" Gull asked him.

"I'd be doing better if I hadn't landed in that godforsaken slash," he said in the fluid Georgia drawl that gave him his nickname. "I thought I knew what it was. I've got two seasons in on wildfires, and that's before we'll-whoop-your-ass recruit training. But it's shit-your-pants hard is what it is. I nearly did just that when I saw I was going to miss the jump spot."

Gull took a heat-softened Snickers out of his pack, pulled it in two. "Snickers really satisfies," Gull said in the upbeat tone of a TV voice-over.

Southern grinned, bit in. "It sure enough does."

They hit the stream, veered northeast toward the sounds of engines and saws.

Rowan came out of a cloud of smoke, a Viking goddess through the stink of war.

"Dry lightning's kicking our ass." She paused only to chug down some water. "We'd beat the head down, nearly had her, then we had a triple strike. We got crown fire along the ridge due north, and the head's building back up west of that. We gotta cut through the middle, stop them from meeting up. Hold here until we're clear. They're sending another load of mud. We got another load from base coming in to take the rear flanks and tail, keep them down. Bulldozer made it through, and he's clearing brush and downed trees. But we need the line."

She scanned faces. "You've got about five minutes till the drop. Make the most of it—eat, drink, because you won't see another five minutes clear today."

She went into a confab with Cards. Gull waited until they stepped apart, then walked to her. Before he could speak, she shook her head.

"Wind changed direction on a dime, and she just blew over. She melted fifty feet of hose before we got clear. Then boom! Boom! Boom! Fourth of July. Trees went up like torches, and the wind carried it right over the tops."

"Anybody hurt?"

"No. Don't look for clean sheets and a pillow tonight. We'll be setting up camp, and going back at her tomorrow. She's not going to die easy." She looked skyward. "Here comes the tanker."

"I don't see it."

"Not yet. You can hear it."

He closed his eyes, angled his head. "No. You must have super hearing. Okay, now I hear it."

She pulled her radio, spoke with the tanker, then with the crew on the ridge.

"Let it rip," she mumbled.

The pink rain tumbled down, caught little stray rainbows of sunlight.

"We're clear!" Rowan shouted. "Let's move. Watch your footing, but don't dawdle."

With that, she disappeared into the smoke.

THEY HACKED, CUT, BEAT at it into the night. Bodies trained to withstand all manner of hell began to weaken. But resolve didn't. Gull caught sight of Rowan a few times, working the line, moving in and out as she coordinated with the other teams and with base.

Sometime toward one, more than twelve hours after he'd landed in the clearing, the fire began to lie down.

To rest, Gull thought, not to surrender. Just taking a little nap. And hell, he could use one himself. They worked another hour before word came down they'd camp a half mile east of the fire's right flank.

"How's the first day on the job going, rook?"

He glanced over at Cards's exhausted face as they trudged. "I'm thinking of asking for a raise."

"Hell, I'd settle for a ham on rye."

"I'd rather have pizza."

"Picky Irishman. You ever been there? Ireland?"

"A couple times, yeah."

"Is it really as green as they say, as it looks in the pictures?"

"Greener."

Cards looked off into the smoky dark. "And cool, right? Cool and damp. Lots of rain."

"That's why it's green."

"Maybe I'll go there one of these days, take Vicki and the kids. Cool and damp and green sounds good after a day like this. There we are." He lifted a chin to the lights up ahead. "Time to ring the supper bell."

Those who'd already arrived had set up tents, or were doing so. Some just sat on the ground and shoveled their Meals Ready to Eat into their mouths.

Rowan, using a rock near the campfire as a table, worked over a map with Gibbons while she ate an apple. She'd taken off her helmet. Her hair shone nearly white against her filthy face.

He thought she looked beautiful, gloriously, eerily so—and was forced to admit she'd probably been right. He was, under it all, a romantic.

He dumped his gear, felt his back and shoulders weep with relief before they cramped like angry fists.

No Box to crawl into this time, he mused as he popped his tent. Then like the others, he dropped down by the campfire and ate like the starving. The cargo drop included more MREs, water, more tools, more hose and, God bless some thoughtful soul, a carton of apples, another of chocolate bars.

He ate his MRE, two apples, a candy bar—and stuffed another in his PG bag. The vague nausea that had plagued him on the hike to camp receded as his body refueled.

He rose, walked over to tap Rowan on the shoulder. "Can I talk to you a minute?"

She stood up, obviously punchy and distracted, and followed him away from the campfire, into the shadows.

"What's the problem? I've got to hit the rack. We're going to be—"

He just yanked her in, covered her mouth with his and feasted on her as he had on the food. Exhaustion became an easier fatigue as he fueled himself with her. The twinges in his back, his arms, his legs gave way to the curls of lust low in the belly.

She took back in equal measure, gripping his hips, his hair, pressing that amazing body against him, diving straight into those deep, greedy kisses.

And that, he thought, was what made it so damn good.

When he drew back he left his hands on her shoulders, studied her face.

"Is that all you have to say?" she demanded.

"I'd say more, but the rest of the conversation requires more privacy. Anyway, that should hold you for the night."

Humor danced into her eyes. "Hold *me*?"

"The crew boss works harder than anybody, to my way of thinking. So, I wanted to give you a little something more to take to bed."

"That's very considerate of you."

"No problem." He watched her eyes shift from amused to puzzled as he tipped down, brushed a kiss on her sooty brow. "'Night, boss."

"You're a puzzle, Gulliver."

"Maybe, but not that hard to solve. See you in the morning."

He went to his tent, crawled in. He barely managed to get his boots off before he went under. But he went under with a smile on his face.

8

Rowan's mental alarm dragged her out of sleep just before
five A.M. She lay where she was, eyes closed, taking inventory. A world of aches, a lot of stiffness and a gut-deep hunger,
but nothing major or unexpected. She rolled out of her sleeping bag and, in the dark, stretched out her sore muscles. She
let herself fantasize about a hot shower, an ice-cold Coke, a
plate heaped with one of Marg's all-in omelets.

Then she crawled out of her tent to face reality.

The camp slept on—and could, she calculated, for about an
hour more. To the west the fire painted the sky grimy red. A
waiting light, she thought. Waiting for the day's battle.

Well, they'd be ready for it.

She rinsed the dry from her mouth with water, spat it out,
then used the glow of the campfire to grab some food. She ate,
washing down the rations with instant coffee she despised but
needed while reviewing her maps. The quiet wouldn't last
long, so she used it to strategize her tasks, directions, organizing teams and tools.

She radioed base for a status report, a weather forecast,
scribbling notes, quick-drawing operational maps.

By first light, she'd organized her tools, restocked her PG

bag, bolted another sandwich and an apple. Alert, energized, ready, she gathered in her small pocket of alone time.

She watched the forest come to life around the sleeping camp. Like something out of a fairy tale, the shadows of a small herd of elk slipped through morning mists veiling the trees like wisps of smoke. The shimmer of the rising sun haloed the ridge to the east, spreading its melting gold. The shine of it trickled down the tree line, flickering its glint on the stream, brushing the green of the valley below.

Birds sang their morning song, while overhead in that wakening sky a hawk soared, already on the hunt.

This, she thought, was just one more reason she did what she did, despite the risks, the pain, the hunger. There was, to her mind, nothing more magical or more intensely real than dawn in the wilderness.

She'd fight beyond exhaustion alongside the best men and women she knew to protect it.

When Cards rolled out of his tent, she smiled. He looked like a bear who'd spent his hibernation rolling in soot. With his hair standing up in grungy spikes, his eyes glazed with fatigue, he grunted at her before stumbling off for a little privacy to relieve his bladder.

The camp began to stir. More grunts and rustles, more dazed and glassy eyes as smoke jumpers grabbed food and coffee. Gull climbed out, his face shadowed by soot and scruff. But his eyes were alert, she noted, and glinted at her briefly before he wandered off into the trees.

"Wind's already picking up." Gibbons came to stand beside her, gulped coffee.

"Yeah." She looked toward the smoke columns climbing the sky. Orange and gold flared through the red now. Like the sky, the magic, the camp, the dragon woke. "We're not going to get any help from the weather gods today. Wind's variable, fifteen to twenty, conditions remain dry with the temps spiking past eighty. She'll eat that up."

Rowan pulled out her hand-drawn maps. "We held her flank along here, but we lost ground at our water source, and when she crowned, she swept straight across this way. The hotshots hit that, kicked her back to about here, but she turned on them, about midnight, and then had to RTO," she added, speaking of reverse tool order, "and retreat back to this line."

"Was anybody hurt?"

"Minor burns, bumps and bruises. Nobody had to be evaced." She glanced over her shoulder as Gull walked up. "They're camped here." She unfolded the main map to show Gibbons. "I'm thinking if we can pump water on the head from about here, and lay line along this sector, intersect the low point of the hotshot line, then cross. We'll head up while they work over. We could box her in. It's a hell of a climb, but we'd smother her tail, block her left flank, then meet up with the pump team and cut off her head."

Gibbons nodded. "We're going to have to hold this line here." He jabbed a finger at the map. "If she gets through that, she could sweep up behind. Then it's the line team that's boxed in."

"I scouted this area yesterday. We've got a couple of safe spots. And they're sending in more jumpers this morning. We'll be up to forty. I want ten on the water team, and for you to head that up, Gib. You're damn good with a hose. Take the nine you want for it."

"All right." He glanced back at the fire. "Looks like recess is over."

"Where do you want me?" Gull asked her when Gibbons stepped off to pick his team.

"Saw line, under Yangtree. You hold that line, or you're going to need those fast feet. If she gets behind you, you make tracks, straight up the ridge and into the black. Here." She looked into his eyes as she laid a finger on the map. "You got that?"

"We'll hold it, then you can buy me a drink."

"Hold the line, cut it up and around to the water team, and maybe I will. Get your gear." She walked over toward the campfire, lifted her voice. "Okay, boys and girls, time to kick some ass."

She caught a ride partway on a bulldozer, then hopped off for a brutal hike to check the hotshots' progress firsthand.

"Winsor, right? Tripp," she shouted at the lean, grim-faced man over the roar of saws. Fire sounded its throaty threat while its heat pulsed strong enough to tickle the skin. "I've got a team working its way up to cross with you. Maybe by one this afternoon."

A scan of the handcrew told her what she'd suspected. They'd downplayed injuries. She gestured to one of the men wielding a Pulaski. His face glowed with sweat and showed raw and red where his eyebrows had been singed off. "You had a close one."

"Shit-your-pants close. Wind bitched on us, and she turned on a freaking dime, rolled right at us. She let out that belly laugh. You know what I mean."

"Yeah." It was a sound designed to turn your bowels to ice. "Yeah, I do."

"We RTO'd. Couldn't see a goddamn thing through the smoke. I swear she chased us like she wanted to play tag. I smelled my own hair burning. We barely got clear."

"You're holding her now."

"These guys'll work her till they drop, but if we don't knock that head down, I think she's going to whip around and try for another bite."

"We're pumping on her now. I'm going to check in with the team leader, see if he wants another drop." She faced the fire wall as ash swirled around her like snow. "They underestimated her, but we're going to turn this around. Look for my team to meet up with yours about one."

"Stay cool," he called after her.

She hiked back around, filling her lungs when she moved into clearer air. Moving, always moving, she checked in with her teams, with base, with the fire coordinator. After jumping a narrow creek, she angled west again. Then stopped dead when a bear crossed her path.

She checked the impulse to run; she knew better. But her feet itched to move. "Oh, come on," she said under her breath. "I'm doing this for you, too. Just move along."

Her heart thumped as he studied her, and running didn't seem like such a stupid idea after all. Then he swung his head away as if bored with her, and lumbered away.

"I love the wilderness and all it holds," she reminded herself when she worked up enough spit to swallow.

She hiked another quarter of a mile before her heart settled down again. And still, she cast occasional cautious looks over her shoulder until she heard the muffled buzz of chain saws.

She picked up her speed and met up with the fresh saw line.

After a quick update with Yangtree, she joined the line. She'd give them an hour before hiking up and around again.

"Pretty day, huh?" Gull commented as they sliced a downed tree into logs.

She glanced up, and through a few windows in the smoke, the sky was a bold blue. "She's a beauty."

"Nice one for a picnic."

Rowan stamped out a spot the size of a dinner plate that kindled at her feet. "Champagne picnic. I always wanted to have one of those."

"Too bad I didn't bring a bottle with me."

She settled for water, then mopped her face. "We're going to do it. I'm starting to feel it."

"The picnic?"

"The fire's a little more immediate. You've got a good hand with the saw. Keep it up."

She headed up to confer with Yangtree again over the maps, then, ripping open a cookie wrapper, headed back into the smoke.

While she gobbled the cookie, she considered the bear— and told herself he was well east by now. She clawed her way up the ridge, checked the time when she met the hotshot line.

Just noon. Five hours into the day, and damn good progress.

She cut up and over, her legs burning and rubbery, to check on the pumpers.

Arcs of water struck the blaze, liquid arrows aimed to kill. Rowan gave in, bent over, resting her hands on her screaming thighs. She couldn't say how many miles she'd covered so far that day, but she was damn sure she felt every inch of it.

She pushed herself up, made her way over to Gibbons. "Yangtree's line is moving up well. He should meet up with the hotshots within the hour. She tried to swish her tail, but they've got that under control. Idaho's on call if you need more on the hoses."

"We're holding her. We're going to pump her hard, go

through the neck here. If you get those lines down, cut them across, we'll have her."

"I want to pull out the fusees, start a backfire here." She dug out her map. "We could fold her back in on herself, and she'd be out of fuel."

"I like it. But it's your call."

"Then I'm making it." She pulled her radio. "Yangtree, we're going with the backfire. Split ten off, lead them up. I'm circling back down. Keep drowning that bitch, Gib."

Rowan stuffed calories into her system by way of an energy bar, hydrated with water as she backtracked. And considered herself lucky when she didn't repeat her encounter with a bear. Nothing stirred in the trees, in the brush. She cut across a trail where the trees still towered—trees they fought to save—and the wildflowers poked their heads toward the smoke-choked sky. Birds had taken wing so no song, no chatter played through the silence.

But the fire muttered and growled, shooting its flames up like angry fists and kicking feet.

She followed its flank, thought of the wildflowers, took their hope with her as she hiked to the man-made burn she'd ordered.

At Yangtree's orders, Gull peeled off from the saw line to deal with spot fires the main blaze spat across the border. Most of his team were too weary for conversation, and as speed added a factor, breath for chat was in limited supply.

Water consumed poured off in sweat; food gulped down burned off and left a constant, nagging hunger.

The trick, he knew from his years as a hotshot, was not to think about it, about anything but the fire, and the next step toward killing it.

"Get your fusees." Gibbons relayed the information in a voice harsh from shouting and smoke. "We're going to burn her ass, pull her back till she eats herself."

Gull looked back toward the direction of the tail. Their line was holding, the cross with the hotshots' cut off her flank—so far. Spot fires flared up, but she'd lost her edge of steam here.

He considered the timing and strategy of the backfire dead-on. Despite his fatigue, it pleased him when Yangtree pulled him off the line and sent him down with a team to control the backfire.

With the others he hauled up his tools, left the line.

He saw the wildflowers as Rowan had, and the holes woodpeckers had drilled into the body of a Douglas fir, the scat of a bear—a big one—that had him scanning the hazy forest. Just in case.

Heading the line, Cards limped a little as he kept in contact with Rowan, other team leaders on his radio. Gull wondered what he'd hurt and how, but they kept moving, and at an urgent pace.

He heard the mumble of a dozer. It pushed through the haze, scooping brush and small trees. Rowan hopped off while it bumped its way along a new line.

"We're going to work behind the Cat line. We got hose." She pointed to the paracargo she'd ordered dropped. "We've got a water source with that stream. I want the backfire hemmed in here, so when she rolls back she burns herself out. Watch out for spots. She's been spitting them out everywhere."

She shifted her gaze to Gull. "Can you handle a hose as well as you do a saw?"

"I've been known to."

"You, Matt, Cards. Let's get pumping. Everybody else, hit those snags."

He liked a woman with a plan, Gull thought as he got to work.

"We light it on my go." Rowan offered Cards one of the peanut-butter crackers from her PG bag. "Are you hurt?"

"It's nothing. Tripped over my own feet."

"Mine," Matt corrected. "I got in the way."

"My feet tripped over his feet. It was pretty crazy on the line for a while."

"And now it's so sane. Soak it down," she told them. "Everything in front of the Cat line, soak it good."

Manning a pumping fire hose took muscle, stability and sweat. Within ten minutes—and hours on the saw and scratch line—Gull's arms stopped aching and just went numb. He dug in, sent his arcs of water raining over the trees, soaking into the ground. Over the cacophony of pump, saw and engine, he heard Rowan shout the order for the light.

"Here she goes!"

He watched fusees ignite, burst.

Special effects, he thought, nothing like it, as flames arrowed up, ignited the forest. It roared, full-throated, and would, if God was good, call to the dragon.

"Hold it here! We don't give her another foot."

In Rowan's voice he heard what flooded him—wonder and determination, and a fresh energy that struck his blood like a drug.

Others shouted, too, infected with the same drug. Steam rose from the ground, melded with smoke as they pushed the backfire forward. Firebrands rocketed out only to sizzle and drown on the wet ground.

This was winning. Not just turning a corner, not just holding ground, but winning. An hour passed in smoke and steam and ungodly heat—then another—before she began to lie down, this time in defeat.

Rowan jogged over to the water line. "She's rolled back. Head's cut off and under control. Flanks are receding. Take her down. She's done."

The fire's retreat ran fitful and weak. By evening she could barely manage a sputter. The pulse of the pump silenced, and Gull let his weeping arms drop. He dug into his pack, found a sandwich he'd ratted in at dawn. He didn't taste it, but since it awakened the yawning hunger in his belly, he wished he'd grabbed more of whatever the hell it was.

He walked to the stream, took off his hard hat and filled it with water. He considered the sensation of having it rain cool over his head and shoulders nearly as good as sex.

"Nice work."

He glanced over at Rowan, filled his hat again. Standing, he quirked a brow. She laughed, took off her helmet, lifted her face, closed her eyes. "Oh, yeah," she sighed when he dumped the water on her. She blinked her eyes open, cool, crystal blue. "You handle yourself pretty well for an ex-hotshot rookie."

"You handle yourself pretty well for a girl."

She laughed again. "Okay, even trade." Then lifted her hand.

He quirked his brow again, the grin spreading, but she shook her head. "You're too filthy to kiss, and I'm still fire boss on this line. High five's all you get."

"I'll take it." He slapped hands with her. "We were holding her, kicking her back some, but we beat her the minute you called for the backfire."

"I'm second-guessing if I should have called it earlier." Then she shrugged. "No point in what-ifs. We took her down." She put her hard hat back on, lifted her voice. "Okay, kids, let's mop it up."

They dug roots, tramped out embers, downed smoldering snags. When the final stage of the fight was finished, they packed out, all but asleep on their feet, shouldering tools and gear. Nobody spoke on the short flight back to base; most were too busy snoring. Some thirty-eight hours after the siren sounded, Gull dragged himself into the barracks, dumped his gear. On the way to his quarters he bumped into Rowan.

"How about a nightcap?"

She snorted out a laugh. He imagined she'd braced a hand on the wall just to stay on her feet. "While a cold beer might go down good, I believe that's your clever code for sex. Even if my brain was fried enough to say sure, I don't believe you could get it up tonight—today—this morning."

"I strongly disagree, and would be willing to back that up with a demonstration."

"Sweet." She gave him a light slap on his grimy face. "Pass. 'Night."

She slipped into her room, and he continued on to his. Once he stripped off his stinking shirt, pants, and fell face-down and filthy on top of his bed, he had time to think, thank God she hadn't taken him up on it, before he zeroed out.

IN THE BUNK in his office, where he habitually stayed when Rowan caught a fire at night, Lucas heard the transport plane go out. Heard it come back. Still, he didn't fully relax until his cell phone signaled a text.

Got nasty, but we put her down. I'm A-OK. Love, Ro

He put the phone aside, settled down, and slid into the first easy sleep since the siren sounded.

LUCAS JUMPED with an early-morning group of eight, posed for pictures, signed brochures, then took the time to discuss moving up to accelerated free fall with two of the group.

When he walked them in to Marcie to sign them up, his brain went wonky on him. Ella Frazier of the red hair and forest-green eyes turned to smile at him.

With dimples.

"Hello again."

"Ah . . . again," he managed, flustered. "Um, Marcie will take you through the rest, get you scheduled," he told the couple with him.

"I watched your skydive." Ella turned her smile on them. "I just did my first tandem the other day. It's amazing, isn't it?"

He stood, struggling not to shuffle his feet while Ella chatted with his newest students.

"Have you got a minute for me?" she asked him.

"Sure. Sure. My office—"

"Could we walk outside? Marcie tells me you've got two more tandems coming in. I'd love to watch."

"Okay." He held the door open for her, then wondered what to do with his hands. In his pockets? At his sides? He wished he had a clipboard with him to keep them occupied.

"I know you're busy today, and I probably should've called."

"It's no problem."

"How's your daughter? I followed the fire on the news," she added.

"She's fine. Back on base, safe and sound. Did I tell you about Rowan?"

"Not exactly." She tucked her hair behind her ear as she angled her face toward his. "I Googled you before I signed up. I love my son, but I wasn't about to jump out of an airplane unless I knew something about who I was hooked to."

"Can't blame you." See, he told himself, sensible. Any man should be able to relax around a sensible woman. A grandmother, he reminded himself. An *educator*.

He managed to unknot his shoulders.

"Your experience and reputation turned the trick for me. So, Lucas, I was wondering if I could buy you a drink."

And his shoulders tensed like overwound springs while his brain went to sloppy mush. "Sorry?"

"To thank you for the experience, and giving me the chance to show off to my grandchildren."

"Oh, well." There went that flush of heat up the back of his neck. "You don't have to . . . I mean to say—"

"I caught you off-guard, and probably sounded like half the women who come through here, hitting on you."

"No, they . . . you—"

"I wasn't. Hitting on you," she added with a big, bright smile. "But now I have to confess to a secondary purpose. I have a project I'd love to speak to you about, and if I could buy you a drink, soften you up, I'm hoping you'll get on board. If you're in a relationship, you're welcome to bring your lady with you."

"No, I'm not. I mean, there isn't any lady. Especially."

"Would you be free tonight? I could meet you about seven, at the bar at Open Range. I could thank you, soften you up, and you can tell me more about training for the AFF."

Business, he told himself. Friendly business. He discussed friendly business over drinks all the damn time. No reason he couldn't do the same with her. "I don't have any plans."

"Then we're set? Thanks so much." She shot out a hand, shook his briskly. "I'll see you at seven."

He watched her walk away, so pretty, so breezy—and reminded himself it was just friendly business.

9

As she had done in her tent, Rowan lay with her eyes closed and took morning inventory. She decided she felt like a hundred-year-old woman who'd been on a starvation diet. But she'd come out of it—as fire boss—uninjured, her crew intact, and the fire down.

Added to it, she thought as she opened her eyes, tracked her gaze around her quarters, during her two days out the pig-blood fairies had not only mopped and scrubbed but rolled a fresh coat of paint on her walls.

She owed somebody, and if she could drag herself out of bed she'd find out who.

When she did, her calves twinged, her quads protested. The bis and tris, she noted, shed bitter tears. The hot shower she'd all but slept through had helped, a little, but the eight hours in the rack after two arduous days required more.

Fuel and movement, she ordered herself. And where was Gull with his breakfast sandwich when she needed one? She settled for a chocolate bar while she dressed, then hobbled off to the gym.

She wasn't the only one hobbling.

She grunted at Gibbons, who grunted back, watched Trigger wince through some floor stretches. She studied Dobie—wiry little guy—as he bench-pressed what she judged to be his body weight.

"I'm back on the jump list tomorrow," he told her as he pumped up with an explosion of breath. "I'm ready. Hell of a lot readier than you guys, from the looks of it."

She shot him the finger, then moaned into a forward bend. She stayed down, just stayed down and breathed for as long as she could stand it, then with her palms on the floor, arched her back and looked up.

The yellow bruising on Dobie's red-with-effort face made him look like a jaundiced burn victim. And he'd shaved off his scraggly excuse for a beard—an improvement, to her mind, since he looked less like a hillbilly leprechaun.

"Somebody cleaned up and painted my room."

"Yeah." With another explosion of breath, he pushed the weights up, then clicked them in the safety. "Stovic and me, we had time on our hands."

She brought herself back to standing. "You guys did all that?"

"Mostly. Marg and Lynn did what they could with your clothes. Salt's what gets blood out; that's what my ma uses."

"Is that so?"

"Doesn't work so well on walls, so we got them painted up. It kept us from going stir-crazy while the rest of you were having all the fun. Hell of a mess in there, and smelled like a hog butchering. Made me homesick," he added with a grin. "Anyhow, that broad must be crazy as a run-over lizard."

She walked over, bent down, kissed him on the mouth. "Thanks."

He wiggled his eyebrows. "It was a big, stinkin' *hell* of a mess."

This time she drilled her finger into his belly. After walking back to her mat, she stretched out her muscles, soothed her mind with yoga. She'd moved to floor work when Gull came in. Fresh, she thought. He looked fresh and clean, with his gait loose and easy as he crossed to her.

"I heard you'd surfaced." He crouched down. "You're looking pretty limber for the morning after."

"Just need some fine-tuning."

"And a picnic."

She lifted her nose from her knee. "I need a picnic?"

"With a big-ass hamper loaded with cuisine by Marg and a fine bottle of adult beverage enjoyed in the company of a charming companion."

"Janis is going with me on a picnic?"

"I've got the big-ass hamper."

"There's always a catch." Danger zone, she warned herself. The man was a walking temptation. "It's a nice thought, but—"

"We're not on the jump list, and L.B. cleared us for the day. Now that we've been through fire together, I think we can take a short break, have some food and conversation. Unless you're afraid a little picnic will drive you into uncontrollable lust until you force yourself on me and take advantage of my friendly offer."

Temptation and challenge—both equally hard to resist. "I'm reasonably sure I can control myself."

"Okay then. We can leave whenever you're ready."

What the hell, she decided. She lived and breathed danger zones. She could certainly handle one appealingly cocky guy on a picnic.

"Give me twenty. And you'd better pick your spot close by because I'm starving."

"I'll meet you out front."

She hunted up Stovic first, gave him the same smack on the lips as Dobie. She paid her debts. She had a report to write and turn in on the fire, but that could wait a couple hours. Check and reorganize her gear, she thought as she pulled on cropped khakis. Deal with her chute, repack her PG bag. She buttoned on a white camp shirt, slapped on some makeup and sunscreen and considered it good enough for a friendly picnic with a fellow jumper.

She shoved on her sunglasses as she walked outside, then narrowed her eyes behind them. Gull leaned on the hood of a snazzy silver convertible chatting it up with Cards.

She sauntered over. "How's the leg?" she asked Cards.

"Not bad. Knee's a little puffy yet. I'm going to ice it down again." He patted the hood beside Gull's hip. "That's some ride, Fast Feet. Some hot ride. Today's word's got to be virile, 'cause that machine's got balls. You kids have fun." He winked at Rowan and, still limping, went back in.

Hands on her hips, Rowan took a stroll around the hot ride. "This is Iron Man's car."

"Since I doubt you're claiming I stole it from your father, I conclude you're a woman who knows her superheroes and her motor vehicles."

She stopped in front of him. "Where's the suit?"

"In an undisclosed location. Villainy is everywhere."

"Too true." She angled her head, skimming a finger over the gleaming fender while she studied Gull. "Iron Man's a rich superhero. That's why he can afford the car."

"Tony Stark has many cars."

"Also true. I'm thinking, smoke jumping pays pretty well, in season. But I can't see selling tokens and tracking games at an arcade's something that pays for a car like this."

"But it's entertaining, and I get free pizza. It's my car," he said when she just kept staring at him. "Do you want to see the registration? My portfolio?"

"That means you *have* a portfolio, and I'm damned if you built one working an arcade." Considering, she pursed her lips. "Maybe if you owned a piece of it."

"You have remarkable deductive powers. You can be Pepper Potts." He stepped over, opened her door. She slid in, looked up.

"How big a piece?"

"I'll give you the life story while we eat if you want it."

She thought it over as he skirted the hood, got behind the wheel. And decided she did.

He drove fast, had a smooth, competent hand on the stick shift—both of which she appreciated.

And God, she did love a slick machine.

"Do I have to sleep with you before you let me drive this machine?"

He spared her a single, mild glance. "Of course."

"Seems fair." Enjoying herself, she tipped her face up to the wind and sky, then lifted her hands up to both. "Riding in it's a pretty decent compromise. How did you manage to get this all set up?"

"Staggering organizational skills. Plus I figured I'd grab a few hours while I had them. The food was the easy part. All I had to do was tell Marg I was taking you on a picnic, and she handled the rest of that section. She's in love with you."

"It's mutual. Still, I'd've had a hard time planning anything when I managed to crawl out of bed."

"I have staggering recuperative powers to go with the organizational skills."

She tipped down her sunglasses to eye him over them. "I know sex bragging when I hear it."

"Then I probably shouldn't add that I woke up feeling like I'd been run over by a sixteen-wheeler after I hauled a two-hundred-pound bag of bricks fifty miles. Through mud."

"Yeah. And it's barely June."

When he turned off on Bass Creek Road, she nodded. "Nice choice."

"It's not a bad hike, and it ought to be pretty."

"It is. I've lived here all my life," she added as he pulled into the parking area at the end of the road. "Hiking the trails was what I did. It kept me in shape, gave me a good sense of the areas I'd jump one day—and gave me an appreciation for why I would."

"We crossed into the black yesterday." He hit the button to bring up the roof. "It's harsh, and it's hard. But you know it's going to come back."

They got out, and he opened the hood with its marginal storage space.

"Jesus, Gull, you weren't kidding about big-ass hamper."

"Getting it in was an exercise in geometry." He hefted it out.

"There's just two of us. What does that thing weigh?"

"A lot less than my gear. I think I can make it a mile on a trail."

"We can switch off."

He looked at her as they crossed to the trailhead. "I'm all about equal pay for equal work. A firm believer in ability, determination, brains having nothing to do with gender. I'm even cautiously open to women players in the MLB. Cautiously open, I repeat. But there are lines."

"Carting a picnic hamper is a line?"

"Yeah."

She slid her hands into her pockets, hummed a little as she strolled with a smirk on her face. "It's a stupid line."

"Maybe. But that doesn't make it less of a line."

They walked through the forested canyon. She heard what she'd missed during the fire. The birdsong, the rustles—the life. Sun shimmered through the canopy, struck the bubbling, tumbling waters of the creek as they followed the curve of the water.

"Is this why you were studying maps?" she asked him. "Looking for a picnic spot?"

"That was a happy by-product. I haven't lived here all my life, and I want to know where I am." He scanned the canyon, the spills of water as they walked up the rising trail. "I like where I am."

"Was it always Northern California? Is there any reason we have to wait for the food to start the life story?"

"I guess not. No, I started out in LA. My parents were in the entertainment industry. He was a cinematographer, she was a costume designer. They met on a set, and clicked."

The creek fell below as they climbed higher on the hillside.

"So," he continued, "they got married, had me a couple years later. I was four when they were killed in a plane crash. Little twin engine they were taking to the location for a movie."

Her heart cracked a little. "Gull, I'm so sorry."

"Me too. They didn't take me, and they usually did if they were on the same project. But I had an ear infection, so they left me back with the nanny until it cleared up."

"It's hard, losing parents."

"Vicious. There's the log dam," he announced. "Just as advertised."

She let it go as the trail approached the creek once more. She could hardly blame him for not wanting to revisit a little boy's grief.

"This is worth a lot more than a mile-and-a-half hike," he said while the pond behind the dam sparkled as if strewn with jewels.

Beyond it the valley opened like a gift, and rolled to the ring of mountains.

"And the hamper's going to be a lot lighter on the mile-and-a-half back."

Near the pond, under the massive blue sky, he set it down.

"I worked a fire out there, the Selway-Bitterroot Wilderness." He stood, looking out. "Standing here, on a day like this, you'd never believe any of that could burn."

"Jumping one's different."

"It's sure a faster way in." He flipped open the lid of the hamper, took out the blanket folded on top. She helped him spread it open, then sat on it cross-legged.

"What's on the menu?"

He pulled out a bottle of champagne snugged in a cold sleeve. Surprised, touched, she laughed. "That's a hell of a start—and you just don't miss a trick."

"You said champagne picnic. For our entrée, we have the traditional fried chicken à la Marg."

"Best there is."

"I'm told you favor thighs. I'm a breast man myself."

"I've never known a man who isn't." She began to unload. "Oh, yeah, her red potato and green bean salad, and look at this cheese, the bread. We've got berries, deviled eggs. Fudge cake! Marg gave us damn near half of one of her fudge cakes." She glanced up. "Maybe she's in love with *you*."

"I can only hope." He popped the cork. "Hold out your glass."

She reached for it, then caught the label on the bottle. "Dom Pérignon. Iron Man's car and James Bond's champagne."

"I have heroic taste. Hold out the glass, Rowan." He filled it, then his own. "To wilderness picnics."

"All right." She tapped, sipped. "Jesus, this is not cheap tequila at Get a Rope. I see why 007 goes for it. How'd you get this?"

"They carry it in town."

"You've been into town today? What time did you get up?"

"About eight. I never made it to the shower last night, and smelled bad enough to wake myself up this morning."

He opened one of the containers, and after breaking off a

chunk of the baguette, spread it with soft, buttery cheese. Offered it. "I'm not especially rich, I don't think."

She studied him as flavors danced on her tongue. Caught in a pretty breeze, his hair danced around his face in an appealing tangle of brown and sun-struck gold.

"I want to know. But I don't want bad memories to screw your picnic."

"That's about it for the bad. I'm not sure I'd remember them, or more than vaguely, if it wasn't for my aunt and uncle. My mother's sister," he explained. "My parents named them as my legal guardians in their wills. They came and got me, took me up north, raised me."

He took out plates, flatware as he spoke, while she gave him room for the story.

"They talked about my parents all the time, showed me pictures. They were tight, the four of them, and my aunt and uncle wanted me to keep the good memories. I have them."

"You were lucky. After something horrible, you were lucky."

His gaze met hers. "Really lucky. They didn't just take me in. I was theirs, and I always felt that."

"The difference between being an obligation, even a well-tended one, and belonging."

"I never had to learn how wide that difference is. My cousins—one's a year older, one's a year younger—never made me feel like an outsider."

That played a part in the balance of him, she decided, in the ease and confidence.

"They sound like great people."

"They are. When I graduated from college, I had a trust fund, pretty big chunk. The money from my parents' estate, the insurance, all that. They'd never used a penny, but invested it for me."

"And you bought an arcade."

He lifted his champagne. "I like arcades. The best ones are about families. Anyway, my younger cousin mostly runs it, and Jared—the older one—he's a lawyer, and takes care of that sort of thing. My aunt supervises and helps plan events, and for the last couple years my uncle's handled the PR."

"For families by family. It's a good thing."

"It works for us."

"How do they feel about your summers?"

"They're okay with it. I guess they worry, but they don't weigh me down with that. You grew up with a smoke jumper." They added chicken and salad to plates. "How'd you handle it?"

"By thinking he was invincible. Talk about superheroes. Mmm," she added when she bit through crisp skin to tender meat. "God bless Marg. I really considered him immortal," Rowan added. "I never worried about him. I was never afraid for him, or myself. He was . . . Iron Man."

Gull poured two more glasses. "I'll definitely drink to Iron Man Tripp. He's why we're both here."

"Weird, but true." She ate, relaxed in the moment and felt easier with him, she realized, than she'd expected to be. "I don't know how much of the story you've heard. About my parents."

"Some."

"A lot of some's glossed over. My father—you've probably seen pictures—he was, still is, pretty wow."

"He passed the wow down to you."

"In a Valkyrie kind of way."

"You're not the sort who decides to die in the battle."

"You know your Norse mythology."

"I have many pockets of strange, inexplicable knowledge."

"So I've noticed. In any case, a man who looks like Iron Man, does what he does . . . women flock."

"I have the same problem. It's a burden."

She snorted, ate some potato salad. "But he wasn't one for coming off a fire, or out of the season, and looking for the handy bang."

She arched a brow as Gull merely grinned. "It's not his way. Like me, he's lived here all his life. If he'd had that kind of rep, it would've stuck. He met my mother when she came to Missoula, picked up work as a waitress. She was looking for adventure. She was beautiful, a little on the wild side. Anyway, they hooked up, and oops, she got knocked up. They got married. They met in early July, and by the middle of September they're married. Stupid, from a rational point of view, but I have to be grateful seeing as I'm sitting here telling the tale."

He'd known he'd been wanted, all of his life. How much did it change the angles when you, as she did, considered yourself an oops?

"We'll both be grateful."

"I think it must've been exciting for her." Rowan popped a fat blackberry into her mouth as she spoke. "Here's this gorgeous man who wore a flight suit like some movie star, one of the elite, one at the top of his game, and he picks her. At the same time, she's rebelling against a pretty strict, stuffy upbringing. She was nearly ten years younger than Dad, and probably enjoyed the idea of playing house with him. Over the winter, he's starting up his business, but he's around. My grandparents are, too, and she's carrying the child of their only son. She's the center. Her parents have cut her off, just severed all ties."

"How do people do that? How do they justify that, live with that?"

"They think they're right. And I think that added to the excitement for her. And in the spring, there I am, so she's got a new baby to show off. Doting grandparents—a husband who's besotted, and still around."

She chose another berry, let it lie on her tongue a moment, sweet and firm. "Then a month later, the season starts, and he's not around every day. Now it's about changing diapers, and walking a squalling baby in the middle of the night. It's not such an adventure now, or so exciting."

She reached for another piece of chicken. "He's never, not once, said a word against her to me. What I know of that time I got from reading letters he'd locked up, riffling through papers, eavesdropping—or occasionally catching my grandmother when she was pissed off and her tongue was just loose enough."

"You wanted to know," Gull said simply.

"Yeah, I wanted to know. She left when I was five months old. Just took me over to my grandparents, asked if they'd watch me while she ran some errands, and never came back."

"Cold." He couldn't quite get his mind around that kind of cold, or what that kind of cold would do to the child left behind. "And clueless," he added. "It says she decided this isn't what I want after all, so I'll just run away."

"That sums it. My dad tracked her down, a couple of times. Made phone calls, wrote letters. Her line, because I saw the letters she wrote back, was it was all his fault. He was the cold and selfish one, had wrecked her emotionally. The least he could do was send her some money while she was trying to recover. She'd promise to come back once she had, claimed she missed me and all that."

"Did she come back?"

"Once, on my tenth birthday. She walks into my party, all smiles and tears, loaded down with presents. It's not my birthday party anymore."

"No, it's her Big Return, putting her in the center again."

Rowan stared at him for a long moment. "That's exactly it. I hated her at that moment, the way a ten-year-old can. When she tried to hug me, I pushed her away. I told her to get out, to go to hell."

"Sounds to me that at ten you had a good bullshit detector. How'd she handle it?"

"Big, fat tears, shock, hurt—and bitter accusations hurled at my father."

"For turning you against her."

"And again, you score. I stormed right out the back door, and I'd have kept on going if Dad hadn't come out after me. He was pissed, all the way around. I knew better than to speak to anyone like that, and I was going back inside, apologizing to my mother. I said I wouldn't, he couldn't make me, and until he made *her* leave, I was never going back in that house. I was too mad to be scared. Respect was god in our house. You didn't lie and you didn't sass—the big two."

"How did he handle it?"

"He picked me right up off the ground, and I know he was worked up enough to cart me right back in there. I punched him, kicked him, screamed, scratched, bit. I didn't even know I was crying. I do know if he'd dragged me in, if he'd threatened me, ordered me, if he who'd never raised a hand to me had raised it, I wouldn't have said I was sorry."

"Then you'd've broken the other big one, by lying."

"The next thing I knew we were sitting on the ground in the backyard, I'm crying all over his shoulder. And he's hugging me, petting me and telling me I was right. He said, 'You're right, and I'm sorry.' He told me to sit right there, and he'd go in and make her go away."

She tipped back her glass. "And that's what he did."

"You got lucky, too."

"Yeah, I did. She didn't."

Rowan paused, looked out over the pond. "A little over two years later, she goes into a convenience store to pick up something, walks in on a robbery. And she's dead, wrong place, wrong time. Horrible. Nobody deserves to die bleeding on the floor of a quick market in Houston. God, how did I get on all this when there's fudge cake and champagne?"

"Finish it."

"Nothing much left. Dad asked me if I'd go to the funeral with him. He said he needed to go, that if I didn't need or want to, that was okay. I said I'd think about it, then later my grandmother came into my room, sat on the bed. She told me I needed to go. That as hard as it might be now, it would be harder on me later if I didn't. That if I did this one thing, I would never have to have any regrets. So I went, and she was right. I did what I needed to do, what my father needed me to do, and I've got no regrets."

"What about her family?"

"Her parents cold-shouldered us. That's who they are. I've never actually spoken to them. I know her sister, my aunt. She made a point of calling and writing over the years, even came out with her family a couple times. They're nice people.

"And that concludes our exchange of life stories."

"I imagine there's another chapter or two, for another time."

She eyed him as he refilled her glass. "You stopped drinking, and you keep filling my glass. Are you trying to get me drunk and naked?"

"Naked's always the goal." He said it lightly as he sensed she needed to change the mood. "Drunk? Not when I've witnessed you suck down tequila shots. I'm driving," he reminded her.

"Responsible." She toasted him. "And that leaves more for me. Did you know Dobie and Stovic scrubbed up and painted my room?"

"I heard Dobie got to first base with you."

She let out that big, bawdy laugh. "If he considers that first base, he's never hit a solid single." She took her fork, carved off a big mouthful of cake right out of the container. Her eyes laughed as she stuffed it in, then closed on a long, low moan. "Now, that is cake, and the equivalent of a grand slam. Enough fire and chocolate, and I can go all season without sex."

"Don't be surprised if the supply of chocolate disappears in a fifty-mile radius."

"I like your style, Gull." She forked up another hefty bite. "You're pretty to look at, you've got a brain, you can fight and you do what needs doing when we're on the line. Plus, you can definitely hit a solid single. But there are a couple of problems."

She stabbed another forkful, this time offering it to him.

"First, I know you've got deep pockets. If I slept with you now, you might think I did it because you're rich."

"Not that rich. Anyway." He considered, smiled. "I can live with that."

"Second." She held out more cake, then whipped it around, slid it into her own mouth. "You're a smoke jumper in my unit."

"You're the kind of woman who breaks rules. Codes, no. Rules, yes."

"That's an interesting distinction."

Full, she stretched out on the blanket, studied the sky. "Not a cloud," she murmured. "The long-range forecast is for hot and dry. There won't be a lot of champagne picnics this season."

"Then we should appreciate this one."

He leaned down, laid his lips on hers in a long, slow, upside-down kiss. She tasted of champagne and chocolate, smelled of peaches on a hot summer day.

She carried scars, body and heart, and still faced life with courage.

When her hands came to his face he lingered over those

flavors, those scents, the fascinating contrasts of her, sliding just a little deeper into the lush.

Then she eased his face up. "You're swinging for a double."

"It worked for Spider-Man."

"He was hanging upside down, in the rain—and that was after he'd kicked bad-guy ass. Not to mention, he didn't get to second."

"I'm in danger of being crazy about you, if only for your deep knowledge of superhero action films."

"I'm trying to save you from that fate." She patted the blanket beside her. "Why don't you stretch out in the next stage of picnic tradition while I explain?"

Gull shifted the hamper aside, lay down hip-to-hip with her.

"If we slept together," Rowan began, "there's no doubt we'd bang all the drums, ring all the bells."

"Sound all the trumpets."

"Those, too. But after, there's the inevitable tragedy. You'd fall in love with me. They all do."

He heard the humor in her voice, idly linked his fingertips with hers. "You have that power?"

"I do and, though God knows I've tried, can't control it. And you—I'm telling you this because, as I said, I like your style. You, helpless, hopeless, would be weak in love, barely able to eat or sleep. You'd spend all the profits you make off quarters pumped into Skee-Ball on elaborate gifts in a vain attempt to win my heart."

"They could be pretty elaborate," he told her. "Skee-Ball's huge."

"Still, my heart can't be bought. I'd be forced to break yours, coldly and cruelly, to spare you from further humiliation. And also because your pathetic pleas would irritate the shit out of me."

"All that," he said after a moment, "from one round in the sack?"

"I'm afraid so. I've lost count of the shoes I've had to throw away because the soles were stained with the bleeding hearts I've crushed along the way."

"That's a fair warning. I'll risk it."

He rolled over, took her mouth.

For a moment, she thought the top of her head simply shot off. Explosions, heat, eruptions burst through her body like a fireball. She lost her breath, and what she thought of as simple common sense, in the wicked whir of want.

She arched up to him, her hands shoving under his shirt—eager to feel her need pressed to him, his skin, his muscles under her hands.

There was a wildness here. She knew it lived inside her, and now she felt whatever animal he caged in leap out to run with hers.

She made him crazy. That lush, greedy mouth, those quick, seeking hands, the body that moved under his with such strength, such purpose, even as, for just a moment, it yielded.

Her breasts, full and firm, filled his hands as her moan of pleasure vibrated against his lips. She was sensation, and bombarded him with feelings he could neither stop nor identify.

He imagined pulling off her clothes, his own, taking what they both wanted there, on a borrowed blanket beside a shining pond.

Then her hands came between them, pushed. He gave himself another moment, gorging on that feast of feelings, before he eased back to look down at her.

"That," he said, "is the next step in a traditional picnic."

"Yeah, I guess it is. And it's a winner. It's a good thing I got off on that fudge cake because you definitely know how to stir a woman up. In fact . . ." She wiggled out from under him, grabbed what was left of the cake and took a bite. "Mmm, yeah, that takes care of it."

"Damn that Marg."

Her lips curved as she licked chocolate from her fingers. "This was great—every step."

"I've got a few more steps in me."

"I'm sure you do, and I have no doubt they'd be winners. Which is why we'd better go."

Her lips had curved, he thought when they began to pack

up, but the smile hadn't reached her eyes. He waited until they'd folded the blanket back into the well-depleted hamper.

"I got to second."

She laughed, as he'd hoped, then snickered with the fun of it as they started the hike back.

10

Lucas poked his head in the kitchen of the cookhouse.

"I heard a rumor about blueberry pie."

Marg glanced back as she finished basting a couple of turkeys the size of Hondas. "I might have saved a piece, and maybe could spare a cup of coffee to go with it. If somebody asked me nicely."

He walked over, kissed her cheek.

"That might work. Sit on down."

He took a seat at the work counter where Lynn prepped hills and mountains of vegetables. "How's it going, Lynn?"

"Not bad considering we keep losing cooks." She shot him a smile with a twinkle out of rich brown eyes. "If you sit here long enough, we'll put you to work."

"Will work for pie. I heard about the trouble. I was hoping to talk to Rowan, but they tell me she's on a picnic with the rookie from California."

"Fast Feet," Lynn confirmed. "He sweet-talked Marg into putting a hamper together."

"Nobody sweet-talks me unless I like the talk." Marg set a warmed piece of blueberry pie, with a scoop of ice cream gently melting over the golden crust, in front of Lucas.

"He's got a way though," Lynn commented.

"Nobody has their way with Rowan unless she likes the way." Marg put a thick mug of coffee beside the pie.

"I don't worry about her." Lucas shrugged.

"Liar."

He smiled up at Marg. "Much. What's your take on this business with Dolly?"

"First, the girl can cook but she doesn't have the brains, or the sense, of that bunch of broccoli Lynn's prepping." Marg waved a pot holder at him. "And don't think I don't know she tried getting her flirt on with you a time or two."

"Oh, golly," Lynn said as both she and Lucas blushed to the hairline.

"For God's sake, Marg, she's Rowan's age."

"That and good sense stopped you, but it didn't stop her from trying."

"Neither here nor there," Lucas mumbled, and focused on his pie.

"You can thank me for warning her off before Rowan got wind and scalped her. Anyway, I'd've butted heads with L.B. about hiring her back, but we needed the help. The cook we hired on didn't last through training."

"Too much work, she said." Lynn rolled her eyes as she filled an enormous pot with the mountain of potatoes she'd peeled and quartered.

"I was thinking about seeing if we could bump one of the girls we have who helps with prep sometimes, and with cleanup, to full-time cook. But then Dolly has the experience, and I know what she can do. And, well, she's got a baby now."

"Jim Brayner's baby." Lucas nodded as he ate pie. "Everybody needs a chance."

"Yeah, and that bromide ended up getting Ro's quarters splattered with pig blood. Nasty business, let me tell you."

"That girl's had it in for Ro since their school days, but this?" Lucas shook his head. "It's just senseless."

"Dolly's lucky Cards was there to hold Ro back long enough for some of the other guys to come on the run and wrestle her down. It would've been more than some oinker's blood otherwise."

"My girl's got a temper."

"And was in the right of it, if you ask me—or anybody else around here. And what does Dolly do after L.B. cans her?" Marg's eyes went hot as she slapped a dishcloth on the counter. "She comes crying to me, asking, can't I put in a word for her? I gave her a word, all right."

Lynn snorted. "Surrounded by others, as in: Get the *word* out of my kitchen."

"I'm sorry for her troubles, but it's best she's gone. And away from my girl," Lucas added. As far as he was concerned, that ended that. "How would you rate the rookies this season?"

Marg hauled out a couple casserole dishes. "The rook your girl's eating fried chicken with, or all of them?"

"All of them." Lucas scraped up the last bit of pie. "Maybe one in particular."

"They're a good crop, including one in particular. I'd say most are just crazy enough to stick it out."

"I guess we'll see. That was damn good pie, Marg."

"Are you after seconds?"

"Can't do it." He patted his belly. "My days of eating like a smoke jumper are over. And I've got some things I've got to get to," he added when he rose to take his plate and mug to the sink. "When you see Ro, tell her I stopped by."

"Will do. You're close enough not to be such a stranger."

"Business is good, and good keeps me pinned down. But I'll make the time. Don't work too hard, Lynn."

"Come back and say that in October, and I might be able to listen."

He headed out to walk down to where he'd left his truck. As always, nostalgia twinged, just a little. Some of the jumpers got in a run on the track. Others, he could see, stood jawing with some of the mechanics.

He spotted Yangtree, looking official in his uniform shirt and hat, leading a tour group out of Operations. Plenty of kids being herded along, he noted, getting a charge out of seeing parachutes, jumpsuits and the network of computer systems— vastly improved since his early days.

Maybe they'd get lucky and see somebody rigging a chute. Anyway, it was a nice stop for a kid on summer vacation.

That made him think of school, and school led him to the high-school principal he'd agreed to meet for a drink.

Probably should've just taken her into the office, had the sit-down there. Professional.

Friendly business started to seem more nerve-racking as the day went on.

No way around it now, he reminded himself, and dug his keys out of his pocket. As he did, he turned toward the lion's purr of engine, frowned a little as he watched his daughter zip up in the passenger seat of an Audi Spyder convertible.

She waved at him, then jumped out when the sleek beast of a car growled to a stop.

"Hey! I was going to try to get over and see you later." She threw her arms around him—was there anything more wonderful than a hard hug from your grown child? "Now I don't have to, 'cause here you are."

"I almost missed you. Gull, right?"

"That's right. It's good to see you again."

"Some car."

"I'm happy with it."

"What'll she do?"

"Theoretically, or in practice—with your daughter along?"

"That's a good answer, without answering," Lucas decided.

"Do you want to try her out?" Gull offered the key.

"Hey!" Rowan made a grab for them, missing as Gull closed his hand. "How come he rates?"

"He's Iron Man."

Rowan hooked her thumbs in her pockets. "He said I had to sleep with him before I could drive it."

Gull sent her smirk a withering look. "She declined."

"Uh-huh. Well, I wouldn't mind giving her a run. I'll take a rain check on it since I've got to get along."

"Can't you stay awhile?" Rowan asked. "We can hang out a little. You can stay and mooch dinner."

"I wish I could, but I've got a couple of things to see to, then I'm meeting a client for a drink—a meeting. An appointment."

Rowan slid off her sunglasses. "A client?"

"Yeah. Yeah. She's, ah, got some project she wants to talk to me about, and she's interested in trying for AFF. So I guess we're going to talk about it. That. Anyway . . . I'll get back over soon, mooch that dinner off you. Maybe try out that machine of yours, Gull."

"Anytime."

Lucas took Rowan's chin in his hand. "See you later."

She watched him get in the truck, watched him drive away.

"Meeting, my ass."

Gull opened the nose to maneuver the hamper out. "Sorry?"

"He's got a date. With a woman."

"Wow! That's shocking news. I think my heart skipped a beat."

"He doesn't date." Rowan continued to scowl as her father's truck shrunk in the distance. "He's all fumbling and flustered around women, if he's attracted. Didn't you see how flustered he was when he talked about his *appointment*? And who the hell is she?"

"It's hard, but you've got to let the kids leave the nest someday."

"Oh, kiss ass. His brain goes to mush when he's around a certain type of woman, and he can be manipulated."

Fascinated with her reaction, Gull leaned on his car. "It's just a wild shot, but it could be he's going to meet a woman he's attracted to, and who has no intention of manipulating him. And they'll have a drink and conversation."

"What the hell do you know?" she challenged, and stomped off toward the barracks.

Amused, Gull hauled the basket back to Marg.

He'd no more than set it down on the counter when someone tapped knuckles on the outside door.

"Excuse me. Margaret Colby?"

Gull gave the man a quick summing-up—dark suit with a tightly knotted tie in dark, vivid pink, shiny shoes, hair the color of ink brushed back from a high forehead.

Marg stood where she was. "That's right."

"I'm Reverend Latterly."

"I remember you from before, from Irene and Dolly."

Catching her tone, and the fact she didn't invite the man in, Gull decided to stick around.

"May I speak with you for a moment?"

"You can, but you're wasting your breath and my time if you're here to ask me to try to convince Michael Little Bear to let Dolly Brakeman back in this kitchen."

"Mrs. Colby." He came in without invitation, smiled, showing a lot of big white teeth.

Gull decided he didn't like the man's tie, and helped himself to a cold can of ginger ale.

"If I could just have a moment in private."

"We're working." She shot a warning glance at Lynn before the woman could ease out of the room. "This is as private as you're going to get."

"I know you're very busy, and cooking for so many is hard work. Demanding work."

"I get paid for it."

"Yes." Latterly stared at Gull, let the silence hang.

In response, Gull leaned back on the counter, drank some ginger ale. And made Marg's lips twitch.

"Well, I wanted a word with you as you're Dolly's direct supervisor and—"

"Was," Marg corrected.

"Yes. I've spoken with Mr. Little Bear, and I understand his reluctance to forgive Dolly's transgression."

"You call it a transgression. I call it snake-bite mean."

Latterly spread his hands, then linked them together for a moment like a man at prayer. "I realize it's a difficult situation, and there's no excuse for Dolly's behavior. But she was naturally upset after Miss Tripp threatened her and accused her of . . . having low morals."

"Is that Dolly's story?" Marg just shook her head, as much pity as disgust in the movement. "The girl lies half the time she opens her mouth. If you don't know that, you're not a very good judge of character. And I'd think that'd be an important skill to have in your profession."

"As Dolly's spiritual advisor—"

"Just stop there because I'm not overly interested in Dolly's spirit. She's had a mean on for Rowan as long as I've known her. She's always been jealous, always wanted what somebody else had. She's not coming back here, not getting another chance to kick at Rowan. Now, L.B. runs this base, but I run this kitchen. If he took it into his head to let Dolly back in here, he'd be looking for another head cook and he knows it."

"That's a very hard line."

"I call it common sense. The girl can cook, but she's wild, unreliable, and she's a troublemaker. I can't help her."

"She is troubled, still trying to find her way. She's also raising an infant on her own."

"She's not on her own," Marg corrected. "I've known her mother since we were girls, and I know Irene and Leo are doing all they can for Dolly. Probably more than they should, considering. Now you're going to have to excuse me."

"Would you, at least, write a reference for her? I'm sure it would help her secure another position as a cook."

"No, I won't."

Gull judged the shock that crossed the man's face as sincere. Very likely the reverend wasn't used to a flat-out no.

"As a Christian woman—"

"Who said I'm a Christian?" She jabbed a finger at him now, pointedly enough to take him back a step. "And how come that's some sort of scale on right and wrong and good and bad? I won't write her a reference because my word and my reputation mean something to me. You advise her spirit all you want, but don't come into my kitchen and try advising me on mine. Dolly made her choices, now she'll deal with the consequences of them."

She took a step forward, and those hazel eyes breathed fire. "Do you think I haven't heard what she's been saying about Rowan around town? About me, L.B., even little Lynn there? About everybody? I hear everything, Reverend Jim, and I won't give a damn thing to anyone who lies about me and mine. If it wasn't for her mother, I'd give Dolly Brakeman a good swift kick myself."

"Gossip is—"

"What plumps the grapes on the vine. If you want to do her a favor, tell Dolly to mind her mouth. Now I've got work to do, and I've given you and Dolly enough of my time."

Deliberately she turned back to the stove.

"I apologize for intruding." He spoke stiffly now, and without the big-toothed smile. "I'll pray the anger leaves your heart."

"I like my anger right where it is," Marg shot back as Latterly backed out the door. "Lynn, those vegetables aren't going to prep themselves."

"No, ma'am."

On a sigh, Marg turned around. "I'm sorry, honey. I'm not mad at you."

"I know. I wish I had the courage to talk like that to people—to say exactly what I think and mean."

"No, you don't. You're fine just the way you are. I just didn't like the sanctimonious prick." She aimed a look at Gull. "Nothing to say?"

"Just he's a sanctimonious prick with too many teeth and an ugly tie. My only critique of your response is I think you should have told him you were a Buddhist woman, or maybe a Pagan."

"I wish I'd thought of that." She smiled. "You want some pie?"

He didn't know where he'd put it after the fudge cake, but understanding the sentiment behind the offer, he couldn't say no.

LUCAS'S STOMACH JITTERED when he walked into the bar, but he assured himself it would settle once they started talking about whatever she wanted to talk about.

Then he saw her, sitting at a table reading a book, and his tongue got thick.

She'd put on a dress, something all green and summery that showed off her arms and legs while her pretty red hair waved to her shoulders.

Should he have worn a tie? he wondered. He hardly ever wore ties, but he had a few.

She looked up, saw him, smiled. So he had no choice but to cross over to the table.

"I guess I'm late. I'm sorry."

"You're not." She closed the book. "I got here a little early, as the errands I had didn't take as long as I thought." She slipped the book into her purse. "I always carry a book in case I have some time on my hands."

"I've read that one." There, he thought, he was talking. He was sitting down. "I guess I figured doing what you do, you'd be reading educational books all the time."

"I do plenty of that, but not with my purse book. I'm liking it a lot so far, but then I always enjoy Michael Connelly."

"Yeah, it's good stuff."

The waitress stepped up. "Good evening. Can I get you a drink?"

When she shifted, Ella's scent—something warm and spicy—drifted across the table and fogged Lucas's brain.

"What am I in the mood for?" she wondered. "I think a Bombay and tonic, with a twist of lime."

"And you, sir? Sir?" the waitress repeated when Lucas remained mute.

"Oh, sorry. Ah, I'll have a beer. A Rolling Rock."

"I'll get those right out to you. Anything else? An appetizer?"

"You know what I'd love? Some of those sweet potato skins. They're amazing," she told Lucas. "You have to share some with me."

"Sure. Okay. Great."

"I'll be right back with your drinks."

"I so appreciate you taking the time to come in," Ella began. "It gives me an excuse to sit in a pretty bar, have a summer drink and some sinful food."

"It's a nice place."

"I like coming here, when I have an excuse. I've come to feel at home in Missoula in a fairly short time. I love the town, the countryside, my work. It's hard to ask for more."

"You're not from here. From Montana." He knew that. Hadn't he known that?

"Born in Virginia, transplanted to Pennsylvania when I went to college, where I met my ex-husband."

"That's a ways from Montana."

"I got closer as time went by. We moved to Denver when the kids were ten and twelve, when my husband—ex—got a difficult-to-refuse job offer. We were there about a dozen years before we moved to Washington State, another job offer. My son moved here, got married, started his family, and my girl settled in California, so after the divorce I wanted fresh. Since I like the mountains, I decided to try here. I get fresh, the mountains, and my son and his family, with my daughter close enough by air I can see her several times a year."

He couldn't imagine the picking up and going, going then

picking it all up again. Though his work had taken him all over the West, he'd lived in Missoula all his life.

"That's a lot of country, a lot of moving around."

"Yes, and I'm happy to be done with it. You're a native?"

"That's right. Born and bred in Missoula. I've been east a few times. We get hired off-season to work controlled burns, or insect eradication."

"Exterminating bugs?"

He grinned. "Bugs that live up in tall trees," he explained, jerking a thumb at the ceiling. "We—smoke jumpers, I mean—are trained to climb. But most of my life's been spent west of St. Louis."

The waitress served their drinks, and Ella lifted hers. "Here's to roots—maintaining them and setting them down."

"Washington State, that's pretty country. I jumped some fires there. Colorado, too."

"A lot of country." Ella smiled at him. "You've seen the most pristine, and the most devastated. Alaska, too, right? I read you fought wildfires there."

"Sure."

She leaned forward. "Is it fantastic? I've always wanted to see it, to visit there."

For a minute, he lost the rhythm of small talk in her eyes. "Ah . . . I've only seen it in the summer, and it's fantastic. The green, the white, the water, the miles and miles of open. All that water's a hazard for jumping fire, but they don't have the trees like we do here, so it's a trade-off."

"Which is more hazardous? Water or trees?"

"Land in the water with all your gear, you're going to go down, maybe not get up again. Land in the trees, land wrong, maybe you just get hung up, maybe you break your neck. The best thing to do is not land in either."

"Have you?"

"Yeah. I hit my share of both. The worst part's knowing you're going to, and trying to correct enough so you'll walk away from it. Any jump you walk away from is a good jump."

She sat back. "I knew it. I knew you'd be perfect for what I'd like to do."

"Ah—"

"I know they give tours of the base, and groups can see the operation, ask some questions. But I had this idea, specifically for students. Something more intimate, more in-depth. Hearing firsthand, from the source, what it takes, what you do, what you've done. Personal experiences of the work, the life, the risks, the rewards."

"You want me to talk to kids?"

"Yes. I want you to talk to them. I want you to teach them. Hear me out," she added when he just stared at her. "A lot of our students come from privilege, from parents who can afford to send them to a top-rated private school like ours. Everyone knows about the Zulies. The base is right here. But I'll guarantee few, if any, unless they have a connection, understand what it really means to be what you are, do what you do."

"I'm not a jumper anymore."

"Lucas." The soft smile teased out the dimples. "You'll always be one. In any case, you gave it half of your life. You've seen the changes in the process, the equipment. You've fought wilderness fires all over the West. You've seen the beauty and the horror. You've felt it."

She laid a fisted hand on her heart. "Some of these kids, the ones I'd especially like to reach with this, have attitudes. The hard work, the dirty work, that's for somebody else—somebody who doesn't have the money or brains to go to college, launch a lucrative career. The wilderness? What's the big deal? Let somebody else worry about it."

She'd tripped something in him the minute she'd said he'd always be a jumper. The minute he saw she understood that.

"I don't know how me talking to them's going to change that."

"I think listening to you, being able to ask you questions, having you take them through, from training to fire, will open some of those young minds."

"And that's what your work is. Even though you don't teach anymore, you'll always be a teacher."

"Yes. We understand that about each other." She watched him as she sipped her drink. "I intend to talk to the operations officer at base. I'd like to, with parental permission, have a group, or groups, go through training. A shortened version obviously. Maybe over a weekend after the fire season."

"You want to put them through the wringer," he said with a glimmer of a smile.

"I want to show them, teach them, bring it home to them that the men and women who dedicate themselves to protecting our wilderness put themselves through the wringer. I have ideas about photographs and videos, and . . . I have ideas," she said with a laugh. "And we'd have all summer to put the project together."

"I think it's a good thing you're trying to do. I'm not much good at speaking. Public speaking."

"I can help you with that. Besides, I'd rather you just be who you are. Believe me, that's enough."

She picked up one of the potato skins the waitress had served while she'd laid out her plan.

She'd caught him up in it, he couldn't deny it. The idea of it, the passion behind it. "I can give it a try, I guess. At least see how it goes."

"That would be great. I really think we can do something that has impact—and some fun. And that brings me to two things." She took another drink. "Let me just get this off the table. I was married for twenty-eight years. I uprooted myself, then my kids as well to support and suit my husband. I loved him, almost all of those twenty-eight years, and for the last of them, I believed in the marriage, the life we'd built. I believed in him. Until on my fifty-second birthday, he took me out to dinner. A beautiful restaurant, candles, flowers, champagne. He even had a rather exquisite pair of diamond earrings for me to top it off."

She sat back a little, crossed her legs. "All of this to set it up, so I wouldn't cause a public scene when he told me he was having an affair with his personal assistant—a woman young enough to be his daughter, by the way. That he was in love with her and leaving me. He still thought the world of me, of course, and hoped I'd understand that these things happened. Oh, and the heart wants what the heart wants."

"I'm sorry. I'm trying to think what I should say, but nothing that's coming into my head seems appropriate."

"Oh, it can't be any less appropriate than what I said—after I picked up the champagne bucket and dumped the ice over his head. When I went to a lawyer—the very next day—she asked if I wanted to play nice or cut him off at the balls. I went for castration. I'd finished playing nice."

"Good for you."

"I wondered if I would regret it. But so far, no. I'm telling you this because I think it's only fair that you understand, right now, I can be mean, and that both my marriage and my divorce taught me to understand myself, virtue and flaw, and to not waste time in going after what I want."

"Time's always wasted if you're not aiming for what you want."

"An excellent point. Which brings me to the second thing. I lied to you earlier today when I said I wasn't hitting on you. I was. I am."

It wasn't just that his mind went blank, but that his whole system hit overload and snapped to an abrupt halt. He couldn't quite manage the simple act of swallowing as he stared into her sparkling eyes.

"I don't believe in absolute honesty in all things," she continued, "because I think a little shading now and then not only softens the edges, but makes things more interesting. But in this case, I decided on the bald truth. If it scares you off, it's better to know at this point, where there really isn't anything on the line for either of us."

She took a small sip from her glass. "So . . . Have I scared you off?"

"I . . . I'm not very good at this."

"I should have put in there that whether you're interested or not, I'm very sincere and serious about the project, and about learning how to skydive. Both of those things might be connected to me being attracted to you, but they're not contingent on it. Or you reciprocating."

She sighed. "And that sounded like a high-school principal when I'd hoped not to. I'm a little nervous."

The idea of that stopped the degeneration of his brain cells. "You are?"

"I like you, and I'm hoping you're interested enough to want to spend time with me, on a personal level. So, yes, I'm a little nervous that pushing that forward so soon might put you off. But it's part of my don't-waste-time policy, so . . . If you're interested, or inclined to consider being interested, I'd like to take you to dinner. There's a nice restaurant a couple blocks away. It's an easy walk—and I made a reservation, just in case."

He considered, shook his head. "No."

"Well. Then we'll just—"

"I'd like to take *you* to dinner." He could hardly believe the words came out of his mouth, and didn't cause a single hitch. "I heard there's a nice restaurant a couple blocks away, if you'd like to take a walk."

He loved watching the way the smile bloomed on her face. "That sounds great. I'm just going to go freshen up first."

She got up from the table, moved toward the restroom.

The minute the door closed behind her, she did a high-stepping dance in the bold purple peek-toe pumps she'd bought that afternoon.

On a foolish giggle, she walked to the sink, studied her giddy face in the mirror. "Let the adventure begin," she said, then took out her lipstick.

A few years before, she'd wondered, worried, all but assumed her life was essentially over. In a way, it had been, had needed to be to push her to start again.

So far, the new life of Ella Frazier brimmed with interesting possibilities.

And one of them was about to take her to dinner.

She nodded to her reflection, dropped the lipstick back in her purse. "Thanks, Darrin," she declared to her ex-husband. "It took that kick in the teeth to wake me up." She tossed her hair, did a stylish half turn. "And just look at me now. I am wide awake."

ROWAN RESISTED calling or texting her father's cell. It struck her as a little too obviously checking up on him. Instead, she opted for his landline at home.

She fully expected him to answer. She'd waited until nine thirty, after all, busying herself with her paperwork. Or trying to. When his machine picked up, she was momentarily at a loss. She had to grope for the excuse it had taken her nearly a half hour to come up with.

"Oh, hey. I'm just taking a quick break from writing up my reports and realized I didn't get the chance to tell you of my brilliance as fire boss. If I can't brag to you, who can I brag to? I'll be at this for another hour or so, then I'll probably take a walk to clear the administrative BS out of my head. So give me a call. Hope your meeting went well."

She rolled her eyes as she clicked off. "Meeting-schmeeting," she muttered. "A drink with a client doesn't go for two and a half hours."

She brooded awhile. It wasn't that she thought her father wasn't entitled to a social life. But she didn't even know who this *client* was. Lucas Tripp was handsome, interesting, a successful businessman. And a prime target for an opportunistic woman.

A daughter held a solemn duty to look after her single, successful, naive and overly-trusting-of-women father. She wanted him to get home and call her back, so she could do just that.

Maybe she should try him on his cell, just in case—

No, no, no, she ordered herself. That crossed the line into interfering. He was sixty, for God's sake. He didn't have a curfew.

She'd just finish the stupid report, take that walk. He was bound to call before she'd gotten it all done.

But she finished the report, sent it to L.B. She took a long, admittedly sulky walk, before going back to her quarters and taking twice as long as necessary to get ready for bed.

Annoyed with herself, she shut off the light. During a brutal mental debate about the justification of trying her father's cell after midnight, she fell asleep.

VOICES WOKE HER. Voices raised outside her window, outside her door. For a bleary moment she thought herself in the recurring dream—the aftermath of Jim's tragic jump when everyone had been shouting, rushing. Scared, angry.

But when her eyes opened in the half-light, the voices continued. Something's wrong, she thought, and instinct had her out of bed, out the door before fully awake.

"What the hell?" she demanded as Dobie pushed by her.

"Somebody hit the ready room. Gibbons said it looks like a bomb went off."

"What? That can't—"

But Dobie continued to run, obviously wanting to see for himself. In the cotton pants and tank she'd slept in, Rowan raced out in her bare feet.

The morning chill hit her skin, but what she saw in the faces of those who hurried with her, or quick-stepped it toward Operations, heated her blood.

Something's *very* wrong, she realized, and quickened her pace.

She hit the door to the ready room in step with Dobie.

A bomb wasn't far off, she thought. Parachutes, so meticulously and laboriously rigged and packed, lay or draped like tangled, deflated balloons. Tools scattered on the torn silks with gear spilling chaotically out of lockers. From the looks of it, tools, once carefully cleaned and organized, had been used to hack and slice at packs, jumpsuits, boots, damaging or destroying everything needed to jump and contain a fire.

On the wall, splattered in bloody-red spray paint, the message read clearly:

JUMP AND DIE

BURN IN HELL

Rowan thought of pig's blood.

"Dolly."

With his hands fisted at his sides, Dobie stared at the destruction. "Then she's worse than crazy."

"Maybe she is." Rowan squatted, slid a hand through the slice in silk. "Maybe she is."

EXTENDED
ATTACK

A little fire is quickly trodden out;
Which, being suffered, rivers cannot quench.

WILLIAM SHAKESPEARE

11

Every able hand worked in manufacturing, in the loadmaster's room, in the loft. They spread through the buildings, making Smitty bags, ponchos, finishing chutes already in for repair, rigging, repacking. Under the hum and clatter of machines, the mutters, Rowan knew everyone's thoughts ran toward the same destination.

Let the siren stay silent.

Until they repaired and restocked, rerigged, inspected, there was no jump list.

Nothing in the ready room could be touched until the cops cleared it. So they worked with what they had in manufacturing, running against the clock and the moods of nature.

"We could maybe send eight in." Cards worked opposite Rowan, painstakingly rigging a chute. "We can put eight together right now."

"I can't think about it. And we can't rush it. It's a damn good thing she didn't get in here. Bad enough as it is."

"Do you really think Dolly did that?"

"Who else?"

"That's just fucked up. She was sort of one of us. I even . . ."

"A lot of the guys even."

"Before Vicki," Cards added. "Before Jim. Anyway, I mean, she worked right here on base, joking and flirting around in the dining hall. Like Marg and Lynn."

"Dolly's never been like Marg and Lynn."

Focusing, Rowan arranged the chute's lines into two perfect bundles. One tangled cord could be the difference between a good jump and a nightmare. "Who else is pissed off and crazy besides Dolly?"

"Painting that crap on the wall, too," Cards agreed. "Like she did in your room. I was up till damn near one, and didn't hear a goddamn thing. Wrecking the place that way, she had to make some noise."

"She snuck onto base late, after everyone was bunked down." Rowan shrugged. "It's just not that hard, especially if you know your way around. It happened, that's for damn sure."

"It doesn't make any sense." Gull stopped on his way to another table with a repaired chute. "If there's a fire when we're not squared away, they'll send in jumpers from other bases. Nobody's going to jump until our equipment's cleared. Who's she trying to hurt?"

"Crazy doesn't have to make sense."

"You've got a point. But all that mess down there accomplishes is to cost time and money—and piss everybody off. Not to mention cops knocking at your door, when you slid by that one last time."

"Vindictive doesn't have to make sense either."

Gull started to speak again, but Gibbons hailed Rowan. "Cops want to talk to you, Ro. To all of us," he added as the machines hummed into silence. "But you're up."

"I'm going to finish packing this chute. Five minutes," she estimated.

"L.B.'s office. Lieutenant Quinniock."

"Five minutes."

"Cards, when you're finished there, you can go on over to the cookhouse. The other one, Detective Rubio'll talk to you there."

Cards jerked his head in acknowledgment. "Looks like you got the short straw, Ro. At least I'll get some breakfast."

"Gull, Matt, Janis, when the cops give us the go-ahead, you'll be working with me on cleanup and inventory. You want chow, Marg's got a buffet set up. Fill your bellies because we're going to be at it awhile. Fucking mess," he said in disgust as he walked out.

Cards signed his name, the time and date on the repacked chute.

"I'll walk down with you," Gull told Cards, and brushed a hand down Rowan's back as he walked by her.

She finished the job, choking down everything but the task at hand. When she was done, she labeled the pack. Chute by Swede.

She shelved it, then gladly left the headachy din of manufacturing. But she detoured to the ready room.

She wanted to see it again. Maybe needed to.

Two police officers worked with a pair of civilians—forensics, Rowan concluded. She knew the woman currently taking photos of the painted message. Jamie Potts, Rowan thought. They'd been stuck in Mr. Brody's insanely boring world history class together their junior year in high school. She recognized one of the cops as well, as she'd dated him awhile about the same time as Mr. Brody.

She started to speak, then just backed out, realizing she didn't want conversation until she had no choice.

Besides, looking at the torn and trampled, the strewn and defaced, only heated up her already simmering temper.

She shoved her hands into the pockets of the hoodie she'd pulled on over her nightclothes.

Halfway to Operations, Gull cut across her path. He handed her a Coke. "I thought you could use it."

"Yeah, thanks. I thought you'd headed down for breakfast."

"I'll get it. It's a bump, Ro."

"What?"

"This." He gestured behind them, toward the ready room. "It's a bump, the kind that gives you a nasty jolt, but it doesn't stop you from getting where you're going. Whoever did that? They didn't accomplish a thing but make everybody on this base more determined to get where we're going."

"Glass half full?"

She honestly couldn't say why that grated on her nerves. "Right now my glass is not only mostly empty, it has a jagged, lip-tearing chip in it. I'm not ready to look at it in sunny terms. I might be once her vindictive batshit crazy ass is sitting in a cell."

"They'll have to call in the rangers or the feds, I guess. U.S. Forest Service property that got messed with, so it's probably a felony. I don't know how it works."

That stopped her. She hadn't thought it through. "L.B. called the locals. The feds aren't going to waste their time with this."

"I don't know. But I'd think if somebody wanted to push it, that's where it would go. Destruction of federal property, that could land her a stiff stint in a cell. What she needs is a big dose of mandatory therapy."

The man, she concluded, was a piece of work. Good work at the core, and right now that core of good made her want to punch something.

Possibly him.

"You're telling me this because you're not sure if I want her to do time in Leavenworth, or wherever."

"Do you?"

"Damn it. Right now I wouldn't shed a tear over that, but at the bottom of it, I just want her out of our hair, once and for all."

"Nobody can argue with that. Whoever did that to the ready room has some serious problems."

"Look, you've had a few weeks' exposure to Dolly. I've had a lifetime, and I'm finished having her problems become mine."

"Nobody can argue with that, either." He cupped a hand at the back of her neck, catching her off-guard with the kiss. "Let's see if we can squeeze in a run later. I could use one."

"Will you *stop* trying to settle me down?"

"No, because you probably don't want to talk to a cop when you're pissed off enough to bite out his throat if he happens to push the wrong button."

He took her shoulders, got a good grip. And, she noted, his eyes weren't so calm, weren't so patient. "You're smart. Be smart. The ready room wasn't a personal attack on you; it was a sucker punch at all of us. Remember that."

"She's—"

"She's nothing. Make her nothing, and focus on what's important. Give the cop what he needs, go back to work on fixing the damage. After that, take a run with me."

He kissed her again, quick and hard, then walked away.

"Take a run. I'll give you a run," she muttered. She veered off toward L.B.'s office, and realized Gull unsettled her nearly as much as Dolly's sudden bent for violence.

Lieutenant Quinniock sat at L.B.'s overburdened desk with a mug of coffee and a notebook. Black-framed cheaters perched on the end of his long, bladed nose while eyes of faded-denim blue peered over them. A small scar rode high on his right cheek, a pale fishhook against the ruddiness. And like a scar, a shock of white, like a lightning bolt blurred at the edges, shot through his salt-and-pepper hair between the left temple and the crown.

She'd seen him before, Rowan realized—in a bar or a shop—somewhere. His wasn't a face easily overlooked.

He wore a dark, subtly pin-striped suit like an executive—pressed and tailored, with a perfectly knotted tie of flashy red.

The suit didn't go with the face, she thought, and wondered if the contrast was deliberate.

He stood when she came into the room. "Ms. Tripp?"

"Yeah. Rowan Tripp."

"I appreciate you taking a few minutes. I know it's a stress-ful day. Would you mind closing the door?"

The voice, she decided, mild, polite, engaging, fit the suit.

"Have a seat," he told her. "I have a few questions."

"Okay."

"I've met your father. I imagine most around these parts have at some time or other. You're following in big footprints, and I'm told you're doing a good job of filling them."

"Thanks."

"So . . . you and a Miss Dolly Brakeman had an altercation a few days ago."

"You could call it that."

"What would you call it?"

She wanted to rage, to jab a finger in the middle of that flashy tie. Be smart, Gull had said—and damn it, he was right.

So she ordered herself to relax in the chair and speak

coolly. "Let's see, I call it trespassing, vandalism, defacing private property and generally being a crazy bitch. But that's just me."

"Apparently not just you, as others I've spoken with share that point of view. You discovered Miss Brakeman in your quarters here on base in the act of pouring animal blood on your bed. Is that correct?"

"It is. And that would be after she'd poured it, tossed it, splattered it over the walls, the floor, my clothes and other assorted items. After she wrote on my wall with it. 'Burn in hell,' to be precise."

"Yes, I've got the photographs of the damage Mr. Little Bear took before the area was cleaned and repainted."

"Oh." That set her back a moment. She hadn't realized L.B. had documented with photos. Should have figured he would, she thought now. That's why he was in charge.

"And what happened when you found her in your quarters?"

"What? Oh, I tried to kick her ass, but several of my colleagues stopped me. Which, given the current situation, is even more of a damn shame."

"You didn't notify the police."

"No."

"Why not?"

"Partially because I was too pissed off, and partially because she got fired and kicked off the base. That seemed enough, considering."

"Considering?"

"Considering, at that time, I figured she was just sublimely stupid, that her stupidity was aimed solely at me—and she's got a baby. Plus, within an hour we caught a fire, so she wasn't a top priority for me after that."

"You and your unit had a long, hard couple of days."

"It's what we do."

"What you do is appreciated." He sipped his coffee as he scanned his notes. "The baby you mentioned is purported to have been fathered by James Brayner, a Missoula smoke jumper who died in an accident last August."

"That's right."

"Miss Brakeman blames you."

It hurt still; she supposed it always would. "I was his jump partner. She blames the whole unit, and me in particular."

"Just for my own edification, what does 'jump partner' mean?"

"We jump in two-man teams. One after the other once we get the go from the spotter. The first one out, that would've been me in this case, checks the location and status of the second man. You might want to make adjustments in direction, trajectory, give the second man a clear stream. If one of you has any problems, the other should be able to spot it. You look out for each other, as much as you can, in the air, on landing."

"And Brayner's accident was ruled, after investigation, as his error."

Her throat burned, making it impossible to keep the emotion out of her voice. "He didn't steer away. We hit some bad air, but he just rode on it. He pulled the wrong toggle, steered toward instead of away. There was nothing I could do. His chute deployed; I gave him space, but he didn't come around. He overshot the jump site, kept riding, and went down into the fire."

"It's difficult to lose a partner."

"Yeah. Difficult."

"At that time Miss Brakeman was employed as a cook on base."

"That's right."

"Did you and she have any problems prior to the accident?"

"She cooked. I ate. That's pretty much it."

"I'm under the impression the two of you knew each other for quite some time. That you went to school together."

"We didn't run in the same circle. We knew each other. For some reason she was always jealous of me. I know a lot of people. I know Jamie and Barry, down doing their cop thing in the ready room; went to school with them, too. Neither one of them ever pulled a Carrie-at-the-prom on my quarters."

He watched her over that long, narrow nose. "Were you aware she was pregnant at the time of Brayner's death?"

"No. As far as I know nobody was aware except, from what she said when she came back, Jim. She took off right after the accident—I don't know where, and don't care. As far as I can tell she came back with the baby, got religion and came here looking for work, armed with her mother, her minister and pictures of her chubby-cheeked baby. L.B. hired her."

To give herself a moment, she took a long drink from her Coke. "I had one conversation with her, figuring we should clear the air, and during which she made it crystal she hated every linear inch of my guts, wished me to hell. She dumped blood all over my room. L.B. fired her. And that brings us up to date."

She shifted in her chair, tired of sitting, tired of answering questions she suspected he already had the answers to. Focus on what's important, she remembered. "Look, I know you've got ground to cover, but I don't see why my past history with Dolly applies. She broke into the ready room and damaged equipment. Essential equipment. It's a lot more than inconvenient and messy. If we're not ready when we're called, people can die. Wildlife and the forests they live in are destroyed."

"Understood. We'll be talking to Miss Brakeman. At this time, the only possible link between her and the vandalism in your ready room is her confirmed vandalism of your quarters."

"She said she wanted us all to die. All of us to burn. Just like she wrote on the wall. I guess she couldn't get her hands on any more pig's blood, so she used spray paint this time."

"Without equipment, you can't jump. If you can't jump, you're not in harm's way."

"Logical. But then logic isn't Dolly's strong suit."

"If it turns out she's responsible for this situation, I'd have to agree. Thanks for your time, and your frankness."

"No problem." She pushed to her feet, stopped on her way to the door. "I don't see how there's any 'if.' People around here understand what we do. We're part of the fabric. Everybody on base is a thread in the fabric, and we do what we do because we want to. We depend on each other. Dolly's the only odd man out."

"There are three men who got their asses kicked last month outside Get a Rope who might enjoy fraying those threads."

She turned fully back into the room. "Do you really think those assholes came back to Missoula, snuck on base, found the ready room and did that crap?"

Quinniock removed his cheaters, folded them neatly on the desk. "It's another 'if.' It's my job to consider all the 'ifs.'"

The interview left Rowan more annoyed than satisfied. Though her appetite barely stirred, she hit the buffet, built herself a breakfast sandwich. She ate on the way back to manufacturing.

Nobody complained. Not about the extra work or the tedium of doing it. While she'd been with Quinniock, Janis set up her MP3 with speakers so R&B, country, rock, hip-hop softened the clamor of the machines. She watched Dobie do a little boot-scoot across the floor to Shania Twain with a load of Smitty bags in his arms.

Could be worse, she thought. It could always be worse, so the smart thing to do was to make the best out of the bad. When Gull hauled in chutes for repair, she figured the cops had cleared the ready room.

She left her machine to go to the counter and help him spread the silks.

"How bad is it?" she asked him.

"Probably not as bad as it looked. Everything's tossed around, but there's not as much actual damage as we thought. Or I thought, anyway. A lot just needs to be sorted and repacked."

"Silver lining." She marked tears and cuts.

"With a rainbow. Maintenance is setting up tables outside. Rumor is Marg is putting a barbecue together, and she's got a truckload of ribs."

Rowan marked another tear. Men who hadn't bothered to shave or shower that morning were singing along with Taylor Swift. It was just a little surreal.

"When the going gets tough," she decided, "the tough eat ribs. We've got nearly all the chutes that were in for rigging and repair done, and nearly all of those packed. Coming along on PG bags, Smitties, ponchos and packs."

She paused, met his eyes. "If it keeps moving, maybe we'll fit in that run."

"Ready when you are."

"I hate being wrong."

"Anybody who doesn't probably has low self-esteem. Low self-esteem can lead to a lot of problems, many of them sexual."

She knew when she was being ribbed, so nodded solemnly. "I'm lucky I have exceptionally high self-esteem. Anyway, I hate being wrong about thinking this was a shot at me. I'd rather she'd taken a shot at me. I'd rather be pissed off about a personal vendetta than this."

"It sucks, but there's something to be said about listening to Southern and Trigger singing a duet of 'Wanted Dead or Alive.' "

"They weren't bad. No Bon Jovi, but not bad."

"If your glass is half empty and has a chip in it, you might as well belly up to the bar and order a fresh one. I've gotta get back."

Bright side, she thought. Silver lining. Maybe it took her longer to find them—or want to—but what the hell. She might as well toss away her crappy glass.

She examined every inch of the chute before turning it over to repair, then started on the next. She was so focused on what she thought of as an assembly line of life and death, she didn't hear L.B. walk up beside her.

His hand came down on her shoulder like a spotter's in the door. "Take a break."

"Some of these need rigging, but most of the ones coming up just need patching."

"I've been getting updates. Let's get some air."

"Fine." The bending, hunching, peering left her stiff and knotted up. She wanted that run, she decided, wanted to burn off the tension and hours of standing.

Then she caught a whiff of the ribs smoking on the grills, and decided she wanted those even more.

"Holy God, that smells good. Marg knows exactly the way to get the mind off problems and on the belly."

"Wait'll you see the cornbread. I just got off the phone with the police."

"Did they arrest her? No," she said before he could speak. "I can tell by your face. Goddamn it, L.B."

"She claims she was home all night. Her mother's backing her up."

"Big surprise."

"The thing is, they can't prove she wasn't. Maybe when

they go through everything, they'll find some evidence. You know, fingerprints or something."

He thumbed out a Life Savers to go with the one already in his mouth, and made her realize the stress had him jonesing for a Marlboro.

"But right now," he continued with cherry-scented breath, "she's denying it. They talked to the neighbors, too. Nobody can say for sure if she was home or wasn't. And since none of us saw her, they can't charge her with anything."

L.B. puffed out his cheeks. "Quinniock wanted us to know she's making noises about suing us for slander."

"Give me a break."

"Right there with you, Ro. She won't, but he thought we should know she got up a pretty good head of steam when he questioned her."

"The best defense is offense."

"That could be it, sure." He looked out over the grill and she imagined the dozens of things on his mind, the load of weight on his shoulders.

"Hell, all that's for cops and lawyers anyway."

"Yeah. The main thing is if we get called out, we're okay. We can send out twenty at this point."

"Twenty?"

"Some of the mechanics pitched in to help out the ready room team. They've been working like dogs. We've got gear and supplies for twenty squared away. I've already requisitioned replacements for what's damaged or ruined. This isn't going to slow us down. You're back on the jump list."

"I guess it wasn't as bad as it looked."

"Well, it looked pretty damn bad." She watched him, very deliberately, roll off some of that weight. "We're smoke jumpers, Swede. We can saw a line from here to Canada. We can sure as hell handle this."

"I want her to pay."

"I know, and by God, so do I. If they find anything to link her to that ready room, I want them to toss her in a cell. I felt sorry for her," he said in disgust. "I gave her a second chance, then a third one when I fired her instead of calling the cops. So believe me, nobody wants her to pay more than I do."

The phone in her pocket jingled.

"Go ahead and take it. I'm going to pass the word on lunch." He headed back, turned around briefly to walk backward. "Keep clear of the stampede," he warned.

Laughing, she pulled out her phone. Seeing her father's ID reminded her of the messages she'd left him.

"Well, it's about time."

"Honey, I'm sorry I didn't get back to you. I got in late, and didn't want to chance waking you up. I've been busy all morning."

"Here, too." She told him about the ready room, the police, about Dolly.

"For God's sake, Ro, what's wrong with that girl? Do you want more help? I can reschedule some things, or at least send over a couple men."

"I think we've got it, but I'll ask L.B."

"Quinniock, you said. I know him a little. I met him when I did one of those charity grip and grins last year. He came out with his kids. We gave them a tour."

"That's where I saw him. He's been through here, too. So . . . how was your meeting last night?"

"It was good. I'm going to work on this project for some of the high-school kids. And Ella—the client—she's signing up for AFF training."

"All that? That was some drink."

"Ha. Well. Ah, you'll probably meet her. She wants to connect up with the base, too. For this project. I've got a group coming in, but you tell L.B. to let me know if he wants extra hands. I can put in some time."

"I will, but I think we're good. You could come over after you close up. You can always put in some time with me."

"I've got a dinner meeting with the accountant on the slate tonight. How about we plan on it tomorrow? I'll come by after work."

"Works for me. See you tomorrow."

She clicked off, then started over to join the horde spilling out of manufacturing in a beeline for the tables.

Her mood improved. Progress, a full stomach, an upcoming date with her best guy. After which, she promised herself, she'd turn in early and bank some sleep.

It lifted her a little more to hear Matt laugh at something Libby said, to watch Cards dazzle one of the rookies with some sleight of hand, to listen to Trigger and Janis bitterly debate baseball.

As irritating as it was, Gull had been right. The Dolly crap? Just a bump.

She nudged him as they started back to their respective work areas. "Four o'clock, on the track."

"I'll be there."

Asking for trouble, she thought, and admitted she liked it. So maybe she'd bend her rule just a little—or a whole lot—for him. Maybe think about it awhile, and stretch out the heat, that sizzle of tension. Or just jump in, go full blast, burn it up, burn it out.

They were both grown-ups. They both knew the score. When the fire between them lay down, they could just step away again. No scars, no worries.

If she opted for the jump, that's just how she'd approach it. Two healthy, single adults who liked each other enjoying some good, tension-snapping sex.

"That's a big, smug smile you're wearing," Janis said as she joined Rowan at the table.

"I'm deciding if I'm going to have sex with Gull sooner or later."

"That would put a big, smug smile on my face. He's just sooo purty—" She gave a shoulder wiggle that sent her ponytail, circled with bluebirds, dancing. "In a manly way. But what happened to the rule?"

"I'm thinking I'll temporarily rescind it. But do I wait, keep getting off, so to speak, on the sexual tension, innuendo, byplay and pursuit? Or do I dive headlong into the hot, steamy, sexy goodness?"

"Both are excellent uses of time. However, I've found, occasionally, that building anticipation can also overbuild expectation. Then nobody can fully meet the overbuild."

"That's a problem, and another factor to consider. The thing is, I don't think I'd be considering it, at least not yet, if this hadn't happened. The Dolly Crapathon. It's thrown me off, Janis."

"If you let that tiny-brained, coldhearted, self-pitying

skank throw you off, you're letting her win. If you let her win, you're going to piss me off. If you piss me off, I'm going to beat the snot out of you."

Rowan went *pfftt*. "You know you can't take me."

"That has not yet been put to the test. I got my fourth-degree black belt this winter. When I make martial arts noises, thousands flee in terror. Don't test me."

"Can you hear that? It's my knees knocking."

"They're wise to fear me. Go, have sex for fun and orgasms, and forget about the Dolly Crapathon."

"You are wise as well as short."

"I can also break bricks with my bare hands." And examined her manicure.

"That's a handy skill if you ever find yourself walled up in the basement of an abandoned house by a psychopath."

"I keep it in my pocket for just that eventuality." She glanced over as Trigger walked between tables on his hands. "A sure sign we're going stir-crazy. Plenty to do, but we're doing it grounded."

"The way we're going, especially with Super-Sewer Dobie, we're going to be in better shape on gear and equipment than before *The Nightmare on Dolly Street*."

"I hope the cops put the fear of God into her." Janis lowered her voice. "Matt gave her five thousand."

"What?"

"For the baby. I heard her crying to Matt after L.B. gave her the boot. How was she going to pay off the hospital bills now, and the pediatrician? He said he could spare five thousand to help her clear up the bills, tide her over until she got work. I guess I get it. His brother's kid and all. But she's going to keep tapping him, you know she is."

"Why work when you can sob-story your dead lover's brother into passing you cash? If he wants to help out with the baby, he should give money to Dolly's mother, or pay some of those bills directly."

"Are you going to tell him that?"

"I just might." Rowan gathered up the chute to take to repair. "I damn well might."

She considered offering unsolicited advice and opinion—which everybody hated—or just staying out of it. By the time she took a break for her run, she'd all but exhausted ideas for a third choice. Maybe the PT would help her think of one.

She changed into her running gear, grabbed a bottle of water. Gull joined her as she walked out of the barracks.

"Right on time," he commented.

"If I'd had to spend another hour indoors, I'd've hurt someone. What've you got in you today?"

"We'll have to find out. I'll tell you this, the ready room looks like Martha Stewart stocked and organized it. And I'm well past done with anything approaching domestic work, but I am looking to get some more rigger training."

"So you've been studying there, too?"

"Knowing how something works isn't the same as making it work. You're a certified Master Rigger. You could tutor me."

"Maybe." She already knew him for a quick study. "Are you looking to work toward your Senior Rigger certification, or to spend more time with me?"

"I'd call it multitasking."

They stopped on the side of the track where Rowan shed her warm-up jacket, laid her water bottle on it. "Distance or time?"

"How about a race?"

"Easy for you to say, Fast Feet."

"I'll give you a head start. Quarter mile of three."

"A quarter mile?" She did a little toe-heel to loosen her ankles. "You think you can beat me with that much of a spread?"

"If I don't, I'll have plenty of time to enjoy the view."

"Okay, sport, if you want my ass in your sights, you've got it."

She took the inside lane, cued her stopwatch, then took off.

Damn nice view, Gull thought as he strolled onto the track, plugged in his earbuds. He took a moment to loosen up, shaking out his arms, lifting his knees. When she hit the quarter mile, he ran.

And God, it felt good to move, to breathe, to have music banging in his head. Warm, dry air streamed over him, the sun splashed on the track, and he had Rowan's curvy body racing ahead of him.

It didn't get much better.

He built up his pace gradually, so by the first mile had cut her lead in half. She'd changed into shorts that clung to her thighs, and a tank that molded her torso. As he closed more distance he let himself enjoy the sexy cut of her calf muscles, the way the sun played on those strong shoulders.

He wanted his hands on both.

Totally in lust with that body, he admitted. Completely fascinated with her mind. The combo left him unable to think of anyone else, and uninterested.

At two miles he advanced to a handful of paces behind her. She glanced back over her shoulder, shook her head and dug for more speed.

Still, at two and a half, he ran with her, shoulder to shoulder. He considered easing off—a sop to her labored breathing—but his competitive spirit kicked in. He hit mile three a dozen strides ahead.

"Jesus, Jesus!" Rowan bent over to catch her wind. "I ought to be pissed off. That was humiliating."

"I thought about letting you win, but I respect you too much to patronize."

She wheezed out a laugh. "Gee, thanks."

"You bet."

"Still." She examined the stopwatch she'd clicked at the finish. "That was a personal best for me. Apparently you push me to excel."

Her face glowed with exertion and sweat; her eyes held his, cool and clear.

He hadn't run far enough, Gull realized. He hadn't nearly run off the need. He hooked his fingers in the bodice of the tank, jerked her to him.

"Hold on. I haven't got my breath back."

"Exactly."

He wanted her breathless, he thought as he took her mouth. Hot and breathless and as needy as he. She tasted like a melted lemon drop, tart and warm. The heat from the run, and from that dominating lust, pulsed off both of them while her heart galloped against his.

For the first time she trembled, just a little. He didn't know whether it came from the run or the kiss. He didn't care.

From somewhere nearby, someone let out a hoot and whistle of approval. And for the first time, like a lemon drop in the sun, she began to melt.

The siren sounded.

They tore themselves apart, their breath quick and jerky as they looked toward the barracks.

"To be continued," Gull told her.

12

In the air the next afternoon, with a golf pro harnessed to him, Lucas watched the base scramble below. He and his daughter wouldn't eat dinner together tonight after all.

The disappointment ran keen, reminding him how many times he'd had to cancel plans with her during his seasons. He wished her safe; he wished her strong.

"This is the best time of my life!" his client shouted.

You're young yet, Lucas thought. Best times come and go. If you're lucky enough, they keep coming.

Once they'd landed, once the routine of photographs, replays, thanks wound down, he read the text on his phone.

Sorry about dinner. Caught one. See you later.

"See you later," he murmured.

Lucas called base to get a summary of the fire.

The one the day before had only required a four-man crew, and they'd been in and out inside ten hours.

This one looked trickier.

Camper fire, off Lee Ridge, load of sixteen jumping it. And his girl was in that load.

Though he could bring the area into his head, he consulted his wall map. Ponderosa and lodgepole pines, he mused, Douglas fir. Might be able to use Lee Creek as a water source or, depending on the situation, one of the pretty little streams.

He studied the map, considered jump sites, and the tricky business of jumping into those thick and quiet forests.

She'd be fine, he assured himself. He'd do some paperwork, then grab some dinner. Then settle in to wait.

He stared at his computer screen for five full minutes before accepting defeat. Too much on his mind, he admitted.

He considered going over to the base, using the gym, maybe scoring a meal from Marg. But it felt too much like what it was. Hovering.

It had been nice to eat in a restaurant the other night, he remembered. Drink a little wine, have some conversation over a hot meal. He'd gotten too used to the grab-and-go when Rowan wasn't around. Not that either of them excelled at cooking, but they managed to get by.

Alone, he tended to hit the little cafe attached to his gift shop, if he remembered before business closed for the day. Or slap a sandwich together unless he wandered down to base. He could mic a packaged meal; he always stocked plenty at home. But he'd never gotten used to sitting down to one without the company of teammates.

There had been times, he knew, when he'd been jumping that he'd felt intensely lonely. Yet he'd come to know he hadn't fully understood loneliness until the nights spun out in front of him in an empty house.

He pulled out his phone. If he let himself think about it, he'd never go through with it. So he called Ella before he had a clear idea what to say, or how to say it.

"Hello?"

Her voice sounded so cheerful, so breezy. He nearly panicked.

Iron Man, my ass, he thought.

"Ah, Ella, it's Lucas."

"Hello, Lucas."

"Yeah, hello."

"How are you?" she asked after ten seconds of silence.

"Good. I'm good. I had a really good time the other night."
Jesus Christ, Lucas.

"So did I. I've had a lovely time thinking about it, and you,
since."

"You did?"

"I did. Now that you've called, I'm hoping you're going to
ask to do it again."

He felt the pleasure rise up from his toes and end in a big,
stupid grin. This wasn't so hard. "I'd like to have dinner with
you again."

"I'd like that, too. When?"

"Actually, I— Tonight? I know it's short notice, but—"

"Let's call it spontaneous. I like spontaneity."

"That's good. That's great. I could pick you up at seven."

"You could. Or we can both be spontaneous. Come to dinner, Lucas, I'm in the mood to cook. Do you like pasta?"

"Sure, but I don't want to put you out."

"Nothing fancy. It's supposed to be a pretty evening; we
could eat out on the deck. I've been working on my garden,
and you'd give me a chance to show it off."

"That sounds nice." A home-cooked meal, an evening on a
deck by a garden—two dinners within three days with a pretty
woman? It sounded flat-out amazing.

"Do you need directions?"

"I'll find you."

"Then I'll see you around seven. Bye, Lucas."

"Bye."

He had a date, he thought, just a little stunned. An official
one.

God, he hoped he didn't screw it up.

HE THOUGHT ABOUT ROWAN while he drove home to
change for dinner. She'd be in the thick of it now, in the smoke
and heat, taking action, making decisions. Every cell in her
body and mind focused on killing the fire and staying alive.

He thought of her when he walked in the house, only minutes from the base. A good-sized place, he reflected. But when
Rowan was home, she needed her space, and his parents came
home several times a year and needed theirs.

Still, during the long stretches without them, the empty seemed to grow.

He kept it neat. All the years of needing to grab whatever he needed the minute he needed it carried over to his private life. And he kept it simple.

His mother liked to fuss, enjoyed having *things* around the place, which he packed up whenever she wasn't in residence and stored away until the next time she was.

Less to dust.

He did the same with the colorful pillows she liked to toss all over the sofa, the chairs. It saved him from shoving them on the floor every time he wanted to stretch out.

In his room a plain brown spread covered his bed, a straight-backed tan chair stood in the corner. Dark wood blinds covered the windows. Even Rowan despaired at the lack of color or style, but he found it easy to keep clean.

Shirts hung tidily in his closet, sectioned off from pants by a set of open shelves he'd built himself for shoes.

Nothing fancy, Ella had said, but what did that mean? Exactly?

When panic tried to tickle his throat, he grabbed his basics. Khaki trousers and a blue shirt. After he'd dressed, he checked in for another fire report.

Nothing to do but wait, he thought, and for a few hours, this time, he wouldn't wait alone.

Because Ella had mentioned her garden, he stopped on the way and bought flowers. Flowers were never wrong, that much he knew.

He plugged her address into the GPS in his truck as backup. He knew the area, the street.

He wondered what they'd talk about. He wondered if he should've bought wine. He hadn't thought of wine. Would wine and flowers be too much?

It was too late to buy wine anyway, plus how would he know what kind?

He pulled into the drive, parked in front of the garage of a pretty, multilevel house in a bold orange stucco he thought suited her. A lot of windows to take in the mountains, flowers in the yard, with more in an explosion of color and shape spiking and tumbling in big native pots on the stones of the covered front entrance.

Now he wondered if the yellow roses he'd bought were over-kill. "Flowers are never wrong," he mumbled to himself as he stepped out of the truck on legs gone just a little bit weak.

He probably should've gotten a burger and fries from the cafe, hunkered down in his office. He didn't know how to do this. He was too *old* to be doing this. Women had never made any sense to him, so how could he make sense to a woman?

He felt stupid and clumsy and tongue-tied, but since retreat wasn't an option, rang the bell.

She answered, her hair swept back and up, her face warm and welcoming.

"You found me. Oh, these are beautiful." She took the roses, and as a woman would, buried her face in the buds. "Thank you."

"They reminded me of your voice."

"My voice?"

"They're pretty and cheerful."

"That's a lovely thing to say. Come in," she said, and, taking his hand, drew him inside.

Color filled the house, and the *things* his mother would have approved of. Bright and bold, soft and textured, a mix of patterns played throughout the living area where candles filled a river stone fireplace.

"It's a great house."

"I love it a lot." She scanned the living area with him with an expression of quiet satisfaction. "It's the first one I've ever bought, furnished and decorated on my own. It's probably too big, but the kids are here a lot, so I like having plenty of room. Let's go on back so I can put these in water."

It was big, he noted, and all open so one space sort of spilled casually into the next. He didn't know much—or anything, really—about decorating, but it felt like it looked. Bright, happy, relaxed.

Then the kitchen made his eyes pop. It flowed into a dining area on one side and a big gathering space—another sofa, chairs, big flat-screen—on the other. But the hub was like a magazine shot with granite counters, a central island, shiny steel appliances, dark wood cabinets, many of them glass-fronted to display glass and dishware. A few complicated small appliances, in that same shiny steel, stood on the counters.

"This is a serious kitchen."

"That and the view sold me on the place. I wanted it the minute I saw it." She chose a bottle of red from a glass rack, set it and a corkscrew on the counter. "Why don't you open this while I get a vase?"

She opened a door, scanned shelves and selected a tall, cobalt vase. He opened the wine while she trimmed the stems under running water in the central island's sink.

"I'm glad you called. This is a much nicer way to spend the evening than working on my doctorate."

"You're working on your doctorate?"

"Nearly there." She held up one hand, fingers crossed. "I put it off way too long, so I'm making up time. Red-wine glasses," she told him, "second shelf in the cupboard to the right of the sink. Mmm, I love the way these roses look against the blue. How did work go today?"

"Fine. We had a big group down from Canada, another in from Arizona, along with some students. Crowded day. Yesterday even more. I barely had time to get over to the base and check after they had the trouble."

"Trouble?" She looked up from her arranging.

"I guess you wouldn't have heard. Somebody got into the ready room over there yesterday—or sometime during the night—tore the place up."

"Who'd do such a stupid thing?"

"Well, odds are it was Dolly Brakeman. She's a local girl who had a . . . a relationship with the jumper who was killed last summer. She had his baby back in the spring."

"Oh, God, I know her mother. We're friends. Irene works at the school. She's one of our cooks."

He'd known that, Lucas realized, known Irene worked in the school's kitchen. "Look, I'm sorry. I shouldn't have said anything about Dolly."

"Irene's one thing, Dolly's another—and believe me, I know that very well." Ella stabbed a trimmed stem into the vase. "That girl's put Irene through hell. In any case, what happened to the father of Dolly's baby—that's tragic for her, but why would she want to vandalize the base?"

"You know Dolly used to be a cook there, and they hired her back on?"

"I knew she'd worked there. I haven't talked to Irene since I went by to take a baby gift. I knew she and Leo went out to . . . Bozeman, I think it was—to bring her and the baby home—so I've been hanging back a little, giving them all time to settle in. I didn't realize Dolly had gone back to work at the base."

"They gave her a chance. You know? She went off after Jim's accident. Before she did, she went after Rowan."

"Your daughter? Irene never mentioned . . . Well, there's a lot she doesn't mention about Dolly. Why?"

"Ro was Jim's partner on that jump. It doesn't make any sense, but that's how Dolly reacted. And she hadn't been back at base but a handful of days when Ro walked in on her splashing pig's blood all over Ro's room."

"For God's sake."

When she planted fisted hands on her hips, Lucas dubbed it her hard-line principal look.

He liked it.

"I haven't heard anything about this." Those deep green eyes flashed as she poured wine. "I'll have to call Irene tomorrow, see if she needs . . . anything. I know Dolly's troublesome, to put it mildly, but Irene really believed the baby, getting Dolly to go to church, taking her back in the house, would settle her down. Obviously not."

Full of sympathy now, and a touch of worry, her eyes met his. "How's your daughter dealing with it?"

"Ro? She deals. They've been working on repairs and manufacturing since, and must've gotten enough done to take some calls. A four-man jump yesterday, basically an in-and-out."

"That's good. Maybe they'll have time to catch their breath."

"Not much chance of that. The siren went off about four-thirty today."

"Rowan's out on a fire? Now? I didn't hear about that, either. I haven't had the news on all day. Lucas, you must be worried."

"No more than usual. It's part of the deal."

"Now I'm even more glad you called."

"And got you upset and worried about Irene."

"I'm glad I know what's going on with her. I can't help if I don't know." She reached out, laid a hand over his. "Why don't you take your wine and the bottle out on the deck? I'll be right out."

He went out wide glass doors to the deck that offered views of the mountains, the endless sky—and her yard that struck him—again—like something out of a magazine.

A squared-off area covered by the colorful, springy mulch he'd seen in playgrounds held a play area for her grandkids. Swings, ladders, bars, seesaws, even a little playhouse with a pint-sized umbrella table and chairs.

He found it as cheerful as the house—and it told him she'd made a home here not just for herself, but for her family to enjoy.

And still, her flowers stole the show.

He recognized roses—he knew that much—but the rest, to his eyes, created fairyland rivers and pools of color and shape all linked together with narrow stone paths. Little nooks afforded space for benches, an arbor covered with a trailing vine, a small, bubbling copper fountain.

While he watched, a Western meadowlark darted to the wide bowl of a bird feeder to help himself to dinner.

Lucas turned when she came out with a tray.

"Ella, this is amazing. I've never seen anything like it outside the movies."

Her dimples winked in cheeks pinked up with pleasure. "My pride and joy, and maybe just a little bit of an obsession. The people who owned the house before were keen gardeners, so I had a wonderful foundation. With some changes, some additions and a whole lot of work, I've made it my own."

She set the tray on a table between two bright blue deck chairs.

"I thought you said no fuss." He looked at the fancy appetizers arranged on the tray.

"I'll have to confess my secret vice. I love to fuss." She picked up her wine. "I hope you don't mind."

"My mother didn't raise a fool."

She sat, angling toward him while her wind chimes picked up the tune of the summer breeze. The meadowlark sang for his supper.

"I love sitting out here, especially this time of day, or early in the morning."

"Your grandkids must love playing out here."

They drank wine, ate her fancy appetizers, talked of her grandchildren, which boosted him to relate anecdotes from Rowan's childhood.

He wondered why he'd had those moments of panic. Being with her was so comfortable once he got off the starting blocks. And every time she smiled, something stirred inside him. After a while it—almost—didn't seem strange to find himself enjoying a pretty summer evening, drinking soft wine, admiring the view while talking easily with a beautiful woman.

It—almost—blocked out memories of how he'd spent so many other summer evenings. How his daughter was spending hers now.

"You're thinking of her. Your Ro."

"I guess it stays in the back of my mind. She's good, and she's with a solid unit. They'll get the job done."

"What would she be doing now?"

"Oh, it depends." So many things, he thought, and all of them hard, dangerous, necessary. "She might be on a saw line. They'd plot out a position, factor in how the fire's reacting, the wind and so on, and take down trees, cut out brush."

"Because those are fuel."

"Yeah. They've got a couple water sources, so she might be on the hose. I know they dropped mud on her earlier."

"Why would they drop mud on Rowan?"

His laugh broke out, long, delighted. "Sorry. I meant the fire. Mud's what we call the retardant the tanker drops. Believe me, no smoke jumper wants to be under that."

"And you call the fire *her* because men always refer to dangerous or annoying things they have to deal with as female."

"Ah . . ."

"I'm teasing you. More or less. Come inside while I start dinner. You can keep me company and tell me about mud."

"You don't want to hear about mud."

"You're wrong," she told him as they gathered up the tray, the glasses, the wine. "I'm interested."

"It's thick pink goo, and burns if it hits your skin."

"Why pink? It's kind of girlie."

He grinned as she got out a skillet. "They add ferric oxide to make it red, but it looks like pink rain when it's coming down. The color marks the drop area."

She drizzled oil into the skillet from a spouted container, diced up garlic, some plump oval-shaped tomatoes, all the while asking him questions, making comments.

She certainly *seemed* interested, he thought, but he was having a hard time concentrating. The way she moved, the way her hands looked when she chopped and diced, the way she smiled and smelled, the way his name sounded when it came from her lips.

Her lips.

He didn't mean to do it. That's what happened when he acted before he thought. But he was a little in her way when she turned away from the work island, and their bodies bumped and brushed. She tipped her face up, smiled, maybe she started to speak, but then . . .

A question in her eyes, or an invitation? He didn't know, didn't think. Just acted. His hands slid onto her shoulders, and he laid his lips over hers.

So soft. So sweet. Yielding under his even as her hands ran up his back, linked there to hold them together. She rose onto her toes, and the sensation of her body sliding up his simmered heat under the soft.

He wanted to burrow into her as he would a blanket at the end of a cold winter's night.

He gave up her lips, rested his forehead to hers.

"It's your smile," he murmured. "It makes it hard for me to think straight."

She framed his face, lifted his head until she could look in his eyes. Sweet man, she thought. Sweet, sweet man.

"I think dinner can wait." She eased away, turned the heat off under the oil, then leaned back to look at him again. "Do you want to go upstairs with me, Lucas?"

"I—"

"We're not kids. We've both got more years behind us than ahead. When we have a chance for something good, we ought to take it. So . . ." She held out a hand. "Come upstairs with me."

He took her hand, let out a shaky breath as she led him through the house. "You don't just feel sorry for me, do you?"

"Why would I?"

"Because I so obviously want . . . this."

"Lucas, if you didn't, I'd feel sorry for me." Humor sparkled over her face when she tipped it up to his. "I've wondered since you called if we'd take each other to bed tonight, then I had to do thirty minutes of yoga to stop being nervous."

"Nervous? You?"

"I'm not a kid," she reminded him as she drew him into her bedroom, where the light through the windows glowed soft. "Men your age often look at thirty-somethings, not fifty-somethings. That's twenty years of gravity against me."

"What would I want with someone young enough to be my kid?"

When she laughed at that, he grinned. "Hell. It'd just make me feel old. I'm already worried I'll mess this up. I'm out of practice, Ella."

"I'm pretty rusty myself. I guess we'll see if we tune up as we go. You could start by kissing me again. We both seemed to have that part down."

He reached for her, and this time her arms went around his neck. He felt her rise up to her toes again as their lips met, as they parted for the slow, seductive slide of tongues.

He let himself stop thinking, stop worrying *what if.* Just act. His hands stroked down her back, over her hips, up her sides, then up again to pull the pins out of her hair.

It tumbled over his hands, slid through his fingers while she tipped back her head so his lips could find the line of her throat.

Nerves floated away on an indescribable mix of comfort and excitement. She shivered when he eased back to unbutton her shirt. As he did when she did the same for him.

She slipped out of her sandals; he toed off his shoes.

"So far . . ."

"So good," he finished, and kissed her again.

And, oh, yes, she thought, he definitely had that part down.

She pushed his shirt aside, splayed her hands over his chest. Hard and fit from a lifetime of training, scarred from a lifetime of duty. She laid her lips on it as he drew her shirt off to join his on the floor. When he took her breasts in his hands, she forgot about gravity. How could she worry when he looked at her as though she were beautiful? When he kissed her with such quiet, such total intensity?

She unhooked his belt, thrilled to touch and be touched, to remember all the things a body felt when it desired, and was desired. The pants it had taken her twenty minutes to decide on after he'd called slid to the floor. Then her heart simply soared as he lifted her into his arms.

"Lucas." Overcome, she dropped her head to his shoulder. "My whole life I've wanted someone to do that. To just sweep me up. You're the first who has."

He looked into her dazzled eyes, and felt like a king as he carried her to bed.

In the half-light, they touched and tasted. They remembered, and discovered. Rounded curves, hard angles, with all the points of pleasure to be savored.

When he filled her, she breathed his name—the sweetest music. Moving inside her, each long, slow stroke struck his heart, hammer to anvil. She met him, matched him, her fingers digging into his hips to urge him on.

The king became a stallion, rearing over his mate.

When she cried out, fisting around him in climax, his blood beat in triumph. And letting himself go, he rode that triumph over the edge.

"Well, God," she said after several moments where they both lay in stunned, sated silence. "I have all these applicable clichés, like it *is* just like riding a bike, or it just gets better with age like wine and cheese. But it's probably enough to simply say: Wow."

He drew her over where she obligingly curled at his side, her head on his shoulder. "Wow covers it. Everything about you is wow to me."

"Lucas." She turned her face into the side of his throat. "I swear, you make my heart skip. Nobody's ever said those kinds of things to me."

"Then a lot of men are just stupid." He twirled her hair around his finger, delighted he could. "I'd write a poem to your hair, if I knew how to write one."

She laughed and had to blink back tears at the same time. "You are the sweetest, sweetest man." She pushed up to kiss him. "I'm going to make you the best pasta you've ever eaten."

"You don't have to go to all that trouble. We could just make sandwiches or something."

"Pasta," she said, "with fresh Roma tomatoes and basil out of my garden. You're going to need the fuel, for later."

As her eyes twinkled into his, he patted her bare butt. "In that case, we'd better get down there and start cooking."

13

As her father slept the sleep of the righteously exhausted in Ella's bed, Rowan headed into her eighth hour of the battle. They'd had the fire cornered, and nearly under control, when a chain of spot fires ignited over the line from a rocket shower of firebrands. In a heartbeat, the crew found itself caught between the main fire and the fresh, spreading spots.

Like hail from hell, embers ripped through the haze, battering helmets, searing exposed skin. With a bellowing roar, a ponderosa torched, whipping flame through clouds of eye-stinging smoke. Catapulted by the wind the fire created, burning coal flew over the disintegrating line, turning near victory into a new, desperate battle.

On the shouted orders, Rowan broke away with half the crew, hauling gear at a run toward the new active blaze.

"Escape route's back down the ridge," she called out, knowing they'd be trapped if the shifting flank fed into the head. "If we have to go, drop the gear and run like hell."

"We're going to catch her. We're going to kill her," Cards yelled back, his face fervent with dragon fever.

They knocked down spots as they went, beating, digging, sawing.

"There's a stream about fifty yards over," Gull said, jogging beside her.

"I know it." But she was surprised he did. "We'll get the pump in, get the hoses going and build a wet line. We'll drown the sister."

"Nearly had her back there."

"Gibbons and the rest will knock the head down." She looked at him, his face glowing in the reflection of the fire while hoarse shouts and wild laughter tangled with the animal growl of the fire.

Dragon fever, she knew, could spread like a virus—for good or ill. It pumped in her own blood now, because make or break was coming.

"If they don't, Fast Feet, grab what gear you can, haul it as far as you can. The way you run, you ought to be able to outrace the dragon."

"You got it."

They worked with demonic speed, dumping gear to set up the pump, run the hose, while others cut a quick saw line.

"Let her rip!" Rowan shouted, planting her feet, bracing her body as she gripped the hose. When it filled, punched out its powerful stream, she let out a crazed whoop.

Her arms, already taxed with the effort of hours of hard, physical work, vibrated. But her lips peeled back in a fierce grin. "Drink this!"

She glanced back over at Gull, laughed like a loon. "Just another lazy, hazy summer night. Look." She jerked her chin. "She's going down. The head's dying. That's a beautiful sight."

AN HOUR shy of dawn, the wildfire surrendered. Rather than pack out, the weary crew coyote'd by the stream, heads pillowed on packs to catch a couple hours' sleep before the mop-up. Rowan didn't object when Gull plopped down beside her, especially when he offered her a swig of his beer.

"Where'd you get this?"

"I have my ways."

She drank deep, then lay back to watch the stars break through the thinning haze of smoke.

This, she thought, was the best—the timeless moment

between night and day—the hush of forest, mountain and sky. No one who hadn't fought the war could ever feel such intense satisfaction in winning it.

"A good night's work should always be followed by beer and starlight," she decided.

"Now who's the romantic?"

"That's just because I'm dazed by the smoke, like a honeybee."

"I dated a beekeeper once."

"Seriously?"

"Katherine Anne Westfield." He gave a little sigh of remembrance. "Long-legged brunette with eyes like melted chocolate. I had the hots enough to help her out with the hives for a while. But it didn't work out."

"You got stung."

"Ha. The thing was, she insisted on being called Katherine Anne. Not Katherine, not Kathy or Kate or Kat, not K.A. It had to be the full shot. Got to be too much trouble."

"You broke up with a woman because her name had too many syllables?"

"You could say. Plus, I have to admit, the bees started to creep me out, too."

"I like to listen to them. Sleepy sound. Cassiopeia's out," she said as the constellation cleared. Then her eyes closed, and she went out.

SHE WOKE curled up against him with her head nestled on his shoulder. She didn't snuggle, Rowan thought. She liked her space—and she sure as hell didn't snuggle while coyote camping with the crew.

It was just embarrassing.

She started to untangle herself, but his arm tucked her in, just a little closer.

"Give it a minute."

"We've got to get started."

"Yeah, yeah. Where's my coffee, woman?"

"Very funny." Actually, it did make her lips twitch. "Back off."

"You'll note I'm the one still in his assigned space, and

you're the one who scooted over and wrapped around me. But am I complaining?"

"I guess I got cold."

He turned his head to kiss the top of hers. "You feel plenty warm to me."

"You know, Gull, this isn't some romantic camping trip in the mountains. We've got a full day's mop-up ahead of us."

"Which I'm happy to put off for another couple minutes while I fantasize we're about to have wake-up sex on our romantic camping trip in the mountains. After which you'll make me coffee and fry me up some bacon and eggs, while wearing Daisy Duke shorts and one of those really skinny tank jobs. After that I have to wrestle the bear that lumbers into camp. Naturally, I dispatch him after a brutal battle. And after *that* you tenderly nurse my wounds, and after *that*, we have more sex."

She didn't snuggle, Rowan thought, and charm cut no ice with her. So why was she snuggling, and why was she charmed? "That's an active fantasy life you've got there."

"Don't leave home without it."

"What kind of bear?"

"It has to be a grizzly or what's the point?"

"And I suppose I'm wearing stilettos with my Daisy Dukes."

"Again, what would be the point otherwise?"

"Well, all that sex and cooking and tending your wounds made me hungry." She pushed away, sat up. "Twenty minutes in a hot, bubbling Jacuzzi, followed by a hot stone massage. That's my morning fantasy."

Rowan dug into her pack for an energy bar. Devoured it while she studied him. He'd scrubbed some of the dirt off his face, but there was plenty left, and his hair looked like he'd used it to mop the basement floor.

Then she looked away, to the mountains, the forest, shimmering away under the bright yellow sun. Who needed fantasies, she thought, when you could wake up here?

"Get moving, rook." She gave him a light slap on the leg. "The morning's wasting."

Gull helped break out some of the paracargo so he could

get to a breakfast MRE—and more importantly, the coffee. He dropped down next to Dobie.

"How'd it go for you?"

"Son, it was the hardest day of my young life." Dobie drenched his hash browns and bacon with Tabasco before shoveling them in as if they were about to be banned. "And maybe the best. You think you know," he added, wagging the bacon, "but you don't. You can't know till you do."

"She gave you a few kisses."

Dobie reached up to rub the burns on the back of his neck. "Yeah, she got in a couple licks. I thought when she started raining fire we might be cooked. Just for a minute. But we beat her back down. You ought to see Trigger. Piece of wood blew back off a snag he was taking down. Got him right here." Dobie tapped a finger to the side of his throat. "When he yanked it out, the hole it left looked like he'd been stabbed with a jackknife."

"I didn't hear about that."

"It happened after your team hightailed it toward the spot on the ridge. Blood all over. So he slaps some cotton on it, tapes it up and hits the next snag. It made me think, if I got cooked, I'd be cooked with the best there is."

"And now we get to sit here and eat breakfast with this view."

"Can't knock it with a hammer," Dobie said, and grabbed another MRE. "What're you going to do about that woman?"

He didn't have to ask what woman, and glanced over in Rowan's direction. "All I can."

"Better pick up the pace, son." Dobie shook his ever-present bottle of Tabasco. "Summer don't last forever."

GULL THOUGHT about that as he worked, sweating through the morning and into the afternoon. He'd approached her along the lines he might have if they'd met outside—where time was abundant, as were opportunities to go to dinner, or the movies, a long drive, a day at the beach. This world and that didn't have much crossover when you came down to it.

Maybe it was time to approach her as he did the work.

Nothing wrong with champagne picnics, but there were times a situation required a less . . . elegant approach.

By the time they packed out, Gull figured all he wanted in the world was to feel clean again, to enjoy a real mattress under him for eight straight.

Hardly a wonder, he decided as he dropped down in the plane, women, despite their wondrous appeal, hit so low on his priority list most seasons.

He shut off his mind and was asleep before the plane nosed into the sky.

With the rest of the crew, he trudged off, dealt with his gear, hung his chute. He watched Rowan texting as she headed for the barracks. He went in behind her, fully intending to walk straight to his quarters, peel off his fire shirt and pants, get his feet out of the damn boots that currently weighed like lead. Everything in him pulsed with fatigue, tension and an irritation that stemmed from both.

If he was hungry, it wasn't for a woman, or for Rowan Tripp in particular. If he was tired, it was because if he wasn't knocked-out exhausted, he spent too much time thinking about her in the middle of the night. So he'd stop. He'd just stop thinking about her.

When she turned into her room, he went in right behind her.

"What do—"

He shut the door—and her mouth—by pushing her back against it. The kiss burned with temper, smoldered with the frustration he'd managed to ignore for the past weeks. Now he let them both go. The hell with it.

He jerked back an inch, his gaze snapping to hers. "I'm tired. I'm pissed off. I don't know exactly why, but I don't give a damn."

"Then why don't you—"

"Shut up. I have something to say." He crushed his mouth to hers again, cuffing her wrists in his hands. "This has gotten stupid. I'm stupid, or maybe you're stupid. I don't care."

"What the hell do you care about?" she demanded.

"Apparently you. Maybe it's because you're goddamn beautiful, and built, and manage to be smart and fearless at the same time. Maybe it's just because I'm horny. That could be it. But something's clicked here; we both know it."

Since she hadn't told him to go to hell, or kneed him in the groin—yet—he calculated he had a short window to make his case.

"So it's time to stop playing around, Rowan. It's time to toss that asinine rule of yours out the window. Whatever we've got going here, we need to hit it head-on. If it's just a flash, fine, we'll take it down and move on. No harm, no foul. But I'm damned if I'm going to keep slapping away at the spot fires. You're in or you're out. Now how do you want to play it?"

She hadn't expected temper and force from him, which, considering she'd seen him take on three men with a ferocity she'd admired, made that her mistake. She hadn't expected anything could stir up her juices after a thirty-six-hour jump, but here he was, looking at her as if he couldn't decide if he wanted to kiss her or strangle her, and those juices were not only stirring, but pumping strong.

"How do I want to play it?"

"That's right."

"Let's drown it." She fisted her hands in his hair, yanked his mouth back to hers. Then she reversed their positions, shoved him back against the door. "In the shower, rookie." She made quick work unbuttoning his shirt.

"Funny, that was first on my list before I got pissed off." He pulled her shirt off as he backed her toward the bathroom. "Then all I could think about was getting my hands on you." He unhooked her pants.

"Boots," she managed as they groped each other. She dropped down on the toilet, fingers flying on laces. He dropped to the floor to do the same.

"This shouldn't be sexy. Maybe I am just horny."

"Just hurry up!" Laughing, she yanked off her pants, then stood to peel off the tank, the bra beneath.

"Sing hallelujah," Gull murmured.

"Get naked!" she ordered, then, wiggling out of her panties, flicked on the water in the shower.

Crazy, she thought. A crazy thing to do, but she felt crazy. Another type of dragon fever, she decided, and turned to pull him in with her under the spray.

"We're very dirty," she said, linking her arms around his neck, pressing her body to his.

"And about to get dirtier. Let's turn up the heat." Reaching behind her, he clicked the hot water up a notch, then gave himself the pleasure of those waiting, willing lips.

Good, so good, she thought, the water on her skin, his hands spreading the wet and hot over her. Why deny what she'd known the first time they'd locked eyes? They'd always been heading here, to this. She ran her hands down his back, over hard planes, tough muscle, instinctively working her fingers over the knots tied tight by hours of brutal effort.

He moaned as she worked her way to his shoulders.

He fixed his teeth at the side of her neck, pressed his own fingers in a line down her spine, then up again until he found points of pain and pleasure at the base of her neck.

"Let me take care of this." She poured shampoo in her palm, rubbed her hands together lightly as she watched him, then slid her fingers through his hair. While she rubbed, massaged, he filled his hands with her shower gel. The shower filled with the scent of ripe peaches as he glided circles, slow circles, over her breasts, her belly.

Lather foamed and dripped, frothing fragrantly between their bodies as he trailed a hand down, his fingers teasing, just teasing when he cupped her.

Her head fell back, and a low sound of pleasure hummed in her throat. Watching her absorb sensation, he gave her a little more, a little more until her hips, her breath picked up the rhythm.

Not yet, he thought, not yet, and made her groan when he turned her to face the wet wall.

"Gull, Jesus—"

"I need to wash your back. Love your back." At the small of it, a tattoo of a red dragon breathed gold flame. He ran his lathered hands over her, followed them with his lips. "Your skin's like milk."

He indulged himself with the subtle curve of the back of her neck, exposed and vulnerable to his teeth and tongue, and when her arm hooked back to press him closer, he glided his hands around, filled them with her breasts.

So firm, so full.

He spun her around, replaced his hands with his mouth.

Not what she'd expected or prepared for. Never what she

expected, she thought as her body quivered. The angry man who'd shoved her against the door should have stormed her. Instead he seduced. She didn't know if she could bear it.

With steam billowing like smoke, he trailed that mouth down her body, until every muscle trembled, until anticipation and sensation squeezed to a pulsing ache inside her.

Then he used his mouth on her until the hot flood of release swamped her.

When she was weak, in that shivering instant where body and mind surrendered, he plunged inside her.

No seduction now, no slow hands or teasing mouth. He gripped her hips and let himself take, and take, and take. Need raged through him, incited by the harsh sound of wet flesh slapping wet flesh, the pounding beat of the water, the wild thrust of her hips as she gave herself over to what they fueled in each other.

The chains of control shattered; madness broke free.

Through the haze of steam and passion he watched her eyes go blind. Still he drove her, himself, greedy for more until pleasure ripped through him and emptied him out.

She let her head drop on his shoulder until she could get her breath back. Might be a while, she realized, as she was currently panting like an old woman.

"Need a minute."

She made some sound of agreement to the statement.

"If we try to move now, we're both going to end up going down and drowning—after we fracture our skulls."

"We're lucky we didn't do that already."

"Probably. But we'd die clean and satisfied. I'm going to turn off the water. It's going cold."

She'd have to take his word for it. Her body still pumped enough heat to melt an ice floe. She managed her first full breath when he brushed his lips over her hair. She simply didn't know how to react to sweetness—after.

"Got your legs under you?" he asked her.

"Steady as a rock." Hopefully.

He let her go to reach out and grab towels. "It's a sacrifice to give you anything to cover up that body with." Before she could take it, he wrapped it around her, laid a warm, lingering kiss on her lips.

"Problem?" he asked her.

"No. Why?"

He trailed a fingertip between her eyebrows. "You're frowning."

"My face is reflecting the mood of my stomach, which is wondering why it's still empty." Which was true enough. "I'm starving." She relaxed again, smiled again. "Between the jump and the shower bonus, I'm out."

"Right there with you. Let's go eat."

She started to move past him to the bedroom, turned. "I've said it before, but it bears repeating. You've got skills."

"I also work well horizontally."

Her laugh rolled out as she pulled out a T-shirt and jeans. "I think you're going to have to prove it."

"Now or after food?"

She shook her head as she pulled on clothes. "After, definitely. I'm in the mood for . . . Aren't you getting dressed?"

"I'm not putting that stinking mess back on. I need to borrow your towel."

She thought of the state of the clothes they'd both dragged off. "Just hang on a minute. I'll get you some clothes."

"Really?"

"I know where your quarters are." She breezed out, strolled into his room.

He kept it tidy, she thought as she pulled open a drawer. Inside spaces, too. She grabbed what she figured he needed, took another quick look around. When she noticed the photograph, she stepped over for a closer study.

Gull, she noted, with what had to be his aunt and uncle, his cousins, all arm in arm in front of big, bright red doors.

Great-looking group, she thought, and the body language spoke of affection and happy. In front of the arcade, which, she realized by what she could see of it, was a lot bigger than she'd envisioned.

She took the clothes back, pushed them into his hands. "Hurry up and get dressed before I start gnawing on my own hand."

"Hurry up and get undressed, hurry up and get dressed. Orders, orders." He sent her an exaggerated smoldering look. "Dominant females make me hot."

"I'll see if I can find my whip and chain later."

"Ah, a brand-new fantasy to explore."

"Don't forget to call me 'Mistress.'"

"If you promise to be gentle. By the way, I like the tat."

"Good-luck charm," she told him. "If I wear the dragon, the dragon doesn't wear me. How about yours?" She walked around to tap the letters scrolled over his left shoulder blade. "Teine," she said.

"It's pronounced 'teen,' not 'The-ine.' Old Irish for fire. I guess if I wear the fire, it doesn't wear me."

"It just gets to try us both on from time to time. How'd you get that one?" she asked, gesturing to the scar along his left ribs.

"Bar fight in New Orleans."

"No, seriously."

"Well, it was, technically, outside the bar. I went down for Mardi Gras one year. Have you ever been?"

"No."

"Not to be missed." His hair, still damp from the shower, curled at the collar of the shirt he pulled on. "I was in college, went down with some friends. After the revelry, we hit a bar. This asshole went after this girl. Sort of like the asshole who hassled you, but this one was drunker and meaner, and she didn't have your style."

"Few do," she said with a grin.

"No argument. So, when I suggested he cease and desist, he objected. One thing led to another. Apparently he didn't like the fact I was kicking his ass in front of witnesses, so he pulled a knife."

The grin changed to openmouthed shock. "Well, sweet baby Jesus, he *stabbed* you?"

"Not exactly. The knife sort of skimmed along my ribs." Gull motioned a careless finger over the spot. "He didn't get much of me, and I had the pleasure of breaking his jaw. The girl was really grateful, so a night well spent."

He tied his sneakers. "I have a spotted and unruly past."

"You're a puzzler."

"Okay." He held out a hand. "How about I buy you dinner and a couple of cold beers?"

"I say since meals come with the job, that makes you a cheapskate, but what the hell."

LATER, AFTER GULL PROVED he did indeed work well horizontally, Rowan gave him a sleepy nudge. "Go home."

"Nope." He simply tucked her in against his side.

"Gull, neither of us is what you'd call petite, and this bed isn't exactly built for two." Besides, sleeping with a guy was different from sex.

"It worked pretty well so far. We'll manage. Besides, you saw the jump list. We're first and second man, first stick. If we get a call, all we have to do is put on the clothes currently strewn all over the floor, and hit it. It's efficient."

"So you always sleep with your jump partner for the sake of efficiency."

"I'm trying it out with you first. Who knows, if it saves enough time, it might become regulation. If we're clear, do you want to take a run in the morning?"

His hand, trailing lightly up and down her back, felt good—soothing. It was late anyway, she thought, she could make an exception on the sleeping rule this one time. Except she'd already made an exception on the sex, and now . . .

"Are we going to keep doing this?" she wondered.

"Okay, but you're going to have to give me about twenty minutes."

"Not tonight. I think we've rung the bell on that."

"Oh, you mean as a continuing series." He gave her ass a light, friendly pat. "Definitely."

"If we continue the series, there's a rule."

"Of course there is."

"If I sleep with a guy, I don't sleep with other guys, or sleep with that guy if he's banging anyone else. If either of us decide someone else looks good, that's fine. Series over. That one's firm. No exceptions."

"That's fair. One question. Why would I want anybody else when I get to take showers with you?"

"Because people tend to want what they don't have."

"I like what I've got." He gave her an easy squeeze. "Ergo, I'm happy to abide by your rule on this matter."

"Ergo." She chuckled, closed her eyes. "You're something else, Gulliver."

Right then, tucked up with Rowan in bed, an owl hooting dourly in the night and the moon shafting through the window, Gull figured he was exactly who, and where, he wanted to be.

IT TOOK LESS TIME to burn a body than a forest. An uglier business, but quicker. Still, collateral damage couldn't be avoided, and probably served as an advantage. She didn't weigh much, considering, so carrying her up the trail, through the lodgepole pines, wasn't as hard as it might have been.

The shimmer of moonlight helped light the way—like a sign—and the music of night creatures soothed.

The trail forked, steepened, but the climb wasn't altogether unpleasant in the cool, pine-scented air.

Better not to think of the unpleasant, of the horror. Better to think of moonlight and cool air and night birds.

In the distance, a coyote called out, high and bright. A wild sound, a *hungry* sound. Burning her would be humane. Better than leaving her for the animals.

They'd probably come far enough.

The task didn't take much effort or require too many tools. Just hacking away some dried brush and twigs, soaking them, her clothes. Her.

Don't think.

Soaking it all with gas from the spare can.

Try not to look at her face, try not to think of what she'd said and done. What had happened. Stick to what had to be done now.

Light the fire. Feel the heat. See the color and shape. Hear the crackle and snap. Then the whoosh of air and flame as that fire began to breathe.

A thing of beauty. Dazzling, dangerous, destructive.

So beautiful and fierce, and *personal*, when started with your own hands. Never realized, never knew.

It would purge. Erase her. Send her to hell. She belonged there. The animals wouldn't get her, tear at her as the dogs had torn at Jezebel. But she'd earned hell.

No more harm, no more threat. No more. In the fire, she would cease to be.

Watching it take her brought a horrible thrill, a bright

tingle of unexpected excitement. Power tasted. No tears, no regrets—not anymore.

That thrill, and the rising voice of the fire, followed down the trail while smoke began to climb toward the shimmering moon.

14

For the second time Rowan woke curled up to Gull with her head on his shoulder. This time she wondered how the hell he could sleep with her weight pressing on him.

Then she wondered, since she was shoehorned into the narrow bed with him, why the hell she wasn't taking advantage of it. She bit his earlobe as her hand trailed down his chest. As she'd expected, she found him already primed.

"I'd've put money on it," she murmured.

"I like your hand on it better."

"Now this . . ." She swung a leg over him, taking him in slowly. Slowly until she sheathed him in the warm and the wet. "This is what I call efficient."

Thinking there was no finer way to greet the morning, he got a firm grip on her hips. "A plus."

When she bowed back, the sun slanting light and shadow over her body, casting diamonds through her crown of hair, a snippet of Tennyson flitted through his mind.

A daughter of the gods, divinely tall, and most divinely fair.

She was that, in that moment, and in that moment took command of his romantic heart.

His grip gentled to a caress. And she began to move, undulating over him in a slow, fluid rhythm. Sensation spooled through him, unwinding a lovely, lazy delight.

Her eyes closed, her hands stroked up her own body, inciting them both.

Through the bars of light, the building beauty, he reached for her. He thought they could drift like this, leisurely awakening body, blood, heart, forever.

The siren screamed.

"Shit!" Her eyes popped open.

"Give me a fucking break." He held on to her for one frustrating moment, then they broke apart to scramble for clothes.

"You did this," she accused him. "You called it last night with that damn efficiency crack."

"Ten minutes more, it would've been worth it."

Instead, in ten minutes they suited up in the ready room.

"Spotted smoke at first light." L.B. gave the outline. "Lolo National Forest, between Grave Creek and Lolo Pass. It's fully active on the south slope above Lolo Creek. Conditions dry. Rowan, I want you in as fire boss; Gibbons, you're on the line."

The ground thundered as the tanker began to roll with the first load of mud.

The minute she boarded the jump ship, Rowan pulled out the egg sandwich and Coke she'd stuck in pockets. She ate and drank while she coordinated with the pilot, the spotter.

"There she is." She pressed her face to the window. "And, damn, she's frisky this morning."

A hundred acres, maybe a hundred and twenty, she estimated, already fully active in some of the most primitive and pristine areas of Lolo. Lewis and Clark had traveled there, and now the fire wanted it for breakfast.

Here we come, she thought, and guarded her reserves as wind rushed in through the open door.

She felt fresh and fueled and ready—and couldn't deny the ride down was beautiful. She checked on Gull, shot him a huge grin. "It's not sex, but it doesn't suck," she shouted.

She heard his laugh, understood exactly what ran through him. It ran through her, free and strong into the sky, the smoke, and down to the soft landing on a sweet little meadow.

Once the unit and the paracargo hit the ground, she strategized with Gibbons. She decided to do a recon up the right flank while the crew headed in to start the line.

She traveled at a trot, gauging the area, the wind, and keeping twenty yards off the flank as the fire burned hot. She heard the head calling in that grumbling, greedy roar as it tossed spot fires into the unburned majesty of forest.

Not going to have it, she thought, using her Pulaski and her bladder pump to smother the spots as she went. It wants to run, wants to feed. She smelled the sharp resin as trees burned, heard their crackling cries, felt the air tremble with the power already unleashed. Smoke spiraled up where spitting embers met dry ground.

She yanked out her radio. "She wants to run, and she's fast, L.B. She's fast. We need another load of mud on the head, and another down the right flank. She's throwing a lot of spots along that line."

"Copy that. Are you clear?"

"I will be." She kept moving, away from a spot that ate ground the size of a tennis court. "We need to contain these spots now, L.B. We're at critical. Gibbons is on the line, southwest, and I'm doubling back."

"Stay clear. We've got another load of jumpers on alert. Say the word and we'll send them in."

"Copy that. Let me finish this recon, check in with Gibbons."

"Tankers on the way. Don't get slimed, Swede."

"I'm clear," she repeated. "And I'm out."

She ran, charging her way down as she checked in with Gibbons, making for the trail where Lewis and Clark had once traveled. At the roar behind her, she cursed, ran through the falling embers, the missiles of burning pinecones hurled by the blasting wind of a blowup. When the ground shook under her feet, she charged through the heart of the fire.

Safer inside it, she thought while smoke gushed through the lick of orange flames.

In the black she took a moment to pull out her compass and get her bearings, to plot the next moves. Gibbons would have sent the crew up the ridge on attack, she thought, and then—

She nearly ran over it. Instinct and atavistic horror stumbled her back three paces from the charred and blackened remains of what had been human. It lay, the crisp bones of its arms and legs curled in. Contracted by the heat, she knew that, but in that terrible moment it seemed as if the dead or dying had tried to tuck into a ball the fire might overlook.

Her fingers felt numb when she pulled out her radio. "Base."

"Base here, come back, Swede."

"I've got a body."

"Say again?"

"I'm maybe ten yards from the Lobo Trail, near the southeast switchback, in the black. There's a body, L.B." She blew out a breath. "It's crisp."

"Ah, Christ. Copy that. Are you safe there?"

"Yeah. I'm in the black. I'm clear."

"Hold there. I'll contact the Forest Service, then get back to you."

"L.B." She rubbed her fingers between her eyebrows. "I can't tell for sure, but the ground under and around the remains, the pattern of the burn . . . Hell, I think maybe somebody lit him—her—up. And there's . . . I don't know, but the angle of the head. It looks like the neck's broken."

"Sweet Jesus. Don't touch anything. Do you copy, Rowan? Don't touch anything."

"Believe me, I won't. I'll radio Gibbons, give him a SITREP. Jesus, L.B., I think it's a woman or a kid. The size . . ."

"Hang in, Rowan. I'll come back."

"Copy that. Out."

She steeled herself. She'd seen burned bodies before. She'd seen Jim, she thought, when they'd finally recovered his remains. But she'd never stumbled over one, alone, in the middle of an operation.

So she took a breath, then radioed Gibbons.

It took her more than an hour and a half to get back to her crew, after holding her position, and guiding two rangers in. She welcomed the heat, the smoke, the battle after her vigil with the dead.

As she'd expected, Gibbons had the crew up the ridge, and the line held.

"Holy shit, Ro." Gibbons swiped a forearm over his blackened face. "You okay?"

The time, the vigil, the hard reality of giving a statement hadn't completely settled the raw sickness in her belly. "I'm a lot better than whoever's back there. The rangers are down there now, and a Special Agent Somebody's coming in. And an arson guy."

"Arson."

"It might be this fire was deliberately set, to cover up murder." Because it felt as if it squeezed her skull, she shifted her helmet—but it did nothing to relieve the steady throbbing.

"They don't know yet," she told him as he cursed. "Maybe it was some dumb kid messing around, but it looked to me like that could've been the point of origin. Putting the fire down's first priority. The feds'll handle the other. Where do you want me?"

"You know you can pack out, Ro. Nobody'll blame you."

"Let's finish this."

She worked the saw line, while another part of the crew reinforced the scratch lines riding up toward the head. A fresher crew of jumpers attacked the other flank, down toward the tail.

Countless times during the hours on the line, she pulled off to radio the other crew for progress, updated base, consulted with Gibbons.

A few more hours to finish her off and mop up, she thought, and the crew would sleep in beds tonight.

"What's up?" Gull stopped by her side. "There are rumors up and down the line something is, and you're the source."

She started to brush him off, but he looked her dead in the eye.

"You can tell me now or tell me later. You might as well get it done."

She'd shared her body with him, she reminded herself, and her bed. "We've got her caged. If Gibbons can spare you, you can come with me to scout out smokes."

Cleared, they moved away from the line. Rowan beat out a spot the size of a basketball, moved on.

And told him.

"You think the person was murdered, and whoever did it started the fire to try to cover it up?"

"I can't know." But her gut, roiling still, told her differently.

"Smarter to bury it." His matter-of-fact tone slowed the churning. "A fire like this brings attention. Obviously."

"I've never done it, but it seems to me killing somebody might impair logic. Or maybe the fire added to it. Plenty of people get off starting fires."

"They spotted this one at first light. From the progress it made by the time we jumped, it must've started late last night, early this morning. It was burning damn hot, had at least a hundred acres involved when we jumped at, what, about eight?"

Odd, she realized, that talking it through, picking out the practical, calmed the jitters. "Yeah."

"The campground's not that far west, but with that burned-out area between where you found the body and the campground, the fire sniffed east. Lucky for the campers."

The drumming inside her skull backed off, a little. Thinking was doing, she decided. Up until now she'd done too much reacting, not enough doing.

"Maybe they were from the camp," she speculated. "And came out on the trail, got into a fight. By accident or design, he kills her."

"Her?"

"The size of the body. I think it was a woman or a kid, and since I don't want to think it was a kid, I'm going with woman. He'd drag or carry her off the trail. Maybe he thinks about burying her, and went back to get tools. Fire's quicker and takes less effort. Dry conditions, some brush."

"If you started it around two, three in the morning," Gull calculated, "it would get a pretty good blaze up by dawn, and buy you a few hours."

Yes, she thought. Sure. Survival had to be the first priority.

"Pack it up, and you're way gone by dawn." She nodded, steadied by working it as a problem to be solved. "It'll take time to identify her, so that buys you more yet. And the fact is, if I hadn't taken that route back to the line, maybe it's hours more, even days, before she's found. I wasn't going that route, but the blowup sent me in and over."

They continued to find and kill spots as they talked. Then she stopped. "I didn't think I wanted to think about it. I found her, I called it in, now it's for the USFS to deal with. But it's been gnawing at me ever since. It . . . it shook me," she confessed.

"It would shake anybody, Rowan."

"Have you ever seen somebody after they've been—"

"Yeah. It sticks with you." And he knew talking about it, thinking about the hows and whys, helped.

"Summers are usually about this." She drowned a bucket-sized spot before it had a chance to grow. "Putting out fires, mopping them up, training and prepping to jump the next. But this summer? We've got crazy Dolly, my father going on a date, dead people."

"Your father dating ranks with vandalism and possible homicide and arson?"

"It's just different. Unusual. Like me sleeping with a rookie—which I haven't done, by the way, since I was one."

"Points for me."

She shifted direction, angled south. Points for him, maybe, but to her mind change, exceptions, the different screwed up the order of things.

After nearly two hours on spots, they rejoined the crew and shifted to mop-up mode.

She pulled out her radio to take a call from the operations desk.

"We want the first load to demob," L.B. told her. "Second load and ground crew will complete the mop-up."

"I hear that."

"The fed wants to talk to you when you get back."

"Can't it wait until tomorrow? I talked to the rangers, gave them all the details."

"Doesn't look like it. You can pack out. There'll be ground transportation for you at the trailhead."

"Copy that." What the hell, she thought, at least this way she'd get it all over with in one day.

SHE'D PLANNED on getting a shower first, but she'd no more
than dumped her gear when the fed came looking for her.

"Rowan Tripp?"

"That's right."

"Special Agent Kimberly DiCicco. I have some questions."

"The rangers already have my answers, but since we both
work for a bureaucracy, I know how it goes."

"Mr. Little Bear offered his office so we can speak in
private."

"I'm not stinking up L.B.'s office. In case you haven't
noticed, I'm pretty ripe with smoke and sweat."

She had to notice, Rowan thought. The agent's compact
body was tucked into a black suit of classic lines with a pristine
white shirt. Without a hair out of place, her sleek nape-of-the-
neck bun left her refined-boned, coffee-with-a-splash-of-cream
face unframed.

DiCicco's eyebrows arched over tawny eyes as she angled
her head. "You've put in a long day. I'm aware. I'll make it as
brief as possible."

"Then let's walk and talk." Rowan stripped down to her
tank and trousers. "Maybe I'll air out a little."

"Heads up."

She turned, caught the cold bottle of Coke Gull sent her in
a smooth underhand pass. "Thanks. Save me some lasagna."

"I'll do what I can."

"Okay, Agent DiCicco." At Rowan's gesture, they walked
outside. "You ask, I'll answer."

"You could start by telling me how you came upon the
body."

Already covered, Rowan thought, but went through it again.
"With the way the fire was running," she continued, "I had to
cut off the recon and make for a safe zone. I headed in, then
hiked across the old burnout section and into the black. The
area adjacent to where the fire had passed through. I was heading for Lolo Trail. I could take that most of the way back to my
crew. And I found her."

"Her?"

"I don't know. The remains were on the small side for a grown man."

"You'd be correct. The victim was female."

"Oh. Well." Rowan stopped, blew out a breath. "That's better than the alternative."

"Excuse me?"

"It could've been a kid. The size again."

"You contacted your operations desk immediately on the discovery?"

"That's right."

"So, if I have this correct." DiCicco read back Rowan's movements, the times she'd radioed in her position and the situation through her recon to the report of the body. "That's a considerable area in a short amount of time."

"When you catch fire, you're not out on a stroll or a nature hike. You move, and you move fast. It's my job to assess the situation on the ground, strategize a plan and approach with Gibbons, the line boss on this one, to recon and to keep Ops apprised of the situation and any additional support we might need."

"Understood. When you contacted Operations, you stated you believed the victim had been murdered and the fire started to cover up the crime."

Should she have kept her mouth shut? Rowan wondered. Would this be done if she'd kept her speculations to herself?

Too late now, she reminded herself.

"I said what it looked like. I've been jumping fires for five years, and I worked with a hotshot crew for two before that. I'm not an arson expert, but I know when a fire looks suspicious. I'm not a doctor, but I know when a head's twisted wrong on a neck."

And now, damn it, *damn* it, that image carved in her brain again. "I acted on what I observed so the proper authorities could be contacted. Is that a problem?"

"I'm gathering facts, Ms. Tripp." DiCicco's tone made a mild counterpoint to Rowan's snap. "The medical examiner's preliminary findings indicate the victim's neck had been broken."

"She was murdered." Better or worse? Rowan wondered.

"The ME will determine if this is homicide, accidental, whether the neck injury was cause of death or postmortem."

"Have you checked with the campground? Lolo Campground isn't far from where I found her, not for a day hike."

"We're working on identifying her. You had some trouble here recently?"

"What?" Rowan pulled her mind back from speculating on just how much force it took to break a neck. "The vandalism?"

"That's plural, isn't it?" DiCicco kept unreadable eyes on Rowan's face. "According to my information, one Dolly Brakeman, employed at that time as a cook here, vandalized your room. You caught her in the act and had to be physically restrained from assaulting her."

Temper burned through fatigue like a brushfire. "You walk into your quarters, DiCicco, and find somebody pouring animal blood on your bed. See how you react. If you want to call my reaction 'attempted assault,' you go right ahead."

"Ms. Brakeman was also questioned by the police regarding the vandalism of the ready room here on base."

"That's right. That little number cost us hours of time and could have cost more if we'd gotten a call out before we'd repaired the damage."

"You and Ms. Brakeman have a history."

"Since you already know that, I'm not going over the ground again. She's a pain in the ass, a vindictive one, and an unstable one. If the locals turned over the vandalism here to your agency, good. I hope it scares the shit out of her. Now look, I'm tired, I'm hungry and I want a goddamn shower."

"Nearly done. When did you last see Dolly Brakeman?"

"Jesus, when she trashed my room."

"You haven't seen or spoken with her since?"

"No, I haven't, and I'd be thrilled if I can keep that record. What the hell does Dolly have to do with me finding a dead woman burned to a crisp in Lolo?"

"We'll need to wait for confirmation of identification, but as Dolly Brakeman failed to return home last night—a home she shares with her parents and her infant daughter—as the victim and Ms. Brakeman are the same height, and thus far the investigation has turned up no other female missing, it's a strong possibility the victim is Dolly Brakeman."

"That's . . ." Rowan felt her belly drop, the blood just drain out of her head while those unreadable eyes never shifted off her face. "A lot of women are Dolly's height."

"But none of them has been reported missing in this area."

"She's probably hooked up with some guy. Take a look at that part of her history." But she had a baby now, Rowan thought. Jim's baby. "Dolly wouldn't be on the trail, in the forest. She likes town."

"Can you tell me your whereabouts last night, from eight P.M. until you reported to the ready room this morning?"

"I'm a suspect?" Anger and shock warred—a short, bloody battle before anger won. "You actually think I snapped her neck, hauled her into the forest, then started a fire? A fire men and women I work with, live with, eat with every day would have to jump. Would have to risk their lives, their *lives*, to beat down?"

"You tried to assault her. Threatened to kill her."

"Fucking A right I did. I was pissed. Who wouldn't be pissed? I wish I'd gotten a punch in, and that's a hell of a long way from killing somebody."

"It'd be easier if you could tell me where you were last night between—"

"I'll make it real easy," Rowan interrupted. "I had dinner in the cookhouse about seven, maybe seven-thirty. About thirty of the crew were in there at the same time, and the kitchen staff. We hung out, bullshitting until close to ten. Then I went to my quarters, where I stayed until the siren went off this morning. Squeezed into bed with the hottie you saw toss me this Coke."

"And his name?" DiCicco asked without a blink of reaction.

"Gulliver Curry. He's probably in the cookhouse by now. Go ask him. I'm getting a goddamn shower."

She stormed off, outrage burning a storm in her belly, slammed into the barracks.

Trigger had the misfortune of getting in her way. "Hey, Ro, are you—"

"Shut up and move." She shoved him aside, then slammed

into her quarters. She kicked the door, then the dresser, causing the little dish she tossed loose change into to jump off and crash onto the floor.

Her boots stamped the shards.

"Stiff-necked, tight-assed *bitch*! And it wasn't Dolly!" Fuming, she tore at the laces of her jump boots, then hurled them.

Dolly was the type who just kept rolling, she thought as she yanked off her clothes, balled them up and threw them. She made people feel sorry for her, or—if they were men—sweetened the pot with sex or the promise of it. She was the type who did whatever the hell she wanted, then blamed somebody else if it didn't work out.

Her mother's type, Rowan decided, and maybe that was just one more reason she'd never liked Dolly Brakeman. Selfish, scheming, whining . . .

Her mother's type, she thought again. Her mother had died bleeding on the floor. Murdered.

Not the same, she told herself firmly. Absolutely not the same.

In the shower, she turned the water on full, braced her hands on the wall and let it run over her. Watched it run black, then sooty gray.

She'd had enough of this shit, enough of the sucker punches.

What right did that federal bitch have to accuse her? She was the reason the body was found so quickly, the reason the feds had been called in the first damn place.

By the time she'd all but scrubbed herself raw, the leading edge of temper had dulled into a sick fear.

Her hands shook as she dressed, but she told herself it was hunger. She hadn't eaten in hours and had burned thousands of calories. So she was shaky. That's all it was.

When the door opened, she whirled, felt the shaking increase as Gull closed it quietly behind him.

"Did you tell that bitch you spent the night nailing me?"

"I told her we spent the night in here, in a bed small enough if you'd managed to roll over I'd've known it."

"Good. Good. She can stick that up her federal ass." She

pushed him back when he came to her. "I don't want to be coddled. Appreciate the alibi and all that. It looks like breaking my rule just keeps paying off. Whoopee."

She pushed at him again, but this time he got his arms around her, hard and tight, and just held on while she struggled against him.

"I said I didn't want to be coddled. I've got a right to blow off some steam after being questioned as a killer, an arsonist, as somebody who'd betray everything that matters to squash some little pissant—"

She broke off, broke down. "Oh, God, oh, God, they think it's Dolly. They think Dolly's dead and I killed her."

"Listen to me." His hands firm on her shoulders, he eased her back until he could see her eyes. "They don't know who it is at this point. Maybe it is Dolly."

"Oh, Jesus, Gull. Oh, God."

"There's nothing anybody can do about that if it is. If it is, nobody thinks you had anything to do with it."

"DiCicco—"

"Was just informed you and I were together all night. There are plenty of people in the barracks who know we came in here together, and we came out together. So, if you're a suspect, I'm one, too. I don't think that's going to play for Di-Cicco or anyone else. She had a job to do. She did it, and now that part's over."

He ran his hands down her arms until he could link them with hers. "You're beat, you're shaky. She wouldn't have gotten to you like this if you'd been in top form."

"Maybe not, but boy, did she."

"Screw her." He kissed Rowan's forehead, then her lips. "Here's what we're going to do. We're going to go get dinner. You can listen to the rest of the unit express their pithy and colorful opinions over the fed asking you for an alibi."

"Pithy." That nearly got a smirk out of her. "I guess that would feel good."

"Nothing like solidarity. Then, we're going to come back here so I can give you an alibi for tonight."

Now the smirk formed, quick and cocky. "Maybe I'll be the one giving you an alibi."

"Either way works. Let's go before those hogs suck down all the lasagna." He gave her ass a light pat as they started out. "And, Ro? Don't worry. If they arrest you, I'll make your bail."

The laugh surprised her. And smoothed out some of the jitters in her belly.

15

After her morning PT, Rowan made a point of going to the cookhouse kitchen. If there was one person who knew something about everything, and most everything about something, it was Marg.

"Lynn's reloading the buffet now," Marg told her. "Or are you looking for a handout?"

"I wouldn't mind."

With silver hoops dancing at the sides of her do-rag—yellow smiley faces over bright blue today—Marg reached for a pitcher. "You don't want to have breakfast with your boyfriend?"

Rowan answered Marg's smirk with an eye roll. "I don't have boyfriends, I have lovers. And I take them and cast them off at my will."

"Ha." Marg poured a glass of juice. "That one won't cast off so easy. Drink this."

Obliging, Rowan pursed her lips. "Your carrot base, some cranberry, and . . ." She sipped again. "It's not really orange. Tangerine?"

"Blood orange. Gotcha."

"Sounds disgusting, and yet it's not. Any word on Dolly?"

Marg shook her head as she whisked eggs. Not a negative gesture, Rowan recognized, but a pitying one.

"They found her car, down one of the service roads in the woods off of Twelve, with a flat tire."

"Just her car?"

"What I heard is her keys were still in it, but not her purse. Like maybe she had some car trouble, pulled off."

"Why would she pull off the main highway if she had a flat?"

"I'm just saying what I heard." After pouring the eggs into an omelet pan, Marg added chunks of ham, cheese, tomatoes, some spinach. "Some of the thinking is maybe she walked on back to the highway, or somebody followed her onto the service road. And they took her."

"They still don't know if the remains in the fire . . . they can't know that for sure."

"Then there's no point in worrying about it."

Marg tried for brisk, but Rowan heard the hitch in her voice that told her Marg worried plenty.

"I wanted to hurt her, and seriously regretted not getting my fist in her face at least once. Now, knowing somebody might've hurt her, or worse? I don't want to feel guilty about Dolly. I hate feeling guilty about anything, but I *hate* feeling guilty about Dolly."

"I've never known anybody better at bringing trouble and drama onto herself than Dolly Brakeman. And if L.B. hadn't fired her, I'd have told him flat he'd have to choose between her and me. I don't feel guilty about that. I can be sorry if something's happened to her without feeling guilty I wanted to give her the back of my hand more than once."

Marg set the omelet and the wheat toast with plum preserves she'd prepared in front of Rowan. "Eat. You've shed a few pounds, and it's too early in the season for that."

"It's the first season I've needed an alibi for a murder investigation."

"I wouldn't mind having an alibi like yours."

Rowan dug into the omelet. "Do you want him when I'm done with him? Ow." Rowan laughed when Marg cuffed the side of her head. "And after I offer you such a studly guy." She smiled, shooting for winsome.

"When do you think you'll be done with him? In case I'm in the market for a stud."

"Can't say. So far he's playing my tune, but I'll let you know."

When Marg set a Coke down by her plate, Rowan leaned into her just a little. "Thanks, Marg. Really."

In acknowledgment, Marg gave her a hard one-armed hug. "Clean your plate," she ordered.

After breakfast, she tracked down L.B. in the gym where he'd worked up a sweat with bench presses.

"I'm on the bottom of the jump list," she said without preamble.

He sat up, wiped his face with his towel. His long braid trailed down his sweaty, sleeveless workout shirt. "That's right." He picked up a twenty-pound free weight and started smooth, two-count bicep curls.

"Why?"

"Because that's where I put you. I'd have taken you off completely for a day or two, but they've caught one down in Payette, and Idaho might need some Zulies in there."

"I'm fit and I'm fine. Move me up. Christ, L.B., you've got Stovic ahead of me, and he's still limping a little."

"You've been on nearly every jump we've had this month. You need a breather."

"I don't—"

"I say you do," he interrupted, and switched the weight to his other arm while he studied her face. "It's my job to decide that."

"This is about what happened yesterday, and that's not right. I need the work, I need the pay. I'm not injured, I'm not sick."

"You need a breather," he repeated. "Put some time in the loft. We're still catching up there. I'll take a look at the list tomorrow."

"I find remains, which I dutifully report, and I get grounded."

"You're still on the list," he reminded her. "And you know jumping fire's not all we do here."

She also knew that when Michael Little Bear used that mild, reasonable tone, she'd have better luck arguing with smoke. She could sulk, she could steam, but she wouldn't change his mind.

"Maybe I'll go down and see my father for a bit."

"That's a good idea. Let me know if you decide you want to go farther off base."

"I know the drill," she grumbled. She started to shove her hands in her pockets, then went stiff when Lieutenant Quinniock walked in. "Cops are here," she said quietly.

L.B. set down his weight, got to his feet.

"Mr. Little Bear, Ms. Tripp. I've got a few follow-up questions."

"I'll get out of your way," Rowan began.

"Actually, I'd like to speak with you, too. Why don't we step out. You can finish your workout," he said to L.B., "then we could talk in your office."

"I'll be there in twenty."

"That works. Miss?" Quinniock, in his polished shoes and stone-gray suit, gestured toward the gym doors.

"Don't 'Miss' me. Make it Tripp," she said as she shoved open the door ahead of him. "Or Rowan, or Ro, but don't 'Miss' me unless you're sad I've gone away."

He smiled. "Rowan. Would you mind if we sat outside? This is a busy place."

"Do you want me to go over my—what would you call it?—altercation with Dolly?"

"Do you have anything to add to what you've already told me?"

"No."

"She got the pig's blood from a ranch, if you're interested. From one of the people who goes to her church."

"Onward, Christian soldiers." She dropped down on a bench outside the barracks.

"She acquired it the day before she came here to ask for work." He nodded when Rowan turned to stare at him. "It leads me to conclude she meant to cause you trouble, even before you and she spoke the day she was hired back on."

"It wouldn't have mattered what I said or did."

"Probably not. I understand you spoke with Special Agent DiCicco."

"She's a snappy dresser. You too."

"I like a good suit. It complicated things for you, finding the remains."

"Complicated because it was during a fire, or because Dolly's missing?"

"Both. The missing person's end is MPD's case, at this time. We're cooperating with the USFS while they work to identify the body. In that spirit, I've shared information with Agent DiCicco."

"My history, as she called it, with Dolly."

"That, and the fact Dolly told several people you were to blame for what happened to James Brayner. You, and everyone here. She's been vocal about her resentment for some time, including the period of time she was away from Missoula."

It didn't surprise her, could no longer anger her. "I don't know how she could work here, be involved with jumpers, and not understand what we do, how we do it, what we deal with."

She looked at Quinniock then, the dramatic hair, the perfectly knotted tie. "And I'm not sure I understand why you're telling me this."

"It's possible she planned to continue to cause trouble—for you, for the base. It's possible she came back here for work so she had easier access. And it's possible she had help. Someone she convinced to help her. Did you see her with anyone in particular after she came back?"

"No."

"She and Matthew Brayner, the brother."

Rowan's back went up. "She blindsided Matt, the Brayner family, with the baby. I know they all took a natural interest in the baby and, being the kind of people they are, would do whatever they could for Dolly. It took guts for Matt to come back here, to work here after what happened to Jim. Any idea you may have that he'd help Dolly destroy my quarters or equipment is wrong and insulting."

"Were they friendly while his brother was alive?"

"I don't think Matt gave Dolly two thoughts, but he was, and is, friendly with everyone. And I'm not talking about another jumper behind his back."

"I'm just trying to get a feel for the dynamics. I'm also told several of the men on base had relationships with Dolly, at least until she became involved with James Brayner."

"Sex isn't a relationship, especially blow-off-some-steam sex with a woman who was willing to pop the cork with pretty much anybody. She popped plenty of corks in town, too."

"Until James Brayner."

"She zeroed in on him last season, and as far as I know that was a first for her. Look, he was a cute guy, fun, charming. Maybe she fell for him, I don't know. Dolly and I didn't share our secrets, hopes and dreams."

"You're probably aware by now that we found her car."

"Yeah, word travels." She squeezed her eyes shut a moment. "It's going to be her, when they finish the ID. I know that. You just have to triangulate the town, where you found the car, where I found the remains, and it's heavy weight on it. I didn't like her. I didn't like her a whole bunch of a lot, but she didn't deserve the way she ended up. Nobody deserves the way she ended up."

"People are always getting what they don't deserve. One way or the other. Thanks for the time."

"When will they know?" she asked when he stood up. "When will they know for sure?"

"Her dentist is local. They'll verify with her dental records, and should have confirmation later today. It's not my case, but just out of curiosity, in your opinion, how long would it take to get from the trailhead to where you found the remains, adding in carrying about a hundred and ten pounds, in the dark."

She got to her feet so they'd be eye to eye. "It depends. It could take an hour. But if you were fit, an experienced hiker, and you knew the area, you could do it in less than half that."

"Interesting. Thanks again."

She sat back down when he walked toward Operations, tried to work her mind around the conversation, the information.

And decided, as much as she hated to admit it, maybe L.B. was right. Maybe she did need a breather. So she'd walk down to see her father, touch base with the rest of his crew. The walk might clear her head, and God knew having a little time with her father never hurt.

She went back in for a bottle of water and a ball cap, then crossed paths with Gull as she came back out.

"I saw you with the cop. Do I need to post that bail?"

"Not so far. They found her car, Gull."

"Yeah, I heard."

"And . . . there's other stuff. I have to get my head around it. I'm going to walk down to the school, see my father."

"Do you want company?"

"I need some solo time."

He ran his knuckles down her cheek in a casually affectionate gesture that threw her off. "Look me up when you get back."

"Sure. You're second load," she called back as she started the walk. "Idaho might need some Zulies. If you jump, jump good."

She watched the show as she walked. Planes nosing up; skydivers drifting down. Clouds gathered in the west, hard and white over the mountains. Smaller, she noted, and puffier overhead and north, drifting east on a slow, leisurely sail.

She heard mechanics working in the hangars, the twang of music, the clink of metal, the roll of voices, but didn't stop as she might have another day. Conversation wasn't what she was after.

Solo time.

The killer had a car, or truck, she decided. Nobody would've carried Dolly from where she'd stopped to where she ended up. Did he kill her when she pulled off 12, dump her body in the trunk of the car, bed of the truck? Or did he give her a ride, maybe park at the trailhead, then do it? Or force her up the trail, then—

Jesus, any way it had happened, she'd ended up dead, and her baby daughter an orphan.

Why had she been heading south on 12, or had she been heading back from farther away? To meet a lover? To meet this theoretical person she'd enlisted to cause trouble? Plenty of motels to choose from. Hard to meet a lover—and Dolly had been famous for using sex as barter—when you lived at home with your parents and your baby.

Why couldn't she have loved the baby enough to just make a life? To treasure what she had, and put some goddamn effort into being a good mother instead of letting this obsession eat away at her?

All the time she'd spent planning her weird revenge,

harboring all that hate, could've been spent on living, on nuzzling her baby.

"Oh, mother issues much?" Annoyed with herself, she quickened her pace.

Enough solo time, she decided. Solo time was overrated. She should've taken Gull up on his offer to come with her. He'd have distracted her out of this mood, made her laugh, or at least annoyed her so she'd stop feeling sad and angry.

When she moved around the people scattered over the lawn, the picnic tables at her father's place, she looked up, as they were.

Coming on final, she thought, watching the plane. She crossed to the fence, tucked her hands in her back pockets and decided to enjoy the show. Her smile bloomed as the skydiver jumped—and taking a breather didn't seem so bad after all. When the second figure leaped out, she settled in, studying their forms on the free fall.

The first, definitely a student, but not bad. Not shabby. Arms out, taking it in. Check out that view! Feel that wind!

And the second . . . Rowan angled her head, narrowed her eyes. She couldn't be sure, not yet, but she'd have laid decent money down Iron Man Tripp rocketed down toward the student.

Then came the moment. The chutes deployed, one then two—to applause and cheers—the blue-and-white stripes of the student's, and the chute she'd designed and rigged for her father's sixtieth birthday with the boldly lettered IRON MAN in red (his favorite color) over a figure of a smoke jumper.

She loved watching him like this, and always had. Perfect form, she thought, absolute control, riding the air from sky to earth while the sun streamed through those drifting clouds.

She'd been exactly right to come here, she realized, when the world tipped crazily all around her. Here, what she loved held constant. Whatever happened, she could count on him.

She willed the stress of the morning into a corner. She couldn't dismiss it, but she could shove it back a little and focus on what made her happy.

She'd hang out here with her father for a while, have lunch with him, talk over what was going on. He'd listen, let her spew, and somehow pull her back in, steady her again.

She always thought more clearly, felt less overwhelmed, after a session with her father.

The student handled the drop well, Rowan observed, managed a very decent landing and was up on his—no her, Rowan realized—feet quickly. Then the Iron Man touched down, soft as butter, smooth as silk.

She added her applause to the rest, sent out a high whistle of approval before waving her arms in hopes of snagging her father's attention.

The student unhooked her harness, pulled off her helmet. Gorgeous red hair seemed to explode in the sunlight. As the woman raced toward her father, Rowan grinned. She understood the exuberance, the charge of excitement, had seen this same scene play out countless times between student and instructor. She continued to grin as the woman leaped into Lucas's arms, something else she'd seen again and again.

What she hadn't seen, and what had her grin shifting to a puzzled frown, was her father swinging a student in giddy circles while said student locked her arms around his neck.

And when Lucas "Iron Man" Tripp leaned down and planted a long, very enthusiastic kiss (and the crowd went wild) on the student's mouth, Rowan's jaw dropped to the toes of her Nikes.

She would've been more shocked if Lucas had pulled out a Luger and shot the redhead between the eyes, but it would've been a close call.

The woman had her hands on Lucas's cheeks, a gesture somehow more intimate than the kiss itself. It spoke of knowledge, familiarity, of privilege.

Who the hell was this bimbo, and when the hell had Iron Man started kissing students? Kissing *anyone*?

And in public.

The woman turned, her face—which didn't look bimboish—warm from the kiss, bright with laughter, and executed a deep, exaggerated curtsy for the still cheering crowd. To Rowan's continued shock, Lucas simply stood there grinning like the village idiot.

Was he on drugs?

Her brain told her to ease back, to find some quiet place to absorb the shock. Her gut told her to hurdle the fence, march right up and demand, what the fuck?!

But her fingers had curled around the fence, and she couldn't seem to uncurl them.

Then her father spotted her. His loopy grin aimed her way as he—Jesus—took the redhead's hand, gave it a little swing. He waved at Rowan with his free hand before he said something to the face-caressing redhead, who actually had the *nerve* to smile in Rowan's direction.

Still holding hands, they strolled toward the fence and Rowan.

"Hi, honey. I didn't realize you were here."

"I . . . I'm low on the jump list, so."

"I'm glad you came by." He laid his fingers over the ones she had curled on the fence, effectively linking the three of them. "Ella, this is my daughter, Rowan. Ro, Ella Frazier. She just did her first AFF."

"It's great to meet you. Lucas has told me so much about you."

"Oh, yeah? Funny, he hasn't told me a thing about you."

"You've been pretty busy." Obviously oblivious, Lucas spoke cheerfully. "We keep missing each other. Ella's principal of Orchard Homes Academy."

A high-school principal. Tony private school. Another strike against bimbo status. Damn it.

"Her son bought her a tandem jump as a gift," Lucas went on, "and she got hooked. You should've had your family here for this, Ella," he continued. "Your grandkids would've loved it."

And a *grandmother*? What kind of father-face-sucking bimbo was this?

"I wanted to make sure I handled it before they came to watch. Next time. In fact, I'm going to go in and talk to Marcie about setting it up. It was nice to meet you, Rowan. I hope we see more of each other."

Though her voice was mild and polite, the quick clash when the two women's gazes met made it clear they understood each other.

"I'll see you inside, Lucas."

Yeah, keep walking, Rowan thought. Make tracks.

"So what did you think?" Lucas asked, eagerly. "I've been hoping you'd get a break so you could meet Ella. It's cool you happened to be here for her first AFF."

"Her form's not bad. She had a good flight. Listen, Dad, why don't we grab some lunch in the cafe? There's—"

"Ella and I are having a picnic lunch out here to celebrate her dive. Why don't you join us? It'll give the two of you a chance to get to know each other."

Was he kidding? "I don't think so, but thanks. Riding third wheel doesn't suit me."

"Don't be silly. If I know Ella, she made plenty. She's a hell of a cook."

"Just—just—" She had to untangle her tongue. "How long has this been going on? *What's* going on? Kissing on the jump spot, hand-holding, picnic lunches? Jesus, Dad, are you *sleeping* with her?"

He pokered up, a look she knew meant she'd hit a nerve.

"I think that would come under the heading of my personal business, Rowan. What's your problem here?"

"My problem, other than the kissing, holding and so on in front of God, crew and visitors, is I came over here because I needed to talk to my father, but you're obviously too busy with Principal Hotpants to spare any for me."

"Watch it." His fingers tightened on hers before she could jerk away. "Don't you use that tone with me. I don't give a damn how old you are. If you need to talk to me, come inside. We'll talk."

"No, thanks," she said, coldly polite. "Go ahead and take care of your personal business. I'll take care of my own. Excuse me." She pulled her fingers free. "I have to get back to base."

She recognized the combination of anger and disappointment on his face, something rarely seen and instantly understood. She swung away from it, strode away from him, her back stiff with resentment. And her heart aching with what she told herself was betrayal.

Her temper only built on the walk back, then took a bitter spike when she heard the siren blast. She broke into a run, covering the remaining distance to the base where she could already see jumpers on the scramble and the jump plane taxiing onto the runway.

She hit the ready room, shoving aside the bitterness as she had the stress—as something to be taken out and examined later.

She grabbed gear off the speed rack for Cards. "Payette?"

"That's the one." He zipped his let-down rope into the proper pocket. "Zulies to the rescue!"

She looked in his eyes. "Have a good one."

"It's in the cards." He let out a chortle before waddling toward the waiting plane.

She went through the same procedure with Trigger while Gull helped Dobie.

In minutes she stood watching the plane take off without her.

"Secondary blaze blew up," Gull told her. "Idaho's already spread thin. One of their second load got hung up on the jump, broke his arm, and they've got two more injuries on the ground."

"Aren't you well informed?"

"I like to keep up with current events." He re-angled his ball cap to gain more shade from the bill as he followed the plane into the sky. "Such as the dry lightning doing a smack-down up in Flathead. You didn't spend much time at your dad's."

"Are you keeping track of me?"

"Just using my keen powers of observation. They also tell me you're severely pissed."

"I don't like being grounded when I'm fit to jump."

"You're on the list," he reminded her. "And?"

"And, what?"

"And what else has you severely pissed?"

"You and your keen powers of observation are about to, so aim them elsewhere." She started to stalk off, then, too riled to hold it in, stalked back. "I go up to see my father, spend some time with him, talk this crap over with him because that's what we do. When I get there he's doing an AFF with a student. A student who happens to be a woman. A redhead. One who, the minute they're on the ground, jumps him like my old dog Butch used to jump a Frisbee. Then he's swinging her around, and then he's kissing her. Kissing her, right there, a serious lip-locking, body-twining kiss no doubt involving tongues."

"The best do. So . . . I'm working my way through that report, trying to pinpoint what pissed you off."

"Did I just tell you my father kissed that redhead?"

"You did, but I'm having a tough time seeing why that flipped your switch. You're acting like you've never seen your old man kiss a woman before."

When she said nothing, only stood with her eyes like smoldering blue ice, he let out a half laugh of genuine surprise. "Seriously? You've seriously never seen him kiss a woman? The man has to have superhuman discretion."

Gull stopped again, shook his head and gave her a light slap on the shoulder. "Come on, Ro. You're not going to tell me you think he actually hasn't bumped lips with a female in—how old are you, exactly?"

"He doesn't date."

"So you said when he had the date with the lady client for drinks . . . Aha. Now my intrepid deductive skills mesh with my keen powers of observation to conclude this would be the same woman."

"She *says* she's a high-school principal. It's pretty damn clear they're sleeping together."

"I guess getting called into the principal's office has taken on a whole new meaning for your dad."

"Fuck you."

"Whoa." He caught her arm as she spun around. "You're jealous? You're actually jealous because your father's interested in a woman—who's not you?"

Heat—temper, embarrassment—slapped into her cheeks. "That's disgusting and untrue."

"You're pissed and jealous, and genuinely hurt because your father may be in a romantic relationship with a woman. That's not disgusting or untrue, Rowan, but it sure strikes me as petty and selfish."

Something very akin to the disappointment she'd just seen on her father's face moved over Gull's. "When's the last time he threw a tantrum because you were involved with someone?"

Now she felt petty, and that only fueled her temper. "My feelings and my relationship with my father are none of your business. You don't know a damn thing about it, or me. And you know what, I'm pretty goddamn sick of being dumped on, from Dolly and vindictive bullshit, to tight-assed special agents, my father's disappointment to your crappy opinion of me. So you can just—"

The shrilling siren sliced off her words.

"Looks like me and my crappy opinion have to get going." Gull turned his back on her and walked back to the ready room.

It was almost more than she could swallow, standing on the ground again while the plane flew north.

"If this keeps up, they'll have to send us up."

She glanced over at Matt. "The way my luck's going, L.B.'ll cross me off and send Marg if we get another call. How did you rate the basement?"

"He feels like I'm too twisted up about Dolly, because of my niece. Maybe I am."

"I'm sorry. I wasn't thinking."

"It's okay. I keep expecting them to come back, say it's all a mistake." He held his cap in his hands, turning it around and around in them and leaving his floppy cornsilk hair uncovered.

"It can't be right, you know, for a baby to lose her father before she's even born, then her mother so soon after." He turned to Rowan, and she thought he looked unbearably young and exposed.

"It isn't right," she said.

"But things, I guess things just aren't always right. I guess . . . it's like fate."

He leaned into her a little when she hooked an arm around his waist. "It's harder on you, maybe," he said, "than me."

"Me?"

"You found her. If it's her. Even if it's not, finding whoever it was. It's awful you were the one who found her."

"We'll both get through it, Matt."

"That's what I keep telling myself. I keep thinking of Shiloh, and telling myself that whatever happens, we'll make sure she's okay. I mean, she's just a baby."

"The Brakemans and your family will take care of her."

"Yeah. Well, I guess I'll go up to the loft, try to get my mind on something else."

"That's a good idea. I'll be up in a few minutes."

She went back to her quarters first, locked herself in. Though she knew it was self-pity, that it was useless, she sat on the floor, leaned back against the bed and had a good cry.

16

The cry emptied out the temper and the self-pity. For a trade-off she accepted the splitting headache, and downed the medication before splashing cold water on her face.

One of the problems with being a true blonde with fair skin, she mused, giving herself the hard eye in the mirror, was that after a jag she resembled someone who'd gotten a brutal sunburn, through cheesecloth.

She splashed some more, then wrung out a cold cloth. She gave herself ten minutes flat on her back on the bed, the cloth over her face, to let the meds and the cool do their job.

So she'd overreacted, she thought. Beat her with a brick.

She'd apologize to her father for sticking her nose in his business since he now had business he didn't want her to stick her nose into.

And she damn well expected the same courtesy from a certain fast-footed, hotshot rookie, so he'd better come back safe.

She checked her face again, decided she'd do. Maybe she didn't look her best, but she didn't look as if she'd spent the last twenty minutes curled up on the floor, blubbering like a big baby.

On her way toward Operations to check on the status of the crews, she caught sight of Special Agent DiCicco walking toward her.

"Ms. Tripp."

"Look, I know you've got a job to do, but we've got two loads out. I'm heading to Ops, and don't have time to go over ground I've already gone over."

"I'm sorry, but I will need to speak with you, as well as members of the crew and staff. The remains you discovered yesterday have been positively identified as Dolly Brakeman."

"Hell." Sick, Rowan pressed her forehead, and rubbed it side to side. "Oh, hell. How? How did she die?"

"Since some of those details will make the evening news, I can tell you cause of death was a broken neck, possibly incurred in a fall."

"A fall? You'd have to fall really hard and really wrong. Not an accidental fall, not when she left her car one place and ended up in another."

DiCicco's face remained impassive, her eyes level. "This is a homicide investigation, coordinated with an arson investigation. Your instincts on both counts appear to have been right on target."

"And being right makes me a suspect."

"I'm not prepared to eliminate anyone as a suspect, but you have an alibi for the time frame. The fact is, you and the victim had an adversarial relationship. It's an avenue I need to explore."

"Explore away. Be Magellan. I didn't look for trouble with her. If I could've punched her on the infamous day of the blood of the pigs, I would have. And she'd have earned it. I think she should've been charged for what she did to our equipment, and spent some quality time in jail. I don't think she should've died for either of those offenses. She was—"

Rowan broke off as a truck roared in, fishtailing as it swerved in her direction. She grabbed DiCicco's arm to yank her back even as DiCicco grabbed hers to do the same.

The truck braked with a shriek, spewed up clouds of road dust.

"Jesus Christ! What the hell are you . . ." She trailed off as she recognized the man leaping out of the truck as Leo Brakeman, Dolly's father.

"My daughter is dead." He stood there, meaty hands balled into white-knuckled fists at his sides, his former All-State left tackle's body quivering, his face—wide and hard—reddened.

"Mr. Brakeman, I'm sorry for—"

"You're responsible. There's nothing left of her but burned bones, and you're responsible."

"Mr. Brakeman." DiCicco stepped between Rowan and Brakeman, but Rowan shifted to the side, refusing the shield. "I explained to you that I and the full resources of my agency will do everything possible to identify your daughter's killer. You need to go home, be with your wife and your granddaughter."

"You'll just cover it up. You work for the same people. My daughter would be alive today if not for that one." When he pointed his finger, Rowan felt the raging grief behind it stab like a blade.

"She got Dolly fired because she couldn't stand being reminded of how she let Jim Brayner die. She got her fired so Dolly had to drive all the way down to Florence to find work. If she didn't kill my girl with her own hands, she's the reason for it.

"You think you're so important?" he raged at Rowan. "You think you can ride on your father's coattails, and because your name's Tripp you can push people around? You were jealous of my girl, jealous because Jim tossed you over for her, and you couldn't stand it. You let him die so she couldn't have him."

"Leo." L.B., with a wall of men behind him, moved forward. "I'm sorry about Dolly. Every one of us is sorry for your loss. But I'm going to ask you once to get off this property."

"Why don't you fire her? Why don't you kick her off this base like she was trash, the way you did my girl? Now my girl's dead, and she's standing there like it was *nothing*."

"This isn't a good time for you to be here, Leo." L.B. kept his voice low, quiet. "You need to go home and be with Irene."

"Don't tell me what I need. There's a baby needs her ma. And none of you give a damn about that. You're going to pay for what happened to my Dolly. You're going to pay dear, all of you."

He spat on the ground, slammed back into his truck. Rowan saw tears spilling down his cheeks as he spun the wheel and sped away.

"Ro."

"Not now, L.B. Please." She shook her head.

"Now," he corrected, and put an arm firm around her shoulders. "You come inside with me. Agent DiCicco, if you need to talk to Rowan, it's going to be later."

DiCicco watched the wall of men close ranks like a barricade, then move into the building behind Rowan.

Inside, L.B. steered her straight to his office, shut the door on the rest of the men. "Sit," he ordered.

When she did, he shoved his hands through his hair, leaned back on his desk. "You know Leo Brakeman's a hard-ass under the best of circumstances."

"Yeah."

"And these are beyond shitty circumstances."

"I get it. It has to be somebody's fault, and Dolly blamed me for everything else, so I'm the obvious choice. I get it. If she told him—people—I was doing the deed with Jim before he tossed me over, why wouldn't her father think I had it out for his kid? And just to clarify, Jim and I were never—"

"You think I don't know you? I'll be talking to DiCicco and setting her straight on that front."

Rowan shrugged. Oddly she'd felt her spine steel up again under Brakeman's assault. "She'll either believe it or she won't. It doesn't matter. I'm okay, or close to being okay. You don't have time to babysit me, L.B., not with our crews out.

"I'm sorry for Brakeman," she said, "but that's the last time he'll use me as an emotional punching bag. Dolly was a liar, and her being dead doesn't change that."

She got to her feet. "I told you this morning I was fit and fine. That wasn't a lie but it wasn't completely true, either. Now it is. Nobody's going to treat me like Dolly and her father have and make me feel bad about it. I'm not responsible for the baggage full of shit they've hauled around. I've got plenty of my own."

"That sounds like you're fit and fine."

"I can help out in Ops if you want, or head up to the loft, see what needs doing there."

"Let's go see how our boys and girls are doing."

DiCicco made her way to the cookhouse kitchen, found it empty, unless she counted the aromas she dubbed as both comforting and sinful. She started to move into the dining area when a movement out the window caught her eye.

She watched the head cook, Margaret Colby, weeding a patch of an impressive garden.

Marg looked up at the sound of the back door opening, pushed at the wide brim of the straw hat she wore over her kitchen bandanna.

"That's some very pretty oregano."

"It's coming along. Are you looking for me, or just out for a stroll?"

"I'd like to talk to you for a few minutes. And to the other cook, Lynn Dorchester."

"I let Lynn go on home for the afternoon since she was upset. She'll be back around four." Marg tossed weeds into the plastic bucket at her feet, then brushed off her hands. "I could use some lemonade. Do you want some?"

"If it's not too much trouble."

"If it was, I wouldn't be getting it. You can have a seat there. I spend enough time in the kitchen on pretty days, so I take advantage of being out when I can."

DiCicco sat in one of the lawn chairs, contemplated the garden, the lay of the land beyond it. The big hangars and outbuildings, the curve of the track some distance off. And the rise and sweep of the mountains dusted with clouds.

Marg came out with the lemonade, and a plate of cookies with hefty chocolate chunks.

"Oh. You hit my biggest weakness."

"Everybody's got one." Marg set the tray down, sat comfortably and toed off her rubber-soled garden shoes.

"We heard it was Dolly. I let Lynn go, as it hit her hard. They weren't best of friends, Dolly didn't have girlfriends. But they'd worked together awhile now, and got along all right for the most of it. Lynn's got a soft core, and punched right into it."

"You worked with Dolly for some time, too. Were her supervisor."

"That's right. She could cook—she had a good hand with it, and she never gave me a problem in the kitchen. Her problem was, or one of them, was she looked at sex as an accomplishment, and as something to bargain with."

Marg picked up a cookie, took a bite. "The men around here, they're strong. They're brave. They've got bodies you'd be hard-pressed not to notice. Dolly wasn't hard-pressed.

"A lot of them are young, too," she continued, "and most all of them are away from home. They're going to risk life and limb and work like dogs, sometimes for days at a time in the worst conditions going. If they get a chance to roll onto a naked woman, there's not many who'd say no thanks. Dolly gave plenty of them a chance."

"Was there resentment? When a woman gives one man a chance, then turns around and gives the same chance to another, resentment's natural."

"I don't know a single one who ever took Dolly seriously. And that includes Jim. I know she said he was going to marry her, and I know she was lying. Or just dreaming. It's kinder to say just dreaming."

Though he'd used different words, L.B. had stated the same opinion.

"Was Jim serious about Rowan Tripp?"

"Ro? Well, she helped train him as a recruit, and worked with him. . . ." Marg trailed off as the actual meaning of *serious* got through. Then she sat back in the chair and laughed until her sides ached. She waved a hand in the air, drank some lemonade to settle down.

"I don't know where you got that idea, Agent DiCicco, but if Jim had tried to *get serious* with Ro, she'd've flicked him off like a fly. He flirted with everything female, myself included. It was his way, and he was so damn good-natured about it. But there was nothing between him and Ro but what's between all of them. A kind of friendship I expect war buddies understand. Added to it, Rowan's never gotten involved with anybody in her unit—until this season. Until Gulliver Curry. I'm enjoying watching how that one comes along."

"Leo Brakeman claims that Rowan and Jim were involved before he broke it off to be with Dolly."

Marg drank more lemonade and contemplated the mountains as DiCicco had. "Leo's grieving, and my heart hurts for him and Irene, but he's wrong. It sounds to me like something Dolly might've said."

"Why would she?"

"For the drama, and to try to take some of the shine off Rowan. I told you, Dolly didn't have girlfriends. She got on with Lynn because she didn't see Lynn as a threat. Lynn's married and happy, and the men tend to think of her as a sister, or a daughter. Dolly always saw Rowan as a threat, and more, she knew Rowan considered her . . . cheap, we'll say."

"It's obvious they didn't get along."

"Up until Jim died they tolerated each other well enough. I've known both of them since they were kids. Rowan barely noticed Dolly. Dolly always noticed Ro. And if you're still thinking Rowan had anything to do with what happened, you're wasting a lot of time better spent finding out who did."

Time wasn't wasted, in DiCicco's opinion, if you found out *something*.

"Did you know anything about Dolly getting work in Florence?"

"No. I don't know why she would. Plenty of places right around here would hire her on, at least for the season."

Marg loosed a long sigh. "I wouldn't give her a reference. Her preacher came out, tried to get me to write her one. I didn't like his way, that's one thing, but I wouldn't do it anyway. She didn't earn it with the way she behaved."

"I guess I'm sorry for that if she felt she had to leave Missoula to work. But there are plenty of places she could've gotten work without a reference."

Marg sat a moment, saying nothing. Just studying the mountains.

"Was she coming back from there when it happened? From work in Florence?"

"It's something I'll have to check out. I hate exaggeration, so you know I'm giving it to you straight when I say this is the best cookie I've ever eaten."

"I'll give you some to take with you."

"I wouldn't say no."

THE CREW IN IDAHO had the fire caged in by sundown. But up north, the battle raged on.

She could see it. As Rowan stepped outside to take the air, she could see the fire and smoke, and the figures in yellow shirts brandishing tools like weapons.

If they called for another load, if they needed relief or re-enforcement, L.B. would send her. And she'd be ready.

Her back stiffened at the glint of headlights, the silhouette of an approaching pickup. Then loosened again, a little, when she saw it wasn't Leo Brakeman back for another shot at her.

Lucas stepped out of the truck, walked to her.

Some anger there, she noted. Still some mad on.

He proved it when he clamped his hands on her shoulders, gave her a little shake. "Why the hell didn't you tell me what happened? Finding the remains, about Dolly, about *any* of it."

"I figured you knew."

"Well, I damn well didn't."

"You've been busy."

"Don't pull that crap with me, Rowan. Your landing text said A-OK."

"I was. I wasn't hurt."

"Rowan."

"I didn't want to tell you in a text, or on the phone. Then it was one thing and another. I came down this morning to talk to you about it, but—"

He simply yanked her against him and hugged.

"I'm a suspect."

"Stop it," he murmured, and pressed his lips to the top of her head.

"The Forest Service agent's questioned me twice. I had altercations with Dolly, then out of all the acres up there, I stumble right over what's left of her. Then, Leo Brakeman came here today."

She unburdened, stripped it out and off because he was there to cover her again.

"Leo's half mad with grief. In his place, I don't know what I'd do." Couldn't bear to think of it. "They'll find whoever did it. Maybe it'll help like they say it does, though I swear I don't know how."

"He was crying when he drove away. I think that was the moment I stopped feeling sorry for myself, because I'd been having a real good time with that."

"You were never able to stretch that out for long."

"I was going for the record. Dad, about before. I'm sorry."

"So am I." He wiped a hand through the air, a familiar gesture. "Clean slate."

"Squeaky clean."

"Where's that guy you've been hanging around with?"

"He's on the Flathead fire."

"Let's go check with Ops, see how they're doing."

"I want him back safe, want all of them back safe. Even though I'm pissed at him. Especially pissed because I think he had a point about a couple things."

"I hate when that happens. Besides, who does he think he is, having a point?"

She laughed, tipped her head to his shoulder. "Thanks."

SHE KEPT VIGIL in Operations, helped update the map tracking the crew's progress and the fire's twists and turns, and watched the lightning strikes blast on radar.

Sometime after two while a booming thunderstorm swept over the base, and up north Gull and his crewmates crawled into tents, she dropped into bed.

And almost immediately dropped into the dream.

The roar of thunder became the roar of engines, the scream of wind the air blasting through the plane's open door. She saw the nerves in Jim's eyes, heard them in his voice and, tossing in bed, ordered herself to stop him. To contact base, alert the spotter, talk to the fire boss.

Something.

"It is what it is," he said to her, with eyes now filled with sorrow. "It's, you know, my fate."

And he jumped as he always did, taking that last leap behind her. Into the mouth of the fire, screaming as its teeth tore through him.

This time she landed alone, the flames behind her snarling, throaty growls that built until the ground shook. She ran, sprinting up the incline, heat drenching her skin while she shoved through billowing clouds of smoke.

She shouted for Jim—there was a chance, always a chance—searching blindly. Fire climbed the trees in pulsing strings of light, blew over the ground in a deadly dance. Through it, someone called her name.

She changed direction and, shouting until her throat burned, stumbled into the black. Charred branches punched out of smoldering spots and beckoned like bony fingers. Snags hunched and towered, seemed to shift and sway behind the curtain of smoke. The scorched earth crackled under her feet as she continued to run toward the sound of her name.

Silence dropped, like a breath held. She stood in that void of sound, dismayed, disoriented. For a moment it was as if she'd become trapped in a black-and-white photo. Nothing moved, even as she ran on. The ground stayed silent under her feet.

She saw him, lying on the ground the fire had stripped bare, facing west, as if positioned to watch the sunset. Her voice echoed inside her head as she called his name. Dizzy with relief, she dropped down beside him.

Jim. Thank God.

She pulled out her radio, but like the air around her, it answered with silence.

I found him! Somebody answer. Somebody help me!

"They can't."

She tumbled back when Jim's voice broke the silence, when behind his mask his eyes opened, behind his mask his lips curved in a horrible smile.

"We burn here. We all burn here."

Flames ignited behind his mask. Even as she drew breath to scream, he gripped her hand. Fire fused her flesh to his.

She screamed, and kept screaming as the flames engulfed them both.

ROWAN DRAGGED HERSELF out of bed, stumbled to the window. She shoved it up, gulping in the air that streamed in. The storm had moved east, taking the rain and the boiling thunder with it. Sometime during the hideous dream the sky had broken clear of the clouds. She studied the stars to steady herself, taking comfort in their cool bright shine.

A bad day, that was all, she thought. She'd had a bad day that had brought on a bad night. Now it was done, out of her system. Put to rest.

But she left the window open, wanting that play of air as she got back in bed, and lay for a time, eyes open, looking at the stars.

As she started to drift something about the dream tapped at the back of her brain. She closed down to it, thought of the stars instead. She kept that cool, bright light in her mind's eye as she slipped into quiet, dreamless sleep.

ROWAN AND A MOP-UP TEAM jumped the Flathead mid-morning. While grateful for the work, the routine—however tedious—she couldn't deny some disappointment that Gull and his team packed out as she came in.

While she did her job, Special Agent Kimberly DiCicco did hers. She met Quinniock at a diner off Highway 12. He slid into the booth across from her, nodded. "Agent."

"Lieutenant. Thanks for meeting me."

"No problem. Just coffee," he told the waitress.

"I'll get right down to it, if that's okay," DiCicco began when the waitress had turned over the cup already in place, filled it and moved off.

"Saves time."

"You know the area better than I do, the people better than I do. You know more of the connections, the frictions, and you just recently questioned the victim over the vandalism. I could use your help."

"The department's always happy to cooperate, especially since your asking saves me from coming to you trying to wrangle a way in. Or working around you if you refused."

"Saves time," she said, echoing him, "and trouble. You have a good reputation, Lieutenant."

"As do you. And according to Rowan Tripp, we're both snappy dressers."

DiCicco smiled, very faintly. "That is a nice tie."

"Thanks. It appears we've taken the time and trouble to check each other out. My thinking, it's your jurisdiction, Agent Di-Cicco, but the victim is one of mine. We'll get what we both want quicker if we play to our strengths. Why don't you tell me who you're looking at, and I might be able to give you some insight."

"Let's take the victim first. I think I have a sense of her after reviewing the evidence, compiling interviews and observations. My leading conclusion is Dolly Brakeman was a liar, by nature and design, with some self-deception thrown in."

"I wouldn't argue with that conclusion. She was also impulsive, while at the same time being what I call a stewer. She tended to hoard bad feelings, perceived insults, and let them stew—then act impulsively with the switch flipped."

"Taking off when Jim Brayner died," DiCicco said, "even though it was a time she'd have most needed and benefited from home, family, support."

"She had a fight with her father."

DiCicco sat back. "I wondered."

"I got this from Mrs. Brakeman, when I talked to her after the vandalism at the base. Dolly came home out of her mind after learning of Jim's accident, and that's when she told her parents she was pregnant, and that she'd quit her job. Brakeman didn't take it well. They went at each other, and he said something along the lines of her getting her ass back to base, getting her job back or finding somebody else to freeload on. Dolly packed up and lit out. A little more maneuvering got me the fact that she packed up her parents' five-hundred-dollar cash emergency envelope for good measure."

"Five hundred doesn't take you far."

"Her mother sent her money now and again. And when Dolly called from Bozeman, in labor, the Brakemans drove out, patched things up."

"Babies are excellent glue."

"Dolly claimed to have been saved, and joined her mother's church when they all came home."

"Reverend Latterly's church. I got that, and I've spoken to him. He made a point of telling me Leo Brakeman didn't attend church." She thought of what Marg had said over lemonade and cookies. "I can't say I liked his way. His passive-aggressive way," she added, and Quinniock nodded agreement. "He seems to feel Little Bear, Rowan Tripp, the rest of them failed to show Christian charity to a troubled soul. As harsh as it was, I prefer Leo Brakeman's honest grief and rage."

"Whatever his way, Irene Brakeman claims he helped the three of them—herself, her husband and Dolly, come to terms once she was back. What Dolly left out when she called her parents for help, and I found after some poking around, was she'd made arrangements for a private adoption in Bozeman, which had paid her expenses."

"She planned to give the baby up?"

"She's the only one who knows what she planned, but she didn't contact the adoptive parents when she went into labor, nor the OB they'd paid for. Instead she went to the ER of a hospital across town and gave her Missoula address. By the time the other party found out what had happened, she was on her way back here. Since birth mothers have a right to change their minds, there wasn't much they could do."

DiCicco flipped open her notebook. "Do you have their names?"

"Yeah. I'll give you all of it, but I don't think we're going to find either of these people tracked Dolly down here and killed her, then set fire to the forest."

"Maybe not, but it's a strong motive."

"Are you still looking at Rowan Tripp?"

DiCicco sat back as the waitress breezed by to top off their coffee. "Let me tell you about Rowan Tripp. She's got a temper. She's got considerable power—physical strength, strength of will. She disliked Dolly intensely, on a personal level and in general terms. Her alibi is a man she's currently sleeping with. Men will lie for sex."

DiCicco paused to tip a fraction of a teaspoon of sugar into her coffee. "Dolly claimed Rowan had it in for her because Brayner tossed Rowan over for her. She was a liar," DiCicco added before Quinniock could respond. "Rowan Tripp isn't. In fact, she's almost brutally up-front. If Dolly had had her face punched in, I'd put my finger on Tripp. But the kill spot off the road, the broken neck, the arson? That doesn't jibe with my observations. Whoever killed her and put her in the forest might have expected the fire to burn her to ash, or at least for it to take more time for the remains to be discovered. It would've been monumentally stupid for Tripp to call the discovery in, and she's not stupid."

"We agree on that."

"Sticking with the victim, I've spent some time trying to verify her claim she had work in Florence. So far, I haven't been able to verify. I've started checking places like this, along the highway, but I haven't found any that hired her, or anyone who remembers her coming in looking for work. And, given her history, I'm wondering why she'd go to the trouble of looking for work down this way when she recently deposited ten thousand dollars in two hits of five—I traced it back to Matthew Brayner—in a bank in Lolo. Not her usual bank," DiCicco added, "which leads me to believe she didn't want anyone knowing about it. Which likely includes her parents."

He hadn't hit on the money—yet—and money always mattered. "She might've been thinking about running again."

"She might have. There's another pattern in her history. Men. Which is why I'm going to start checking motels along the route from Florence to Missoula. Maybe she decided to try out the other Brayner brother."

"Sex and money and guilt." Quinniock nodded. "The trifecta of motives. Want to get started?"

17

Gull sat on his bed with his laptop. He'd answered personal e-mail, attached a couple of pictures he'd taken that morning of the mountains, of the camp. He'd done a little business and now brought up his hometown paper to scan the sports section.

He knew the jump ship was back, and wondered how long it would take Rowan to knock on his door.

She would, he thought, even if just to pick up the fight where they'd left off. She wasn't the avoid-and-evade type, and, even if she were, it was damn near impossible to avoid and evade him while working on the same base.

He could wait.

Out of curiosity he did a Google search for wildfire arson investigation, and while he sifted through the results, considered heading into the lounge to see what was up, or maybe see if Dobie wanted to drive into town.

Always easier to wait when you're occupied, he thought. Then an article caught his interest. He answered the knock on the door absently.

"Yeah, it's open."

"Unlocked is different than open."

He glanced over. Rowan leaned on the jamb.

"It's open now."

She left the door ajar as she stepped in, and angled to see the laptop screen. "You're boning up on arson?"

"Specific to wildfire. It seemed relevant at the moment. How'd the mop-up go?"

"You left a hell of a mess." She shifted her gaze from the screen to his face. "I heard things got hairy up there."

"There were moments." He smiled. "Missed you."

"Because I'm so good or so good-looking?"

"All of the above." He shut down the computer. "Why don't we take a walk, catch the sunset."

"Yeah, all right."

When they went out, she pulled her sunglasses out of her pocket. "The fact that I'm surprised and not happy that my father's involved with a woman I don't know and he didn't tell me about doesn't make me jealous."

"Is that what we're calling it? Surprised and not happy. I'd've defined it as outraged and incensed."

"Due to the surprise." She clipped the words off.

"I'll give you that," Gull decided, "since you've apparently gone your entire life without witnessing a lip-lock."

"I don't think I overreacted. Very much."

"Why quibble about degrees?"

"I'm not apologizing for telling you to butt the hell out."

"Then I don't have to be gracious and accept a nonexistent apology. I'm not apologizing for expressing my opinion over your not very much of an overreaction."

"Then I guess we're even."

"Close enough. It's a hell of a sunset."

She stood with him, watching the sun sink toward the western peaks, watched it drown in the sea of red and gold and delicate lavender it spawned.

"I don't have to like her, and I sure as hell don't have to trust her."

"You're like a dog with a bone, Rowan."

"Maybe. But it's my bone."

Silence, Gull thought, could express an opinion as succinctly as words. "So. I heard about Dolly's father coming down on you."

"Over and done."

"I don't think so."

"Are you butting in again, Gull?"

"If you want to call it that. You've got to have sympathy for a man dealing with what he's dealing with, so maybe he gets a pass this time. But that's what's over and done. Nobody lays into my girl."

"Your girl? I'm not your girl."

"Are we or are we not together here and watching the sunset? And isn't it most likely you and I will end up naked in bed together tonight?"

"Regardless—"

"Regardless, my ass." He grabbed her chin, pulled her in for a kiss. "That makes you my girl."

"Holy hell, Gull, you're making my back itch."

Amused, he scratched it, then hooked an arm around her shoulders and kept walking. "So, later. Your place or mine?"

With the light softening, she pulled her sunglasses off, then swung them by the earpiece. "Some people are intimidated or put off by a certain level of confidence."

"You're not."

"No, I'm not. Fortunately for you, I like it. Let's—" She jerked back at the sharp crack in the air. "Jesus, was that—"

The breath whooshed out of her lungs when Gull knocked her to the ground and landed on top of her.

"Stay down," he ordered, and saw a bullet dig into the ground six feet away. "Hold on to me. We're going to roll." The minute her arms clamped around him, he pushed his body over, felt her do the same, so they covered the ground in a fast, ungainly roll to shield themselves behind one of the jeeps parked outside a hangar.

A third report snapped, pinging metal overhead.

"Where's it coming from? Can you tell?"

Gull shook his head, keeping his body over hers while he waited for the next shot. But silence held as seconds ticked by, then shattered with the shouts and rushing feet.

"For Christ's sake, get down, get cover," he called out. "There's a sniper."

Dobie bolted for the jeep, dived. "Are you hit? Are you— Goddamn, Gull, you're bleeding."

Rowan bucked under him. "Get off, get off. Let me see."

"Just scraped up from the asphalt. I'm not shot. Stay down."

"Rifle." Dobie shifted to a crouch. "I know a rifle shot when I hear one. From over there in the trees, I think. Damn good thing he's a shitty shot 'cause the two of you were sitting ducks. Standing ducks."

"Hey!" Trigger called from the far side of the hangar. "Is anybody hurt?"

"We're okay," Rowan answered. "Don't come out here. He may be waiting for somebody to step into the clear."

"L.B.'s got the cops coming. Just stay where you are for now."

"Copy that. Get off me, Gull."

"He tackled you good," Dobie commented when Gull pushed off. "You know he played football in high school. Quarterback."

"Isn't that interesting?" Rowan muttered it as she turned Gull's arm over to examine the bloody scrapes on his elbows and forearms. "You got grit in these."

"I liked basketball better," Gull said conversationally. "But I didn't have the height to compete. Had the speed, but I'd topped out at six feet until senior year when I had a spurt and added two more. Baseball, now, I like that better than either. Had a pretty good arm back in the day."

Maybe talking kept his mind off the scrapes, she decided, because they had to sting like hell.

"I thought you were the track star."

"My best thing, but I like sports, so I dabbled. Anyway, I liked collecting letters. I graduated a four-letter man."

Rowan studied him in the fading light. "We're sitting behind this jeep, hiding from some nutcase with a rifle, and you're actually bragging about your high-school glory days?"

"It passes the time. Plus I had very impressive glory days." He brushed dirt off her cheek. "We're okay."

"If you two are going to get sloppy, I'm not looking the other way." Dobie leaned back against the tire. "Wish I had a beer."

"Once this little interlude's over," Gull told him, "the first round's on me."

"I was thinking about going to the lounge, kicking back

with some screen and a beer. Just stepped outside for a minute, and *bam! bam!*"

"So you ran out, in the open, instead of back in?" Rowan demanded.

"I wasn't sure if either of you were hit or not, the way you both went down."

Rowan leaned over Gull, kissed Dobie on the mouth. "Thanks."

"I'm not kissing you. He's gone," Gull added. "He took off after the third shot."

"I expect so," Dobie agreed. "It's full dusk now. He can't see squat, unless he's got infrared."

"Let's go." Rowan pushed up to her haunches. "If he wants to shoot us, he could circle around in the dark and get us while we're sitting here."

"She's got a point. Don't run in a straight line. That's what they say in the movies," Gull pointed out. "Barracks?"

"Barracks," Dobie agreed.

Before either man could react, Rowan sprang up, a runner off the blocks, and revved straight into a sprint.

"Goddamn it."

Gull raced after her—could have caught her, passed her, they both knew. But he stayed at her back, zigging when she zigged, zagging when she zagged.

"We're coming in!" Rowan called out, then hit the door.

"What the hell were you thinking?" Gull grabbed her, spun her around. "Taking off like that?"

"I was thinking you weren't going to be my human shield twice in one day. I appreciate the first, I'm not stupid."

"You don't get to decide for me."

"Right back at you."

They shouted at each other while people shouted around them. Libby let out a piercing whistle. "Shut up! Shut the hell up. Everybody!" She shoved her hands through the hair dripping from the shower she'd leaped out of. "Gull, you're bleeding on the floor. Somebody get a first-aid kit and clean him up. The cops are on their way. Okay, the cops are here," she amended when the sirens sounded. "L.B. wants everybody inside until . . . until we know something."

"Come on, Gull." Janis gave him a light pat on the butt. "I'll be Nurse Betty."

"Is everybody accounted for?" Rowan asked.

"Between here, the cookhouse and Operations, we're all good." Yangtree stepped forward, drew her in for a hug that nearly cracked her ribs. "I was watching TV. I thought it was a backfire. Then Trig came running through, said somebody was shooting, and you were out there." He drew her back. "What the fuck, Ro?"

"My thought exactly. Why would somebody shoot at us?"

"People are batshit." Dobie shrugged. "Maybe one of those government's-our-enemy types. Y'all got those militia types out here."

"Three shots isn't much of a statement."

"It would've been," Trigger pointed out, "if one of them had hit you or Gull."

"Your father's going to hear about this, Ro," Yangtree commented. "You call him now before he does, tell him you're okay."

"Yeah, you're right." She glanced down toward Gull's quarters before she stepped into her own to make the call.

Steaming, Gull endured the sting as Janis cleaned out cuts and scrapes. "What the hell's wrong with her?"

"Since the blood on her appeared to be mostly yours, not much. And I know you're talking about how she thinks or acts, but you'll have to be more specific."

"How can somebody trained to be a team player, who *is* a team player in ninety percent of her life, be the damn opposite the other ten?"

"First, smoke jumpers work as a crew, but you know damn well we all have to think, act and react individually. But more to the point, with Rowan it's defense mechanism, pride, an instinctive hesitation to trust."

"Defense against what?"

"Against having her pride smacked and her trust betrayed. Personally, I think she's dealt pretty well with being abandoned by her mother as an infant. But I don't think anybody ever gets all the way over being abandoned. Okay, I'm going to need to use the tweezers to get some of this debris out. Feel free to curse me."

He said, "Fuck," then gritted his teeth. "You trust every time you get in the door. The spotter, the pilot, yourself. Hell, you have to trust fate isn't going to send a speeding bus your way every time you step out of your house. If you can't take that same leap with another human being, you end up alone."

"I think she's always figured she would. She's got her father, us, a tight pack of people. But a serious, committed one-to-one? She's not sure she believes in them in general, much less for herself."

A bit of gravel hit the bowl with a tiny ting. "I've worked with Ro a long time. She's a proactive optimist in general. In that she—or we, depending—will find a way to make this work. In her personal life, she's a proactive pessimist who has no problem living in the moment because this isn't going to last anyway."

"She's wrong."

"Nobody's proven that to her yet." She glanced up. "Can you?"

"If I don't bleed to death from this sadistic game of Operation you're playing."

"I haven't hit the buzzer yet. You're the first guy, in my opinion, who has a shot at proving her wrong. So don't screw it up. There." She dropped more grit into the bowl. "I think that's it. You lost a lot of skin here, Gull," she began as she applied antiseptic. "Banged up your elbows pretty good, but it could've been a hell of a lot worse."

"Not to knock the results, but I keep wondering why it wasn't a hell of a lot worse."

He looked over at the rap on the door frame. As she had earlier, Rowan leaned on the jamb, but now she had two beers hooked in her fingers. "I brought the patient a beer."

"He could probably use one." Janis bandaged the gouges around his right elbow. "Any word?"

"The cops have the grounds lit up like Christmas. If they've found anything, they're not sharing it yet."

"Okay. You're as done as I can do." Janis picked up the bowl filled with grit, bloodied cloths and cotton swipes. "Take two ibuprofen and call me in the morning."

"Thanks, Janis."

She gave his leg a squeeze as she rose. "None but the brave," she said, then walked out.

Rowan stepped over, offered a beer. "Do you want to fight?"

Watching her over the bottle, he took a long swallow. "Yeah."

"Seems like a waste, considering, but fine. Pick your topic."

"Let's start with the latest—we can always work back— and how you ran, alone, into the open out there."

"We'd decided to try for the barracks, so I did."

"Of the three of us, I'm the fastest—and the one best qualified to draw and evade fire, if there'd been any."

"I said I like overconfidence, but this idea you can dodge bullets might be taking it too far. I can and do take care of myself, Gull. I do it every day. I'm going to keep doing it."

He considered himself a patient, reasonable man—mostly. But she'd just about flipped his last switch.

"The fact you can and do take care of yourself is one of the most appealing things about you. You idiot. Handling yourself on a jump, in a fire or in general, no problem. This was different."

"How?"

"Have you ever been shot at before?"

"No. Have you?"

"First time for both of us, and clearly a situation where you should have trusted me to take care of you."

"I don't want anybody to take care of me."

"You know, that's just stupid. Janis just took care of me, yet somehow my pride and self-esteem remain unbattered and unbowed."

"Bandaging somebody up isn't the same as falling on them like they were a grenade you were going to smother with your own body to save the guys in the trenches. And look at you, Gull. I've barely got a scrape because you took the brunt of that roll instead of letting me take my share."

"I protect what I care about. If you've got a problem with that, you've got a problem with me."

"I protect what I care about," she tossed back at him.

"Were you protecting a fellow smoke jumper, or me?"

"You *are* a fellow smoke jumper."

He stepped closer. "Is it what I do, or who I am? And don't try the 'you are what you do' because I'm a hell of a lot more, and less, and dozens of other things. So are you. I care about you, Rowan. The you who's got a laugh like an Old West saloon girl, the you who picks out constellations in the night sky and smells like peaches. I care about that woman as much as I do the fearless, smart, tireless one who puts her life on the line every time the siren goes off."

Wariness clouded her eyes. "I don't know what to say when you talk like that."

"Is the only thing you see when you look at me another jumper you'll work with for the season?"

"No." She let out an unsteady breath. "No, that's not all, but—"

"Stop at no." He cupped a hand at the back of her neck. "Do us both a favor and stop at no. That's enough for now."

She moved into him, wrapping her arms tight around his waist when their lips met. She felt her equilibrium shift, as if she'd nearly overbalanced on a high ledge. With it came a flutter, under her heart, at the base of her throat. She gripped harder, wanting to find the heat, the buzz, an affirmation that they were both alive and whole.

Nothing more than that, she told herself. It didn't have to be more than that.

"Getting a room's not always enough," Trigger said from the doorway. "Sometimes you gotta close the door."

"Go ahead," Gull invited him, then slid back into the kiss.

"Sorry, they want you in the lounge."

"Who are 'they'?" Rowan demanded, and gave Gull's bottom lip a nip.

"The lieutenant guy and the tree cop. If you're not interested in finding out who the hell *shot* at you tonight, I can tell them, gee, you're out on a date."

Gull lifted his head. "Be right there." He looked at Rowan, ran his hands over her shoulders, down her arms. "My place," he said. "The decision that was so rudely interrupted earlier. My place tonight because it's closer to the lounge."

"Not a bad reason." She picked up the beers, handed him his. "Let's get this done so we can close the door."

DiCicco sat with Quinniock and L.B. in the lounge. Generally at that time of the evening, people sprawled on sofas and chairs watching TV, or gathered around one of the tables playing cards. Somebody might've buzzed up some microwave pizza or popcorn. And there would always be somebody willing to talk fire.

But now the TV screen remained blank and silent, the sofas empty.

L.B. got up from the table, walked quickly over to wrap an arm around Gull and Rowan in turn. "You're okay. That matters most. Next is finding the bastard."

"Did they find anything?" Rowan asked.

"If we could get your statements first." DiCicco gestured to the table. "It should help us get a clearer picture."

"The picture's clear," Rowan countered. "Somebody shot at us. He missed."

"And when you file a fire report, does it just say: 'Fire started. We put it out'?"

"If we could just take it from the beginning." Quinniock held up his hands for peace. "The witness, Dobie Karstain, says he stepped outside the barracks around nine thirty. A few minutes later, he noticed the two of you walking together between the training field and the hangar area, approximately thirty yards from the trees. Does that sound accurate?"

"That's about right." Gull took the lead, as it seemed obvious to him DiCicco put Rowan's back up. "We went for a walk, took a couple of beers, watched the sunset. You'd narrow down where we were if you find the bottles. We dropped them when the shooting started."

He took them through it, step by step.

"Dobie said it sounded like rifle fire," he continued, "and it was coming from the trees. He grew up hunting in rural Kentucky, so I'm inclined to believe he's right. We couldn't see anyone. The first shot fired right around sunset. The whole thing probably only lasted about ten minutes. It seemed longer."

"Have either of you had trouble with anyone, been threatened?" When Rowan merely arched her eyebrows, DiCicco inclined her head. "Other than Leo Brakeman."

"We're a little too busy around here to get into arguments with the locals or tourists."

"Actually, there was an incident with you, Mr. Curry, Ms. Tripp and Mr. Karstain in the spring."

"That would be when Rowan objected to one of those three yahoos' behavior toward her, and them sopping their pride by ganging up on Dobie when he came out of the bar."

"And you kicking their asses," Rowan concluded. "Good times."

"The same holds true on them as it did when we had the vandalism," Gull continued. "It's pretty hard to see them coming back here. And harder still to see any one of them staking us out from the woods and taking shots at us when we went for a walk. We're in and out all the damn time anyway. Together, separately. It's stretching it even more to figure those bozos from Illinois came all the way back, then got lucky when Ro and I walked out to give them some target practice."

"How do you know they're from Illinois?" DiCicco asked.

"Because that's what the plate on the pickup said—and I did some checking on it after the ready room business."

"You never told me that."

Gull shrugged at Rowan. "It didn't amount to anything to tell you. The big guy—and he was the alpha—owns a garage out in Rockford. He's an asshole, and he's had a few bumps for assaults—bar fights his specialty—but nothing major." He shrugged again when DiCicco studied him. "The Internet. You can find out anything if you keep looking."

"All right. You two have recently become involved," DiCicco said. "Is there anyone who might resent that? Any former relationship?"

"I don't date the kind of woman who'd take a shot at me." He gave Rowan the eye. "Until maybe now."

"I shoot all my former lovers, so your fate's already set."

"Only if we get to the former part." He covered her hand with his. "It was either a local with a grudge against one or both of us specially, or the base in general. Or a wacko who wanted to shoot up a federal facility."

"A terrorist?"

"I think a terrorist would've used more ammo," Gull said to DiCicco. "But any way you slice it, he was a crap shot.

Unless he's a really good shot and was just trying to scare and intimidate."

Rowan's gaze sharpened. "I didn't think of that."

"I think a lot. I can't swear to it, but I think the closest one hit about six or seven feet away from where we hit the ground. That's not a comfortable distance when bullets are involved, but it's a distance. Another sounded like it hit metal, the hangar. Way above our heads. Maybe it'll turn out to be a couple of kids on a dare. Smoke jumpers think they're so cool, let's go make them piss their pants.

"It's a theory," he claimed when Rowan rolled her eyes.

"Lieutenant." A uniformed cop stepped in.

"Hi, Barry."

"Ro. Glad you're okay. Sir, we found the weapon, or what we believe to be the weapon."

"Where?"

"About twenty yards into the trees. A Remington 700 model—bolt action. The special edition. It was covered up with leaves."

"Stupid," Rowan mumbled. "Stupid to leave it there."

"More stupid if it's got a brass name plaque on the stock," L.B. said. "I went hunting with Leo Brakeman last fall, and he carried a special edition 700. He was real proud of it."

Rowan's hand balled into a fist under Gull's. "So much for theories."

When DiCicco and Quinniock went out to examine the weapon, L.B. walked over to the coffeemaker.

"You know," Ro said, "she told those lies to her father. All those lies, and they drove him to come out here with a gun and try to kill me."

"I'd say you're half right." L.B. sat with his coffee, sighed. "The lies drove him to come out here with a gun, but, like I said, I've been hunting with Leo. I saw him take down a buck with that rifle, at thirty yards with the buck on the run. If he'd wanted to put a bullet in you, you'd have a bullet in you."

"I guess it was my lucky day then."

"Something snapped in him. I'm not excusing him, Ro. There's no excuse for this. But something's snapped in him. What the hell's Irene going to do now? Her daughter murdered, and her husband likely locked up, an infant to care for. She hasn't even buried Dolly yet, and now this."

"I'm sorry for them. For all of them."

"Yeah, it's a damn sorry situation. I'm going to go see if the cops will tell me what happens next." He went out, leaving his untouched coffee behind.

18

Too wound up to sit, Rowan pushed up, wandered the room, peeked out the window, circled back. Gull propped his feet on the chair she'd vacated and decided to drink L.B.'s abandoned coffee.

"I want to *do* something," Rowan complained. "Just sitting here doesn't feel right. How can you just sit here?"

"I'm doing something."

"Drinking coffee doesn't count as something."

"I'm sitting here, I'm drinking coffee. And I'm thinking. I'm thinking if it's Brakeman's rifle, and if Brakeman was the one shooting it, did he just go stand in the trees and assume you'd eventually wander out into range?"

"I don't know if it had to be me. He's pissed at all of us, just mostly at me."

"Okay, possible." He found the coffee bitter, wished for a little sugar to cut the edge. But just didn't feel like getting up for it. "So Brakeman stands in the woods with his rifle, staking out the base. He gets lucky and we come along. If he's as good a shot as advertised, why did he miss?"

"Because it has to be a hell of a lot different to shoot a

human being than a buck. Nerves. Or he couldn't bring himself to kill me—us—and decided to scare us to death instead."

"Also possible. Why leave the weapon? Why leave a special edition, which had to cost, which he cared enough about to put his name on, under a pile of leaves? Why leave it behind at all when he had to know the cops would do a search?"

"Panic. Impulse. He wasn't thinking clearly—obviously. Hide it, get out, come back for it another time. And maybe take a few more shots." She stopped, rubbed at the tension in the back of her neck as she studied Gull. "And you don't think Leo Brakeman shot at us."

"I think it might be interesting to know who had access to his gun. Who might've liked causing him trouble, and wouldn't feel too bad about scaring you doing it." He sipped at the coffee. "But it could've been Brakeman following impulse, getting lucky, being nervous and panicking."

"When you say it like that, it's a lot to swallow."

She plopped down in L.B.'s chair as Gull had opened her mind to alternatives. And thinking *was* doing, she reminded herself.

"I guess his wife would have access, but I have a hard time seeing her doing this. Plus, I've never heard of her going hunting or target shooting. She's more the church-bake-sale type. And it's easier to believe she might panic because she's more the quiet, even a little timid, type. If you get past the first step, her actually coming out here with a rifle, the rest goes down.

"Maybe a double bluff," she considered aloud. "He left the rifle so he could say, hey, would anybody be that stupid? But I don't know if he'd be that cagey. I just don't know these people very well. We've never had much interaction, even when Dolly worked here. Which means I don't know if anybody's got a grudge against Brakeman, or would know enough to use him as a fall guy. It's easier if it's Brakeman. Then it would be done, and there wouldn't be anything to worry about."

"It's up to the cops anyway. We can let it go."

"That's passive, and that's what's driving me crazy. Who killed Dolly? That's the first question. Jesus, Gull, what if her father did?"

"Why?"

"I don't know." She hooked her feet around the legs of the

chair, leaned forward. "Say they had a fight. Say she's coming back from Florence—if she got work there like she claimed—gets the flat. Calls her father to come fix it. I can't picture Dolly with a lug wrench and jack. He comes out, and they get into it over something. Her dumping the baby on her mother so much, maybe having the kid in the first place, or just dragging him out that time of night. Things get out of hand. She takes a fall, lands wrong, breaks her neck. He freaks, puts her body in the truck. He's got to figure out what to do, decides to destroy the evidence—and the rest follows. He knows the area, the trails, and he's strong enough to have carried her in."

"Plausible," Gull decided. "Maybe he confesses to his wife, and you get part two. There's another hypothesis."

"Share."

"You said you didn't know Dolly that well, but you had definite opinions about her. Jim died last August. We're moving toward July. Is she the type to be without a man for a year?"

Rowan opened her mouth, shut it again, then sat back. "No. And why didn't I think of that? No, she'd never go this long without a man. There's a stronger case for that knowing that her whole I-found-Jesus deal was bogus."

"Maybe the current guy's in Florence. Maybe that's why she got work there, or said she did. Or maybe they just met up in a motel on Twelve or thereabouts."

"Lovers' quarrel, and *he* kills her. If there's a he. There had to be—it's Dolly. Or her father found out, and so on. But if she had one on the line in Florence, why come back here anyway? Why not just go there, be with him? Because he's married," Rowan said before Gull could comment. "She fooled around with married men all the time."

"If so, it's more likely he's in Missoula. She came back here, got work here at the base. She'd want to be close to whoever she was sleeping with. Say, he's married, or there's some other reason why they can't be open about a relationship. Then you have the meet-up somewhere away from where people know you, would recognize you."

"You're good at this."

"It's like playing a game. You work the levels." He took her hand again. "Except it's not characters, it's real people."

"It still feels better to play it through. And here's another thing. Dolly wasn't nearly as smart or clever as she liked to think. If she was sleeping with somebody, she'd have dropped hints. Maybe to Marg. More likely to Lynn. She was going to church, so maybe to somebody she made friends with there."

"It would be interesting to find out."

"It would." She needed to move again, do more than think. "Why don't we go outside, see what's going on?"

"Good idea."

"Quinniock likes me, I think. Maybe he'll give us a couple of nibbles."

When they went out, she spotted Barry heading toward his patrol car. "Hey, Barry. Is Lieutenant Quinniock around?"

"He and Agent DiCicco just left. Do you need something, Ro?"

She gave Gull a quick glance. "I could sure use a little reassurance. I'd sleep better tonight."

"I can tell you the weapon we found is Leo Brakeman's. The lieutenant and DiCicco are on their way to his place to talk to him."

"Talk."

"That's the first step. I had to back up Little Bear when he told them Leo's a damn good shot. I don't know if it makes you feel better or not, but I don't think he was aiming for you."

"It doesn't make me feel worse."

"He was wrong blaming you for what happened to Dolly. Some people just can't get their lives together."

"I meant to ask Lieutenant Quinniock if they found out where she'd gotten work. Maybe somebody she knew or met there killed her."

Barry hesitated, then shrugged. "It doesn't look like she was working. It's nothing for you to worry about, Ro."

"Barry." She put a hand on his arm. "Come on. I'm in the middle of this whether I want to be or not. What was she doing coming back from down that way if she didn't have a job?"

"I can't say for sure, and I shouldn't say at all." He puffed out his cheeks as she kept looking into his eyes. "All I know is the police artist is scheduled to work with somebody tomorrow. The word is it's a maid from some motel down off Twelve.

Whoever he is, if we can ID him, the lieutenant's going to want to talk to him."

"Thanks, Barry." She moved in to hug him. "Erin got lucky with you. Tell her I said so."

"I'll do that. And you don't worry. We're looking out for you."

Gull slipped his hands in his pockets as Barry got in the car. "You didn't come down on him for saying he was looking out for you."

"Cops are supposed to look out for everybody. Besides, Barry gets a pass. He was my first. Actually we were each other's firsts, a scenario I don't necessarily recommend unless both participants have a solid sense of humor. That was several years before he met Erin, his wife, and the mother of his two kids."

"My first was Becca Rhodes. She was a year older and experienced. It went quite smoothly."

"Are you still friends with Becca Rhodes?"

"I haven't seen her since high school."

"See? Humor wins out. Dolly never worked in Florence," Rowan added. "Our little what-if session hit a mark. A man, a motel—possibly a murderer." She tipped her head back, found the sky. "I feel less useless and victimized. That counts for a lot. I'm going to talk to Lynn first chance I get, just to see if Dolly dropped any crumbs."

Time to put it away for the night, Gull decided, and draped an arm over her shoulders. "Pick one out for me. A constellation. Not the Dippers. Even I can find them. Usually."

"Okay. Then you'll spot Ursa Minor there." She took his hand, used it to outline the connection of stars. "Now, the stars in this one aren't very bright, but if you follow that west, connect the dots, going south and over—it winds around the Little Dipper, see? There. You've got Draco. The dragon. It seems apt for a couple of smoke jumpers."

"Yeah, I get it. Pretty cool. Now that we've got our constellation, we just need to decide on our song."

He lightened her load, she thought. No doubt about it. "You're so full of it, Gulliver."

"Only because I have so much depth."

"Hell." She turned into him, indulged them both with a deep, dreamy kiss. "Let's go to bed."

"You read my mind."

"DID YOU FIND who killed my girl?" Leo demanded the minute he opened the door.

"Let's go inside and sit down," Quinniock suggested.

He and DiCicco had discussed their approach on the drive, and, as agreed, Quinniock took the lead. "Mrs. Brakeman, we'd like to talk with both of you."

Irene Brakeman linked her hands together at her heart. "It's about Dolly. You know who hurt Dolly."

"We're pursuing several avenues of investigation." DiCicco kept her voice clipped. It wasn't quite good cop/bad cop, but more cold cop/warm cop. "There are some matters we need to clear up with you. To start with, Mr. Brakeman—"

Quinniock touched a hand to her arm. "Why don't we all sit down? I know it's late, but we'd appreciate if you gave us some time."

"We answered questions. We let you go through Dolly's room, through her things." Leo continued to bar the door with his knuckles white on the knob. "We were going up to bed. If you don't have anything new to tell us, just leave us in peace."

"There is no peace until we know who did this to Dolly." Irene's voice pitched, broke. "Go up to bed if you want to," Irene told her husband with a tinge of disgust. "I'll talk to the police. Go on upstairs and shake your fists at God, see if that helps. Please, come in."

She moved forward, a small woman who pushed her burly husband aside so that he stepped back, his head hung down like a scolded child's.

"I'm just tired, Reenie. I'm so damn tired. And you're wearing yourself to the bone, tending the baby and worrying."

"We're not asked to lift more than we can carry. So we'll lift this. Do you want some coffee, or tea, or anything?"

"Don't you worry about that, Mrs. Brakeman." Quinniock took a seat in the living room on a chair covered with blue and red flowers. "I know this is hard."

"We can't even bury her yet. They said you need to keep

her awhile more, so we can't give our daughter a Christian burial."

"We'll release her to you as soon as we can. Mrs. Brakeman, the last time we spoke, you said Dolly got a job in Florence, as a cook."

"That's right." She twisted her fingers together in her lap, a working woman's hands wearing a plain gold band. "She felt like she didn't want to take a job in Missoula after what went on at the base. I think she was embarrassed. She was embarrassed, Leo," Irene snapped as he started to object. "Or she should have been."

"They never treated her decent there."

"You know that's not true." She spoke more quietly now, briefly touched a hand to his. "You can't take her word as gospel now that she's gone when you know Dolly didn't tell the real truth half the time or more. They gave her a chance there," she said to Quinniock when Leo lapsed into brooding silence. "And Reverend Latterly and I vouched for her. She shamed herself, and us. She got work down there in Florence," Irene continued after she'd firmed quivering lips. "She was a good cook, our girl. It was something she liked, even when she was just a little thing. She could be a good worker when she put her mind to it. The hours were hard, especially with the baby, but the pay was good, and she said she could go places."

"You didn't remember the name of the restaurant when we spoke before," DiCicco prompted.

"I guess she never mentioned it." Irene pressed her lips together again. "I was angry with her about what she did to Rowan Tripp, and embarrassed my own self. It's hard knowing Dolly and I were at odds when she died. It's hard knowing that."

"I have to tell you, both of you, that Agent DiCicco and I have contacted or gone to every restaurant, diner, coffee shop between here and Florence, and Dolly didn't work in any of them."

"I don't understand."

"She wasn't working in a restaurant," DiCicco said briskly. "She didn't get a job, didn't leave here the night she died to go to work."

"Hell she didn't," Leo protested.

"On the night she died, and on the afternoon prior, the evening prior to that, Dolly spent several hours in a room at the Big Sky Motel, off Highway Twelve."

"That's a lie."

"Leo, hush." Irene gripped her hands together tighter.

"Several witnesses identified her photograph," Quinniock continued. "I'm sorry. She didn't spend those hours alone. She met a man there, the same man each time. We have a witness who'll be working with our police artist to reconstruct his face."

With tears trickling down her face, Irene nodded. "I was afraid of it. I knew in my heart she was lying, but I was so upset with her. I didn't care. Just go on then, I thought. Go on and do what you want, and I'll have this baby to tend. Then, after . . . after it happened, I took that out of my mind. I told myself I'd been harsh and judgmental, a cold mother."

"I knew she was lying," she said, turning to her husband. "I knew all the signs. But I couldn't let myself believe it when she was dead. I just couldn't have that inside me."

"Do you have any idea who she was involved with?"

"I swear to you I don't. But I think maybe it'd been going on awhile now. I know the signs. The way she'd whisper on the phone, or how she'd say she just needed to go out for a drive and clear her head, or had to run some errands so could I watch Shiloh? And she'd come home again with that look in her eye."

She let out a shuddering breath. "She never meant to change." Dissolving, Irene turned to press her face to Leo's shoulder. "Maybe she just couldn't."

"Why do we have to know this?" Leo demanded. "Why do you have to tell us this? You don't leave us anything."

"I'm sorry, but Dolly was with this man the night she died. We need to identify him and question him."

"He killed her. This man she gave herself to, this man she lied to us about."

"We need to question him," Quinniock repeated. "If you have any idea who she was meeting, we need to know."

"She lied to us. We don't know anything. We don't have anything. Just leave us alone."

"There's something else, Mr. Brakeman, we need to discuss." DiCicco took the ball. "At approximately nine thirty tonight, Rowan Tripp and Gulliver Curry were fired on while walking on the base."

"That's nothing to do with us."

"On the contrary, a Remington 700 special edition rifle was found hidden in the woods flanking the base. It has your name engraved in a plaque on the stock."

"You're accusing me of trying to kill that woman? You come into my home, tell me my daughter was a liar and a whore and say I'm a killer?"

"It's your gun, Mr. Brakeman, and you recently threatened Ms. Tripp."

"My daughter was *murdered*, and she . . . My rifle's in the gun safe. I haven't had it out in weeks."

"If that's the case, we'd like you to show us." DiCicco got to her feet.

"I'll show you, then I want you out of my house."

He lunged up, stomped his way back to the kitchen to yank open a door that led to a basement.

Or a man cave, DiCicco thought as she followed. Dead animal heads hung on the paneled wall in a wildlife menagerie that loomed over the oversized recliner and lumpy sofa. The table that fronted the sofa showed scars from years of boot heels and faced an enormous flat-screen television.

The room boasted an ancient refrigerator she imagined held manly drinks, a worktable for loading shot into shells, a utility shelf that held boxes of clay pigeons, shooting vests, hunting caps—and, oddly, she thought, several framed family photos, including a large one of a pretty baby girl with one of those elasticized pink bows circling her bald head.

A football lamp, a computer and piles of paperwork sat on a gray metal desk shoved in a corner. Above it hung a picture of Leo and several other men beside what she thought was a 747 aircraft, reminding her he worked at the airport as a mechanic.

And against the side wall stood a big, orange-doored gun safe.

Pumping off waves of heat and resentment, Leo marched to the safe, spun the dial for the combination, wrenched it open.

DiCicco had no problems with guns; in fact she believed in them. But the small arsenal inside the safe had her eyes widening. Rifles, shotguns, handguns—bolt action, semiauto, revolvers, under and overs, scopes. All showing the gloss of the well-cleaned, well-oiled, well-tended weapon.

But her scan didn't turn up the weapon in question, and her hand edged toward her own as Leo Brakeman's breathing went short and quick.

"You have an excellent collection of firearms, Mr. Brakeman, but you seem to be missing a Remington 700."

"Somebody stole it."

Her hand closed over the butt of her weapon when he whirled around, his face red, his fists clenched.

"Somebody broke in here and stole it."

"There's no record of you reporting a break-in." Quinniock stepped up.

"Because I didn't *know*. Somebody's doing this to us. You have to find out who's doing this to us."

"Mr. Brakeman, you're going to have to come with us now." She didn't want to draw on the man, hoped she wouldn't have to, but DiCicco readied to do so.

"You're not taking me out of my home."

"Leo." Quinniock spoke calmly. "Don't make it worse now. You come quietly, and we'll go in and talk about this. Or I'm going to have to cuff you and take you in forcibly."

"Leo." Irene simply collapsed onto a step. "My God, Leo."

"I didn't do anything. Irene, as God is my witness. I've never lied to you in my life, Reenie. I didn't do anything."

"Then let's go in and talk this out." Quinniock moved a step closer, laid a hand on Leo's quivering shoulder. "Let's try to get to the bottom of it."

"Somebody's doing this to us. I never shot at anybody out at the base, or anywhere else." He jerked away from Quinniock's hand. "I'll walk out on my own."

"All right, Leo. That would be best."

Stiff-legged, he walked toward the steps. He stopped, reached for his wife's hands. "Irene, on my life, I didn't shoot at anybody. I need you to believe me."

"I believe you." But she dropped her gaze when she said it.

"You need to lock up now. You be sure to lock up the house. I'll be home as soon as we straighten this out."

ROWAN GOT THE WORD when she slipped into the cookhouse kitchen the next morning.

Lynn set down the hot bin of pancakes she carried, then wrapped Rowan in a hug. "I'm glad you're all right. I'm glad everybody's all right."

"Me too."

"I don't know what to think. I don't know what to say." Shaking her head, she picked up the bin again. "I have to get these on the buffet."

At the stove, Marg scooped bacon from the grill, set it aside to drain before shifting over to pour a glass of juice. She held it out to Rowan. "Drink what's good for you," she ordered, then turned back to pull a batch of fresh biscuits from the oven. "They picked up Leo Brakeman last night."

Rowan drank the juice. "Do you know what he's saying?"

"I don't know a lot, but I know they talked to him for a long time last night, and they're holding him. I know he's saying he didn't do it. I'm feeling like Lynn. I don't know what to think."

"I think it was stupid to leave the rifle. Then again, the cops would do their CSI thing since they found at least one of the bullets. Then again, with his skill, at that range, he could've put all three of them into me."

"Don't say that."

At the crack of Marg's voice, Rowan walked over, rubbed a hand down Marg's back. "He didn't, so I can come in here and drink a juice combo of carrots, apples, pears and parsnips."

"You missed the beets."

"So that's what that was. They're better in juice than on a plate."

Marg moved aside to take a carton of eggs out of the refrigerator. "Go on in and eat your breakfast. I've got hungry mouths to feed."

"I wanted to ask you. I wanted to ask both of you," she said when Lynn came back with another empty tub. "Was Dolly seeing someone? Did she say anything about being involved?"

"She knew better than to start that business up around me," Marg began, "when she kept saying how she was next thing to a grieving widow, and finding her comfort in God and her baby. But I doubt she stepped outside on a break to giggle on her cell phone because she'd called Dial-A-Joke."

"She didn't tell me anything, not directly," Lynn put in. "But she said, a couple of times, how lucky I was to have a daddy for my kids, and how she knew her baby needed one, too. She said she spent a lot of time praying on it, and had faith God would provide."

Lynn shifted, obviously uncomfortable. "I don't like talking about her this way, but the thing is, she was a little sly when she said it, you know? And I thought, well, she's already got her eye on a candidate. It wasn't very nice of me, but it's what I thought."

"Did you tell the cops?"

"They just asked if she had a boyfriend, and like that. I told them I didn't know of anybody. I wouldn't have felt right telling them I thought she was looking for one. Do you think I should have?"

"You told them what you knew. I think I'm going to go get in my run, work up an appetite." She saw Lynn bite her lip. "The cops have the rifle, and they have Brakeman. I can't spend my life indoors. I'll be back with an appetite."

She walked outside. The shudder that went through her as she glanced toward the trees only stiffened her spine. She couldn't live her life worried she had a target on her back. She put on the sunglasses—the ones Cards found where Gull had tackled her—and started the walk toward the track.

She could run on the road, she considered, but she was on the jump list, first load. The clouds over the mountains confirmed the forecast from the morning briefing. *Cumulus overtimus,* she thought, knowing the buildup could hurl lightning. She'd likely jump fire today, and get plenty of that overtime.

Better to stay on base in case.

"Hey." Gull caught up with her at a light jog. "We running?"

"I thought you had things to do."

"I said I wanted coffee, maybe some calories. And that was

mostly to give you time to talk to Marg and Lynn. A straight three miles?"

"I . . ." Behind him, she saw Matt, Cards and Trigger come out of the cookhouse and head in her direction. Her eyes narrowed. "Did Lynn go in and tell the dining hall I was heading to the track?"

"What do you think?"

Now Dobie, Stovic and Gibbons herded out.

"Did she call up the Marines while she was at it? I don't need a bunch of bodyguards."

"What you've got is people who care about you. Are you really going to carp about that?"

"No, but I don't see why . . ." Yangtree, Libby and Janis headed out from the direction of the gym. "For Christ's sake, in another minute the whole unit's going to be out here."

"It wouldn't surprise me."

"Half of you aren't even in running gear," she called out.

Trigger, in jeans and boots, reached her first. "We don't wear running gear on a fire."

She considered him. "Nice save."

"When you run, we all run," Cards told her. "At least everybody who's not on duty with something else. We voted on it."

"I didn't get a vote." She jabbed a finger at Gull. "Did you get a vote?"

"I got to add mine to the unanimous results this morning, so your vote is moot."

"Fine. Dandy. We run."

She took off for the track, then geared up to a sprint the minute she hit its surface. Just to see who'd keep up, besides Gull, who matched her stride for stride. She heard the scramble and pounding of feet behind her, then the hoots and catcalls as Libby zipped up to pass.

"Have a heart, Ro," she shouted. "We've got old men like Yangtree out here."

"Who're you calling old!" He kicked it up a notch, edged out of the pack on the turn.

"Gimps like Cards hobbling back there in his boots."

Amused, Ro glanced over her shoulder to see Cards shoot

up his middle finger. And Dobie begin to run backward to taunt him.

She cut her pace back a bit because he was hobbling just a little, then laughed herself nearly breathless when Gibbons jogged by with Janis riding on his shoulders pumping her arms in the air.

"Bunch of lunatics," Rowan decided.

"Yeah. The best bunch of lunatics I know." Gull's grin widened as Southern puffed by with Dobie on board. "Want a ride?"

"I'll spare you the buck and a half on your back. Show them how it's done, Fast Feet. You know you wanna."

He gave her a pat on the ass and took off like a bullet to a chorus of cheers, insults and whistles.

By the time she made her three, Gull was sprawled on the grass, braced on his elbows to watch the show. Highly entertained, she stood, hands on hips, doing the same. Until she saw her father drive up.

"It's a good thing he didn't get here sooner," she commented, "or he'd have been out on the track, too."

"I'm betting he can hold his own."

"Yeah, he can." She started toward him, trying for an easy smile. But the expression on his face told her easy wouldn't work.

He grabbed her, pulled her hard against him.

"I'm okay. I told you I was A-OK."

"I didn't come to see for myself last night because you asked me not to, because you said you had to talk to the cops, and needed to get some sleep afterward." He drew her back, took a long study of her face. "But I needed to see for myself."

"Then you can stop worrying. The cops have Brakeman. I texted you they found his gun and were going to get him. And they got him."

"I want to see him. I want to look him in the eye when I ask him if he thinks hurting my daughter will bring his back. I want to ask him that before I bloody him."

"I appreciate the sentiment. I really do. But he didn't hurt me, and he's not going to hurt me. Look at that bunch." She gestured toward the track. "I came out here for my run, and every one of them came out of their various holes."

"All for one," he murmured. "I need to talk to your boyfriend."

"He's not my . . . Dad, I'm not sixteen."

"Boyfriend's the easiest term for me. Have you had breakfast?"

"Not yet."

"Go on in, and I'll sweet-talk Marg into feeding me with you—when I'm done talking to your boyfriend."

"Just use his name. That should be easy."

Lucas merely smiled, kissed her forehead. "I'll be in in a minute."

He crossed over to Gull, slapped hands with Gibbons, gave Yangtree a pat on the back as the man bent over to catch his breath.

"I want to talk to you a minute," he said to Gull.

"Sure." Gull pushed to his feet. His eyebrows lifted when Lucas walked away from the group, but he followed.

"I heard what you did for Rowan. You took care of her."

"I'd appreciate it if you wouldn't say that to her."

"I know better, but I'm saying it to you. I'm saying I'm grateful. She's the world to me. She's the goddamn universe to me. If you ever need anything—"

"Mr. Tripp—"

"Lucas."

"Lucas, first, I figure mostly anyone would've done what I did, which wasn't that big a deal. If Rowan's instincts had kicked in first, she'd have knocked me down, and I'd've been under her. And second, I didn't do it so you'd owe me a favor."

"You scraped a lot of bark off those arms."

"They'll heal up, and they're not keeping me off the jump list. So. No big."

Lucas nodded, looked off toward the trees. "Am I supposed to ask what your intentions are regarding my daughter?"

"God, I hope not."

"Because to my way of thinking, if you were just in it for the fun, me saying I owed you wouldn't put your back up. So I'm going to give you that favor whether you want it or not. And here it is." He looked back into Gull's eyes. "If you're serious about her, don't let her push you back. You'll have to hold on until she believes you. She's a hard sell, but once she believes, she sticks.

"So." Lucas held out a hand, shook Gull's. "I'm going to go have breakfast with my girl. Are you coming?"

"Yeah. Shortly," Gull decided.

He stood alone a moment, absorbing the fact that Iron Man Tripp had just given his blessing. And thinking over just what he wanted to do with it.

He mulled it over, taking his time walking toward the cookhouse. The siren sounded just before he reached it. Cursing the missed chance of breakfast, Gull turned on his heel and ran for the ready room.

19

After forty-eight hours battling a two-hundred-acre wildfire in the Beaverhead National Forest, getting shot at a few times added up to small change. Once she'd bolted down the last of a sandwich she'd ratted away, Rowan worked with her team, lighting fusees in a bitter attempt to kick the angry fire back before it rode west toward the national battlefield.

The head changed direction three times in two days, snarling at the rain of retardant and spitting it out.

The initial attack, a miserable failure, moved into a protracted, vicious extended one.

"Gull, Matt, Libby, you're on spots. Cards, Dobie, we're going to move west, take down any snags. Dig and cut and smother. We stop her here."

Nobody spoke as they pushed, shoved, lashed the backfire east. The world was smoke and heat and noise with every inch forward a victory. About time, Rowan thought, about damn time their luck changed.

The snag she cut fell with a crack. She positioned to slice it into smaller, less appetizing logs. They'd shovel and drag limbs and coals away from the green, into the black, into a bone pile.

Starve her, Rowan thought. Just keep starving her.

She straightened a moment to stretch her back.

She saw it happen, so fast she couldn't shout out much less leap forward. A knife-point of wood blew out of the cut Cards was carving and shot straight into his face.

She dropped her saw, rushing toward him even as he yelped in shock and pain and lost his footing.

"How bad? How bad?" she shouted, grabbing him as he staggered. She saw for herself the point embedded in his cheek, half an inch below his right eye. Blood spilled down to his jaw.

"For fuck's sake," he managed. "Get it out."

"Hold on. Just hold on."

Dobie trotted up. "What're you two . . . Jesus, Cards, how the hell did you do that?"

"Hold his hands," Rowan ordered as she dug into her pack.

"What?"

"Get behind him and hold his hands down. I think it's going to hurt when I pull it out." She set a boot on either side of Cards's legs, pulled off her right glove. She clamped her fingers on the inch of jagged wood protruding from his cheek. "On three now. Get ready. One. Two—"

She yanked on two, watched the blood slop out, watched his eyes go a little glassy. Quickly, she pressed the pad of gauze she'd taken out of her pack to the wound.

"You've got a hell of a hole in your face," she told him.

"You said on three."

"Yeah, well, I lost count. Dobie, hold the pad, keep the pressure on. I have to clean that out."

"We don't have time for that," Cards objected. "Just tape it over. We'll worry about it later."

"Two minutes. Lean back against Dobie."

She tossed the bloody pad aside, poured water over the wound, hoping to flush out tiny splinters. "And try not to scream like a girl," she added, following up the water with a hefty dose of peroxide.

"Goddamn it, Ro! Goddamn, fucking shit!"

Ruthless, she waited while the peroxide bubbled out dirt and wood, then doused it with more water. She coated another pad with antibiotic cream, added another, then taped it over what she noted was a hole in his cheek the size of a marble.

"We can get you out to the west."

"Screw that. I'm not packing out. It was just a damn splinter."

"Yeah." Dobie held up the three-inch spear of wood. "If you're fifty feet tall. I saved it for you."

"Holy shit, that's a fucking missile. I got hit with a wood missile. In the face. My luck," he said in disgust, "has been for shit all season." He waved off Rowan's extended hand. "I can stand on my own."

He wobbled a moment, then steadied.

"Take some of the ibuprofen in your PG bag. If you're sure you're fit, I want you to go switch off to scout spots. You're not running a saw, Cards. You know better. Switch off, or I'll have to report the injury to Ops."

"I'm not leaving this here until she's dead."

"Then switch off. If that hole in your ugly face bleeds through those pads, have one of your team change it."

"Yeah, yeah." He touched his fingers to the pad. "You'd think I cut off a leg," he muttered, but headed down the line. When he'd gone far enough, she pulled out her radio, contacted Gull. "Cards is headed to you. He had a minor injury. I want one of you to head up to me, and he'll take your place down there."

"Copy that."

"Okay, Dobie, get that saw working. And watch out for flying wood missiles. I don't want any more drama."

The backfire held. It took another ten hours, but reports from head to tail called the fire contained.

The sunset ignited the sky as she hiked back to camp. It reminded her of watching the sun set with Gull. Of bullets and blind hate. She dropped down to eat, wishing she could find that euphoria that always rose in her once a fire surrendered.

Yangtree sat down beside her. "We're going to get some food in our bellies before we start mop-up. Ops has eight on tap for that. It's up to you since he was on your team, but I think Cards should demob, get that wound looked at proper."

"Agreed. I'm going to pack out with him. If they can send eight, let's spring eight from camp."

"My thinking, too. I tell you, Ro, I say I'm too old for this, but I'm starting to mean it. I might just ask your daddy for a job come the end of the season."

"Hell. Cards is the one with the hole in his face."

He looked toward the west, the setting sun, the black mountain. "I'm thinking I may want to see what it's like to sit on my own porch on a summer night, drink a beer, with some female company if I can get it, and not have to think about fire."

"You'll always think about fire, and sitting on a porch, you'd wish you were here."

He gave her a pat on the knee as he rose. "It might be time to find out."

She had to browbeat Cards into packing out. Smoke jumpers, she thought, treated injuries like points of pride, or challenges.

He sulked on the flight home.

"I get why he's in a mood." Gull settled down beside her. "Why are you?"

"Sixty hours on fire might have something to do with it."

"No. That's why you're whipped and more vulnerable to the mood, but not the reason for the mood."

"Here's what I don't get, hotshot: why, after a handful of months, you think you know me so damn well. And another is why you spend so much time psychoanalyzing people."

"Those are both pretty easy to get. The first is it may be a handful of months, but people who live and work together, particularly under intense conditions, tend to know and understand each other quicker than those who don't. Add sleeping together, and it increases the learning curve. Second."

He pulled out a bag of shelled peanuts, offered her some, then shrugged and dug in himself when she just glowered at him.

"Second," he repeated. "People interest me, so I like figuring them out."

He munched nuts. Whatever her mood or the reasons for it, he wasn't inclined to lower his to match it. A hot shower and hot food, followed by a bed with a warm woman in it, ranged in his immediate future.

Who could ask for better?

"You're starting to think about what's waiting back at base. All the crap we've been too busy to worry about. What's happened while we were catching fire, if the cops charged Brakeman, found Dolly's killer. If not, what next?"

He glanced over toward Cards, who snored with his head on his pack, a fresh bandage snowy white against his soot-smeared face. "And you're mixing in worrying how bad Cards messed his face up. Whatever Yangtree and you talked about before we demobbed topped it off."

She said nothing for a moment. "Know-it-alls are irritating." Leaning her head back, she closed her eyes. "I'm getting some sleep."

"Funny, I think having somebody understand you is comforting."

She opened one eye, cool, crystal blue. "I didn't say you were an understand-it-all."

"You've got me there." Gull shut his eyes as well, and dropped off.

ROWAN HEADED STRAIGHT to the barracks after unloading her gear. To settle down, Gull decided, as much as clean up. Maybe she'd label it as "taking care of her," and that was too damn bad, but he postponed his own agenda to hunt down L.B.

He waited in Operations while L.B. coordinated with the mop-up crew boss.

"Got a minute?"

"For the first time in three days, I've got a few. I'm stepping out," L.B. announced, then jerked his head toward the door. "What's on your mind?"

"You telling me the status of things around here so I can pass it on to Rowan."

"I don't know how much they're keeping me in the loop, but let's find a place to sit down."

WHEN ROWAN STEPPED OUT of the bathroom wrapped in a towel, a still filthy Gull was sitting on the floor.

"Is something wrong with your shower?"

"I don't know. I haven't been in it yet."

"I've got a lot to do before I'm done, so we'll have to reschedule the hot-sex portion of the evening."

"You've got a one-track mind, Swede. I like the track, but there are more than one."

She opened a drawer, selected yoga pants and a top.

"I'll give you the rundown," Gull began. "Trigger dragged Cards to the infirmary. The wound's clean. No infection, but it's pretty damn deep. Plastic surgeon recommended, and after some bullshit, he's going into town to see one in the morning. He wants to keep his pretty face."

"That's good." She pulled on the pants and top without bothering with underwear—something Gull appreciated whatever the circumstances. "And it'll be fun to rag him about plastic surgery," she added, stepping back into the bath to hang the towel. "We ought to get some fun out of it."

"Trigger already suggested they suck the lard out of his ass while they're at it."

"That's a start."

"They've charged Leo Brakeman."

He watched her jerk, just a little, then cross over to sit on the side of the bed. "Okay. All right."

"His rifle, prior threats and the fact he can't verify his whereabouts for the time of the shooting. He admitted he and his wife had a fight, and he went out to drive around for a couple hours. He'd only just gotten back when the cops showed up at the door."

"His wife could've lied for him."

"He never asked her to. Some of this came from the cops, some of it's via Marg. I could separate it out, but being a know-it-all, I figure Marg's intel is as solid as the cops'."

"You'd be right."

"They fought about him coming out here, going off on you. About Dolly in general. I think losing a child either sticks the parents together like cement, or rips them up."

"My father had a brother. A younger one. You probably know that, too, since you studied Iron Man."

Gull said nothing, gave her room. "He died when he was three of some weird infection. He'd never been what you'd call robust, and, well, they couldn't fix it. I guess it cemented my grandparents. Has he admitted it? Brakeman?"

"No. He's claiming he was driving around, just tooling the backroads, that somebody broke in, took his rifle. Somebody's framing him. His wife finally convinced him to get a lawyer. They held the bail hearing this morning. She put up their house to post his bond."

"Jesus."

"He's not coming back around here, Ro."

"That's not what I mean. She's dealing with more than anybody should have to deal with, and it just doesn't feel like any of it's her doing. I don't know how she's standing up to it."

"She's dealing with more yet. They identified a man Dolly met at a motel off Twelve the night she died. One she met there a number of times in the past few months. Reverend Latterly."

"Their pastor? For the love of—" She broke off, slumped back. "Dolly was putting out for her mother's *padre*, all the while claiming she'd been washed in the light of the Lord or whatever. It makes sense," she said immediately. "Now it makes sense. God will provide. That's what she said to Lynn. Her baby would need a father, and God would provide."

"I don't think God had the notion to provide Dolly with a married man who's already got three kids. He's denying it, all righteously outraged, and so far, anyway, his wife's sticking with him. The cops are working on picking that apart."

"He met her the night she was killed. She wanted a father for her baby, and Dolly always pushed when she wanted something. She pushed, maybe threatened to tell his wife, ruin him with his congregation. And he kills her."

"Logical," Gull agreed.

"It still doesn't explain why he didn't just leave her, why he took her into the forest, started the fire. But odds are it's the first time he killed anyone. It's probably hard to be rational after doing something like that.

"Gull . . . If he and Dolly were heating the sheets, all this time—and he's been preaching to Mrs. Brakeman for years—he could've gotten into their house."

She tilted her head. "And you've already thought about that."

"Speculated. I expect he's had Sunday dinner there a time or two, he and his wife probably brought a covered dish to summer cookouts and so on. Yeah, I think he knew how to get in, and he might've known or been able to access the combination to the safe."

"It would be a way to have the cops looking at Brakeman, and that worked. Maybe have them speculating. This violent man, this man with a violent temper, one who'd already pushed his daughter out of the house once, has been known to have heated arguments with her. It could be."

"It's not out of the realm. You lost your mood."

She smirked, just a little. "Know-it-all. Maybe I was feeling useless again, a comedown from three days when I know everything I did mattered, made a difference, was needed. Then I'm coming back here where I can't do a damn thing. I can't be in charge, so I guess it helps some to think it all through, and to figure out what I'd do if I could be in charge. Maybe it helps to talk it through with somebody who understands me." She smirked again. "At least understands parts of me."

"You know, I could sit here and look at you all night. All gold and cream and smelling like a summer orchard. It's a nice way to transition back after an extended attack. But, how about I clean up, and we go get ourselves a late supper?"

"That's a solid affirmative."

"Great." He pushed to his feet. "Can I use your shower?"

She laughed, waved toward the bathroom. Since she had some time she decided to call the other man who understood her.

"Hi, Dad."

ELLA TURNED when Lucas opened the door to the deck. She'd slipped out when his cell phone rang to give him some privacy for the call, and to admire the fairy lights she'd strung on the slender branches of her weeping plum.

"Everything okay?"

"Yeah. Rowan just wanted to check in, and to update me on what's going on."

"Is there anything new?"

"Not really." As he sipped a glass of the wine they'd

enjoyed with dinner, he brushed his fingertips up and down her arm.

She loved the way he touched her—often, like a reassurance she was with him.

"She sounded steady, so I feel better about that. With Ro, when bad things happen, or wrong things, she tends to take it in. What could she have done to prevent it, or what should she do to fix it?"

"I can't imagine where she gets that from. Who's been fiddling around here every chance he gets? Fixing the dripping faucet in the laundry room sink, the drawer that kept sticking in that old table I bought at the flea market?"

"I have to pay for all those dinners you cook me. And breakfasts," he added, gliding his hand down to her waist.

"It's nice to have a handy man around the house."

"It's nice to be around the house, with you." He hooked his arm around her waist so they looked out at the garden together, at the pretty lights, the soft shadows. "It's nice to be with you."

"I'm happy," she told him. "I tend to be a happy person, and I learned how to be happy on my own. It was good for me, to have that time, to find out a little bit more about myself. What I could do, what I could do without. I'm happier with you."

She hooked an arm around his waist in turn. "I was standing here before you came out thinking how lucky I am. I've got a family I love and who loves me, a career I'm proud of, this place, good friends. Now the bonus round. You."

Lights sparkling, she thought, in her garden, and in her heart. And all the while her friend lived in the terrible dark.

"I talked with Irene earlier."

"She's got a terrible load to carry now."

"I went to see her, hoping to help, but . . . I can't even begin to conceive what she's lost. The most devastating loss a mother can know. What she may lose yet. Nothing in her life is certain now, or steady or happy. She's burying her daughter, Lucas. She's facing the very real possibility her husband will go to prison. The man she trusted with her spiritual guidance, her faith, betrayed her in a horrible way. The only thing she has to hold on to now is her grandchild, and caring for that sweet little girl must bring Irene incredible pain and joy.

"I'm lucky. And I guess I'm enough like you and Rowan to wish there were some way I could fix things. I wish I knew what I could do or say or be to help Irene."

"You're helping her plan the service, and you'll be there for her. That'll matter. Do you want me to go with you?"

"Selfishly yes. But I think it would embarrass her if you did."

He nodded, having thought the same. "If you think it's right, you could tell her I'm sorry for her loss, sorry for what she's going through."

"I've made us both sad, and here I was thinking about being happy."

"People who are together get to share both. I want to . . . share both with you."

Almost, she thought as butterflies on the wing filled her belly. They were both almost ready to say it. Had she said she felt lucky? She'd been blessed.

"Let's take a walk in the moonlight," she decided. "In the garden. We can finish drinking this wine, and make out."

"You always have the best ideas."

USING A DEAD WOMAN'S phone to lure a man to his death felt . . . just. A man of God should understand that, should approve of the sentiment of an eye for an eye. Though Latterly was no man of God, but a fraud, a liar, an adulterer, a fornicator.

In a very real sense Latterly had killed Dolly. He'd tempted her, led her onto the path—or if the temptation and leading had been hers, he had certainly followed.

He should have counseled her, advised her, helped her be the decent person, the honorable woman, the good mother. Instead he'd betrayed his wife, his family, his God, his church, for sex with the daughter of one of his faithful.

His death would be justice, and retribution and holy vengeance.

The text had done its job, so simple really.

it wasnt me u have 2 come bring money dont tell not yet
talk first need to know what 2 do meet me 1 am Lolo Pass
Vistor Center fs rd 373 2 gate URGENT Can help u Dolly

Of course, the soon-to-be-dead man called the dead woman. The return text when the call went unanswered had been full of shock, panic, demands. Easy enough to deflect.

must c u face 2 face explain then will do what u say when you know what i know cant txt more they might find out

He'd come. If he didn't, there would be another way.

Planning murder wasn't the same as an accident. How would it feel?

The car rolled in ten minutes early, going slow. A creep along the service road.

Easy after all. So easy. Should there be talk first? Should the dead man know why he was dead? Why he would burn in fiery hell?

He called for Dolly, his voice a harsh whisper in the utter peace of the night. At the gate, he sat in his car, silhouetted in the moonlight.

Death waited patiently.

He got out, his head turning right, left, as he continued to call Dolly's name. As he continued up the road.

Yes, it was easy after all.

"An eye for an eye."

Latterly looked over, his face struck with terror as shadow moved to moonlight.

The first bullet struck him in the center of the forehead, a small black hole that turned terror to blank shock. The second pierced his heart, releasing a slow trickle of blood that gleamed black in the shimmer of light.

Easy. A steady hand, a just heart.

No shock, no grief, no trembling, not this time.

A long way to drag a body, but it had to be done right, didn't it? Anything worth doing was worth doing well. And the forest at night held such beauty, such mystery. Peace. Yes, for a little while, peace.

All the effort came to nothing in that moment when the body rested at the burn site, on the pyre, already prepared.

Reverend Latterly didn't look so good, didn't look so *pious* now with his clothes and flesh torn and dirty from the trail.

A click of the lighter, that's all it took to send him to hell.

Flames kindled with a whoosh as they gulped fuel and oxy-gen. Burning the body as the soul would burn. Peace settled while the fire climbed and spread.

How did it feel to murder and burn?

It felt right.

20

The fire chewed its way east, consuming forest and meadow, its head a rage of hunger and greedy glee leading the body across two states.

Gull dug his spikes into a lodgepole pine, climbing up, up into a sky of sooty red. Sweat dripped down his face to soak the bandanna he'd tied on like a latter-day outlaw as he ground the teeth of his saw through bark and wood. Logs tumbled, crashed below as he worked his way down.

The blaze they sought to cage danced, leaped nimbly up trees to string their branches with light as it roared its song.

He hit the ground, unhooked his harness, then moved down the saw line.

He knew Rowan worked the head. Word traveled down the crew, and the jumpers from Idaho had twice had to retreat due to unstable winds.

He heard the roll of thunder, watched the tanker pitch through the smoke. So far the dragon seemed to swallow the retardant like candy.

He'd lost track of the hours spent in the belly of the beast since the siren had sounded that morning. Only that morning, looking into Rowan's eyes as she moved under him, feeling her body rise and fall beneath him. Only that morning he'd had the taste of her skin, warm from sleep, on his tongue.

Now he tasted smoke. Now he felt the ground move as another sacrificial tree fell to earth. He looked into the eyes of the enemy, and knew her lust.

What he didn't know, as he set down his saw to gulp down water, was if it was day or night. And what did it matter? The only world that mattered lived in this perpetual red twilight.

"We're moving east." Dobie jogged out of the smoke, his eyes red-rimmed over his bandanna. "Gibbons is taking us east, digging line as we go. The hoses are holding her back on the right flank at Pack Creek, and the mud knocked her back some."

"Okay." Gull grabbed his gear.

"I volunteered you and me to go on south through the burn-out and scout spots and snags along the rim, circle on up toward the head."

"That was real considerate of you to include me in your mission."

"Somebody's got to do it, son." Those red-rimmed eyes laughed. "It's a longer trip, but I bet we beat the rest of the crew to the head, get back into the real action sooner."

"Maybe. The head's where I want to be."

"Fighting ass-to-ass with your woman. Let's get humping."

Spots bloomed like flowers, burst like grenades, simmered like shallow pools. The wind colluded, thickened the smoke, giving loft to sailing firebrands.

Gull smothered, dug, doused, beat, then laughed his way through the nasty work as Dobie started naming the spots.

"Fucking Assistant Principal Brewster!" Dobie stomped out the licking flames. "Suspended me for smoking in the bathroom."

"High school sucks."

"Middle school. I got an early start."

"Priming your lungs for your life's work," Gull decided as he moved on to another.

"That's fucking Gigi Japper. Let me at her. She dumped me for a ball player."

"Middle school?"

"Last year. Bastard plays slow-pitch softball. Can you beat that? Slow-pitch softball. How does that count for anything?"

"You're better off without her."

"Damn straight. Well, Captain, I believe we've secured this line, and recommend we cut across from here and start scouting north. I'm still looking for crazy old Mr. Cotter, used to shoot at my dog just because the pup liked to shit in his petunias."

"We'll beat the hell out of old Mr. Cotter together."

"That's a true friend."

They ate lunch, dinner, breakfast—who the hell knew?— on the quickstep hike, chowing down on Hooah! bars, peanut-butter crackers, and the single apple from Gull's pack they passed back and forth.

"I love this job," Dobie told him. "I didn't know as I would. I knew I could do it, knew I would. Figured I'd like it okay. But I didn't know it's what I was after. Didn't know I was after anything."

"If it gets its hooks in you, you know it's what you were after." That, Gull thought, covered smoke jumping and women.

Murdered trees stood, black skeletons in the thinning smoke. Wind trickled through, sending them to moan, scooping up ash that swirled like dirty fairy dust.

"It's like one of those end-of-the-world movies," Dobie decided. "Where some meteor destroys most every goddamn thing, and what's left are mutant scavengers and a handful of brave warriors trying to protect the innocent. We can be the warriors."

"I was counting on being a mutant, but all right. Look at that." Gull pointed east where the sky glowed red above towers of flame. "Half the time I can't understand how I can hate it and still think it's beautiful."

"I felt that way about fucking Gigi Japper."

Laughing, somehow completely happy to be hot and filthy alongside his strangely endearing friend, Gull studied the fire as they hiked—the breadth of it, the colors and tones, the shapes.

On impulse, he pulled his camera out of his PG bag. A

photo couldn't translate its terrifying magnificence, but it would remind him, over the winter. It would remind him.

Dobie stepped into the frame, set his Pulaski on his shoulder, spread his legs, fixed a fierce expression on his face. "Now, take a picture. 'Dragon-slayer.'"

Actually, Gull thought when he framed it in, the title seemed both apt and accurate. He took two. "Eat your heart out, Gigi."

"Fucking A! Come on, son, time's a'wasting."

He took off with a swagger as Gull secured his camera.

"Gull."

"Yeah." He glanced up from zipping his PG bag to see Dobie in nearly the same pose, reversed with his back to him. "Camera's secured, handsome."

"You better come on over here. Take a look at this."

Alerted by the tone, Gull moved fast, stared when Dobie pointed. "Is that what I think it is?"

"Aw, shit."

The remains lay, a grim signpost on the charred trail.

"Jesus, Gull, looks like the mutants have been through here." Dobie staggered a few feet away, braced his hands on his knees, and puked up his energy bars.

"Like Dolly," Gull murmured. "Except . . ."

"Christ, I feel like a pussy. Losing my lunch." Bone-white beneath the layer of soot, Dobie took a pull of water, spat it out. "He started the fire, the cocksucker, right here. Like with Dolly." He rinsed again, spat again, then drank. "He did all this."

"Yeah, except I don't think he did this to try to hide the body, or destroy it. Maybe it's so we'd find it, or for attention, or because the son of a bitch likes fire. And it's not like Dolly because this one's got what's got to be a bullet hole dead in the forehead."

Bracing himself, Dobie stepped over again, looked. "Christ, I think you're right about that."

"I guess I should've taken that bet." Gull pulled out his radio. "Because I don't think we're going to get back to action before the rest of the crew."

While they waited, Dobie took two mini bottles of Kentucky bourbon from his bag, took a swig. "Who do you think it is?" he asked, and passed the second bottle to Gull.

"Maybe we've just got some homicidal firebug picking people at random. More likely it's somebody connected to Dolly."

"Jesus please us, I hope it's not her ma. I really hope it's not her ma. Somebody's got to take care of that baby."

"I saw her mother that day she and the preacher came to thank L.B. for hiring Dolly again. She's short, little like Dolly was. I think what's there's too tall. Pretty tall, I think."

"Her daddy, maybe."

"Maybe."

"If I hadn't volunteered us, somebody else would've found it. It's right on the damn trail. Ro said Dolly was off it. Right on the trail. The rangers would've found it if we hadn't. It really makes you think about what the fire'll do to you, it gets the chance."

Gull looked out at the red, the black, the stubborn lashing gold. And downed the bourbon.

The rangers let them go to rejoin the war. The fury built up in Gull all the way up to that snarling, snapping head. He channeled that fury into the attack so every strike of his ax fed his anger. This war wasn't fought against God or nature or fate, but against the human being who'd given birth to the fire for his own pleasure or purpose or weakness.

For those hours the battle burned, he didn't care about the reasons why. He only cared about stopping it.

"Take a breath," Rowan told him. "We've got her now. You can feel it. Take a breath, Gull. This isn't a one-man show."

"I'll take a breath when she's down."

"Look, I know how you feel. I know exactly how—"

"I'm not in the mood to be reasonable." He pushed her hand off his arm, eyes hot and vivid. "I'm in the mood to kill this bitch. We can discuss our mutual traumas later. Now let me do my job."

"Okay, fine. We need men up on that ridge digging line before she rides this wind and shifts this way for fresh eats and builds again."

"All right."

"Take Dobie, Matt, Libby and Stovic."

NIGHT, HE THOUGHT—or morning, probably—when he dragged himself to the creek. The fire trembled in its death throes, coughing and sputtering. Overhead, stars winked hopefully through thinning smoke.

He pulled off his boots, his socks, and stuck his abused feet in the gorgeously cool water. The postfire chatter ran behind him in voices raw with smoke and adrenaline. Jokes, insults, rewinds of the long fight. And the expected what-the-fuck? question about what he and Dobie had found.

More work waited, but would keep until daybreak. The fire hadn't lain down to rest. She'd lain down to die.

Rowan sat down beside him, dropped an MRE in his lap, pushed a drink into his hand. "They dropped a nice load down for camp, so I made you dinner."

"A woman's work is never done."

"More in the mood to be reasonable, I see."

"I needed to burn it off."

"I know." She touched a hand to his briefly, then picked up the fork to shovel in beef stew. "I put some of Dobie's famous Tabasco in this. Nice kick."

"I was taking his picture. Him standing there in the black, and behind him the fire, and the sky. Surreal. I'd just taken his picture when we found it. It didn't get to me, really, until we started up to meet you, and it just got bigger and bigger in me. Christ, I wasn't even thinking about some guy burned to bone after taking a shot in the head."

"Shot?"

Gull nodded. "Yeah, but I wasn't thinking about him. All I could think about was this, and us. All the loss and waste, the risks, the sweat and blood. And for what, Ro? Since I couldn't beat the hell out of whoever caused it, I had to beat the hell out of the fire."

"Matt got hung up on the jump. He let down okay, but it could've gone bad. A widowmaker as thick as my arm nearly hit Elf when we had to retreat, and Yangtree's got a Pulaski gash on his calf to go with his swollen knee. One of the Idaho crew took a bad fall, broke his leg. You were right to be mad."

For a while, they ate in silence. "They want you back in the morning, you and Dobie, so DiCicco and Quinniock can talk to you. I can pack out with you."

He glanced over, grateful—grateful enough not to mention she was taking care of him. "That'd be good."

"I figured you're pretty tired, so I can save you the time popping your tent. You can share mine."

"That'd be even better. I love this job," he said after a moment, thinking of Dobie. "I don't know why exactly but what this bastard's done makes me love it even more. The cops have to find him, catch him, stop him. But we're the ones cleaning up his goddamn mess. We're the ones doing whatever it takes to keep it from being worse. The wild doesn't mean anything to him, what lives in it, lives off it. It means something to us."

He looked at her then, slowly leaned in to take her lips in a kiss of surprising gentleness. "I found you in the wild, Rowan. That's a hell of a thing."

She smiled, a little uncertainly. "I wasn't lost."

"Neither was I. But I'm found, too, just the same."

When they walked the short distance to the tents, they crossed paths with Libby.

"How you doing, Gull?"

"Okay. Better since I hear I get to skate out of mop-up. Have you seen Dobie?"

"Yeah, he just turned in. He was feeling . . . I guess you know. Matt and I sat up with him awhile after the rest bunked down. He's doing okay."

"You did good work today, Barbie," Rowan told her.

"Never plan to do any other kind. Good night."

Rowan yawned her way into the tent and, with her mind and body already shutting down, worked off her boots. "Don't wake me unless there's a bear attack. In fact, even then."

She stripped down to her tank and panties. As she rolled toward the sleeping bag, Gull considered.

"You know, thirty seconds ago I figure I was too tired to scratch my own ass. And now, strangely, I'm filled with this renewed energy."

She opened one eye, shut it again. "Do what you gotta do. Just don't wake me up doing it."

He climbed in beside her, smiling, drew her already-limp-

with-sleep body to his. When he closed his eyes he thought of
her, of nothing but her, and slid quietly into the dark.

IT WAS HER KNEE pressing firmly into his crotch that woke
him. His eyes crossed before they opened. Easing back
relieved the worst of the pressure on his now throbbing balls.

Had she aimed, he wondered, or had it just been blind luck?
Either way, perfect shot.

She didn't budge when he rolled out to pull on his pants,
fresh socks, boots. He left the pants and boots unfastened and
crawled out into soft morning light.

Nothing and no one stirred. Then again, as far as he knew
the other tents held occupants of one—with no one to jab a
knee into their balls. Should they have them.

He stood, adjusted himself—carefully—then chose a direction out of camp to empty his bladder. Coffee, and filling his
belly, would be next on the list, he decided. Being the first
awake meant he had first dibs on the breakfast MREs. He'd sit
outside, maybe down by the creek, give Rowan the tent for
more sleep and enjoy a quiet, solitary if crappy meal until . . .

He stopped and looked. Looked over a meadow brilliant
with wild lupines, regally purple. The faintest ground mist
shimmered through them, giving them the illusion of floating
on a thin, white river while dozens of deep blue butterflies
danced over those bold lances.

Untouched, he thought. The fire hadn't touched this. They'd
stopped it, and now the wildflowers bloomed, the butterflies
danced in the misty morning light.

It was, he thought, as beautiful, as vivid as the finest work
of art. Maybe more. And he'd had a part in saving it, and the
trees beyond it, and whatever lay beyond the beyond.

He'd fought in the smoke and the blistering red air, walked
through the black that stank with death. And to here, where
life lived, where it thrived in quiet and simple grace.

To here, which held all the answers to why.

HE BROUGHT HER THERE, dragging her away from camp
before they packed out.

"We've got to get going," she protested. "If we haul our asses down to the visitors' center, they can van us back to base. Clean bodies, clean clothes. And, *God*, I want a Coke."

"This is better than a Coke."

"Nothing's better than a Coke first thing in the morning. You coffee hounds have it all wrong."

"Just look." He gestured. "That's better than anything."

She'd seen meadows before, seen the wild lupine and the butterflies it seduced. She started to say so, grumpy with caffeine withdrawal, but he looked so . . . struck.

And she got it. Of course she got it. Who better?

Still, she had to give him a dig, one with the elbow in the side, the other verbal. "There's that mushy romantic streak again."

"Stand right there. I'm going to get a picture."

"Hell you are. Jesus, Gull, look at me."

"One of my favorite occupations."

"If you want a shot of a woman in front of a meadow of flowers, get one with clean, shiny hair and a flowy white dress."

"Don't be stupid, you look exactly right. Because you're part of why it's here. This is like a bookend to the one I took of Dobie in the black. It shows how and why and who go into everything between those two points."

"Romantic slob," she repeated. But it moved her, the truth of it, the knowing they shared.

So she hooked her thumbs in her front pockets, cocked her hip and sent him and his camera a big, bold grin.

He took the shot, lowered the camera slowly and just stared at her as he had at the meadow. Struck.

"Here, switch off. I'll take one of you."

"No. It's you. It's Dobie in the black, the fire raging behind him, telling me how much he loves this job, what he's found in it. And it's you, Rowan, in the sunlight with preserved beauty at your back. You're the end of the goddamn rainbow."

"Come on." Mildly embarrassed, she shrugged it off, started toward him. "You must be punchy."

"You're the answer before I even asked the question."

"Gull, it weirds me out when you start talking like that."

"I think you're going to have to get used to it. I've fallen pretty deep in . . . care with you. We'll go with that for now, because I think it's more, and that's a lot to figure out."

A touch of panic speared through embarrassment. "Gull, getting wound up in . . . care for people like us—for people like me—it's a sucker bet."

"I don't think so. I like the odds."

"Because you're crazy."

"You have to be crazy to do this job."

She couldn't argue with that. "We've got to get going."

"Just one more thing."

He took her shoulders, drawing her in. His fingers glided up to her face as he guided them into a kiss made for meadows and summer shine, the flutter of butterflies and music of birdsong.

Unable to find a foothold, she tumbled into it, lost herself in the sweetness, the promise she told herself she didn't want. Her heart trembled in her chest, ached there.

And, for the first time in her life, yearned there.

Unsteady, she stepped away. "That's just heat."

"Keep telling yourself that." He hooked an arm around her shoulders in a lightning switch to friendly. The man, she thought, could make her dizzy.

DICICCO AND QUINNIOCK stepped out of Operations even as the vans pulled up to base.

"It'd be nice if they let us clean up first," Gull commented, then he got off the van, nodded to the cop and the fed. "Where do you want to do this?"

"L.B.'s office is available for us," Quinniock told him.

"Look, there are tables outside the cookhouse. I wouldn't mind airing out some and getting some food while we're at it. I expect Dobie feels the same."

"You got that right, son. Did you figure out who's dead?"

"We'll talk about it," DiCicco told him.

"We'll take care of your gear." Rowan gestured to Matt, Janis. "Don't worry about it."

"Appreciate it." Gull gave her a quick look.

"Are we suspects?" Dobie wanted to know as they walked toward the cookhouse.

"We haven't made any determinations, Mr. Karstain."

"Loosen up, Kim," Quinniock suggested. "We have no reason to suspect you in this matter. You can tell us where you were the night before you jumped the fire, between eleven P.M. and three A.M., if you'd like."

"Me? I was playing cards with Libby and Yangtree and Trigger till about midnight. Trig and me had a last beer after. I guess we bunked down about one."

"I was with Rowan," Gull said, and left it at that.

"We'd like to go over the statements you gave the rangers on scene." DiCicco sat at the picnic table, pulled out her notebook, her mini recorder. "I'd like to record this."

"Dobie, why don't you go ahead? I'll go see what Marg can put together for us. Do you two want anything?" Gull asked.

"I wouldn't mind a cold drink," Quinniock told him, and, remembering the lemonade, DiCicco nodded.

"That'd be good. Now, Mr. Karstain—"

"Can you leave off calling me mister? Just Dobie."

"Dobie."

He went over what happened. What he'd seen, done, what he'd already told the rangers.

"You know, the black looks like a horror show anyhow, then you add that. Gull said it must be connected to Dolly."

"Did he?" DiCicco said.

"Makes sense, doesn't it?" Dobie looked from one to the other. "Is it?"

"Dobie, how was it only you and Mr. Curry were in that area?"

Dobie shrugged at DiCicco just as Gull came out, two steps in front of Lynn. Both carried trays.

"We needed most everybody up at the head, digging line toward it, but somebody still needed to scout spots along the flank. So I volunteered me and Gull."

"You suggested that you and Mr. Curry take that route?"

"She's big on the misters," he said to Gull. "Yeah. It's a longer hike, but I like killing spots. Me and Gull, we work good together. Thanks." He gave Lynn a smile when she set a loaded plate in front of him. "It sure looks good."

"Marg said to save room for cherry pie. You just let me know if you need anything else."

"Let's save some time." Gull took his seat. "We took that route because we were scouting spots. You see a spot, you put it out, and you move on. We had that duty while making our way east to join the rest of the crew. The fire'd been moving east, but the winds kept changing, so the flanks shifted. We found the remains because we cut across the burnout, heading to the far flank in case any spots broke out and took hold. If they did, and we didn't, it could've put the visitor center in the line. Nobody wanted that. Clear?"

"That's the way it is." Dobie took his bottle of Tabasco out of his pocket, lifted the top of his Kaiser roll and dumped some on the horseradish Marg had piled on his roast beef.

Gull shook his head when Dobie offered the bottle. "Mine's fine as it is. And, yeah, I speculated this body was related to Dolly. It could be we've got a serial killer–arsonist picking victims at random, but I like the odds on connection a lot better."

"Shot this one," Dobie said with his mouth full. "Couldn't miss the bullet hole."

"Jumpers got hurt on that fire. I heard on the way in a couple of hotshots I know were injured. I watched acres of wilderness go up. I want the person responsible to pay for it, and I want to know why killing wasn't enough. Because I can speculate again that the fire was just as important as the kill. Otherwise, there wasn't a reason for it. The fire itself had to matter."

"That's an interesting speculation," DiCicco commented.

"Since we've already told you what we know, speculation's all that's left. And since neither of you look particularly stupid, I have to assume you've already entertained those same speculations."

"He's feeling a little pissed off 'cause he's out here talking to cops instead of taking a shower with the Swede."

"Jesus, Dobie." Then Gull laughed. "Yeah, I am. So, since you cost me, maybe you could tell us if you've identified the remains."

"That information . . ." DiCicco caught Quinniock's look, huffed out a breath. "While we're waiting for verification, we found Reverend Latterly's car parked on the service road alongside the visitors' center. His wife can't tell us his where-

abouts, only that he wasn't home or at his church when she got
up this morning."

"Somebody shot a preacher?" Dobie demanded. "That's
hell for sure."

"The Brakemans' preacher," Gull added. "And the one
rumor has it Dolly was screwing around with. I heard Leo
Brakeman made bail."

"Sumbitch better not come back around here."

DiCicco gave Dobie a glance, but kept her focus primarily
on Gull. "We'll be speaking to Mr. Brakeman after his daughter's funeral this afternoon."

"I've got a couple of men on him," Quinniock added.
"We've got a list of his registered weapons, and we'll take
another look at his gun safe."

"It'd be pretty stupid to use one of his own guns, at least a
registered weapon, to kill the man who was screwing his
daughter and preaching to his wife."

"Regardless, we'll pursue every avenue of the investigation. We can speculate, too, Mr. Curry," DiCicco added. "But
we have to work with facts, with data, with evidence. Two
people are dead, and that's priority. But those wildfires matter.
I work for the Forest Service, too. Believe me, it all matters."

She got to her feet. "Thanks for your time." She offered
Gull the ghost of a smile. "Sorry about the shower."

"Why, Agent DiCicco," Quinniock said as they walked
away, "I believe you just made an amusing, smart-ass comment. I feel warm inside."

"Well, hold on to it. Funerals tend to cool things off."

BLOWUP

To burn always with this hard, gem-like flame,
to maintain this ecstasy, is success in life.

WALTER PATER

21

Rowan dawdled. She lingered in the shower, took her time selecting shorts and a top as if it mattered. She even put in a few minutes with makeup, pleased when the dawdling transformed her into a girl.

Time enough, she decided, and went to hunt for Gull.

When she stepped out of her quarters, Matt stepped out of his.

"Wow." She gave him and his dark suit and tie a lusty eyebrow wiggle. "And I thought I looked good."

"You do."

"What, do you have a hot date? Going to a wedding, a funer—" She broke off, mentally slapped herself. "Oh, God, Matt, I forgot. I wasn't thinking. You're going to Dolly's funeral."

"I thought I should, since we're off the fire."

"You're not going by yourself? I'd go with you, but I've got to be the last person the Brakemans want to see today."

"It's okay. I'm just . . . I feel like I have to, to represent Jim, you know? I don't want to, but . . . the baby." He shoved at his floppy, sun-bleached hair with his fingers. "I almost wish we were still out on the fire, so I couldn't go."

"Get somebody to go with you. Janis packed out with us, or Cards would go if he's up to it. Or—"

"L.B.'s going." Matt stuck his hands in his pockets, pulled them out again to tap his fingers on his thigh. It reminded her painfully of Jim. "And Marg and Lynn."

"Okay then." She walked over, fussed with his tie though it didn't need it. "You're doing the right thing by your family by going. If you want to talk later, or just hang out, I'll be around."

"Thanks." He put a hand over hers until she met his eyes. "Thanks, Rowan. I know she caused you a lot of trouble."

"It doesn't matter. Matt, it really doesn't. It's a hard day for a lot of people. That's what matters."

He gave her hand one hard squeeze. "I'd better get going."

She changed direction when he left, headed to the lounge. Cards sprawled on the sofa watching one of the soaps on TV.

"This girl's telling this guy she's knocked up, even though she's not, because he's in love with her sister but banged her—the one who's not knocked up—when she put something in his drink when she went over to his place to tell him the sister was cheating on him, which she wasn't."

He slugged down some Gatorade. "Women suck."

"Hey."

"Fact is fact," he said grimly. "So I'm riveted. I could get hooked on this stuff taking my afternoon, medically ordered lie-down. I get to malinger for another day while I get pretty again."

She sat, studied the bandage over his cheek. "I don't know. The hole in your face added interest, and it would've distracted from the fact your eyes are too close together."

"I have the eyes of an angel. And a hawk. An angel hawk."

"Matt's leaving to go to Dolly's funeral."

"Yeah, I know. He's wearing Yangtree's tie."

"We should get a couple more of the guys to go with him. Libby's still on mop-up, but Janis packed out."

"Let it be, Ro. You can't fix every damn thing."

He hissed through his teeth when she said nothing. "Look, L.B.'s going to stand for the base, and Marg and Lynn, because they worked with her. Matt, well, he's like kin now with Jim's baby and all. But L.B. and I talked about it. The way things ended up here with Dolly, it's probably best to keep it to a minimum. Probably be easier on Dolly's mom."

"Probably," she agreed, but frowned as she studied him. She knew that face, with or without the hole, and those big camel eyes. "What's up?"

"Nothing except your interrupting my soap opera. Orchid's going to get hers when Payton finds out she's been playing him for a sap."

She knew a brood when she was sitting next to one. "You're sulking."

"I've got a frigging hole in my face and I'm watching soap operas, then you come along and start carping about dead Dolly and funerals." He shot her a single hot look. "Go find somebody else to rag on."

"Fine."

She shoved up.

"Women suck," he repeated with a baffled bitterness that had her easing down again. "We're better off without them."

She opted not to remind him she happened to be a woman. "Altogether, or one in particular?"

"You know the one I hooked up with last winter."

Since he'd mentioned her about a hundred times, shown off her picture, Rowan had a pretty good idea. "Vicki, sure."

"She was coming out in a couple weeks, with the kids. I was getting a few days off to show her around. The kids were all juiced up to see the base."

Were, Rowan thought. "What happened?"

"That's just it. I don't know. She changed her mind, that's all. She doesn't think it's a good idea—I've got my life, she's got hers. She dumped me; that's it. She won't even tell me why, exactly, just how she has to think of the kids, how she needs a stable, honest relationship and all that shit."

He turned, aiming those angry, baffled eyes at Rowan. "I never lied to her, that's the thing. I told her how it was, and she said she was okay with it. Even that she was proud of what I did. Now she's done, just like that. Pissed off, too. And . . . she cried. What the hell did I do?"

"I guess . . . the theory of being attached to somebody who does what we do is different from the reality. It's hard."

"So I'm supposed to give it up? Do something else? Be something else? That's not right."

"No, it's not right."

"I was going to ask her to marry me when she came out."

"Hell. I'm sorry."

"She won't even talk to me now. I keep leaving messages, and she won't answer. She won't let me talk to the kids. I'm crazy about those kids."

"Write her a letter."

"Do what?"

"Nobody writes letters anymore. Write her a letter. Tell her how you feel. Lay it all out."

"Shit, I'm not good at that."

"And that'll make it even better. If you're hung up enough to want to marry her, you can write a damn letter."

"I don't know. Maybe. Hell."

"Women suck."

"Tell me about it. Write a letter," he repeated, brooded into his Gatorade. "Maybe. Talk about something else. If I keep talking about her, I'm going to try to call her again. It's humiliating."

"How about those Cubs?"

He snorted. "I need more than baseball to get my mind off heartbreak, especially since the Cubbies suck more than women this year. We've got murder, and fire starters. I heard there was another one, another body. And whoever did it started the fire. The cops better catch this bastard before he burns half of western Montana. We can all use the fat wallet, but nobody wants to earn it that way."

"He got a good chunk of Idaho, too. It's scary," she said because they were alone. "We know fire wants to kill us when we're going there. We know nature couldn't give a damn either way. But going in, knowing there's somebody out there killing people and lighting it up who maybe wants to see some of us burn. Maybe doesn't give a shit either way. That's scary. It's scary not knowing if he's done, or if the next time the siren sounds, it's because of him."

She looked over as Gull came in. "What did the cops say?" she demanded.

"It's not official, but it's a pretty good bet what we found out there is what's left of Reverend Latterly."

Cards bolted up. "The priest?"

"Loosely." Gull dropped down in a chair. "They found his car out there, and nobody can find him. So, either we did, or he's taken off. They're going to be talking to Brakeman after the funeral."

"They think he killed him and burned him up?" Cards said. "But . . . wouldn't that mean . . . or do they think he killed Dolly and— Her own father? Come on."

"I don't know what they think."

"What do you think?" Rowan asked him.

"I'm still working on it. So far I think we've got somebody who's seriously pissed off, and likes fire. I've got to clean up."

Rowan followed him into his quarters. "Why do you say 'likes fire'? Using it's not the same as liking it."

"I guess since you're dressed—and you look good, by the way—you're not going to wash my back."

"No. Why do you say 'likes fire'?"

Gull pulled off his shirt. "I increased my passing acquaintance with arson after Dolly."

"Yeah, you study. It's a thing with you."

"I like to learn. Anyway," he continued, dragging off his boots. "Arsonists usually fall into camps. There's your for-profit—somebody burning property to collect insurance, say, or the torch who lights them up for a fee. That's not this."

"You've got the torching to cover up another crime. I have a passing acquaintance, too," she reminded him as he took off his pants. "Murder's sure as hell another crime."

"Maybe that's what it was with Dolly." Naked, he walked into the bathroom, turned on the shower. "The accident or on purpose, the panic, the cover-up. But this, coming on top of it, when the first didn't really work?"

He stepped under the spray, let out a long, relieved groan. "All hail the god of water."

"Maybe it was a copycat. Somebody wanted to kill Latterly. Brakeman had motive, so did Latterly's wife if she found out about him and Dolly. One of his congregation who felt

outraged and betrayed. And they mirrored Dolly because of
the connection. It's the same motive."

"Could be."

She whipped back the shower curtain. "It makes the most
sense."

"In or out, Blondie." He skimmed those feline eyes down
her body. "I'd rather in."

She whipped the curtain back closed. "The third type
doesn't play out, Gull. The firebug who gets off starting fires,
watching them burn. It doesn't play because of the murders."

"Maybe he's getting a twofer."

"It's bad enough if it's to cover the murders. That's plenty
bad enough. What you're thinking's worse."

"I know it. If the vibe I got from the cops is right, it's something they're thinking about, too."

She leaned her hands on the sink, stared at her own reflection. "I don't want it to be somebody I know."

"You don't know everybody, Ro."

No, she didn't know everybody, and was suddenly, desper-
ately grateful she knew only a few people who were connected
to Dolly and Latterly.

But . . . what if it was one of those few?

"Dolly's funeral. Where can they have it?" she wondered.
"They couldn't have planned on Mrs. Brakeman's church,
even before this happened."

"Marg said they're having the service in the funeral parlor.
They don't expect much of a crowd."

"God." She shut her eyes. "I hated her like a hemorrhoid,
but that's just depressing."

He shut off the water, pulled back the curtain. "You know
what you need?" He reached for a towel.

"What do I need? Gee, let me guess."

"Gutter brain. You need a drive with the top down and an
ice-cream cone."

"I do?"

"Yeah, you do. We're third load on the jump list, so we can
cruise into town, find ourselves an ice-cream parlor."

"I happen to know where one is."

"Perfect. And you look nice. I should take my girl out for
ice cream."

"Cut that out, Gull."

"Uh-uh." He wrapped the towel around his waist and, still dripping, grabbed her in for a kiss.

"You're getting me wet!"

"Sex, sex, sex. Fine, if that's what you want."

He managed to chase the blues away, make her laugh as she shoved him back. "I want ice cream." Since he'd already dampened her shirt, she grabbed his face, kissed him again. "First. Get dressed, big spender. I'll go check with Ops, make sure we're clear for a few hours."

PHOTOGRAPHS OF DOLLY BRAKEMAN, from birth to death, were grouped together in a smiling display. Pink roses softened with sprigs of baby's breath flanked them. The coffin, closed, bore a blanket of girlish pink and white mums over polished gloss.

As she'd helped Irene by ordering her choice of flowers, Ella sent pink and white lilies. She noted a couple other floral offerings, and even such a sparse tribute overpowered the tiny room with scent.

Irene, pale and stark-eyed in unrelieved black, sat on the somber burgundy sofa with her sister, a woman Ella knew a little who'd come in from Billings with her husband. The man sat, stiff and grim, on a twin sofa across the narrow room with Leo.

Sacred music played softly through the speakers. No one spoke.

In her life, Ella thought, she'd never seen such a sad testament to a short life, violently ended.

Ella crossed the room, took her friend's limp hands. "Irene."

"The flowers look nice."

"They do."

"I appreciate you taking care of that for me, Ella."

"It was no trouble at all."

Irene's sister nodded at Ella, then rose to sit with her husband. "The photographs are lovely. You made good choices."

"Dolly always liked having her picture taken. Even as a baby," she said as Ella sat down beside her, "she'd look right at the camera. I don't know how to do this. I don't know how to bury my girl."

Saying nothing—what was there to say?—Ella put her arms around Irene.

"I've got pictures. All I've got's a lot of pictures. That one there, of Dolly and the baby, is the last one I have. My sister Carrie's bringing the baby soon. She's been a help to me, coming up from Billings. She's bringing Shiloh. I know Shiloh won't understand or remember, but I thought she should be here."

"Of course. You know you can call me, anytime, for anything."

"I don't know what to do, with her things, with her clothes."

"I'll help you with that when you're ready. There's Reverend Meece now."

Irene's hand clutched at Ella's. "I don't know him. It's good you asked him to come do the service, but—"

"He's kind, Irene. He'll be kind to Dolly."

"Leo didn't want any preacher. Not after what . . ." Her eyes welled again. "I can't think about that now. I'll go crazy if I think about that now."

"Don't. Remember the pretty girl in the photographs. Let me bring Reverend Meece over. I think he'll be a comfort to you. I promise."

Though she wasn't much of a churchgoer, Ella liked Meece, his gentle ways. Irene needed gentle now.

"Thank you so much for doing this, Robert."

"No need for thanks. It's a hard day," he said, looking at the coffin. "The kind of day that shakes a mother's faith. I hope I can help her."

As she led him to Irene, she saw a trio of staff from the school come in. Thank God, she thought. Someone came. Leaving Irene with Meece, she went over to take on greeter duties, as Irene's older sister seemed unwilling or unable to shoulder the task.

She excused herself when Irene's younger sister arrived with the baby, her husband and her two children. "Carrie, would you like me to take the baby? I think Irene could use you."

As people formed their groups, quiet conversations began, Ella cuddled the chubby, bright-eyed orphan.

And Leo surged to his feet. "You've got no business here. You've got no right to be here."

The outraged tone had Shiloh's lip quivering with a whimper. Ella murmured reassurance as she turned, saw the small contingent from the base.

"After what you did? The way you treated my girl? You get out. You get the hell *out*!"

"Leo." Across the room, Irene sank back into the sofa. "Stop. Stop." Covering her face with her hands, she burst into harsh sobs.

Ignoring Leo, Marg marched straight to Irene, sat to embrace the woman, to let Irene cry on her shoulder.

"Mr. Brakeman." Irene watched a ruddy-faced, towheaded young man step forward—his jaw as clenched as Leo's fists. "That baby there is my blood as much as yours, and Dolly was her ma. Wasn't a year ago I buried my brother. We both lost something, and Shiloh's what we've got left. We've come to pay Shiloh's ma our respects."

The livid color in Leo's cheeks only deepened. For one horrible moment, Ella imagined the worst. Fists, blood, chaos. Then Lieutenant Quinniock and a woman stepped in, and fear flickered briefly in Leo's eyes.

"Stay away from me," he told the young man. Matt, Ella realized. Matt Brayner.

"That's your uncle," Ella whispered. "That's Uncle Matt. It's okay now."

Leo turned his back, moved as far away as the narrow confines of the room allowed, folded his arms over his chest.

Ella stepped to Matt. "Would you hold her? I'd like to take Irene out for a minute or two, get her some fresh air."

"I'd be pleased." Matt's eyes watered up when the baby reached a chubby hand to his face.

"She favors Jim a little." Lynn spoke quietly. "Don't you think, Matt? She favors Jim?"

Matt's throat worked as he nodded, as he bent his head to press his cheek to Shiloh's.

"Come on with us, Irene." With Marg's help, Ella got Irene to her feet. "Come on with us for a bit."

As they led the sobbing woman out, Ella heard Meece's gentle voice coat over the ugly tension in the room.

ROWAN LICKED her strawberry swirl, enjoying the buzz of
pedestrian and street traffic as she strolled with Gull.

"That's not really ice cream," she told him.

"Maple walnut is not only really ice cream, it's macho ice
cream."

"Maple's for syrup. It's like a condiment. It's like mustard.
Would you eat mustard ice cream?"

"I'm open to all flavors, even your girlie strawberry
parfait."

"This is refreshing." As the drive had been, she thought.
A long, aimless drive on winding roads, and now a slow, pur-
poseless stroll along the green shade of boulevard trees toward
one of the city's parks.

With two of the four-hour breaks ahead of them, she could
let go, relax. Unless the phones in their pockets signaled a call
back to base.

For now she'd just appreciate the respite, the ice cream, the
company and the blissful rarity of a free summer afternoon.

"I'll ignore your syrup ice cream because you had a really
good idea. Twenty-four hours ago, we're in the belly of
the beast, and here we are poking along like a couple of
tourists."

"One makes the other all the more worthwhile."

"You know what, if we're not catching fire, we should complete our tequila shot competition tonight. We can pick up a
bottle of the good stuff before we head back."

"You just want to get me drunk and take advantage of me."

"I don't have to get you drunk for that."

"Suddenly I feel cheap and easy. I like it."

"Maybe we can get Cards into it. He could use the
distraction."

She'd told Gull the situation on the drive in. "The letter's a
good idea. He should follow through."

"Maybe you could help him."

"Me?"

"You've got good words."

"I don't think Cards wants me playing Cyrano for his
Roxanne."

"See?" She drilled a finger into his arm, and put on a bumpkin accent. "You got all that there book-larning."

"Rowan?"

She glanced over at the sound of her name. Feeling awkward, mildly annoyed and uncertain what came next, Rowan lowered her ice cream. "Ah, yeah. Hi."

Ella stayed seated on the bench. "It's nice to see you. I heard you got back this morning." Ella mustered up a smile for Gull. "I'm Ella Frazier, a friend of Rowan's father."

"Gulliver Curry." He stepped over, offered his free hand. "How're you doing?"

"Honestly? Not very well. I've just come from Dolly's funeral, which was as bad as you can imagine. I wanted to walk it off, then I thought I could sit it off. It's so pretty here. But it's not working."

"Why were you . . . Mrs. Brakeman works at your school," Rowan remembered.

"Yes. We've gotten to be friends the last year or so."

"How is she . . . It's stupid to ask how she's doing, if she's okay. She couldn't be okay."

"She's not, and I think it may be worse yet. The police were there, too, and took Leo in for questioning after the service. Irene's in the middle of a nightmare. It's hard to watch a friend going through all this, knowing there's little to nothing you can do to help. And I'm sorry." She caught herself, shook her head. "Here you are on what I'm sure is very rare and precious free time, and I'm full of gloom."

"You need ice cream," Gull decided. "What flavor?"

"Oh, no, I—"

"Ice cream," he repeated, "is guaranteed to cut the gloom. What would you like?"

"You might as well pick something," Rowan told her. "He'll just keep at you otherwise."

"Mint chocolate chip. Thank you."

"I'll be back in a minute."

Only more awkward now, Rowan thought as Gull jogged back in the direction of the ice-cream parlor. "I guess you saw the group from the base."

"Yes. Leo started to cause a scene, which might have escalated. But between Matt, then the police coming in, it died off into awful tension, resentment, grief, smothered rage. And, enough." She closed her eyes. "Just enough of all that. Will you sit? You know your delightful man took off not only to get me ice cream but to give us a few minutes on our own."

"Probably. He likes to put things in motion."

"He's gorgeous, and strikes me as tough and sweet. That's an appealing blend in a man." Ella angled on the bench, putting them face-to-face. "You're uncomfortable with me, with my relationship with your father."

"I don't know you."

"No, you don't. I feel like I know you, least a little, because Lucas talks about you all the time. He loves you so much, is so proud of you. You have to know there's nothing he wouldn't do for you."

"It's mutual."

"I know it. Just as I know if you made it a choice between you and me, I wouldn't stand a chance."

"I'm not going to—"

"Just let me finish, because you don't know me and, at this point, don't particularly like me. Why should you? But since we have this opportunity I'm going to tell you your father is the most wonderful, the most endearing, the most exciting man I've ever known. I made the first move, he was so shy. Oh, God." She pressed a hand to her heart, her face lighting up in the dappled sunlight. "I'd hoped we'd get to know each other, date, enjoy each other's company. And we did. What I never expected was I'd fall in love with him."

Battling a dozen conflicting emotions, Rowan stared at her melting ice cream.

"You're so young. And I know you don't think you are. But you're so young, and it has to be impossible to understand how someone my age can fall just as hard, as deep and terrifyingly as someone yours. But I have, and I know where the power is, Rowan. I hope you'll give me a chance."

"He's never . . . He hasn't been involved with anyone since my mother."

"I know. That makes me very, very lucky. Here comes Gull. From where I'm sitting, we're both very lucky."

Gull skimmed his gaze over Rowan's face before shifting to Ella. "Here you go."

"That was quick."

"We call him Fast Feet." Not sure what to think, Rowan attacked the drips running down her cone.

"Thank you." After the first taste, Ella smiled, tasted again. "You were right, this cuts the gloom. Take my seat," she said as she got up. "I think I can walk this off now. It was nice to talk to you, Rowan."

"Yeah. You too." Sort of, Rowan thought, as Ella walked away.

Gull sat, looked after her. "She's hot."

"Jesus Christ. She's old enough to be your mother."

"My aunt's also hot. A guy doesn't have to want to sleep with a woman to acknowledge the hotness."

"She said she's in love with my father. What am I supposed to say to that? Do about that? Feel about that?"

"Maybe that she has good taste in men." He patted her thigh. "You've got to let these crazy kids work these things out on their own. Anyway, my first—if brief—impression. I liked her."

"Because she's hot."

"Hot is a separate issue. She was sitting here grieving for a friend's loss, worried for that friend and what she might still have to face. Empathy and compassion. She's pissed off at Leo Brakeman, which shows good sense and a lack of hypocrisy. She told you how she felt about your father, when it's pretty clear you're not too crazy about the whole matchup. That took guts, and honesty."

"Maybe you could be her campaign manager." Rowan sat back. "She dropped it in my court, and that was smart. I have the power. So you can add smart to her list of virtues."

"Would you rather see your dad with somebody dumb, self-ish, cold-hearted and hypocritical?"

"You're no dummy, either. Hell, let's buy two bottles of tequila. I could use a good drunk tonight."

"Who says I'm a good drunk?"

ROWAN CHECKED in on Matt when they got back to base, and found him sitting on the side of his bed tying his running shoes.

"I heard it was pretty bad."

"It was, but it could've been worse. Why he wants to blame me and L.B. and, jeez, Marg and Lynn for Dolly getting fired? She brought that on herself."

Good, she thought, he was pissed off, not broody. "Because people suck and generally want anything crappy to be somebody else's fault."

"At the damn funeral? He starts yelling and threatening us at his daughter's funeral?"

"At my mother's funeral, her parents wouldn't even speak to me. They wouldn't speak to me really loud."

"You're right. People suck."

"We're going to have a tequila shooter contest in the lounge later. You're on third load, too. I'll float your entry fee."

That got a smile. "You know I can't compete with you there. I'm going for a run. It's cooled off a little." He fixed on his cap. "I got to see the baby anyway, and even held her a few minutes. I'm thinking my parents ought to talk to a lawyer, about custody or rights and all that."

"That's a tough call, Matt."

He gave the bill of his cap a quick jerk into place as he frowned at Rowan. "She's their blood, too. I don't want to screw with Mrs. Brakeman. I think she's a good person. But if that dickhead she's married to goes to jail, how is she supposed to take care of Shiloh all alone? How's she supposed to pay for all the stuff Shiloh needs on her salary cooking in the school cafeteria?"

"It's a hard situation, and, well, I know you already gave Dolly money for the baby."

Those faded blue eyes flattened out. "It's my money, and my blood."

"I know that. It was good of you to want to help with Shiloh's expenses, to stand in for Jim that way."

He relaxed a little. "It was the right thing to do."

"And it's not always easy to do the right thing in a hard situation. I guess I'd worry bringing lawyers in might murk it up even more. At least right now."

"It doesn't hurt to talk. Everybody should do whatever's best for the baby, right?"

"They should. I . . . I'm probably the wrong person to ask about something like this. Maybe, I don't know, Matt, if your

mother came out . . . if she and Mrs. Brakeman talked about
everything, they could work out what's best, what's right."

"Maybe. She looks like a Brayner, you know? The baby?
Even Lynn said so. I've got to think about it."

She supposed they did, Rowan decided when he headed out
for his run. Matt, his family, the Brakemans, they'd all have to
think about it. But she knew what it was to be the child everybody was thinking about.

It wasn't an easy place to be.

22

Rowan watched Dobie painfully swallow shot number ten. His eyes had gone glassy on eight, and now his cheeks took on a faint, sickly green hue.

"That's twenty."

"Count's ten, Dobie," Cards, official scorekeeper, told him.

"I'm seeing double, so it's twenty." Laughing like a loon, he nearly tipped out of his chair.

Janis, official pourer, filled shot number eleven for Yangtree. "Experience," he said, and knocked it back smooth. "That's the key."

Rowan smirked, licked salt off the back of her hand, then drank hers down. "I'd like to thank the soon-to-be loser for springing for the prime."

"You're welcome." Gull polished off eleven.

"I got another in me." Stovic lifted his glass, proved he did—before he slid bonelessly to the floor.

"And he's out." Cards crossed Stovic off the board.

"I am not out." From the floor, Stovic waved a hand. "I'm fully conscious."

"You leave your chair without calling for a piss break, you're out."

"Who left the chair?"

"Come on, Chainsaw." Gibbons got his hands under Stovic's arms and dragged him out from under the table.

Dobie made it to thirteen before surrendering. "It's this foreign liquor, that's what it is. Oughta be homegrown bourbon." He got down, crawled on his hands and knees and lay down next to a snoring Stovic.

"Rookies." Yangtree got number fourteen down, then laid his head on the table and moaned, "Mommy."

"Did you mean uncle?" Cards demanded, and Yangtree managed to shoot up his middle finger.

Rowan and Gull went head-to-head until Janis split the last shot between them. "That's all there is, there ain't no more."

"Shoulda bought three bottles." Rowan closed one eye to focus and click her glass to Gull's. "On three?"

Those still conscious in the room counted off, then cheered when the last drops went down.

"And that's a draw," Cards announced.

"I'm proud to know you." Janis dropped a hand on each shoulder. "And wish you the best of luck with tomorrow's hangover."

"Gull doesn't get 'em."

He smiled, a little stupidly, into Rowan's eyes. "This might be the exception. Let's go have lotsa drunk sex before it hits."

"'Kay. Drunk sex for everybody!" She waved her hands and smacked a barely awake Yangtree in the face. "Oops."

"No, I needed that. Everybody still alive?"

"Can't make that much noise dead." Rowan gestured to snoring-in-stereo Stovic and Dobie as she swayed to her feet. "Follow me, stud."

"I'm with the blonde." Gull staggered after her.

"We can do this." She fumbled at his shirt when he booted the door shut on the third try. "Soon as the room stops spinning around."

"Pretend we're doing it on a merry-go-round."

"Naked at the carnival." On a wild laugh she defeated his shirt, but started to teeter. When he grabbed for her, she took them both onto the floor, hard.

"I think that hurt, but it's better down here, 'cause of the gravity."

"Okay." He shifted off her to struggle with her clothes. "We should do naked tequila shots. Then we wouldn't have to take them off after."

"Now you think of it. Alley-oop!" She held up her arms to help him strip off her shirt. "Gimme, gimme." She locked her legs around his waist, her arms around his neck, then latched her mouth onto his.

The heat burned through the tequila haze, fired in the senses. The world rolled and turned, yet she remained constant, chained around him. Caged, he met the desperate demand of her mouth, rocking center to center until he thought he'd go mad.

The chains broke. She rolled on top of him, biting, grasping, lapping, then rolled off again.

"Get naked," she ordered. "Beat ya."

They tugged at shoes, clothes in a panting race. With clothes still landing in heaps, they dived at each other. Wrestling now, skin damp and slick, they rolled over the floor. Knees and elbows banged, and still her laughter rang out. The moonlight turned her dewed skin to silver, glowing and precious, irresistible.

Breathless with pleasure, crazed with a whirling, spinning need, she threw her head back when he plunged into her.

"Take me like you mean it."

And he did, God, he did, filling her up, wringing her out while she pushed for more. Catching fire, she thought, leaping into the heart of the blaze. She rode the heat until it simply consumed her.

"Merry-go-round," she murmured. "Still turning. Stay right here." This time she drew him close before they slept.

ANOTHER FIRE WOKE HER, the fire that killed, that hunted and destroyed. It growled behind her, pawing at the ground as she ran. She flew through the black, yet still it came, stalking her to the graveyard where the dead lay unburied on the ground. Waiting for her.

Jim's eyes rolled up in the sockets of the charred skull. "Killed me dead."

"I'm sorry. I'm so sorry."

"Plenty of that going around. Plenty of dragon fever. It's not finished. More to come. Fire can't burn it away. But it can sure try."

From behind her, it breathed, and its breath ignited her like kindling.

"HEY, HEY." Gull pulled her to sitting, shaking her by the shoulders on the way. "Snap out of it."

She shoved at him, gulping for air, but he tightened his grip. He couldn't see her clearly, but he could feel her, hear her. The shakes and tremors, the cold sweat, the whistle of air as she fought for breath.

"You had a nightmare." He spoke more calmly now. "A bad one. It's done."

"Can't breathe."

"You can. You are, just too fast. You're going to hyperventilate if you keep it up. Slow it down, Rowan."

Even as she shook her head, he started rubbing her shoulders, moving up her neck where the muscles strained stiff as wire. "It's a panic attack. You know that in your head. Let the rest of you catch up. Slow it down."

He saw her eyes now as his own vision adjusted, wide as planets. She pressed a hand to her chest where he imagined the pressure crushed like an anvil. "Breathe out, long breath out. Long out, slow in. That's the way. Let go of it. Do it again, smooth it out. You're okay. Keep it up, in and out. I'm going to get you some water."

He let her go to roll to her cooler, grab a bottle.

"Don't guzzle," he warned her. "We're in slow mode." When she gulped the first swallow, he tipped the bottle down. "Easy."

"Okay." She took another, slower sip. She stopped, went back to breathing, with more control, less trembling. "Wow."

He touched her face, leaned in to rest his brow on hers. The shudder he'd held back rocked through him.

"You scared the shit out of me."

"That makes two of us. I didn't scream, did I?" She glanced toward the door as she asked.

Trust her, Gull thought, to worry about embarrassing herself with the rest of the crew. "No. It was like you were trying to and couldn't get it out."

"I was on fire. I swear I could feel my skin burning, smell my hair going up. Pretty damn awful."

"How often do you have them?" Now that the crisis had passed, he could coddle her a little—a comfort to himself, too. So he touched his lips to her forehead as he shifted to rub her back and shoulders.

"I never used to have them. Or just the usual monster-in-the-closet deal once in a while when I was a kid. But I started having them after Jim. Replaying the jump, then how we found him. They eased off over the winter, but started coming back at the start of the season. And they're getting worse."

"You found another fire victim, someone else you knew. That would kick it up some."

"He's started to talk to me in them—cryptic warnings. I know it's my head putting words in his mouth, but I can't figure it out."

"What did he say tonight?"

"That it wasn't finished. There'd be more coming. I guess I'm worried there will be, and that's probably all there is to it."

"Why are you worried?"

"Well, Jesus, Gull, who isn't?"

"No, be specific."

"Be specific at half past whatever in the morning after twisting myself up into a panic attack?"

The irritation in her tone settled him down. "Yeah."

"I don't *know*. If I knew, I'd . . . Dolly and Latterly, obviously that's connected. The odds of them both running afoul of some homicidal arsonist are just short of nil. If we were dealing with random, that would be cause for some serious worry. But this isn't, and they're probably going to bust Brakeman for the whole shot. But . . ."

"But you're having a hard time buying he'd set fire to his own daughter's body. So am I."

"Yeah, but that's what makes the most sense. He finds out Dolly's not only lying but screwing the preacher. They fight about it, he kills her—in a rage, by accident, however. Then panics, does the rest. It broke something in him."

Tears running down his face, she remembered.

"He shoots at us, kills Latterly. Case closed."

"Except you don't quite believe it. Hence—"

"Hence," she repeated, and snickered.

"That's right. Hence you have nightmares where Jim—who's connected to you and to Dolly—verbalizes what you're already thinking, at least on a subconscious level."

"Thanks, Dr. Freud."

"And your fifty minutes are up. You should catch the couple hours' sleep we've got left."

"We're still on the floor. The floor was most excellent, but for sleep, the bed's better."

"The bed it is." He rose, grabbed her hand to pull her up. Then, to make her laugh, swept her up in his arms.

Laugh she did. "I may have shed a few this season, but I'm still no lightweight."

"You're right." He dropped her onto the bed. "Next time, you carry me." He stretched out beside her. "One thing, it looks like your nightmare blew any potential tequila hangover out of me."

"Always the bright side."

He snuggled her in, gently stroking her back until he felt her drop off.

AFTER THE MORNING BRIEFING, she got in her run, some weight training and power yoga with Gull for company. She had to admit, having someone who could keep up with her, and more, made the daily routine more fun.

They hit the dining hall together where Dobie slumped over a plate of toast and what Rowan recognized as a glass of Marg's famed hangover cure.

"Mmm, look at these big, fat sausages." Rowan clattered the top back on the warmer. "Nothing like pig grease in the morning."

"I'll hurt you when I can move without my head blowing up."

"Hangover?" she asked sweetly. "Gosh, I feel *great*." There might have been a dull, gnawing ache at the base of her skull, but all things considered, small price to pay.

"Hurt you, and all your kin. Your pets, too."

She only grinned as she sat down with a full plate. "Not much appetite this morning?"

"I woke up on the floor with Stovic. I may never eat again."

"How's Stovic?" Gull asked.

"Last I saw him, his eyes were full of blood, and he was crawling toward his quarters. If I ever pick up a glass of tequila again, shoot me. It'd be a mercy."

"Drink that," Rowan advised. "It won't make you jump up and belt out 'Oh, What a Beautiful Morning,' but it'll take the edge off."

"It's brown. And I think something's moving in there."

"Trust me."

When he picked up the Tabasco Lynn kept on the table for him, Rowan started to tell him he wouldn't need it—then smiled to herself as she cut into a sausage.

Dobie doused the concoction liberally, gave a brisk, bracing nod. "Down the hatch," he announced. Closing his eyes, he drank it down fast.

And his eyes popped open as his face went from hangover gray to lobster red. "Holy shitfire!"

"Burns like a helitorch." Struggling with laughter, Rowan ate more sausage. "It may scorch some brain cells while it's at it, but it fires through the bloodstream. You've been purified, my child."

"He's not going to speak in tongues, is he?" Gull asked.

"Holy shitfire. *That's* a drink. All it needs is a shot of bourbon. Man, makes me sweat."

Fascinated, Gull watched sweat pop out on Dobie's red face. "Flushing out the toxins, I guess. What the hell's in there?"

"She won't tell. She makes you start with the M-and-M Breakfast—Motrin and Move-Free—with a full glass of water, then drink that, eat toast, drink more water."

"Said I had to do my run, too."

"Yeah." Rowan nodded at Dobie. "And by lunchtime, you'll feel mostly human and be able to eat. Somebody ought to drag Stovic down here—and Yangtree. Hey, Cards," she said when he walked in. "How about hauling Stovic's and Yangtree's pitiful asses down here so we can pour some of Marg's hangover antidote into them?"

He said nothing until he'd taken the chair beside hers, angled it toward her. "L.B. just got word from the cops. The rangers found a gun, half buried a few yards from where they found the preacher's car. They ran it. It's one of Brakeman's."

"Well." Deliberately she spread huckleberry jelly on a breakfast biscuit. "I guess that answers that."

"They went to pick him up this morning. He's gone, his truck's gone."

Jelly dripped off her knife as she stared at him. "You don't mean as in gone to work."

"No. It looks like he took camping gear, a shotgun, a rifle, two handguns and a whole hell of a lot of ammo. His wife said she didn't know where he'd gone, or that he'd packed up in the first place. I don't know if they believe her or not, but from what L.B. says, nobody seems to have the first goddamn clue where he is."

"I thought— I heard they were going to take him in after the funeral yesterday."

"For questioning, yeah. But he has a lawyer and all that, and until they had the gun, Ro, they didn't have anything on him for this shit."

"For Christ's sake," Gull exploded. "Didn't they have him under surveillance?"

"I don't know. I don't know dick-all about it, Gull. But L.B. says he wants you to stay on base, Ro, unless we catch a fire. He wants you to stay inside as much as possible until we know what the fuck. And he doesn't want to hear any carping about it."

"I'll work in the loft."

"They'll get him, Ro. It won't take them long."

"Sure."

He gave her arm an awkward pat. "I'll roust Yangtree and Stovic. It'll be fun watching the smoke come out of their ears when they drink the hangover cure."

In the silence that followed Cards's exit, Dobie got up, poured himself coffee. "I'm going to say this 'cause I have a lot of respect for you. And because Gull's got more than that for you. If I took off into the hills back home, if I had the gear—hell, even without it, but if I had the gear, a good gun, a good knife, I could live up there for months. Nobody'd find me I didn't want finding me."

Rowan made herself continue eating. "They'll find his truck, maybe, but they won't find him. He'll lose himself in the Bitter-roots, or the Rockies. His wife'll lose her home. She put it up for his bond, and he just fucking broke that. I didn't believe he'd done it—or not Dolly. He's running, and left his wife and grand-daughter twisting in the wind. He abandoned them.

"I hope he screws up." She shoved to her feet. "I hope he screws up and they catch him, and they toss him in a hole for the rest of his life. I'll be in the loft, sewing goddamn Smitty bags."

As she stomped out, Dobie dumped three heaping spoons of sugar into his coffee. "How do you want to play this, son?"

"Intellectually, I don't think Brakeman's coming back around here, or worrying about Rowan right now."

"Mmm-hmm. How do you want to play it?"

He looked over. Sometimes the most unlikely person became the most trusted friend. "When we're on base, some-body's with her, round the clock. We make sure she has plenty to do inside. But she needs to get out. If we hole her in, she'll blow. I guess we mix up the routine. We usually run in the mornings, early. We'll start running in the evening."

"If everybody wore caps, sunglasses, it'd be a little harder to tell who's who at a distance. The trouble is, that woman's built like a brick shithouse. You just can't hide that talent. I don't guess she'd transfer to West Yellowstone, or maybe over to Idaho for a stretch."

"No. She'd see that as running. Abandonment."

"Maybe. But maybe not, if you went, too."

"She's not there yet, Dobie."

Dobie pursed his lips, watching Gull as he drank coffee. "But you are?"

Gull stared down at his half-eaten breakfast. "Fucking lupines."

"What the hell's lupines?"

Gull just shook his head. "Yeah, I'm there," he said as he got to his feet. "Goddamn it."

Southern, Gibbons and Janis came in, still sweaty from PT, as Gull stormed out.

"What's that about?" Gibbons demanded.

"Sit down, boys and girls, and I'll tell you."

TEMPER BUBBLING, Gull tracked down L.B. outside a hangar in conversation with one of the pilots.

"How the fuck did this happen?"

"Do you think I didn't ask the same damn thing?" L.B. tossed back. "Do you think I'm not pissed off?"

"I don't care if you're pissed off. I want some answers."

L.B. jerked a thumb, headed away from the hangar and toward one of the service roads. "If you want to jump somebody's ass, find a cop. They're the ones who screwed this up."

"I want to know how."

"You want to know how? I'll tell you how." L.B. picked up a palm-sized rock, heaved it. "They had two cops outside the Brakeman house. Shit, probably looking at skin mags and eating donuts."

He found another rock, heaved that. "My fucking brother's a cop, over in Helena, and I know he doesn't do that shit. But goddamn it."

Gull leaned over, picked up a rock, offered it. "Go ahead."

"Thanks." After hurling it, L.B. rolled his shoulder. "They were out in the front, watching the house. Brakeman's truck is around the side, under a carport. So he loads it up sometime in the middle of the night, then he pushes it right across the backyard, cuts a truck-sized hole in the frigging fence, then pushes it right across the neighbor's yard to the road. Then God knows where he went."

"And the cops don't see the truck's gone until this morning."

"No, they fucking don't."

"Okay."

"Okay? That's it?"

"It's an answer. I do better with answers. She's third load. Can you put her on Ops if we get a call for one or two?"

"Yeah." L.B. picked up another rock, just stared at it a moment, then dropped it again. "I'd figured on it. I just wanted to wait until she'd cooled off."

"I'll tell her."

"She's been known to kill the messenger. That's why I sent Cards," L.B. added with a slow smile. "He's just off the DL, so I figured she'd take it easy on him."

"That's why you're chief."

Gull swung by the barracks to grab a Coke, considered, and though he thought it the lamest form of camouflage outside a Groucho mustache, he grabbed caps and sunglasses.

On the way to the loft, he pulled out his phone, called Lucas.

Since most of the unit was doing PT or still at breakfast, he found only a handful working in the loft along with Rowan. She inspected, gore by gore, a canopy hanging in the tower.

"Busy," she said shortly.

He tipped the Coke from side to side. "You know you're jonesing by now."

"Very busy." Using tweezers, she removed some pine needles lodged in the cloth.

"Fine, I'll drink it." He popped the top. "L.B. wants you in Ops if we catch a fire."

She jerked around. "He's not grounding me."

"I didn't say that. You're third load, so unless we catch a holocaust, you're probably not going to jump on the first call. You're a qualified assistant Ops manager, aren't you?"

She grabbed the Coke from him, gulped some down. "Yeah." She shoved it back at him, returned to her inspection. "Thanks for letting me know."

"No problem. About this situation."

"I don't want or need to be reassured, protected, advised or—"

"Jesus, shut up." He shook his head at the ceiling towering above, took another drink.

"*You* shut up."

He had to grin. "I'm rubber; you're glue. You really want to sink that low? I don't think Brakeman's your problem."

"I'm not worried about him. I can take care of myself, and I'm not stupid. I've got plenty to keep me busy, here, in manufacturing, in the gym when I'm not out on a fire."

Meticulously she removed a twig, marked a small, one-inch tear for repair before she lowered the apex to examine higher areas.

"Last night, Brakeman eluded two cops by pushing his full-size pickup across his backyard, cutting a fence, pushing it across another yard until he reached the road. He loaded up everything he'd need to live in the wild. That tells me he's not stupid, either."

"So he's not stupid. Points for him."

"But he leaves weapons, *twice*, so they're easily found. A handgun properly registered to him, a rifle that has his name on it. That's pretty damn stupid."

"You're back to thinking he didn't do any of this."

"I'm back to that. I'd rather not be, because this way, we've got nothing. We don't know who or why. Not really. On the other hand, I'm also thinking it's unlikely anyone's going to be using you or the base for target practice. Unlikely isn't enough, but it's comforting."

"Because it would be stupid for somebody else to shoot at me, when Brakeman's on the run and the cops know what weapons he's got with him."

No, she wasn't stupid, she reminded herself, but she'd been too angry to think clearly. Gull, it seemed, didn't have the same problem.

"But if it's not him, Gull, why is somebody working so hard to make it look like him?"

"Because he's an asshole? Because he's plausible? Because they want to see him go down? Maybe all three. But the point is, you've got to be smart—and you are—but I don't think you have to sweat this."

She nodded, inspected the apex bridle cords, then the vent hoods.

"I wasn't sweating it. I'm pissed off."

"Your subconscious sweats it, then."

"All right, all right." She inspected the top of each slot, then the anti-inversion net. There she marked a line of broken stitching.

Gull waited her out until she'd attached the inspection tag to the riser.

"I guess I have to call my father. Word travels, and he'll get worried."

"I talked to him before I came up. We went over it."

"He came by? Why didn't he—"

"I called him."

She faced him with one quick pivot. "You did what? What do you mean calling my father about all this before I—"

"It's called male bonding. You'll never get it. I believe women are as capable as men, deserve equal pay—and that one day, should be sooner than later, in my opinion, the right woman can and should be leader of the free world. But you can't understand the male bonding rituals any more than men can understand why the vast majority of women are obsessed with shoes and other footwear."

"I'm not obsessed with shoes, so don't try to make this something cultural or—or gender-based."

"You have three pairs of jump boots. Two is enough. You have four pairs of running shoes. Again, two's plenty."

"I'm breaking in a third pair of jump boots before the first pair gets tossed so I don't get boot-bit. And I have four pairs of running shoes because . . . you're trying to distract me from the point."

"Yes, but I'm not done. You also have hiking boots—two pairs—three pairs of sandals and three of really sexy heels. And this is just on base. God knows what you've got in your closet at home."

"You've been counting my shoes? Talk about obsessed."

"I'm just observant. Lucas wants you to call him when you get a chance. Leave him a text or voice message if he's in the air, and he'll come by to see you tonight. He likes knowing I've got your back. You'd have mine, wouldn't you?" he asked before she could snap at him.

So she sighed. "Yes. You defeat me with your reason and your diatribe over shoes. Over which I am *not* obsessed."

"You also have a good dozen pairs of earrings, none of which you wear routinely. But we can discuss that another time."

"Oh, go away. Go study something."

"You could give me a rigging lesson. I want to work on getting certified."

"Maybe. Come back in an hour, and we'll—"

When the siren sounded she stepped back. "I guess not. I'm switching to Ops."

"I'll walk you over. Here."

He handed her her cap and sunglasses, then put on his own while she frowned at them.

"What is this?"

"A disguise." He grinned at her. "Dobie wants you to wear them. Let's give him a break, or he might order fake mustaches and clown noses off the Internet."

She rolled her eyes, but put them on. "And what, this makes us look like twins? Where are your tits?"

"You're wearing them, and may I say they look spectacular on you."

"I can't disagree with that. Still, everybody should stop worrying about Rowan and do their jobs."

By four P.M., she was jumping fire, doing hers.

23

July burned. Hot and dry, the wild ignited, inflamed by light-ning strikes, negligence, an errant spark bellowed by a gust of wind.

For eighteen straight days and nights Zulies jumped and fought fire. In Montana, in Idaho, Colorado, California, the Dakotas, New Mexico. Bodies shed weight, lived with pain, exhaustion, injury, battling in canyons, on ridges, in forests.

The constant war left little time to think about what lived outside the fire. The manhunt for Leo Brakeman heading into its third week hardly mattered when the enemy shot firebrands the size of cannonballs or swept on turbulent winds over bar-riers so effortfully created.

Along with her crew, Rowan rushed up the side of Mount Blackmore, like a battalion charging into hell. Beside her another tree torched off, spewing embers like flaming confetti. They felled burning trees on the charge, sawed and cut the low-hanging branches the fire could climb like snakes.

Can't let her climb, Rowan thought as they hacked and dug. Can't let her crown.

Can't let her win.

So they fought their way up the burning mountain, sweat running in salty rivers in the scorched air.

When Gull climbed up the line to her position, she pulled down her bandanna to pour water down her aching throat.

"The line's holding." He jerked a thumb over his shoulder. "A couple of spots jumped it, but we pissed them out. Gibbons is going to leave a couple down there to scout for more, and send the rest up to you."

"Good deal." She took another drink, scanning and counting yellow shirts and helmets through the smoke. On the left the world glowed, eerie orange with an occasional spurt of flame that picked out a hardened, weary face, tossed it into sharp relief.

In that moment, she loved them, loved them all with a near religious fervor. Every ass and elbow, she thought, every blister and burn.

Her eyes lit when she looked at Gull. "Best job ever."

"If you don't mind starving, sweating and eating smoke."

Grinning, she shouldered her Pulaski. "Who would? Head on up. We're still making line here so—" She broke off, grabbed his arm.

It spun out of the orange wall, whipped by the wind. The funnel of flame whirled and danced, spinning a hundred feet into the air. In seconds, screaming like a banshee, it uprooted two trees.

"Fire devil. *Run!*" She pointed toward the front of the line as its wind blasted the furnace heat in her face. She grabbed her radio, watching the flaming column's spin as she shouted to the crew, "Go up, go up! *Move* your asses. Gibbons, fire devil, south flank. Stay *clear.*"

It roared toward the line, a tornadic gold light as gorgeous as it was terrifying, spewing flame, hurling fiery debris. The air exploded with the call of it, with its lung-searing heat. She watched Matt go down, saw Gull haul him up, take his weight. Keeping her eye on the fire devil, she shifted, got her shoulder under Matt's other arm.

"Just my ankle. I'm okay."

"Keep moving! Keep moving!"

It snaked toward them, undulating. They'd never outrun it,

she thought, not with Matt stumbling and limping between them. Behind Matt's back, Gull's hand gripped her elbow, and in acknowledgment, she did the same.

This is it. Even thinking it she pushed up the ridge. No time for emergency gear, for the shelters.

"There!" Gull jerked her, with Matt between them, to the right, and another five precious feet. He shoved her under the enormous boulder first, then Matt, before crawling under behind them.

"Here we go," Gull breathed, and stared into Rowan's eyes while the world erupted.

Rock exploded and rained down like bullets. Through smoke black as pitch, Rowan saw a blazing tree crash and vomit out a flood of flame and sparks.

"Short, shallow breaths, Matt." She gripped his hand, squeezed hard. "Just like in a shake and bake."

"Is this what Jim felt?" Tears and sweat rolled down his face. "Is this what he felt?"

"Short and shallow," she repeated. "Through your bandanna, just like in a shelter."

For an instant, another, the heat built to such mad intensity she wondered if they'd all just torch like a tree. She worked her other hand free, found Gull's. And held on.

Then the screaming wind silenced.

"It's cooling. We're okay. We're okay?" she repeated, in a question this time.

"What can you see?" Gull asked her.

"The smoke's starting to thin, a little. We've got a lot of spots. Spots, no wall, no devil." She shifted as much as she could. "Get behind me, Matt, so I can look out." She angled beside Gull, cautiously eased her head out to look out, up. "It didn't crown, didn't roll the wall. Just spots. Jesus, Gull, your jacket's smoking." She beat at it with her hands as he worked to shrug out of it. "Are you burned?" she demanded. "Did it get you?"

"I don't think so." He crab-walked back. "The ground's still hot. Watch yourselves."

Rowan crawled out, reaching for her radio. On it Gibbon shouted her name.

"It's Ro, Gull, Matt. We're good. We're clear. Is everybody all right? Is everybody accounted for?"

"We are now." Relief flooded his voice. "Where the hell are you?"

She stood, scanned the area to give him the best coordinates. "Matt's bunged up his ankle. Gull and I can handle these spots, but we dumped most of the gear on the run so . . . Never mind," she said as she heard the shouts, saw the yellow shirts through the smoke. "Cavalry's coming this way."

Dobie came on the run with Trigger right behind him. "Jesus Christ, why don't you just give us all heart attacks and get it over with?"

He grabbed Gull, slapped his back. "What the hell happened to you?"

"A little dance with the devil. Better put out those spots before we end up having to run again."

Trigger crouched beside Matt, held out a scorched and mangled helmet. "Found your brainbucket, snookie. You're a lucky bastard." He put Matt in a headlock, a sign of relief and affection. "A lucky son of a bitch. Have a souvenir."

He set the helmet beside Matt before hurrying over to help Dobie with the spot fires.

"Let's check that ankle out." Rowan knelt to undo his boot.

"I thought we were finished. I would've been finished if you and Gull hadn't gotten me in there. You saved my life. You could've lost yours trying."

She probed gently at his swollen ankle. "We're Zulies. When one of us goes down, we pick them up. I don't think it's broken. Just sprained bad enough to earn you a short vacation."

She looked up, smiled at him as she started to wrap it. "Lucky bastard."

Though he protested, they medevaced Matt out, while the rest of the crew beat the fire back, finally killing it in the early hours of the morning. Mop-up took another full day of digging, beating, dousing.

"You volunteered to stay back, confirm the put-out," Rowan told Gull.

"I've got to quit all this volunteering."

"With me. The rest are packing out."

"That's not such a bad deal."

"We've got MREs, a cool mountain spring, in which the beer fairy has snugged a six-pack."

"And people say she doesn't exist."

"What do people know? I wanted to see this one through, all the way, and take a breath, I guess. So you're good with it?"

"What do you think?"

"Then let's take a hike, start doing a check before the sun goes down."

They moved through the burnout at an easy pace, looking for smoke and smolder.

"I wanted to wait until it was over—all the way—before I said anything about it," Rowan began. "I didn't think we were going to make it back there against the fire devil. If you hadn't spotted those boulders, reacted fast, we'd have all ended up like Matt's now-famous helmet."

"I don't plan on losing you. Anyway, if you'd been on my side, you'd've seen the boulders."

"I like to think so. It was beautiful," she said after a moment, and with reverence. "It might be crazy to say that, think that, about something that really wants to kill you, but it was beautiful. That spinning column of fire, like something from another world. In a way, I guess it is."

"Once you see one, it changes things because you know you can't beat it. You run and hide and you pray, and if you live through it, for a while, all the bullshit in real life doesn't mean dick."

"For a while. I guess that's why I wanted to stay out, stick with it a little longer. There's a lot of bullshit waiting out there. Leo Brakeman's still out there. He's no fire devil, but he's still out there."

She blew out a breath. "Every time we get a call, I wonder if we're going to stumble over another body. His, someone else's. Because he's out there. And if he didn't start those fires, whoever did is out there, too."

"It's been three weeks. That's a long time between."

"But it doesn't feel over and done."

"No. It doesn't feel over and done."

"That's the bullshit waiting." She gestured. "Why don't you

take that direction, I'll take this one. We'll cover more ground, then meet back at camp." She checked her watch. "Say six-thirty."

"In time for cocktails and hors d'oeuvres."

SHE BEAT HIM BACK to the clearing by the bubbling stream. The campsite, a hive the night before of very tired, very grungy bees, held quiet as a church now, and shimmered in the rays of evening sun. She stowed her gear, checked on the six-pack of beer and the six-pack of Coke she'd asked L.B. to drop.

She'd rather have that, she realized, in this remote spot on the mountain than a bottle of the finest champagne in the fanciest restaurant in Montana.

In anywhere.

She went back for her PG bag and her little bottles of liquid soap and shampoo.

Alone in the sunlight, she pulled off her boots, socks, stripped off the tired work clothes. The stream barely hit her knees, but the cool rush of the water felt like heaven. She sat down, let it bubble over her skin as she looked up to the rise of trees, the spread of sky.

She took time washing, as another woman might in a hot, fragrant bubble bath, enjoying the cool, the clean, the way the water rushed away with the froth she made.

Drawing her knees up, she wrapped her arms around them, laid her cheek on her knees, closed her eyes.

She opened them again as a shadow fell over her, and smiled lazily up at Gull. Until she saw the camera.

"You did not take my picture like this. Am I going to have to break that thing?"

"It's for my private collection. You're a fantasy, Rowan. Goddess of the brook. How's the water?"

"Cold."

He, as she did, pulled off his boots. "I could use some cold."

"You're late. It's got to be close to seven."

"I had a little detour."

"Did you find fresh spots?"

"No, all clear. But I found these." He picked up a water bottle filled with wildflowers.

"You know you're not supposed to pick flowers up here." But she couldn't stop the smile.

"Since we save them, I figured the mountain could spare a few. Yeah, it's pretty damn cold," he said as he stepped into the water. "Feels great."

She pulled out the bottle of soap she'd shoehorned between rocks, tossed it to him. "Help yourself. It feels like we're the only two people in the world. I wouldn't want to be the only two people in the world for long—who'd do the cooking?—but it's nice for right now."

"I heard birds in the black. They're already coming back, at least to see what the hell happened. And in the green, across the meadow where I got the flowers, I saw a herd of elk. We may be the only people here, but life rolls on."

"I'm going to get dressed before I freeze." She stood, water sliding down her body, sun glinting to turn it to tiny diamonds.

"Wow," Gull said.

"For that, and the bottle of wildflowers, I guess you've earned a beer." She got out, shivering now, rubbing her skin to warm and dry it. "We've got spaghetti and meat sauce, fruit cups, crackers and cheese spread and pound cake for dinner."

"Right now I could eat cardboard and be happy, so that sounds amazing."

"I'll get the campfire going," she told him as she dressed. "And you get the beer when you get out. I guess cocktails and hors d'oeuvres will consist of— Holy shit."

"That I don't want to eat, even now."

"Don't move. Or do—*really* fast."

"Why?"

"Life rolls along, including the big-ass bear on the other bank."

"Oh, fuck me." Gull turned slowly, watched the big-ass bear lumber up toward the stream.

"This may be your fantasy come true, but I really think you should get out of the water."

"Crap. Throw something at him," Gull suggested as he stayed low, edging through the water.

"Like what, harsh words? Shit, shit, he's looking at us."

"Get one of the Pulaskis. I'm damned if I'm going to be eaten by a bear when I'm naked."

"I'm sure it's a more pleasant experience dressed. He's not going to eat us. They eat berries and fish. Get out of the water so he doesn't think you're a really big fish."

Gull pulled himself out, stood dripping, eyeing the bear and being eyed. "Retreat. Slowly. He's probably just screwing with us, and he'll go away, but in case."

Even as Rowan reached down for the gear, the bear turned its back on them. It squatted, shat, then lumbered away the way it came.

"Well, I guess he showed us what he thinks of us." Overcome, Rowan sat on the ground, roared with laughter. "A real man would go after him, make him pay for that insult—so I could then tend your wounds."

"Too bad, you're stuck with me." Gull scooped both hands through his dripping hair. "Christ, I want that beer."

AS FAR AS GULL was concerned, ready-to-eat pasta and beer by a crackling campfire in the remote mountain wilderness scored as romantic as candlelight and fine wine in crystal. And beat the traditional trappings on the fun scale by a mile.

She'd relaxed for the first time in weeks, he thought, basking in the aftermath of a job well done and the solitude of what they'd preserved.

"Does your family do the camping thing?" she asked him.

"Not so much. My aunt's more the is-there-room-service? type. I used to go with some buddies. We'd head up the coast—road trip, you know? Pick a spot. I always figured to head east, take on the Appalachian Trail, but between this and the arcade, I haven't pulled that one off."

"That'd be a good one. We mostly stuck to Montana, for recreation. There's so much here anyway. My dad would work it out so he'd have two consecutive days off every summer, and take me. We'd never know when he'd get them, so it was always spur-of-the-moment."

"That made it cooler," Gull commented, and she just beamed at him.

"It really did. It didn't occur to me until after I'd joined the unit that wilderness camping on his days off probably wouldn't have been his first choice. I imagine he could've used that room service."

"Kids come first, right? The universal parental code."

"I guess it should be. I was thinking about Dolly and her father earlier, and the way they'd tear into each other. Was it their fractured dynamic that made her the way she was, or did the way she was fracture the dynamic?"

"Things are hardly ever all one way or the other."

"More a blend," she agreed. "A little from each column. Don't you wonder what aimed her at Latterly? There are plenty of unmarried men she could've hooked up with. And he was, what, about fifteen years older and not what you'd call studly."

"Maybe he was a maniac in bed."

"Yeah, still waters and so on, but you've got to get into bed to find that out. A married guy with three kids. A God guy. If she'd really planned on reeling him in toward the 'I do's,' didn't she consider what her life would be like? A preacher's wife, and stepmother of three? She'd have hated it."

"It might just have been a matter of proving something. Married God guy, father of three. And she thinks, I could get him if I wanted."

"I don't get that kind of thinking," she stated. "For a one-night stand, I can see it. You've got an itch, you scope out the talent in the bar, rope one out of the herd to scratch it. I don't see wrecking a family for another notch on the bedpost."

"Because you're thinking like you." Gull opened the last two beers. "The older-man thing. He'd probably be inclined to indulge her, and be really grateful that a woman her age, with her looks, wanted to sleep with him. It's a pretty good recipe for infatuation on both sides."

She angled her head. "You know, you're right. A guy a little bored in his marriage, a needy young single mother. There's a recipe. Of course, for all we know Latterly might've been a hound dog boning half the women in his congregation, and Dolly was just the latest."

"If so, the cops'll find out, if they haven't already. Sex is never off the radar."

"Maybe they'll have this thing wrapped up when we get

back." She broke off a piece of pound cake. "Nobody talks about it much, but it's on everybody's mind. L.B.'s especially because he's got to think about everybody, evaluate everybody, worry about everybody."

"Yeah, he's handling a lot. He has a smooth way of juggling."

"My rookie season, we had Bootstrap. He was okay, ran things pretty smooth, but you could tell, even a rook could tell, his head was already halfway into retirement. He had this cabin up in Washington State, and that's where he wanted to be. Everybody knew it was his last season. He kept a distance, if you know what I mean, with the rookies especially."

Gull nodded, sampled pound cake. Ambrosia. "He didn't want to get close. Didn't want to make any more personal bonds."

"I think that was a good part of it. Then L.B. took over. You know how he is. He's the boss, but he's one of us. Everybody knows if you need to bitch or whine or let off steam, you can go to him."

"Here's to L.B."

"Bet your ass." She tipped her head as they clinked beer cans. "I like having sex with you."

Those cat eyes gleamed in the firelight. "That's a non-sequitur I can get behind."

"Seriously. It occurs to me that the season's half over, and I've never had another one like it. Murder, arson, mayhem, and I'm having sex regularly."

"Let's hope the last element is the only one that spills over into the second half."

"Absolutely. The thing is, Gulliver, while I really like sex with you, I also realize that if we stopped having sex—"

"Bite your tongue."

"If we did," she said with a laugh, "I'd still like sitting around the fire with you, and talking about whatever."

"Same here. Only I want the sex."

"Handy for both of us. What makes it better, over and above the regular, is you don't secretly wish I'd be something else. Less tied up with the job, more inclined to fancy underwear."

He pulled out a cigar, lit it. Blew out a long stream. "I like fancy underwear. Just for the record."

"It doesn't bother you that I had a hand in training you, and I might be the one giving you orders on a fire."

She took the cigar when he offered it, enjoyed the tang. "Because you know who you are, and that matters. I can't push you around, and that matters, too. And there's this thing I didn't think mattered because it never did. But it does when it's mixed in with the rest. When it's blended, like we said before. You bring me flowers in a bottle."

"I think of you," he said simply.

She pulled on the cigar again, giving her emotions time to settle, then passed it back to him. "I know, and that's another new element for the season. And here's one more. I guess the thing is, Gull, I'm in care with you, too."

He reached out for her hand. "I know. But it's nice to hear you say it."

"Know-it-all." Still holding his hand, she tipped her head back, looked at the star-swept sky. "It'd be nice to just stay here a couple of days. No worries, no wondering."

"We'll come back, after the season's over."

She couldn't see that far. Next month, she thought, next year? As distant as the stars. As murky as smoke. Always better, to her way of thinking, to concentrate on the right now.

TOWARD DAWN, Gull slipped through a dream of swimming under a waterfall. He dove deep into the blue crystal of the pool where sunbeams washed the gilded bottom in shimmering streaks. Overhead water struck water in a steady, muted drumbeat while Rowan, skin as gold and sparkling as the sand, eyes as clear and cool as the pool, swam toward him.

Their arms entwined, their mouths met, and his pulse beat like the drumming water.

As he lay against her, his hand lazily stroking along her hip, he thought himself dreaming still. He drifted toward the surface, in the dream and out of the dream, and the water drummed on.

It echoed in the confines of the tent when he opened his eyes. Smiling in the dark, he gave Rowan a little shake.

"Hey, do you hear that?"

"What?" Her tone, sleepy and annoyed, matched the nudge

back she gave him. "What?" she repeated, more lucidly. "Is it the bear? Is it back?"

"No. Listen."

"I don't want . . . It's rain." She shoved him with more force as she pushed to sit up. "It's raining!"

She crawled to the front of the tent, opened the flap. "Oh, yeah, baby! Rain, rain, don't go away. Do you *hear* that?"

"Yeah, but I'm a little distracted by the view right this minute."

He caught the glint of her eyes as she glanced over her shoulder, grinned. Then she was out of the tent and letting out a long, wild cheer.

What the hell, he thought, and climbed out after her.

She threw her arms up, lifted her face. "This isn't a storm, or a quick summer shower. This is what my grandfather likes to call a soaker. And about damn time."

She pumped her fists, her hips, high stepped. "Give it up, Gulliver! Dance! Dance to honor the god of rain!"

So he danced with her, naked, in the rainy gloom of dawn, then dragged her back in the tent to honor the rain gods his way.

The steady, soaking rain watered the thirsty earth, and made for a wet pack-out. Rowan held on to the cheer with every step of every mile.

"Maybe it's a sign," she said as rain slid off their ponchos, dripped off the bills of their caps. "Maybe it's one of those turning points, and means the worst of the crap's behind us."

Gull figured it was a lot to expect from one good rain in a dry summer—but he never argued against hope.

24

Rowan refused to let the news that Leo Brakeman remained at large discourage her, and instead opted for Gull's glass half full of no further arson fires or connected murders in almost a month.

Maybe the cops would never find him, never solve those crimes. It didn't, and wouldn't, change her life.

While she and Gull packed out, a twelve-man team jumped a fire in Shoshone, putting the two of them back on the jump list as soon as they'd checked in.

That was her life, she thought as she unpacked and re-organized her gear. Training, preparing, doing, then cleaning up to go again.

Besides, when she studied the big picture, she couldn't complain. As the season edged toward August, she'd had no injuries, had managed to maintain a good, fighting weight by losing only about ten pounds, and had justified L.B.'s faith in her by proving herself a solid fire boss on the line. Most important, she'd had a part in saving countless acres of wildland.

The fact she'd managed to accomplish that *and* build what

she had to admit had become an actual relationship was cause to celebrate, not a reason to niggle with the downsides.

She decided to do just that with something sweet and indulgent from the cookhouse.

She found Marg out harvesting herbs in the cool, damp air.

"We brought the rain down with us," Rowan told her. "It followed us all the way in. Didn't stop until we flew over Missoula."

"It's the first time I haven't had to water the garden in weeks. Ground soaked it right up, though. We're going to need more. Brought out the damn gnats, too." Marg swatted at them as she lifted her basket. She spritzed a little of her homemade bug repellant on her hands, patted her face with it and sweetened the air with eucalyptus and pennyroyal. "I guess you're looking for some food."

"Anything with a lot of sugar."

"I can fix you up." Marg cocked her head. "You look pretty damn good for a woman who hiked a few hours in the rain."

"I feel pretty damn good, and I think that's why."

"It wouldn't have anything to do with a certain good-looking, green-eyed jumper?"

"Well, he was hiking with me. It didn't hurt."

"It's a little bright spot for me." Inside, Marg set her herb basket on the counter. "Watching the romances. Yours, your father's."

"I don't know if it's . . . My father's?"

"I ran into Lucas and his lady friend at the fireworks, and again a couple days ago at the nursery. She was helping him pick out some plants."

"Plants? You're talking about my father? Lucas black-thumb Tripp?"

"One and the same." As she spoke, Marg cut a huge slice of Black Forest cake. "Ella's helping him put in a flower bed. A little one to start. He was looking at arbors."

"Arbors? You mean the . . ." Rowan drew an arch with her forefingers. "Come on. Dad's gardening skills start and stop with mowing the lawn."

"Things change." She set the cake and a tall glass of milk in front of Rowan. "As they should or we'd all just stand in the same place. It's good to see him lit up about something that doesn't involve a parachute or an engine. You ought to be happy about that, Rowan, especially since there's a lot of lights dimming around here right now."

"I just don't know, that's all. What's wrong with standing in the same place if it's a good place?"

"Even a good place gets to be a rut, especially if you're standing in it alone. Honey, alone and lonely share the same root. Eat your cake."

"I don't see how Dad could be lonely. He's always got so much going on. He has so many friends."

"And nobody there when he turns off the lights—until recently. If you can't see how much happier he is since Ella, then you're not paying attention."

Rowan searched around for a response, then noticed Marg's face when the cook turned away to wash her herbs in the sink. Obviously she hadn't been paying attention here, Rowan realized, or she'd have seen the sadness.

"What's wrong, Marg?"

"Oh, just tough times. Tougher for some. I know you'd probably be fine if Leo Brakeman wasn't seen or heard from again. And I don't blame you a bit for it. But it's beating down on Irene."

"If he comes back, or they find him, he'll probably go to prison. I don't know if that's better for her."

"Knowing's always better. In the meantime, she had to take on another job, as her pay from the school isn't enough to cover the bills. Especially since she leveraged the house for his bail. And taking on the work, she can't see to the baby."

"Can't her family help her through it?"

"Not enough, I guess. It's the money, but it's also the time, the energy, the wherewithal. The last time I saw her, she looked worn to the nub. She's ready to give up, and I don't know how much longer she can hold out."

"I'm sorry, Marg. Really. We could take up a collection. I guess it wouldn't be more than a finger in the dike for a bit, but the baby's Jim's. Everybody'd do what they could."

"Honestly, Ro, I don't think she'd accept it. On top of it all, that woman's shamed down to the root of her soul. What her husband and her daughter did here, that weighs on her. I don't think she could take money from us. I've known Irene since we were girls, and she could hardly look at me. That breaks my heart."

Rowan rose, cut another, smaller slice of cake, poured another glass of milk. "You sit down. Eat some cake. We'll fix it," she added. "There's always a way to fix something if you keep at it long enough."

"I like to think so, but I don't know how much long enough Irene's got left."

WHEN ELLA CAME BACK DOWNSTAIRS, Irene continued to sit on the couch, shoulders slumped, eyes downcast. Deliberately Ella fixed an easy smile on her face.

"She's down. I swear that's the sweetest baby, Irene. Just so sunny and bright." She didn't mention the time she'd spent folding and putting away the laundry in the basket by the crib, or the disarray she'd noticed in Irene's usually tidy home.

"She makes me want more grandbabies," Ella went on, determinedly cheerful. "I'm going to go make us some tea."

"The kitchen's a mess. I don't know if I even have any tea. I didn't make it to the store."

"I'll go find out."

Dishes were piled in the sink of the little kitchen Ella always found cozy and charming. The near-empty cupboards, the sparsely filled refrigerator, clearly needed restocking.

That, at least, she could do.

She found a box of tea bags, filled the kettle. As she began filling the dishwasher, Irene shuffled in.

"I'm too tired to even be ashamed of the state of my own kitchen, or to see you doing my dishes."

"There's nothing to be ashamed of, and you'd insult our friendship if you were."

"I used to have pride in my home, but it's not really my home now. It's the bank's. It's just a place to live now, until it's not."

"Don't talk like that. You're going to get through this. You're just worn out. Why don't you let me take the baby for a day or two, give yourself a chance to catch your breath? You know I'd love it. Then we could sit down, and if you'd let me, we could go over your financial situation, see if there's anything—"

She broke off when she turned to see tears rolling down Irene's face. "Oh, I'm sorry. I'm sorry." Abandoning the dishes, she hurried over to wrap Irene in her arms.

"I can't do it, Ella. I just can't. I've got no fight left. No heart."

"You're just so tired."

"I am. I am tired. The baby's teething, and when she's fretful in the night, I lie there wishing she'd just stop. Just be quiet, give me some peace. I'm passing her off to anybody who'll take her for a few hours while I work, and even with the extra work, I'm not going to make the house payments, unless I let something else go."

"Let me help you."

"Help me what? Pay my bills, raise my grandchild, keep my house?" Even the hard words held no life. "For how long, Ella? Until Leo gets back, if he comes back? Until he gets out of prison, if he goes to prison?"

"With whatever you need to get you through this, Irene."

"I know you mean well, but I don't see getting through. I wanted to believe him. He's my husband, and I wanted to believe him when he told me he didn't do any of it."

With nothing to say, Ella kept silent while Irene looked around the room.

"Now he's left me like this, left me alone, and taking money I need out of the ATM on the way gone. What do I believe now?"

"Sit down here at the table. Tea's a small thing, but it's something."

Irene sat, looked out the window at the yard she'd once loved to putter in. The yard her husband had used to escape, to run from her.

"I know what people are saying, even though it doesn't come out of their mouths in my hearing. Leo killed Reverend Latterly, and if he killed him, he must've killed Dolly. His own flesh and blood."

"People say and think a lot of hard things, Irene."

The bones in Irene's face stood out too harshly under skin aged a decade in two short months. "I'm one of them now.

I may not be ready to say it, but I think it. I think how he and Dolly used to fight, shouting at each other, saying awful things. Still . . . he loved her. I know that."

She stared down at the tea Ella put in front of her. "Maybe loved her too much. Maybe more than I did. So it cut more, the things she'd do and say. It cut him more than me. Love can turn, can't it? It can turn into something dark in a minute's time."

"I don't know the answers there. But I do know that you can't find them in despair. I think the best thing for you now is to concentrate on the baby and yourself, to do what you have to do to make the best life you can make for the two of you, until you have those answers."

"That's what I'm doing. I called Mrs. Brayner this morning before I went into work. Shiloh's other grandmother. She and her husband are going to drive out from Nebraska, and they'll take Shiloh back with them."

"Oh, Irene."

"It's what's best for her." She swiped a tear away. "That precious baby deserves better than I can give her now. She's the innocent in all this, the only one of us who truly is. She deserves better than me leaving her with friends and neighbors most of the day, better than me barely able to take care of her when I'm here. Not being sure how long I can keep a roof over her head, much less buy her clothes or pay the baby doctor."

Her voice cracked, and she lifted the tea, sipped a little. "I've prayed on this, and I talked with Reverend Meece about it. He is kind, Ella, like you told me."

"He and his church could help you," Ella began, but Irene shook her head.

"I know in my heart I can't give Shiloh a good life the way things are, and I can't keep her, knowing she has family who can. I can't keep her wondering if her grandpa's the reason she doesn't have her mother."

Ella reached over, linked her hands with Irene's. "I know this isn't a decision you've come to lightly. I know how much you love that child. Is there anything I can do? Anything?"

"You didn't say it was the wrong decision, or selfish, or weak. That helps." She took a breath, drank a little more tea.

"I think they're good people. And she said—Kate, her name's Kate. Kate said they'd stay in Missoula a couple days or so, to give Shiloh time to get used to them. And how we'd all work together so Shiloh could have all of us in her life. I . . . I said how they could have all the baby stuff, her crib and all, and Kate, she said no, didn't I want to keep that? Didn't I want it so when we fixed it so Shiloh could come see me, it would all be ready for her?"

Ella squeezed Irene's hands tighter as tears plopped into the tea. "They do sound like good people, don't they?"

"I believe they are. I'm content they are. Still, I feel like another part of me's dying. I don't know how much is left."

HER CONVERSATION WITH MARG had Rowan's wheels turning. The time had come, she decided, for a serious sit-down with her father. Since she wanted to have that sit-down off base, she walked over to L.B.'s office.

She saw Matt step out. "Hi. Is he in there?"

"Yeah, I just asked him for a couple days at the end of the week." His face exploded into a grin she'd rarely seen on his face since Jim's accident. "My parents are driving in."

"That's great. They get to see you, and Jim's baby."

"Even more. They're taking Shiloh home with them."

"They got custody? That's so fast. I didn't think it worked so fast."

"They didn't get a lawyer. They were talking about maybe, but they didn't get one yet. Mrs. Brakeman called my ma this morning and said she needed—wanted—them to have Shiloh."

"Oh." Not enough long enough, Rowan thought, and felt a pang of sympathy. "That's great for your family, Matt. Really. It's got to be awfully rough on Mrs. Brakeman."

"Yeah, and I'm sorry for her. She's a good woman. I guess she proved it by doing this, thinking of Shiloh first. They're going to spend a couple days, you know, give everybody a chance to adjust and all that. I figured I could help out. Shiloh knows me, so that should make it easier. It's like I'm standing in for Jim."

"I guess it is. It's a lot, for everybody."

"The way Brakeman ran?" The light in his face died into something dark. "He's a coward. He doesn't deserve to even see that baby again, if you ask me. Mrs. Brakeman's probably going to lose her house because of him."

"It doesn't seem right," Rowan agreed, "for one person to lose so much."

"She could move to Nebraska if she wanted, and be closer to Shiloh. She ought to, and I hope she does. I don't see how there's anything here for her now anyway. She oughta go on and move to Nebraska so the baby has both her grans. Anyway, I've got to go call my folks, let them know I got the time off."

One family's tragedy, another family's celebration, Rowan supposed as Matt rushed off. The world could be a harsh place. She gave L.B.'s door a tap, poked her head in.

"Got another minute for somebody looking for time off?"

"Jesus, maybe we should just blow and piss on the next fire."

"An interesting new strategy, but I'm only looking for a few hours."

"When?"

"Pretty much now. I wanted to hook up with my father."

"Suddenly everybody wants family reunions." Then he shrugged. "A night off's okay. We've got smoke over in Payette, and up in Alaska. The Denali area's getting hammered with dry lightning. Yellowstone's on first attack on another. You should count on jumping tomorrow."

"I'll be ready." She started to back out before he changed his mind, then hesitated. "I guess Matt told you why he wanted the time."

"Yeah." L.B. rubbed his eyes. "It's hard to know what to think. I guess it's the best thing when it comes down to it, but it sure feels like kicking a woman in the teeth when she's already taken a couple hard shots in the gut."

"Still no word on Leo?"

"Nothing, as far as I know. Fucker. It makes me sick he could do all this. I went hunting with the bastard, even went on a big trip up to Canada with him and some other guys once."

"Did you tell the cops all the places you knew he liked to go?"

"Every one, and I didn't feel a single pang of guilt. Fucker," he repeated, with relish. "Irene's a decent woman. She doesn't deserve this. You'd better go while the going's good. If we get a call from Alaska, we'll be rolling tonight."

"I'm already gone." As she left, Rowan pulled out her phone and opted to text, hoping that would make her plans a fait accompli.

Got a couple hours. Meet you at the house. I'm cooking!
Really want to talk to you.

Now she had to hope he had something in the house she could actually cook. She stopped by the barracks, grabbed her keys, then stepped into the open doorway of Gull's quarters.

"I cleared a few hours so I can go over and see my father." Gull shifted his laptop aside. "Okay."

"There are some things I want to air out with him. One-on-one." She jingled her car keys. "We've got potential situations out in Yellowstone, down in Wyoming, up in Alaska. We could be up before morning. I won't be gone very long."

"Are you waiting to see if I'm going to complain because you're going off base without me?"

"Maybe I was wondering if you would."

"I'm not built that way. Just FYI, I wouldn't mind maybe having dinner with you and your father sometime, maybe when things slow down."

"So noted. See you when I get back." She jingled her keys again. "Hey, I just remembered, my car's low on gas. Maybe I can borrow yours?"

"You know where the base pumps are."

"Had to try."

She'd talk him into letting her drive it before the end of the season, she promised herself as she headed out to her much less sexy Dodge. She just had to outline the right attack plan.

The minute she drove off the base, something shifted inside her. As much as she loved what she did, she felt just a bit lighter driving down the open road. Alone, away from the pressure, the intensity, the dramas, even the interaction.

Maybe, for the moment, she realized, especially the interaction. A little time to reconnect with Rowan, she thought, then in turn for Rowan to reconnect with her father.

She could admit to the contrary aspect of the feeling. If L.B. had insisted she take time off, had pulled her off the jump list, she'd have fought him tooth and nail. Asking for the little crack in the window was more a little gift to herself, and one where she chose the wrapping and the contents.

Maybe, too, it hit just close enough to the camping trips her father had always carved out during the season—this one evening together, her making dinner in the house they shared half the year. Just the two of them, sitting at the table with some decent grub and some good conversation.

Too much had happened, too many things that kept running around inside her head. So much of the summer boomeranged on her, making her think of her mother, and all those hard feelings. She'd shaken off most of them, but there remained a thin and sticky layer she'd never been able to peel away.

She liked to think that layer helped make her tougher, stronger—and she believed it—but she'd started to wonder if it had hardened into a shield as well.

Did she use it as an excuse, an escape? If she did, was that smart, or just stupid?

Something to think about in this short time alone, and again in the company of the single person in the world who knew her through and through, and loved her anyway.

When she pulled up in front of the house, the simple white two-story with the wide covered porch—the porch she'd helped her father build when she was fourteen—she just sat and stared.

The slope of lawn showed the brittleness of the dry summer, even in the patches of shade from the big old maple on the east corner.

But skirting that porch, on either side of the short steps, an area of flowers sprang out of a deep brown blanket of mulch. Baskets hung from decorative brackets off the flanking posts and spilled out a tangle of red and white flowers and green trailing vines.

"I'm looking at it," she said aloud as she got out of the car, "but I still can't quite believe it."

She remembered summers during her youth when her grandmother had done pots and planters, and even dug in a little vegetable garden in the back. How she'd cursed the deer and rabbits for mowing them down, every single season.

She remembered, too, her father's rep for killing even the hardiest of houseplants. Now he'd planted—she didn't know what half of them were, but the beds hit hot, rich notes with a lot of deep reds and purples, with some white accents.

And she had to admit they added a nice touch, just as she had to admit the creativity of the layout hadn't come from the nongardening brain of Iron Man Tripp.

She mulled it over as she let herself into the house.

Here, too, the difference struck.

Flowers? Since when did her father have flowers sitting around the house? And candles—fat white columns that smelled, when she sniffed them, faintly of vanilla. Plus, he'd gotten a new rug in the living room, a pattern of bold-colored blocks that spread over a floor that had certainly been polished. And looked pretty good, she had to admit, but still . . .

Hands on hips, she did a turn around the living room until her jaw nearly landed on her toes. Glossy magazines fanned on the old coffee table. Home and garden magazines, and since when had her father . . . ?

Stupid question, she admitted. Since Ella.

A little leery of what she'd find next, she started toward the kitchen, poked into her father's home office. Bamboo shades in spicy tones replaced the beige curtains.

Ugly curtains, she remembered.

But the powder room was a revelation. No generic liquid soap sat on the sink, no tan towels on the rack. Instead, a shiny and sleek chrome dispenser shot a spurt of lemon-scented liquid into her hand. Dazed, she washed, then dried her hands on one of the fluffy navy hand towels layered on the rack with washcloths in cranberry.

He'd added a bowl of potpourri—*potpourri*—and a framed print of a mountain meadow on a freshly painted wall that matched the washcloths.

Her father had cranberry walls in the powder room. She might never get over it.

Dazed, she continued on to the kitchen, and there stood blinking.

Clean and efficient had always been the Tripp watchwords. Apparently fuss had been added to them since she'd last stood in the room.

A long oval dish she thought might be bamboo and had never seen before held a selection of fresh fruit. Herbs grew in small red clay pots on the windowsill over the sink. An iron wine rack—a filled wine rack, she noted—graced the top of the refrigerator. He'd replaced the worn cushions on the stools at the breakfast counter, and she was pretty damn sure the glossy magazines in the living room would call that color pumpkin.

In the dining area, two place mats—bamboo again—lay ready with cloth napkins rolled in rings beside them. If that didn't beat all, the pot of white daisies and the tea lights in amber dishes sure rang the bell.

She considered going upstairs, decided she needed a drink first, and a little time to absorb the shocks already dealt. A little time, like maybe a year, she thought as she opened the refrigerator.

Okay, there was beer, that at least was constant. But what the hell, since he had an open bottle of white, plugged with a fancy topper, she'd go with that.

She sipped, forced to give it high marks as she explored supplies.

She felt more at home and less like an intruder as she got down to it, setting out chicken breasts to soften, scrubbing potatoes. Maybe she shook her head as she spotted the deck chairs out the kitchen window. He painted them every other year, she knew, but never before in chili pepper red.

By the time she heard him come in, she had dinner simmering in the big skillet. She poured a second glass of wine.

At least he looked the same.

"Smells good." He folded her in, held her hard. "Best surprise of the day."

"I've had a few of them myself. I poured you this." She offered him the second glass. "Since you're the wine buff now."

He grinned, toasted her. "Pretty good stuff. Have we got time to sit outside awhile?"

"Yeah. That'd be good. You've been busy around here," she commented as they walked out onto the deck.

"Fixing things up a little. What do you think?"

"It's colorful."

"A few steps out of my comfort zone." He sat in one of the hot-colored deck chairs, sighed happily.

"Dad, you planted flowers. That's acres outside your zone."

"And I haven't killed them yet. Soaker hose."

"Sorry?"

"I put in a soaker hose. Keeps them from getting thirsty."

Wine, soaker hoses, cranberry walls. Who was this guy?

But when he looked at her, laid his hand over hers, she saw him. She knew him. "What's on your mind, baby?"

"A lot. Bunches."

"Lay it on me."

She did just that.

"I feel like I can't get a handle on things, or keep a handle on. This morning, I thought I did, then it started slipping again. I've been having the dreams about Jim again, only worse. But with everything that's gone on this season, how am I supposed to put that aside anyway? Everything Dolly did, then what happened to her. Add on her crazy father. And the thing is, if he did what they say he did, if he killed her, the preacher, started the fires—and he probably did—why am I more pissed off and disgusted that he ran, left his wife twisting in the wind? And I know the answer," she said, pushing back to her feet.

"I know the answer, and *that* pisses me off. My mother ditching us doesn't define my life. I sure as hell don't want it to define me. I'm smarter than that, damn it."

"You always have been," he said when she turned to him.

"I'm tangled up with Gull so I'm not sure I'm thinking straight. Really, where can that go? And why am I even thinking that because why would I want it to go anywhere? And you, you're planting flowers and drinking wine, and you have potpourri."

He had to smile. "It smells nicer than those plug-in jobs."

"It has berries, and little white flowers in it. While that's screwing with my head, Dolly's mother's giving the baby to the Brayners because she can't handle it all by herself. It's probably the best thing, it's probably the right thing, but it makes me feel sick and sad, which pisses me off all over again because I *know* I'm projecting, and I *know* the situation with that baby isn't the same as with me.

"I may be jumping fire in Alaska tomorrow, and I'm stuck on pumpkin-colored cushions, a baby I've never even seen and a guy who's talking about being with me after the season. How the hell did this happen?"

Lucas nodded slowly, drank a little wine. "That is a lot. Let's see if we can sift through it. I don't like hearing you're having those nightmares again, but I can't say I'm surprised. The pressure of any season wears on you, and this hasn't been just any season. You're probably not the only one having hard dreams."

"I hadn't thought about that."

"Have you talked to L.B.?"

"Not about that. Piling my stress on his doesn't work for anybody. That's why I pile it on you."

"I can tell you what we talked about before, after it happened. We all live with the risks, and train body and mind to minimize them. When a jumper has a mental lapse, sometimes he gets lucky. Sometimes he doesn't. Jim didn't, and that's a tragedy. It's a hard blow for his family, and like his kin, the crew's his family."

"I've never lost anybody before. She doesn't count," she said, referring to her mother. "Not the same way."

"I know it. You want to save him, to go back to that jump and save him. And you can't, baby. I think when you've really settled your mind on that, the dreams will stop."

He got up, put an arm around her shoulders. "I don't know if you'll really be able to settle your mind until this business with Leo is resolved. It's in your face, so it's in your head. Dolly tried to put the blame for what happened to Jim on you, and it looks like her telling him she was pregnant right before a jump contributed to his mental lapse. Then Leo came at you about Jim, about Dolly—and the cops think he's the one responsible for her murder. Time to use your head, Ro." He kissed the top of it. "And stop letting the people most responsible lay the weight on you. Feeling sorry for Irene Brakeman, that's just human. Maybe you and me tend to be a little more human than most on that score. Ella's over there right now helping her get through it, and I feel better knowing that."

"I guess it's good that she—Mrs. Brakeman—has somebody."

"I had your grandparents, and I leaned on them pretty hard. I had my friends, my work. Most of all I had you. When somebody walks out, it leaves a hole in you. Some people fill it up, the good and the bad, and get on that way. Some people leave it open, maybe long enough to heal, maybe too long, picking at it now and then so it doesn't heal all the way. I hate knowing it as much as you, but I think we've been like the last."

"I don't even think about it, most of the time."

"Neither do I. Most of the time. Now you've got this guy, who'd be the first one you've ever mentioned to me as giving you trouble. And that makes me wonder if you've got feelings for him you've managed to avoid up till now. Are you in love with him?"

"How does anybody answer that?" she demanded. "How does anyone know? Are you in love with this Ella?"

"Yes."

Stunned, Rowan stepped back. "Just like that? You can just . . . poof, I'm in love."

"She filled the hole, baby. I don't know how to explain it to you. I never knew how to talk about this kind of thing, and maybe that's where I fell down with you. But she filled that hole I never let all the way heal, because if I did, there could be another. But I'd rather take that chance than not have her. I wish you'd get to know her. She . . ."

He lifted his hands as if to grab something just out of reach. "She's funny and smart, and has a way of speaking her mind that's honest instead of hurtful. She can do damn near anything. You should see her on a dive. I swear she's a joy to watch. She could give Marg a run for her money in the kitchen, and don't repeat that or I'll call you a liar. She knows about wine and books and flowers. She has her own toolbox and knows how to use it. She's got great kids and they've got kids. She listens when you talk to her. She'll try anything.

"She makes me feel . . . She makes me feel."

There it was, Rowan realized. If there'd been an image in the dictionary for the definition of "in love," it would be her father's face.

"I have to get dinner on the table." She turned away to the door, then turned back to see him looking after her, that light dimmed. "Are you, more or less, asking for my blessing?"

"I guess. More or less."

"Anybody who makes you this happy—and who talked you into getting rid of those ugly curtains in your office—is good with me. You can tell me more about her while we eat."

"Ro. That means more than I can say."

"You don't have heart-shaped pillows on your bed now, do you?"

"No. Why?"

"Because that's going to be my line in the sand. Anything else I think I can adjust to. Oh, and none of those crocheted things over spare toilet paper. That's definitely a deal breaker."

"I'll take notes."

"Good idea because I probably have a few more." She walked to the stove, pleased that light had turned back on full.

25

Feeling sociable, Gull plopped down in the lounge with his book. That way he could ease out of the story from time to time, tune in on conversations, the ball game running on TV and the progress of the poker game he wasn't yet interested in joining.

Or he could just let all of it hum at the edges of his mind like white noise.

With the idea he might be called up at any time, he opted for a ginger ale and a bag of chips to snack him through the next chapter or two.

"Afraid of losing your paycheck?" Dobie called out from the poker table.

"Terrified."

"Out?" An outraged Trigger lurched out of his chair at a call on second. "That runner was safe by a mile. Out my ass! Did you see that?" he demanded.

He hadn't, but Gull's mood hit both agreeable and sociable. "Damn right. The ump's an asshole."

"He oughta have his eyes popped out if he can't use them better than that. Where's the ball to your chain tonight?"

Amused, Gull turned a page. "Ditched me for another man."

"Women. They're worse than umps. Can't live with them, can't beat them with a brick."

"Hey." Janis discarded two cards at the poker table. "Having tits doesn't mean I can't hear, buddy."

"Aw, you're not a woman. You're a jumper."

"I'm a jumper with tits."

"Unless you're going to toss them in the pot," Cards told her, "the bet's five to you."

"They're worth a lot more than five."

Better than white noise, Gull decided, and likely better than his book.

Across the room, Yangtree—with an ice bag on his knee— and Southern played an intense, nearly silent game of chess. Earbuds in, Libby ticked her head back and forth like a metronome to her MP3 while she worked a crossword puzzle.

A lot of sociable going around, he mused. About half the jumpers on base gathered, some in groups, some solo, more than a few sprawled on the floor, attention glued to the Cardinals v. Phillies matchup on-screen.

Waiting mode, he decided. Everybody knew the siren could sound anytime, sending them north, east, south, west, where there would be camaraderie but little leisure. No time to insult umpires or figure out 32 Across. Instead of raking in the pot, as Cards did now with relish, they'd rake through smoldering embers and ash.

He watched Trigger throw up his hands in triumph as the runner scored, saw Yangtree take Southern's bishop and Dobie toss in chips to raise the bet, causing Stovic to fold on a grunt of disgust.

"What's a five-letter word for boredom?" Libby asked the room.

"TV ads," Trigger volunteered. "Ought to be outlawed."

"Boredom, not boring. Besides, some of them are funny."

"Not funny enough."

"Ennui," Gull told her.

"Damn it, I knew that."

"He can spout off all those pussy words," Dobie commented.

Gull only smiled. He definitely didn't feel ennui. Contentment, he thought, best described his current state. He'd be

ready to roll if and when the call came, but for now knew the
contentment of lounging with friends, enjoying the cross talk
and bullshit while he waited for his woman to come home.

He'd found his place. He didn't know, not for certain, when
he'd first understood that. Maybe the first time he'd seen
Rowan. Maybe his first jump. Maybe that night at the bar
when he'd kicked some ass.

Maybe looking over a meadow of wild lupine.

It didn't matter when.

He'd liked his hotshot work, and the people he'd worked
with. Or most of them. He'd learned to combine patience,
action and endurance, learned to love the fight—the violence, the
brutality, the science. But what he found here dug deeper, and
deep kindled an irresistible love and passion.

He knew he'd sprawl out in the lounge, listening to cross
talk and bullshit season after season, as long as he was able.

He knew, he thought as Rowan came in, he'd wait for her
to come home whenever she went away.

"Man, they let anybody in the country club these days."
She dropped down beside Gull, shot a hand into the chip bag.
"Score?"

"Tied," Trigger told her, "one to one due to seriously blind
ump. Top of the fifth."

She stole Gull's ginger ale, found it empty. "What, were
you waiting for me to get back, fetch you a refill?"

"Caught me."

She pushed up, got a Coke. "You'll drink this and like it."
She downed some first, then passed it to him.

"Thanks. And how's the ball to my chain?"

"*What* did you call me?"

"He said it." Gull narked on Trigger without remorse.

"Skinny Texas bastard." She angled her head to read the
cover of the book Gull set aside. "*Ethan Frome*? If you've
been reading that, I'm surprised I didn't find you lapsed into a
coma drooling down your chin."

He gave the Coke back to her. "I thought I'd like it better
now, being older, wiser, more erudite. But it's just as blind-
ingly boring as it was when I was twenty. Thank God you're
back, or I might have been paralyzed with ennui."

"Get you."

"It was a crossword answer a while ago. How's your dad?"

"He's in love."

"With the hot redhead."

Rowan's eyebrows beetled. "I wish you wouldn't call her the hot redhead."

"I call them like I see them. How's by you?"

"I had to get by the flower beds he's planted, the flowers in vases, candles, the potpourri in the powder room—"

"Mother of God! Potpourri in the powder room. We need to get a posse together *ASAP*, go get him. He can be deprogrammed. Don't lose hope."

Since he'd stretched his legs across her lap, she twisted his toe. Hard. "He's got all this color in the place all of a sudden. Or all of an Ella. I told myself it was fussy, she'd pushed all this fussy stuff on him. But it's not. It's style, with an edge of charm. She brought color to the beige and bone and brown. It makes him happy. She makes him happy. She filled the hole he couldn't let heal—that's what he said. And I realized something, that she was right that day we saw her in town. Ice cream day. She said that if I made him choose between her and me, she didn't stand a chance. And if I'd done that, I'd be just enough like my mother to make myself sick. Either/or, pal, you can't have both."

"But you're not."

"No. I'm not. I have to get used to it—to her, but she's put a light in him so I think I'm going to be a fan."

"You're a stand-up gal, Swede."

"If she screws him up, I'll peel the skin off her ass with a dull razor blade."

"Fair's fair."

"And then some. I need to walk off the not-too-shabby skillet cuisine I prepared, then I'm going to turn in."

"Wait a minute. You cooked?"

"I have a full dozen entrées in my repertoire. Four of them are variations on the classic grilled cheese sandwich."

"A whole new side of you to explore while we walk. I want my shoes."

Gibbons came in as Gull tossed the Edith Wharton onto the table for someone else.

"You might want to wrap up that card game. Everybody's

on standby. It's not official, but it looks like we'll roll two loads to Fairbanks tonight, or maybe straight to the fire. L.B.'s working out some details. And it's looking like Bighorn might need some help come tomorrow."

"Just when my luck's starting to turn," Dobie complained.

"New shoes for baby," Cards reminded him.

"I rake another couple pots in, I can buy the new shoes without eating smoke."

"Anybody on the first and second loads might want to check their gear while they've got a chance," Gibbons added.

"I've never been to Alaska," Gull commented.

"It's an experience." Rowan shoved his feet off her lap.

"I'm all about them."

SHE STUFFED more energy bars into her PG bag, and after a short debate added two cans of Coke. She'd rather haul the weight than do without. She changed from the off-duty clothes she'd worn to her father's, and was just buckling her belt when the siren sang out.

Along with the others, she ran to the ready room to suit up.

The minute she stepped onto the plane, she staked her claim, arranging her gear and stretching out with her head on her chute. She intended to sleep through the flight.

"What's it like?" Gull poked her with the toe of his boot.

"Big."

"Really? I hear it's cold and dark in the winter, too. Can that be true?"

She let the vibration of the engines lull her as other jumpers settled in. "Plenty of daylight this time of year. It's not the trees as much there to worry about on the jump. It's the water. They've got a lot of it, and you don't want to miss the spot and land in it. A lot of water, a lot of land, mountains. Not a lot of people, that's an advantage."

She shifted, found a more comfortable position. "The Alaskan smoke jumpers know their stuff. It's been dry up there this season, too, so they're probably spread pretty thin, probably feeling that midseason fatigue."

She opened her eyes to look at him. "It's beautiful. The snow that never melts off those huge peaks, the lakes and rivers, the glow of the midnight sun. They've also got mosquitoes the size of your fist and bears big as an armored truck. But in the fire, it's pretty much the same. Kill the bitch; stay alive. Everybody comes back."

She closed her eyes. "Get some sleep. You're going to need it."

She slept like a rock; woke stiff as a board. And grateful they put down at Fairbanks, giving the crew time to loosen up, fuel up, and the bosses time to cement a strategy.

With nearly four hundred acres involved, and the wind kicking flare-ups, they'd need solid communication with the Alaskan team. She managed to scrounge up a cold soda, preserving the two in her bag, before they performed a last buddy check and loaded.

"You're right," Gull said when they flew southwest out of Fairbanks. "It's beautiful. Not far off midnight, either, local time, and bright as afternoon."

"Don't get enchanted. You'll lose focus. And she'll eat you alive."

He had to change his angle to get his first glimpse of the fire, shift his balance as the plane hit turbulence and began to buck.

"Just another maw of hell. I'm focused," he added when she sent him a hard look.

He saw the white peaks of the mountain through the billows of smoke. Denali, the sacred, with the wild to her north and east burning bright.

He continued to study and absorb as she moved to the rear to confer with Yangtree, and with Cards, who worked as spotter. Others lined the windows now, looking down on what they'd come to fight.

"We're going to try for a clearing in some birch, east side. The Alaska crew used it for their jump spot. Cards is going to throw some streamers, see how they fly."

"Jesus, did you see that?" somebody asked.

"Looks like a blowup," Gull said.

"It's well west of the target jump spot. Everybody stay chilly," she called out. "Settle in, settle down. Stay in your heads."

"Guard your reserves!" Cards pulled in the door.

Gull watched the streamers fly, adjusted with the bank and bounce of the plane. The wind dragged the stench and haze of smoke inside, a small taste of what would come.

Rowan got in the door, shot him a last grin. She propelled herself out, with Stovic seconds behind her.

When it came his turn, he evened his breathing, listened to Cards tell him about the drag. He fixed the clearing in his head and, at the slap on his shoulder, flew.

Gorgeous. He could think it while the wind whipped him. The staggering white peaks, the impossibly deep blue in glints and curls of water, the high green of summer, and all of it in sharp contrast with the wicked blacks, reds, oranges of the fire.

His chute ballooned open, turning fall into glide, and he shot Gibbons, his jump partner, a thumbs-up.

He caught some hard air that tried to push him south, and he fought it, pushing back through the smoke that rolled over him. It caught him again, gave him a good, hard tug. Again he saw that deep dreamy blue through the haze. And he thought no way, goddamn it, no way he'd end up hitting the water after Rowan had warned him.

He bore down on the toggles, saw and accepted he'd miss the jump spot, adjusted again.

He winged through the birch, cursing. He didn't land in the water, but it was a near thing, as his momentum on landing nearly sent him rolling into it anyway.

Mildly annoyed, he gathered his chute as Rowan and Yangtree came running.

"I thought for sure you'd be in the drink."

"Hit some bad air."

"Me too. I nearly got frogged. Be grateful you're not wet or limping."

"Tore up my canopy some."

"I bet." Then she grinned as she had before jumping into space. "What a ride!"

Once all jumpers were on the ground, Yangtree called a briefing with Rowan and Gibbons while the others dealt with the paracargo.

"They thought they could catch it, had forty jumpers on it, and for the first two days, it looked like they had it. Then it turned on them. A series of blowups, some equipment problems, a couple injuries."

"The usual clusterfuck," Gibbons suggested.

"You got it. I'll be coordinating with the Alaska division boss, the BLM and USFS guys. I'm going to take me a copter ride, get a better look at things, but for right now."

He picked up a stick, drew a rough map in the dirt. "Gibbons, take a crew and start working the left flank. They've got a Cat line across here. That's where you'll tie in with the Alaska crew. You've got a water source here for the pumpers. Swede, you take the right, work it up, burn it out, drown it."

"Take it by the tail," she said, following his dirt map. "Starve the belly."

"Show 'em what Zulies can do. We catch her good, shake her by the tail and push up to the head." He checked the time. "Should reach the head in fifteen, sixteen hours if we haul our asses."

They discussed strategy, details, directions, crouched in the stand of birch, while on the jump site the crew unpacked chain saws, boxes of fusees, pumpers and hose.

Gibbons leaped up, waved his Pulaski toward the sky. "Let's do it!" he shouted.

"Ten men each." Yangtree clapped his hands together like a team captain before the big game. "Get humping, Zulies."

They got humping.

As planned, Rowan and her team used fusees to set burn-outs between the raging right flank and the service road, sawing snags and widening the scratch line as they moved north from the jump spot.

If the dragon tried to swing east to cross the roads, move on to homesteads and cabins, she'd go hungry before she got there. They worked through what was left of the night, into the day with the flank crackling and snarling, vomiting out fire-brands the wind took in arches to the dry tundra.

"Chow time," she announced. "I'm going to scout through the burn, see if I can find how close Gibbons's crew is."

Dobie pulled a smashed sandwich out of his bag, looked up at the towering columns of smoke and flame. "Biggest I've ever seen."

"She's a romper," Rowan agreed, "but you know what they

say about Alaska. Everything's bigger. Fuel up. We've got a long way to go."

She couldn't give them long to rest, she thought as she headed out. Timing and momentum were as vital tools as Pulaski and saw because Dobie hadn't been wrong. This was one big mother, bigger, she'd concluded, than anticipated and, she'd already estimated by the staggered formation of her own line, wider in the body.

Pine tar and pitch tanged in the air, soured by the stench of smoke that rose like gray ribbons from the peat floor of the once, she imagined, pristine forest. Now mangled, blackened trees lay like fallen soldiers on a lost battlefield.

She could hear no sound of saw, no shout of man through the voice of the fire. Gibbons wasn't as close as she'd hoped, and she couldn't afford to scout farther.

She ate a banana and an energy bar on the quickstep hike back to her men. Gull gulped down Gatorade as he walked to her.

"What's the word, boss?"

"We're shaking her tail, as ordered, but she's got a damn long one. We'll be hard-pressed to meet Yangtree's ETA. We've got a water source coming up. It should be about a hundred yards, and a little to the west. We'll put the baby hoses on her, pump it up and douse her like Dorothy doused the Wicked Witch."

She took his Gatorade, chugged some down. "She's burning hot, Gull. Some desk jockey waited too long to call in more troops, and now she's riding this wind. If she rides it hard enough, she can get behind us. We've got to bust our humps, get to the water, hose her down and back."

"Busting humps is what we do."

Still, it took brutal, backbreaking time to reach the rushing mountain stream, while the fire fought to advance, while it threw brands like a school-yard bully throws rocks, its roar a constant barrage of taunts and threats.

"Dobie, Chainsaw, beat out those spots! Libby, Trigger, Southern, snags and brush. The rest of you, get those pumps set up, lay the hose."

She grabbed one of the pumps, connected the fuel can line to the pump, vented it. Moving fast, sweat dripping, she attached the foot valve, checked the gasket, tightened it with a spanner wrench from her tool bag.

Beat it back here, she thought, had to, or they'd be forced to backtrack and round east, giving up hundreds of acres, risk letting the fire snake behind them and drive them farther away from the head, from Gibbons. From victory.

She set the wye valve on the discharge side of the pump, began to hand-tighten it. And found it simply circled like a drain.

"Come on, come on." She fixed it on again, blaming her rush, but when she got the same result, examined the valve closely.

"Jesus Christ. Jesus, it's stripped. The wye valve's threads are stripped on this pump."

Gull looked over from where he worked. "I've got the same deal here."

"I'm good," Janis called out on the third pump. "It's priming."

"Get it warmed up, get it going."

But one pump wouldn't do the job, she thought. Might as well try a goddamn piss bag.

"We're screwed." She slapped a fist on the useless pump.

Gull caught her eye. "No way two stripped valves end up on the pumps by accident."

"Can't worry about that now. We'll hold her with one as long as we can, use the time to saw and dig a line. We'll double back to that old Cat line we crossed, then retreat east. Goddamn it, give up all that ground. There's no time to get more pumps or manpower in here. Maybe if I had some damn duct tape we could jerry-rig them."

"Duct tape. Hold on." He straightened, ran to where Dobie shoveled dirt over a dying spot fire.

Rowan watched in amazement as he ran back with a roll of duct tape. "For Dobie it's like his Tabasco. He doesn't leave home without it."

"It could work, or work long enough."

They worked together, placing the faulty valve, wrapping it tight and snug to the discharge. She added another insurance layer, continued the setup.

"Fingers crossed," she said to Gull, and began to stroke the primer. "She's priming," she mumbled as water squirted out of the holes. "Come on, keep going. Duct tape heals all wounds. Keep those fingers crossed."

She closed the valve to the primer, opened it to the collapsible hose.

"It's going to work."

"It *is* working," she corrected, and flicked the switch to start and warm the engine. "Trigger, on the pump! Let's get the other one going," she said to Gull.

"Not two of them," Gull repeated while they worked.

"No, not two of them. Somebody majorly fucked up or—"

"Deliberately."

She let the word hang when she met his eyes. "Let's get it running. We'll deal with that when we get out of this mess."

They beat it back, held the ground, laying a wet line with hoses, hot shoveling embers right back in the fire's gullet. But Rowan's satisfaction was tempered with a simmering rage. Accident or deliberate, carelessness or sabotage, she'd put her crew at risk because she'd trusted the equipment.

When they reached Yangtree's proposed rendezvous time, they were still over a half mile south of the head with fourteen hours' bitter labor on their backs. She deployed most of the crew north, sending two back to check the burnout, and once again cut across the burn.

She took the time to calm, to radio back to Ops with a report of the faulty equipment and the progress. But this time when she crossed the dead land, she heard the buzz of saws.

Encouraged, she followed the sound until she came to Gibbons's line.

"Did I call this a clusterfuck?" He paused long enough to swipe his forearm over his brow. "What's the next step up from that?"

"Whatever this is. We've run into everything but Bigfoot on this. I had two pumps with stripped wye valves."

"I had three messed-up chain saws. Two with dead spark plugs, one with a frayed starter cord that snapped first pull. We had to—" He stopped, and his face reflected the shock and suspicion in hers. "What the fuck, Ro?"

"We need to brief on this, but I've got to get back to my

crew. We'll be lucky to make the head in another three hours the way it's going."

"How far east are you now?"

"A little more than a third of a mile. We're tightening her up. We'll talk about this when we camp. We may catch her tonight, but we're not going to kill her."

"The crew's going to need rest. We'll see how it goes. Check back in—if we don't tie up before—around ten, let's say."

"You'll hear from me."

She caught up with her men, following the sound of saws as she had with Gibbons, found them sawing line through black spruce.

They'd been actively fighting for nearly eighteen hours. She could see the exhaustion, the hollow eyes, slack jaws.

She laid a hand on Libby's arm, waited until the woman took out her earplugs. "Extended break. An hour. Nappie time. Pass it up the line."

"Praise Jesus."

"I'm going to recon toward the head, see what we have in store for us."

"Whatever it is, I'll kick its ass, if I have my nappie time."

She signaled to Gull. "I'm going to recon the head. You could come with me, but you'd miss an hour's downtime."

"I'd rather walk through the wilderness with my woman."

"Then let's go."

They walked through the spruce while around them jumpers dumped their tools, dropped down on the ground or sprawled on rocks.

"Gibbons had three defective chain saws—two dead spark plugs, one bad starter cord."

"I'd say that makes it officially sabotage."

"That's unofficial until the review, but, yeah, that's what it was."

"Cards was spotter. That puts him as loadmaster."

"Load being the operative word," she reminded him. "He wouldn't check every valve and spark plug. He just makes sure everything gets loaded on, and loaded right."

"Yeah, that's true enough. Look, I like Cards. I don't want

to point fingers at anybody, but this kind of thing? It has to be one of us."

She didn't want to hear it. "A lot of people could get to the equipment. Support staff, mechanics, pilots, cleaning crews. It's not just who the hell—it's why the hell."

"Another good point."

Because she felt shaky, she took out one of her precious Cokes for a shot of caffeine and sugar, and used it to make yet another energy bar more palatable.

"We wouldn't have been trapped," she added. "We had time to take an escape route, get to a safe zone. If we hadn't fixed the hoses and held that line, we'd have gotten out okay."

"But," he prompted.

"Yeah, but if the situation had been different, if we'd gotten in a fix and needed the hoses to get out, some of us could've been hurt, or worse."

"So the why could be one, wanting to screw around, cause trouble. Two, wanting to give fire an advantage. Or three, wanting somebody to get hurt or worse."

"I don't like any of those options." Each one of them made her sick. "But the way this summer's been going, I'm afraid it might be three. L.B.'s ordering a full inspection of all equipment, right down to boot snaps." She pulled off her gloves to rub her tired eyes.

"I don't want to waste the energy being pissed about it," she told him, "not until we demob anyway. God, Gull. Look at her burn."

They stopped a moment, stood staring at the searing wall.

She'd fought fire on more than one front before. She knew how.

But she'd never fought two enemies in the same war.

26

Ella studied Lucas across the pretty breakfast table she'd set up on the deck. She'd gone to a little trouble—crepes and shirred eggs on her best china, fat mixed berries in pretty glass bowls, mimosas in tall, crystal flutes, and one of her Nikko Blue hydrangeas sunk into a low, square glass vase for a centerpiece.

She liked to go to the trouble now and again, and Lucas usually showed such appreciation. Even for cold cereal and a mug of black coffee, she thought, he always thanked her for the trouble.

But this morning he said little, and only toyed with the food she'd so carefully prepared.

She wondered if he was regretting taking the day off to be with her, to go poking around the Missoula Antique Mall. Her idea, she reminded herself, and really, did any man enjoy the prospect of spending the day shopping?

"You know, it occurs to me you might like to do something else today. Lucas," she said when he didn't respond.

"What?" His gaze lifted from his plate. "I'm sorry."

"If you could do anything, what would you want to do today?"

"Honestly. I'd be up in Alaska with Rowan."

"You're really worried about her." She reached over for his hand. "I know you must worry every time, but this seems more. Is it more?"

"I talked to L.B. while you were fixing breakfast. He thought I should know— No, she's fine. They're fine," he said when her fingers jerked in his. "But the fire's tougher and bigger than they thought. You get that," he added with a shrug. "The thing that's got me worried is it turns out they jumped with several pieces of defective equipment, tools."

"Aren't those kinds of things inspected and maintained? That shouldn't happen."

"Yeah, they're checked and tested. Ella, they think these tools may have been tampered with."

"You mean . . . Well, God, Lucas, no wonder you're worried. What happens now?"

"They'll examine the equipment, investigate, review. L.B.'s already ordered a complete inspection of everything on base."

"That's good, but it doesn't help Rowan or the rest of them on the fire."

"When you're on a fire, you've got to depend on yourself, your crew and, by God, on your equipment. It could've gone south on my girl."

"But she's all right? You're sure?"

"Yeah. They worked nearly twenty-four hours before making camp. She's getting some sleep now. They'll hit it early today; they'll have the light. They dropped them more equipment, and they're sending in another load of jumpers, more hotshots. They're sending in another tanker, and . . ." He trailed off, smiled a little, waved his hand. "Enough fire talk."

She shook her head. "No. You talk it through. I want you to be able to talk it through with me."

"What they had was your basic clusterfuck. Delays in calling in more men and equipment, erratic winds and a hundred percent active perimeter. Fire makes its own weather," he continued, and pleased her when talking relaxed him enough to have him cutting into a crepe. "This one kicked up a storm, kept bumping the line—that means it spots and rolls, delays containment. Blowups, eighty-foot flames across the head."

"Oh, my God."

"She's impressive," he said, and amazed Ella by smiling.

"You really do wish you were there." She narrowed her eyes, pointed at him. "And not just for Rowan."

"I guess it never goes away, all the way away. Bottom line is they've made good progress. They're going to have a hell of a day ahead of them, but they'll have her crying uncle by tonight."

"You know what you should do—the next best thing to flying yourself to Alaska and jumping out over Rowan's campsite? You should go on over to the base."

"They don't need me over there."

"You may have retired, but you're still Iron Man Tripp. I bet they could use your expertise and experience. And you'd feel closer to Rowan and to the action."

"We had plans for the day," he reminded her.

"Lucas, don't you know me better by now?"

He looked at her, then took her hand to his lips. "I guess I do. I guess you know me, too."

"I like to think so."

"I wonder how you'd feel . . . I'd like to ask if I could move in here with you. If I could live with you."

It took a minute for her brain to catch up. "You—you want to live together? Here?"

"I know you've got everything you want here, and we've only been seeing each other a few months. Maybe you need to—"

"Yes."

"Yes?"

"I mean, I'll have everything I want here when you are. So, yes, absolutely yes." Delighted by his blank stare, she laughed. "How soon can you pack?"

He let out a breath, then picked up the mimosa, drank deep. "I thought you'd say no, or that we should wait awhile more."

"Then you shouldn't have asked. Now you're stuck."

"Stuck with a beautiful woman who knows me and wants me around anyway. For the life of me, I can't figure out what I did right." He set the glass back down. "I did this backward because first I should've said—I should've said, I love you, Ella. I love you."

"Lucas." She got up, went around the table to sit in his lap.

Took his face in her hands. "I love you." She kissed him, sinking in. "I'm so happy my son wanted me to jump out of a plane." She sighed as she laid her cheek against his. "I'm so happy."

WHEN HE LEFT, she adjusted her plans for the day. She had to make room for a man. For her man. Closet space, drawer space. Space for manly things. The house she'd made completely her own would become a blend, picking up pieces of him, shades of him.

It amazed her how much she wanted that, how very much she wanted to see what those shades would be once blended.

She needed to make a list, she realized, of what should be done. He'd want some office space, she decided as she took out a notebook and pen to write it down. Then she tapped the pen on the table, calculating which area might work best.

"Oh, who can think!" Laughing, she tossed down the pen to dance around the kitchen.

She had to call her kids and tell them. But she'd wait until she'd settled down a little so they didn't think she'd gone giddy as a teenager on prom night.

But she felt like one.

When the phone rang, she boogied to it, then sobered when she saw Irene's readout.

She took two quiet breaths. "Hello."

"Ella, Ella, can you come? Leo. Leo called."

"Slow down," she urged when Irene rushed over the words. "Leo called you?"

"He turned himself in. He's at the police station, and he wants to talk to me. They let him call me, and he said he's not saying anything about anything until he talks to me. I don't know what to do."

"Don't do anything. I'll be right over."

She grabbed her cell phone out of the charger, snagged her purse on the run. On the way out the door, she called Lucas.

"I'm on my way over to Irene's. Leo's turned himself in."

"Where?" Lucas demanded. "Where is he?"

"He called her from the police station." She slammed her car door, shifted the phone to yank on her seat belt. "He says he won't talk to anyone until he talks to her. I'm going with her."

"Don't you go near him, Ella."

"I won't, but I don't want her to go alone. I'll call you as soon as I'm back."

She closed the phone, tossed it in her purse as she reversed down the drive.

WAKING TO THE VIEW of the Alaska Range and Denali lifted the spirits. As she stood in camp, Rowan felt the mountain was on their side.

The crews had worked their hearts out, had the burns and bruises, the aches and pains to prove it. They hadn't slayed the dragon, not yet, but they'd sure as hell wounded it. And today, she had a good, strong feeling, today they'd plunge the sword right through its heart.

She knew the crew was banged up, strung out, but they'd gotten a solid four hours' sleep and even now filled their bellies. With more equipment, more men, an additional fire engine and two bulldozers, she believed they could be flying home by that evening, and leave the final beat-down and mopping up to Alaska.

Sleep, she decided, the mother of optimism.

She pulled out her radio when it signaled. "Ro at base camp, go ahead."

"L.B., Ops. I've got somebody here who wants to talk to you."

"How's my girl?"

"Hey, Dad. A-OK. Just standing here thinking and looking at a big-ass mountain. Wish you were here. Over."

"Copy that. It's good to hear your voice. Heard you had some trouble yesterday. Over."

"Nothing we couldn't handle with some bubble gum and duct tape. We softened her up yesterday." She watched the cloud buildup over the park, and puffs of smoke twining up from islands of green. We're coming for you, she thought. "Today, we'll kick her ass. Over."

"That's a roger. Ro, I've got something you should know," he began, and told her about Leo.

When she'd finished the radio call, Rowan walked over, sat down by Gull.

"Hell of a view," he commented. "Libby's in love. She's talking about moving up here. Ditching us for the Alaska unit."

"People fall for the mountain. Gull, Leo turned himself in this morning. He's in custody."

He studied her, then drank more coffee. "Then it's a damn good day."

"I guess it is." She heaved out a breath. "Yeah, I guess it is. Let's make it better and kill this dragon dead."

"I hear that," he said, and leaned over to kiss her.

IT SHOOK IRENE to the core to walk into the room and see Leo shackled to the single table. He'd lost weight, and his hair, thinner, straggly, hung over the collar of the bright orange prison suit. He hadn't shaved for God knew how long, she thought, and the beard had grown in shockingly gray around his gaunt face.

He looked wild. He looked like a criminal.

He looked like a stranger.

Had it only been a month since she'd seen him?

"Irene." His voice broke on her name, and the shackles rattled obscenely in her ears when he reached out.

She had to look away for a moment, compose herself.

The room seemed airless, and much too bright. She saw the reflection in the wide mirror—two-way glass, she thought. She watched *Law & Order*, and she knew how it worked.

But the reflection stunned her. Who was that woman, that old, bony woman with dingy hair scraped back from her haggard face?

It's me, she thought. I'm a stranger, too.

We're not who we were. We're not who we're supposed to be.

Were they watching behind that glass? Of course they were. Watching, judging, condemning.

The idea struck what little pride she had left, kindled it. She straightened her shoulders, firmed her chin and looked into her husband's eyes. She walked to the table, sat, but refused to take the hands he held out to her.

"You left me."

"I'm sorry. I thought it'd be better for you. They were looking to arrest me, Irene, for *murder*. I thought if I was gone, you'd be better off, and they'd find the real killer so I could come back."

"Where did you go?"

"I went up in the mountains. I kept moving. I had the radio, so I kept listening for word they'd arrested somebody. But they didn't. Somebody did this to me, Reenie. I just—"

"To you? To you, Leo? I signed my name with yours, putting up our home for your bail. You left, and now I'm going to lose my home because even taking another job isn't enough to meet the payments."

Pain, and she judged it sincere, cut across his face. "I didn't think about that until I'd already gone. I wasn't thinking straight. I just thought you and the baby would do better if I left. I didn't think—"

"You didn't think I'd be alone with no idea where my husband was, if he was dead or alive? You didn't think I'd have a baby to tend to, bills to pay, questions to answer, and all this right after I put my daughter's bones in the ground?"

"Our daughter, Reenie." Under the beard his cheeks reddened as he pounded his fist on the table. "And they think I killed my own girl. That I broke her neck, then burned her like trash in a barrel. Is that what you think? Is it?"

"I stopped thinking, Leo." She heard her own voice, thought it as dull as her hair, her face. "I had to, just to get from one day to the next, one chore to the next, one bill to the next. I lost my child, my husband, my faith. I'm going to lose my home, and my grandchild."

"I've been living like an animal," he began. Then stopped, squinted at her. "What are you talking about? They can't take Shiloh away."

"I don't know if they can or not. But I know I can't raise her right on my own without a good home to give her, or enough time. The Brayners will be here tomorrow, and they're taking her home to Nebraska."

"No." That stranger's face lit with fury. "Irene, no. Goddamn it, you listen to me now."

"Don't you swear at me." The slap in her voice had his head

snapping back. "I'm going to do what's right by that baby, Leo, and this is what's best. You've got no say in it. You left us."

"You're doing this to punish me."

She sat back. Funny, she realized, she didn't feel so tired now, so worn, so full of grief. No, she felt stronger, surer, clearer of mind than she had since they'd come to tell her Dolly was dead.

"Punish you? Look at yourself, Leo. Even if I had a mind to punish you, and I just don't, you've already done plenty of it on your own. You say you lived like an animal—well, that was your choice."

"I did it for you!"

"Maybe you believe that. Maybe you need to. I don't care. There's an innocent baby in all this, and she comes first. And for the first time in my life I'm putting myself next. Ahead of you, Leo. Ahead of every-damn-body else."

Something stirred in her. Not rage, she thought. She was sick of rage, and sick of despair. Maybe, just maybe, what stirred in her was faith—in herself.

"I'm going to do what I have to do for me. I have some thinking to do about that, but I'll be leaving, most likely to move closer to Shiloh. I'll take my half of whatever's left once this is said and done, and leave you yours."

He jerked back as if she'd slapped him. "You're going to leave me like this, when I'm locked up, when I need my wife to stand with me?"

"You need," she repeated, and shook her head. "You're going to have to get used to your needs being down the line. After Shiloh's and after mine. I'd've stood with you, Leo. I'd've done my duty as your wife and stuck by you, whatever it took and for however long. But you changed that when you proved you wouldn't do the same for me."

"Now you listen to me, Irene. You listen to me. Somebody took that rifle, took that gun, right out of my house. They did that to ruin me."

"I hope for the sake of your soul that's true. But you and Dolly made our house a battlefield, and neither one of you cared enough about me to stop the war. She left me without a second thought, and when we took her back, because that's what a parent does for a child, she lied and schemed just like always. And you fought and clawed at each other, just like always. With me in the middle, just like always."

God help her, Irene thought. She'd mourn her child for the rest of her life, but she wouldn't mourn the war.

"Now she's gone, and my faith's so broken I don't even have the comfort of believing it was God's will. I don't have that. You left me alone in the dark when I most needed a strong hand to hold on to.

"I don't know what you've done or haven't done, but I know that much. I know I can't depend on you to give me that strong hand, so I have to start depending on me. It's past time I did."

She got to her feet. "You should call your lawyer. He's what you need now."

"I know you're upset. I know you're mad at me, and I guess you've got a right to be. But please, don't leave me here alone, Irene. I'm begging you."

She tried, one last time, to reach down inside herself for love, or at least for pity. But found nothing.

"I'll come back when I can, and I'll bring you what they say I'm allowed to bring. Now I've got to go to work. I can't afford to take any more time off today. If I can find it in me to pray again, I'll pray for you."

L.B. HAILED MATT as Matt came back from his run.

"Have you got your PT in for the day?"

"Yeah. I was going to grab a shower and some breakfast. Have you got something you want me to do?"

"We could use some help restocking gear and equipment as it gets inspected. The crew got in from Wyoming while you were out."

"I saw the plane overhead. Man, L.B., did they have trouble, too?"

"Another bad pumper."

"Well, shit."

"We've got mechanics going over every inch of the rest of them, the saws and so on. We're unpacking all the chutes, and

I've got master riggers going over them. Iron Man's here, so he's helping with that."

"Jesus Christ, L.B., you don't think somebody messed with the chutes?"

"Are you willing to risk it?"

Matt pulled off his cap, scrubbed a hand over his hair. "I guess not. Who the hell would do something like this?"

"We're damn sure going to find out. Iron Man had news. Leo Brakeman turned himself in this morning."

"He's back? In Missoula? The cops have him?"

"That's exactly right. It makes me wonder how long he's been around these parts."

"And he could've done this. Screwed with us like this." Matt looked away, stared off, shaking his head. "Threatening Ro, shooting at her, for God's sake. Now messing with equipment. We never did anything to him or his. Never did a damn thing, and he can't say the same."

"Right now, we take care of our own, so grab that shower and some chow, then report to the ready room."

"Okay. Listen, if you need me back on the jump list—"

"We'll leave you off for now."

"I appreciate it, a lot. My parents should be in late this afternoon. I'm going to let them know I might have to cut it short. I don't want you having to shuffle somebody into my spot with the other crap on your plate, too. You call me in if you need me."

"Copy that." He gave Matt a slap on the shoulder.

He headed back into Operations. He had twenty-one men in Alaska, and didn't expect to see them back until the next day, soonest. Another load barely touched down, and a fire in California where they might need some Zulies before it was said and done. Dry conditions predicted for the next two weeks.

He'd be damned if he'd send the first load up without being sure, absolutely sure, every strap, every buckle, every fucking zipper and switch passed the most rigorous inspection.

He thought of Jim, felt the familiar heartsickness. Accidents couldn't be controlled, but he could and would control this human-generated bullshit.

AT THE END of a very long day, Lieutenant Quinniock drove out to the base. He wanted to go home, see his wife and kids, have dinner with them the way men who weren't cops did.

Most of all he wanted to be done with Leo Brakeman.

The man was a stone wall, wouldn't give an inch.

Every pass he or DiCicco had taken at him—together or separately—met with the same result.

Zero.

Brakeman just sat there, arms folded, eyes hard, jaw tight under that scruffy man-of-the-mountain beard. He'd lost ten pounds, gained ten years, and still wouldn't budge from his I'm-being-framed routine.

Now he demanded—through his lawyer, as he'd stopped talking altogether—a polygraph. So they'd have to go through that dance and shuffle.

Quinniock suspected if the polygraph results indicated Brakeman was a lying sack of shit who couldn't tell the truth over the size of his own dick, he'd claim the polygraph framed him.

They had circumstantial evidence aplenty. They had motive, means, opportunity and the fact that he'd run. What they didn't have was a confession.

The DA didn't want to charge Leo Brakeman, former All-State tackle, a Missoula native, with no priors and deep ties to the community, with the murder of his own daughter without a confession.

And since every goddamn bit of that evidence tied Dolly's murder with Latterly's, they couldn't charge him with that, either.

Need a break, Quinniock thought. Need a little off-the-clock before going back the next day to beat his head against the DA's. But first he had to see what the hell Michael Little Bear wanted.

Once on base, he aimed directly for Little Bear's office.

"You looking for L.B.?"

Quinniock stopped, nodded at the man who hailed him. "That's right."

"He just walked over to the loft. Do you know where that is?"

"Yeah, thanks."

He changed direction. It struck him how quiet the base seemed. None of the crew training outside or hustling from building to building, though he had seen a couple of them hauling ass down one of the service roads in a jeep. Either a test or a joyride, he decided.

When he made his way to the loft, passed what he knew they called the ready room, he saw why.

Here the hive of activity buzzed. Men and a handful of women worked on tools, taking them apart or putting them back together. Others pulled equipment off shelves or replaced it.

Routine inspection? he wondered, considered the organized chaos as he entered the loft.

There he saw chutes spread on counters, being unpacked or meticulously repacked. More hung in the tower waiting to be inspected or already tagged for repair or repacking.

He spotted Little Bear standing beside Lucas Tripp at one of the counters.

"Iron Man." Quinniock offered a hand with genuine pleasure. "Have they talked you back on the team?"

"Just helping out for the day. How's it going, Lieutenant?"

"I've had better days, and I've had worse. You wanted to talk to me?" he said to L.B.

"Yeah. Where's the tree cop?"

"Seeing to some tree cop business. Did you want her here?"

"Not especially. I have crews in Alaska, and another just back this morning from Wyoming."

"I heard about the fires in Alaska, threatening Denali Park. What's the status?"

"They hope to have it contained within a few hours. It's been a long, hard haul and my people jumped that fire with defective equipment."

"Is that what this is about?" Quinniock took another look around the loft. "You're running an equipment inspection?"

"What this is about is the fact that the equipment was tampered with. Stripped valves in pumpers, and one of them went into Wyoming. Chain saws with burned-out spark plugs and a frayed starter cord."

"I don't want to tell you your business, but all of that sounds like it could easily be simple wear and tear, something that got overlooked during the height of a busy season."

L.B.'s face went hard as stone. "We don't overlook a damn thing. Equipment comes in from a fire, it's gone over, checked out and checked off before it goes back in rotation. The same valve stripped on three pumpers, and two in the load that went to Denali?"

"Okay, that's a stretch."

"You're damn right. We're inspecting everything, and we've already found two more defective saws, and four piss bags with the nozzles clogged with putty. We're not careless; we can't afford to be. We don't overlook."

"All right."

"We have to inspect every chute, drogue, reserve. And thank God so far none of the ones we've gone over show any signs of tampering. Do you know how long it takes to repack a single chute?"

"About forty-five minutes. I've taken the tour. All right," Quinniock repeated, and took out his notebook. "You have a list of who checked off the equipment?"

"Sure I do, and I've gone over it. I'll give you the names, and the names of the mechanics who did any of the repairs or cleaning. It doesn't fall on one person."

"Are any of your crew dealing with more than the usual stress?"

"My people in Alaska who had to jerry-rig pumpers with duct tape, goddamn it, or lose their ground."

As he also sent men out into the field, bore the weight of those decisions, Quinniock understood the simmering rage. He kept his own tone brisk. "Have you had to discipline anyone, remove anyone from active?"

"No, and no. Do you think one of the crew did this? These people don't know when they'll have to jump or where or into what conditions until they do. Why in the hell would somebody do this when they might be the one with a starter cord snapping off in their hands, or scrambling with a useless pump with a fire bearing down on him?"

"Your support staff, your mechanics, your pilots and so on don't jump."

"And Leo Brakeman walked into your house this morning. He's already shot up mine, and isn't shy about starting fires. Tampering with the equipment here takes a little mechanical know-how."

"And he has more than a little." Quinniock blew out a breath. "I'll look into it. If it was him, I can promise you he's going to be sitting just where he's sitting for some time to come."

"His wife's leaving him," Lucas put in. He'd finished packing the chute, tagged it, then turned to address Quinniock. "She's giving the baby to the Brayners, the father's parents. They're coming in from Nebraska. She's making arrangements to turn the house over, to sell whatever she can sell, cash out whatever she can cash out. She's thinking about moving out near the Brayners so she can be near the baby, help out, watch her grow up."

"You're well informed."

"My . . ." Did a sixty-year-old man have a girlfriend? he wondered. "The woman I'm involved with is a close friend of Irene's."

"Ella Frazier. I'm well informed, too," Quinniock added. "I met her at the funeral."

"She's helping Irene as much as she can. Irene told Leo all this when she went to see him this morning."

Quinniock passed a weary hand over his face. "That explains why he shut down."

"It seems to me he's got nothing left to lose now."

"He wants to take a polygraph, but that could be the lawyer's idea. He's sticking with the same story, and the more we twist it up, the harder he bears down. Maybe tossing this tampering at him will shake him. I want the timelines, when each piece was last used, last inspected, by whom in both cases if you can get that for me. I have to make a call first."

He flipped out his phone, called the sergeant on duty and ordered a suicide watch on Leo Brakeman.

27

The plane touched down in Missoula shortly after ten A.M. They'd hit very rocky air over Canada, with hail flying like bullets while the plane rode the roller coaster of the storm.

Half the crew landed queasy or downright sick.

Since she'd slept the entire flight, Rowan calculated she felt nearly three-quarters human. Human enough to take a year-long shower, and eat like a starving horse.

As she and Gull walked to the barracks, she spotted L.B. with Cards, supervising the off-loading. She suspected L.B. had been waging his own war while they had waged theirs.

She didn't want to think about either battle for a little while.

She dropped down to sit on the bed in her quarters, remove her boots. "I want lots and lots of sex."

"You really are the woman of my dreams."

"First round, wet shower sex, after we scrape off a few layers of the Alaskan tundra, then a short and satisfying lunch break." She unbuckled her belt, dropped her pants. "Then a second round of make-the-mattress-sing sex."

"I feel a tear of gratitude and awe forming in the corner of my eye. Don't think less of me."

God, the man just tickled every inch of her. And, she decided, even with the scruff on his face, his hair matted, twanged her lust chords.

"Then a quickie just to top things off before I start my reports. I'll have to brief with L.B. at some point, and squeeze in daily PT, after which there must be more food."

"There must."

"Then I believe it's going to be a time for relax-into-a-nap sex."

"I can write up an agenda on this, just so we don't miss anything."

"It's all here." She tapped her temple. "So . . ." She strolled naked into the bathroom. "Let's get this party started."

Rowan considered the first round a knockout. Now that she felt a hundred percent human, and with Gull shaving off the scruff in her bathroom, she went out to dress.

She picked up the note someone must have shoved under her door in the last forty minutes.

FULL BRIEFING ALL CREW
OPS
THIRTEEN HUNDRED

"Oh, well. Round two's going to have to be postponed." She held the note up for Gull to read.

"Maybe he has some answers."

"Or maybe he's just got a whole lot of questions. Either way, we'd better scramble if we're going to get any food before thirteen hundred."

"Marg might know something."

"I'm thinking the same."

Since Marg liked him well enough, Gull went with Rowan to the kitchen.

Probably not the best timing, he realized as they walked into the heat and the rush. Marg, Lynn and the new cook—Shelley, he remembered—turned, hauled, chopped and scooped with a creative symmetry that made him think of a culinary Cirque du Soleil.

"Hey." Lynn filled a tub with some sort of pasta medley. "Shelley, we need more rolls, and the chicken salad's getting low."

"I'm all over it!"

"Bring the barbecue pan back when you come," Marg told Lynn while she swiped a cloth over her heat-flushed face. "They'll be ready for it by then. I know how they suck this stuff down.

"Briefing at one o'clock," she muttered, and wagged a spoon at Rowan. "Right in the middle of things, so they all storm this place before noon like Henry the Fifth stormed, wherever the hell that was."

"I could chop something," Rowan volunteered.

"Just stay clear. Once we get this second round of barbecue out to them, they'll hold awhile."

"You were right." Lynn bustled back in with a near-empty pan. Together, she and Marg filled it.

"This tops everything off but the dessert buffet. Shelley and I can get that."

"Good girl." Marg flipped out two plates, tossed the open rolls on them, dumped barbecue on the bottom, scooped the pasta medley beside it, added a serving of summer squash. Then pointed at Gull. "Get three beers and bring 'em out to my table. Take this." She shoved one of the plates at Rowan before grabbing up flatware setups.

She sailed outside and, after setting the plate and setups down, pressed her hands to her lower back. "God."

"Sit down, Marg."

"I need to stretch this out some first. Go on and eat."

"Aren't you going to?"

Marg just waved a hand in the negative. "That's what I'm after," she said, taking the beer Gull held out to her. "I've got the AC set to arctic blast, but by the time we're into the middle of the lunch shift, it's like Nairobi. Eat. And don't bolt it down."

Gull lifted the sloppy sandwich, got in the first bite. Warm, tangy, with the pork melting into sauce and the combination melding into something like spiced bliss.

"Marg, what'll it take for you to come and live with me?"

"A lot of sex."

"I'm good for that," he said over another bite, pointing to Rowan for verification. "I'm good for that."

"Everybody's got to be good for something," Rowan commented. "What's the word, Marg?"

"L.B.'s on a tear, that's for certain. You don't see that man get up a head of steam often. It's why he's good at the job. But he's been puffing it out the last couple days. He had every chute, every pack, every jumpsuit gone over. He'd have used microscopes on them if he could have. Every piece of equipment, every tool, every damn thing. He's having the jeeps gone over, the Rolligons, the planes."

She took a long, slow sip of beer, set it aside, then surprised Gull by lowering smoothly into a yoga down dog. "God, that feels better. He called Quinniock out here."

"He wants a police investigation?" Rowan asked.

"He's made up his mind Leo managed to do this. He may be right." She walked her feet up to a forward fold, hung there a moment, then straightened. "Irene's leaving him. She's already packing up. The Brayners are taking the baby tomorrow, and I don't think she plans to be far behind. She's going to move into your daddy's place for a couple weeks, until she clears up her business."

"She's moving in with Dad?"

"No, into the house. He offered it to her. He'll be in Ella's."

"Oh."

"Don't give me that WTF look. Talk to your father about it. Meanwhile, I hear they have Leo on suicide watch and he's clammed up tight. He wants to take a lie detector test. I think they're going to do that today or tomorrow.

"That's about it. I've got to get back."

Gull waited a moment, then scooped up some pasta. "All that, and I bet the only thing you're thinking is your father's going to be living with the hot redhead."

"Shut up. Besides, he's just doing a favor for Mrs. Brakeman."

"Yeah, I bet it's a real sacrifice. You know what I'm thinking?"

Deliberately she stared up at the sky. "I don't care."

"Yes, you do. I'm thinking, the way this is working out, I'll move in with you. You're going to have the room, then I can be closer to Marg and get this barbecue on a regular basis."

"I don't think this is something to joke about."

"Babe, I never joke about barbecue." He licked some off

his thumb. "I wonder how a Fun World would go over in Missoula."

Rowan tried to squeeze out some stress by pinching the bridge of her nose. "I'm losing my appetite."

"Too bad. Can I have the rest of your sandwich?"

The snort of laughter snuck up on her. "Damn it. Every time I should be annoyed with you, you manage to slide around it. And no." With a smirk, she stuffed the rest of her sandwich into her mouth.

"Just for that I'm going to get some pie. And I'm not bringing you any."

"You don't have time." She tapped her watch. "Briefing."

"I'll take it to go."

He didn't get her any pie, but he did bring her a slab of chocolate cake. They ate dessert out of their palms on the way to Ops.

Jumpers poured out of the woodwork, heading in from the training field and track, striding out of the barracks, filing in from the loft. A grim-faced Cards, shoulders hunched, hands deep in his pockets, turned out of the ready room.

Rowan nudged Gull's arm with her elbow and shifted direction to intersect.

"You look like somebody stole your last deck," she commented.

"Do you think I didn't do my job? Didn't pay attention to what I load?"

"I know you did. You do."

"That equipment was inspected and checked. I've got the goddamn paperwork. I checked the goddamn manifest."

"Are you taking heat on this?" Rowan demanded.

"It's got to go up the chain, something like this, and when shit goes up the chain, the hook drops on somebody. What're we supposed to do, check every valve, nozzle, cord and strap before we load it, when every damn thing's been checked before it goes into rotation? Are we supposed to start everything up before we put it on the damn plane?

"Fuck it. Just fuck it. I don't know why I do this damn job anyway."

He stalked off, leaving Rowan looking after him with a

handful of cake crumbs and smeared icing. "He shouldn't take a knock for this. This is nobody's fault except whoever messed up the equipment."

"He's right about the way things drop back down the chain. Even if they pin it on Brakeman, on anybody, Cards could take a hit."

"It's not right. L.B. will go to bat for him. It's bad enough, what we've been dealing with, without one of us getting dinged for it." She stared down at her chocolate-smeared hand. "Hell."

"Here." Gull dug a couple of wet naps out of his pocket. "Some problems have easy solutions."

"He's a damn fine jumper." She swiped at the chocolate. "As good a spotter as they come. He can be annoying with the card games and tricks, but he puts a lot into this job. More than most of us."

Gull could have pointed out that putting more than most into it meant Cards had regular and easy access to all the equipment, and that as spotter he hadn't jumped the Alaska fire.

No point in it, he decided. Her attachment there ran deep.

"He'll be all right."

They went into the building where people milled and muttered.

He saw Yangtree sitting, rubbing his knee, and Dobie leaning against a wall, eyes closed in a standing-up power nap. Libby played around with her iPhone while Gibbons sat with a hip hitched on a counter, his nose in a book.

Some drank coffee, some huddled in conversations, talking fire, sports, women—the three top categories—or speculating about the briefing to come. Some zoned out, sitting on the floor, backs braced against the wall or a desk.

Every one of them had dropped weight since the start of the season, and plenty of them, like Yangtree, nursed aching knees. The smoke jumper's Achilles' heel. Strained shoulders, pulled hamstrings, burns, bruises. Some of the men had given up shaving, sporting beards in a variety of styles.

Every one of them understood true exhaustion, real hunger, intense fear. And every one of them would suit up if the siren called. Some would fight hurt, but they'd fight all the same.

He'd never known people so stubbornly resilient or so willing to put body, mind and life on the line, day after day.

And more, to love it.

"L.B. hasn't started." Matt maneuvered in beside him. "I thought I'd be late."

"Not yet. I didn't expect to see you for a couple more days."

"I'm just in for this. L.B. wanted all of us, unless we caught a fire. What's the word?"

"As far as I know they're still inspecting. They found a few more pieces of equipment tampered with."

"Son of a bitch."

"Did your parents get in all right?" Rowan asked him.

"Yeah. They're over visiting with Shiloh. We're going to take her out for a couple hours later, so she gets used to being with us. She's already taken to my ma."

"How's Mrs. Brakeman doing?"

He lifted his shoulders, stared toward the Ops desk. "She's being real decent about it. It shows how much she loves the baby." He let out a little sigh. "She and my ma had a good cry together. L.B.'s getting ready to start."

"All right, settle down," L.B. called out. "I've got some things to say, so pay attention. Everybody knows about the equipment failures on the jumps in Alaska and Wyoming. I want to tell you all that we're continuing a full inspection, any equipment or gear not yet inspected and passed doesn't go out. I called in a couple extra master riggers to help reinspect, clear, repack every chute on this base. I don't want anybody worrying about the safety of their gear."

He paused a moment.

"We've got a good system of checks on this base, and nobody cuts corners. Everyone here knows it's not just important, it's fucking *essential* that every jumper have confidence the gear and equipment needed to jump and attack will be safe, meet the highest standards and be in good working order. That didn't happen on these jumps, and I take responsibility."

He hard-eyed the protests until they died off.

"I've been in touch with the Management Council so they're aware of what we're dealing with. The local police and the USFS are also aware and conducting their own investigations."

"They know damn well Leo Brakeman did this," somebody shouted out and started everybody else up again.

"He shouldn't have been able to." L.B. roared it over the rise of chatter, smashing it like a boot heel on an anthill. "He shouldn't have been able to get to us the way he did. The fact he's locked up is all fine and good, but we're going to be a lot more security-conscious around here. We're going to do spot checks, regular patrols. If I could suspend the tours, I would, but since that's not an option, two staff members will go with each group.

"Until the investigations and reviews are complete, and we know who and how, we're not taking any chances."

He stopped again, took a breath. "And I'm recommending everybody toss a roll of duct tape into their PG bags."

That got a laugh, succeeding in lowering the tension.

"I want you to know I've got your backs, on base, in the air and on a fire. I've posted a new jump list and a rotation of assignments. If you don't like it, come see me in my office so I can kick your ass. Anybody's got any questions, suggestions, public bitching, now's the time."

"Can we get the feds to pay for the duct tape?" Dobie asked, and earned hoots and applause.

Gull sent his friend an appreciative look. The right attitude, he thought. Keep it cocky, keep it steady, maintain unity.

Whether the sabotage had been an inside or outside job, unity equaled strength.

He had questions, but not the sort he wanted to ask here.

"I've got something I need to work on," he told Rowan over the cross talk. "Catch up with you later."

He noted her disapproving frown, but slipped out and walked straight to his quarters. There, he booted up his laptop and got to work.

He shut down, passcoding his work when the siren sounded. He wasn't on the first or second loads, but he ran to the ready room to assist those who were. He loaded gear on speed racks, hefted already packed and strapped paracargo onto the electric cart.

He listened, and he observed.

With Rowan and Dobie, he watched the plane rise into the wide blue cup of the sky.

"It's good L.B. got that briefing in before the call." Rowan shaded her eyes from the sun with the flat of her hand. "The sky looks a little dicey to the east."

"Might be jumping ourselves before long."

Hearing the eagerness in his voice, Rowan angled her body toward Dobie. "You've got jump fever. The best thing for you is to go sleep it off."

"I got me an assignment. I'm on PC," he said, using the shorthand for paracargo. "Packing and strapping in the load-master's room. You, too, pal," he told Gull. "Swede pulled the loft."

"Yeah, I saw that, and that anybody on the Alaska jump could take a two-hour break first. But what the hell." He leaned over, kissed Rowan. "We'll get back to our agenda later."

"Count on it."

"I don't see how it's right and fair you got a woman right on base," Dobie said as they walked toward the loadmaster's room together. "The rest of us have to hunt one up, if we're lucky and get a turn at a bar."

"Life's just full of not right and not fair. Otherwise I'd be stretched out on a white sand beach with that woman, drinking postcoital mai tais."

"Postcoital." Dobie snickered like a twelve-year-old. "You beat all, Gull. Beat all and back again."

SINCE HE DIDN'T FIND her in her quarters, Gull assumed he'd finished up his duties before her, and went back to his room to continue on his project.

He sat on the bed, left the door open in a casual, nothing-to-see-here mode.

People walked by now and then, but for the most part his section stayed quiet.

Since he'd left his window open as well, he caught snippets of conversation as people wandered outside. A small group not on the jump list made plans to go into town. Somebody muttered to himself about women as the shimmering afternoon light dimmed.

He took a moment to shift to look out, and saw Rowan had

been right about the eastern sky. Clouds gathered now, sailing in like warships.

A storm waiting to happen, he thought, toying with getting his run in before it did, then decided to wait for Rowan.

She and the first grumble of thunder arrived at the same time.

"Lightning strikes all over hell and back," she told him, and flopped on the bed. "I ran up to check the radar. Tornadoes whipping things up in South Dakota."

She circled her neck, rubbing hard at the back of her left shoulder as she spoke.

"We'll probably have to run on the damn treadmill. I hate that."

He pressed his fingers where she rubbed. "Jesus, Rowan, you got concrete in here."

"Don't I know it. I haven't had a chance to work it out today. I need that run, some yoga . . . or that." She sighed when he shifted and dug his fingers and thumbs into the knotted muscles.

"We'll do our run after the storm's over," he said. "Use the track."

Lightning struck, a flash and burn, and the wind rattled the blinds at his window. But no rain followed.

"When things slow down, we'll hit L.B. up for a night off and get a fancy hotel suite. One with a jet tub in the bathroom. We'll soak in it half the night."

"Mmm." She sighed her way into the image he painted. "Room service with fat, juicy steaks, and a great big bed to play on. Sleeping with somebody who has money and doesn't mind spending it has advantages."

"If you've got money and mind spending it, you can't be having much fun."

"I like that attitude. Are you e-mailing back home?"

"No, something else. You're not going to like it."

"If you're e-mailing your pregnant wife to ask about your two adorable children and frisky puppy, I'm not going to like it." She angled around. "That's the kind of tone you used. Like you were going to tell me something that meant I had to punch you in the face."

"My wife's not pregnant, and we have a cat." He gave her shoulders a last squeeze, then got up to close the door.

"You didn't do that because we're going to continue our planned agenda from this morning."

"No. It's the tampering, Rowan. Brakeman thinking of it, then pulling it off—all while eluding the cops. That's just not working for me."

"He knows this area better than most. He's a mechanic, and he has a grudge against us. It works for me."

On the surface, he thought, but you only had to scratch off a layer.

"Why tamper with some of the equipment?" Gull began working off his mental list. "He doesn't know how we roll here, or in a fire. Not all the ins and outs."

"His daughter worked here three seasons," Rowan pointed out. "She had a working knowledge of how we roll, and he's spent time on base."

"If he wanted to hurt us, there are more direct ways. He had weapons; he could've used them. Sure, he could've known or found out where the equipment is," Gull conceded, "and he could've gotten to it. This stretch of the season, most of us would sleep through a bomb blast. We'd hear the siren, the same way a mother hears her baby crying in the night even when she's exhausted. We're tuned, but otherwise, we're out for the count.

"This was subtle, and sneaky, and it was the kind of thing, it seems to me, you'd know to do if you knew just how broken equipment could impact a crew on a fire. Because you've been there."

He was right, Rowan thought. She didn't like it. "You're actually saying one of us did this?"

"I'm saying one of us could have done it, because we know how to access the equipment, how to screw it up and how it could impact an attack."

"How stupid would that be since you could be the one impacted?"

"There's that. Let's take that first. Who didn't jump either fire?"

He toggled his screen back to the document he'd worked on.

"You're right; I don't like it one damn bit. And first, Yangtree jumped with us."

"He spent nearly the entire jump coordinating, doing flyovers."

"That's crap. And L.B.? Seriously?"

"He didn't jump. Cards worked as spotter, so he didn't jump. Neither did any of these. That's over twenty, with six of them off the list altogether for personal reasons or injuries."

"Yangtree's been jumping thirty *years*. What, suddenly he decides to find out what'll happen if he screws up equipment? Cards has ten years in, and L.B. more than a dozen. And—"

"Look, I know how you feel about them. They're friends—they're family. I feel the same."

"In my world people don't make up a suspect list of friends and family."

"How often in your world has your equipment been sabotaged?" He laid a hand on her knee to soften the words. "Look, it's more with you because you've been with them a long time. But I trained with a lot of the names on this list, and you know going through that makes a tight bond."

"I don't even know why you're doing this."

"Because, damn it, Rowan, if it wasn't Brakeman, then we can do our patrols, our rechecks and spot checks, but . . . If you wanted to get in the ready room, the loadmaster's room, any damn place on base tonight and mess something up, could you?"

She didn't speak for a moment. "Yeah. I could. Why would I? Why would any of us?"

"That's another deal entirely. Before that, there's the possibility, if it's one of us, it *is* somebody who jumped, who knew they were high on the list. Who wanted to be there, be part of it. We're in a stressful line of work. People snap, or go too far. The firefighter who starts fires, then risks himself and his crew to put it out. It happens."

"I know it happens."

He hit another key, took her to another page.

"I divided the crews, the way we were that day."

"You're missing some names."

"I think we can eliminate ourselves."

"Dobie's not here."

"He had the duct tape."

"Yeah, that was real handy."

"He always carries . . . Okay, you're right." It burned his belly and his conscience, but he added Dobie's name. "I should add us because you wished for the damn tape, and I remembered he'd have it."

"What's our motive?"

"Maybe I want to scare you off the job so you'll stay home and cook me a hot dinner every night."

"As if. But I mean the question. What's any motive?"

"Okay, let's roll with that. Yangtree." He toggled back again. "He's talking about giving it up. His knees are shot. Thirty years, like you said. He's given this more than half his life, and now he knows he can't keep it up. The younger and stronger are moving in. That's a pisser."

"He's not like that." She snapped it out—knee-jerk—then subsided when Gull only looked at her. "All right. This is bogus, but all right."

"Cards? He's had a bad-luck season. Injuries, illness. It wears. The woman he wanted to marry dumped him. Last summer, when he was spotter, Jim Brayner died."

"That wasn't—"

"His fault. I agree. It wasn't yours, either, Rowan, but you have nightmares."

"Okay. Okay. I get it. We could walk down your lists and find a plausible motive for everyone. That doesn't make it true. And if it's such a good theory, the cops would've thought of it."

"What makes you think they haven't?"

That stopped her. "That's a really ugly thought. The idea they're looking at us, investigating us, scraping away to hunt for weaknesses, secrets. That they're doing what we're doing here, only more."

"It is ugly, but I'd rather take a hard look than ignore what might be right here with us."

"I want it to be Brakeman."

"Me too."

"But if it's not," she said before he could, "we have to think of the safety of the unit. It's not L.B."

He started to argue, then backed off. "What's your reasoning?"

"He worked hard for his position, and he takes a lot of pride in it. He loves the unit and he also loves its rep. Anything that damages or threatens that reflects on him. He could've closed ranks and kept this internal, but he opened it up. He's the one shining the light on it when he knows he may pay consequences."

Good points, Gull decided. Every one a good point. "I'll agree with that."

"And it's not Dobie. He's too damn good-natured under it all. And he loves what he's doing. He loves it all. Mostly he loves you. He'd never do anything that put you at risk."

"Thanks."

"I didn't say that for you."

"I know." But it soothed both his belly and his conscience. "Thanks anyway."

She looked out the window where lightning flashed, and thunder echoed over the gloom-shrouded peaks. "The wind's pushing the rain south. We just can't catch a break."

"We don't have to do this now. We can let it alone, hit the gym."

"I'm not a weak sister. Let's work it through. I'll tell you why it's not Janis."

"All right." He took her hand, disconcerting her by bringing it briefly to his lips. "I'm listening."

28

Gull figured he had an hour, tops. With Rowan hip-deep on her reports for the Alaska fire, she'd be occupied for at least that long. He came down from his duties in the loft, checking the time as he struck out on the service road at a light jog.

Nobody would question a man doing his PT, and there'd be no reason to suspect he'd arranged a meeting away from any casual observers.

Especially Rowan.

In any case, he liked being out, taking a short extra run, getting inside his own head.

The storm the night before hadn't squeezed out more than a piss pot of rain, but it had managed to drop the temperature. They'd rolled a load that morning to jump a fire east, so he didn't want to go far in case the siren went off.

He didn't have to.

Half a mile out, Lucas stood in running sweats and a T-shirt talking on his cell.

"Sure, that'd be great." He gave Gull a slight nod. "Perfect. I'll see you then." After closing the phone, he tucked it in the pocket of his sweats. "Gull."

"Thanks for meeting me."

"No problem. I still run here some days, so I got a mile or so in. I have to figure this has to do with Rowan since you didn't want to talk to me on base."

"With her, with everybody. Nobody knows the players better than you, Lucas. The staff and crew, the Brakemans, the cops. Maybe not the rookies as much as the long-timers, but I'm betting you've got some insight there, as they jump with your daughter."

Lucas cocked an eyebrow at that, but Gull just shrugged.

"You'd size them up, ask some questions, get some answers."

"I know you're fast on your feet, had a good rep with the hotshots, and L.B. considers you a solid asset to the crew. You don't mind a fight, like fast cars, have a head for business and good taste in women."

"We've got the last in common. Let me ask you straight out, does Leo Brakeman have the brains, the canniness, let's say, the aptitude to do all that's being laid down here? Forget motive and opportunity and all that cop shit." Gull shrugged it off. "Is he the man for this?"

Lucas said nothing for a moment, only nodding his head as if affirming his own thoughts. "He's not stupid, and he's a damn good mechanic. Starting from the back, yeah, he could've figured how to disable equipment without it showing until it was too late. Killing Latterly . . ."

Lucas stuck his hands in his pockets, looked away at the mountains. "I'd see him going after the son of a bitch once he found out Latterly was messing with his daughter. I'd see him beating the man bloody for it, especially considering Irene's connection to the church. It's harder to see Leo putting a bullet in him, but not impossible to see."

He sighed once. "No, not impossible. He'd be capable of shooting up the base. Aiming for anybody, I don't think so. But if he had, he wouldn't have missed. And that's one I've thought long and hard on since he'd have had Rowan in the crosshairs.

"Dolly? They kept at each other like rottweilers over the same bone. He's got a temper, that's no secret, and it's no secret she caused him a lot of shame and disappointment."

"But?"

"Yeah, but. The only way I can see him killing her is an accident. I don't know if I'm putting myself into it, or if that's a fact, but it's how I see it. I guess what I'm saying is I can see him doing any of those things, in the heat. He's got a short fuse, burns hot. But it burns out."

"You've been giving all of this some long, hard thought."

"Rowan's in the middle of it."

"Exactly. Hot temper. Hot and physical." And, Gull thought, straight down the line of his own take on it. "Latterly and the tampering. Those were cold and calculated."

"You're thinking some of this, maybe all of it, comes from somebody who works on base. Maybe even one of your own."

He thought of the men and women he'd trained with, the ones he fought with. "I haven't wanted to think it."

"Neither have I, but I started asking myself these same questions after L.B. told me about the tampering. After I settled down some. We've skirted around it, but I'm pretty sure L.B.'s asking himself the same."

"Are you leaning in any particular direction?"

"I worked with some of these people. You know as well as I that's not like sharing an office or a watercooler. I can't see anyone I know the way I know those men and women in this kind of light. And I don't know if that's because of what we were—still are—to each other or because it's just God's truth."

He waited a beat, watching Gull's face carefully. "You haven't told Rowan your line of thinking?"

"I did."

Approval and a little humor curved Lucas's lips. "We can add you've got balls to what I know about you."

"I'm not going behind her back." He thought of where he stood right now, and with whom. And grinned. "Much. Anyway, I made a spreadsheet. I like spreadsheets," he said when Lucas let out a surprised laugh. "They're efficient and orderly. She doesn't want to think it could be true, but she listened."

"If she listened, and didn't kick the balls I know you have up past your eyes for suggesting it, it must be serious between the two of you."

"I'm in love with her. She's in love with me, too. She just hasn't figured it out yet."

"Well." Lucas studied Gull's face for a long moment. "Well," he repeated, and sighed a second time. "She's got a hard view of relationships and their staying power. That's my fault."

"I don't think so. I think it's circumstances. And she may have a hard head and a guarded heart, but she's not closed up. She's too smart, too self-aware, not to mention a bred-in-the-bone risk-taker to deny herself what she wants once she's decided she wants it. She'll figure out she wants me."

"Cocky bastard, aren't you? I like you."

"That's a good thing, because if you didn't, she'd give me the boot. Then she'd be sad and sorry the rest of her life."

At Lucas's quick, helpless laugh, Gull glanced at his watch. "I've got to start heading back."

"I'll walk back with you. I run here off and on," he reminded Gull. "And I have something I need to tell Rowan, face-to-face."

"If it's that you're moving in with Ella, she heard."

"Hell." Lucas scrubbed a hand over the back of his neck as they walked. "I should've known it'd bounce through the base once I so much as thought about doing it. You'd think with everything going on, my personal life wouldn't make the cut.

"Well?" Lucas jabbed an elbow in Gull's ribs. "How'd she take it?"

"It knocked her back some. She'll get used to it because she loves you, she respects Ella, and she's not an idiot. Anyway, before we get back—and I'd as soon, unless she asks directly, Rowan assume we ran into each other on the road."

"Probably for the best."

"Generally I don't mind pissing her off, but she's got a lot on her plate. So, before we get back, I wanted to ask if I can e-mail you the spreadsheet."

"Jesus Christ. A spreadsheet."

"I've listed names in multiple categories, along with general data, then my take on each. Rowan's take. Adding yours might help narrow the field."

"Send me the damn spreadsheet." Lucas rattled off his e-mail address. "Want me to write it down?"

"No, I've got it."

"Even if Brakeman didn't do all this—or any of it, for that

matter—as long as he's behind bars it should end. You can't frame him if you do any of this crap when the cops know exactly where he is twenty-four/seven. I guess the question we should ask is, who's got this kind of grudge against Leo?"

Lucas lifted his eyebrows when Gull said nothing. "You're thinking something else?"

"I think it could be that, just exactly that. But I also think Brakeman, with his temper, his history with Dolly, makes a pretty good patsy. And I know whoever's responsible for this is one sick son of a bitch. I don't think sick sons of bitches stop just because it's smart."

"I wish you hadn't said that and made me think the same. Fear the same. If I could I'd make Rowan take the rest of the season off, get the hell away from this."

"I won't let anything happen to her." Gull looked Lucas dead in the eye. "I know that's a stupid and too usual a thing to say, but I won't. She can handle just about anything that comes at her. What she can't, I will."

"I'm going to hold you to that. Now, you might want to make yourself scarce while I go talk to her. Not too scarce," Lucas added. "It's likely she'll need to take out how she feels about my new living arrangements on somebody after I'm gone. It might as well be you."

Rowan finished her reports, rechecked the attached list of paracargo she'd requested and received the second day of the attack. All in order, she decided.

Once she'd turned it over to L.B., she could get the hell outside for a while, and then . . .

"It's open," she called out at the two-tap knock on her door. "Hey." Her face brightened as she rose to greet her father. "Great timing. I just finished my reports. Got your run in?"

"I thought I'd take it this way, get a twofer and see my girl."

"I tell you what, I'll dig out a cold drink from the cooler, trade you for glancing over my work here."

"If you've got any 7UP, you've got a deal."

"I always keep my best guy's favorite in stock," she reminded him as he braced his hands on her desk, scanning the work on her laptop.

"Thorough and to the point," he said after a moment. "Are you bucking for L.B.'s job?"

"Oh, that's a big hell no. I don't mind spending the time on reports, but if I had to deal with all the paperwork, personalities, politics and bullshit L.B. does, I'd just shoot myself and get it over with. You could've done it," she added. "Gotten in a couple more years."

"If I'm going to do administrative crap, it's going to be *my* administrative crap."

"Yeah, I guess that's where I got it. Do you want to walk over to the lounge? Or maybe the cookhouse? I imagine Marg has some pie we could talk her out of."

"I don't really have enough time. Ella's picking me up in a little bit."

"Oh."

"I wanted to see you, talk to you about some things."

"I heard Irene Brakeman's letting her house go, and she's probably moving to Nebraska. That you're letting her use your house until she's got it all dealt with. That was good of you, Dad. It has to be hard for her, being alone in the house, with all the memories. Added on to knowing it's not really hers anymore."

"She's moving in tomorrow. I need to pack up a few more things I'll need with me now. Ella's been helping her do the same—pack up what she'll need—and pack up what she wants to take with her when she goes."

"It's a big step she's taking. A lot of big steps. Leaving Missoula, leaving her husband, her friends, her job."

"I think she needs it. She looks better than she has since this all started. Once she decided what she needed to do for herself, for the baby, I think it took some of the weight off."

He took a long, slow drink. "Speaking of decisions, big ones. I won't be moving back into the house. I'm going to live with Ella."

"Jesus, are you going to marry her?"

He didn't choke, but he swallowed hard. "One step at a time, but I think that one's right down the road."

"I'm just getting used to you dating her, now you're moving in together."

"I love her, Rowan. We love each other."

"Okay, I guess I'm going to sit down for a minute." She chose the side of the bed. "Her place?"

"She's got a great place. A lot of room, her gardens. She's done it up just the way she wants it. Her house means a lot to her. Ours?" He let his shoulders lift and fall. "Half the year or more it's just where I sleep most nights."

"Well." She didn't know what she felt because there was too much to feel. "I guess if I'd known that would be our last dinner in the house together, I'd've . . . I don't know, done something more important than skillet chicken."

"I'm not selling the house, Ro." He sat beside her, laid a hand on her knee. "Unless you don't want it. I figured you'd take it over. We can get somebody to cut the grass and all that during the season."

"Maybe I can think about that awhile."

"As long as you want."

"Big changes," she managed. "You know how it takes me a while to navigate changes."

"Whenever you got sick as a kid, we had to dig out the same pajamas."

"The blue puppies."

"Yeah, the blue ones with puppies. When you outgrew them there was hell to pay."

"You cut them up and made me a little pillow out of the fabric. And it was okay again. Crap, Dad, you look so happy." Her eyes stung as she reached for his face. "And I didn't even notice you weren't."

"I wasn't unhappy, baby."

"You're happier now. She's not the only one who loves you," she told him, and kissed his cheeks. "So consider I've got my blue puppy pillow, and it's okay."

"Okay enough that you'll take some time when you have it to get to know her?"

"Yeah. Gull thinks she's hot."

Lucas's eyebrows winged up. "So do I, but he'd better not get any ideas."

"I'm running interference there."

"You've had some changes yourself since he came along."

"Apparently. This is the damnedest season. Gull's got it

into his head that somebody on base might be responsible for what's been going on, instead of Brakeman."

"Does he?"

"Yeah, and in his Gull way he's got all the data and suppositions organized in a file. I think it's whacked, but then I start wondering, once he's done laying it out. Then I go about my business and decide it's whacked again. Until he points out this and that. I end up not sure what to think. I hate not knowing what to think."

Gently, he skimmed a hand over her crown of hair. "Maybe the best thing to do is keep your eyes, your ears and your mind open."

"The first two are easy. It's the last that's hard. Everybody's edgy and trying to pretend they aren't. We've jumped nearly twice as many fires as we did by this time last season, and the success rate's good, injuries not too bad. But outside of that? This season's FUBAR, and we're all feeling it."

"Do me a favor. Stick close to the hotshot, as much as you can. Do it for me," he added before she could speak. "Not because I think you can't take care of yourself, but because I'll worry less if I know somebody's got your back."

"Well, he's hard to shake off anyway."

"Good." He patted her leg. "Walk me out."

She got up with him, chewing over everything they'd talked about while they walked outside. "Is it different with her, with Ella, than it was with my mother? Not the circumstances, or rate of maturity, or any of that. I mean . . ." She tapped a fist on her heart. "I'm okay with however you answer. I'd just like to know."

He took a moment, and she knew he sought out the words.

"I was dazzled by your mother. Maybe a little overwhelmed, a lot excited. When she told me she was pregnant, I loved her. And I think it was because I loved what was inside her, what we'd started without meaning to. Sometimes I wonder if she knew that, even before I did. That would've been hurtful. I cared about her, Rowan, and I did my best by her. But you were why.

"I can say Ella dazzled me, overwhelmed me, excited me. But it's different. I know what I didn't feel for your mother because I feel it now, for Ella."

"What is it you're supposed to feel?" she demanded. "I can never figure it out."

He cleared his throat. "Maybe you should ask another woman about this kind of thing."

"I'm asking you."

"Ah, hell." Now he shuffled his feet, the big man, the Iron Man. "I'm not going to talk about sex. I did that with you once already, and that was scarier than any fire I ever jumped."

"And embarrassing for both of us. I'm not asking about sex, Dad. I know about sex. You tell me you love her, and I can see it all over you. I can see it, but I don't know how it feels—how it's supposed to feel."

"There's a lot that goes around it. Trust and respect and—" He cleared his throat again. "Attraction. But the center's a reflection of all of those things, all your strengths and weaknesses, hopes and dreams. They catch fire there, in the center. Maybe it blazes, maybe it simmers, smolders, but there's the heat and the light, all those colors, and what's around it feeds it.

"Fire doesn't only destroy, Rowan. Sometimes it creates. The best of it creates, and when love's a fire, whether it's bright or a steady glow, hot or warm, it creates. It makes you better than you were without it."

He stopped, colored a little. "I don't know how to explain it."

"It's the first time anyone ever explained it so I could understand it. Dad." She took his hands, looked into his eyes. "I'm really happy for you. I mean it, all the way through. Really happy for you."

"That means more than I can tell you." He drew her in, held her tight as Ella drove up. "You were my first love," he whispered in Rowan's ear. "You always will be."

She knew it, but now let go enough to accept he could love someone else, too. She nodded as Ella stepped out of the car.

"Hi."

"Hi." Ella smiled at Lucas. "Am I late?"

"Right on time." Keeping his hand in Rowan's, he leaned down, kissed Ella. "How'd it go with Irene?"

"Packing up, organizing, deciding over the contents of a house a woman's lived in for twenty-five years is a monumental project—and you know I love projects. It's helping her,

I think, the work, the planning. Helping her get through the now."

"Did Jim's parents . . ." Rowan trailed off.

"They're leaving this afternoon. I met them, and they're lovely people. Kate's asked Irene to come stay with them if and when she goes to Nebraska. To stay until she finds a place of her own. I don't think she will, but the offer touched her."

"Don't be sad," Lucas said, sliding an arm around Ella's shoulders as her eyes filled.

"I can't figure out what I am." She blinked the tears back. "But I called my son, asked him to bring the kids over later. I know how I feel after a few hours with my grandchildren. Happy and exhausted."

Grandchildren, Rowan thought. She'd forgotten. Did that make her father kind of an unofficial grandfather? What did he think about *that*? How did he—

"Oh, hell, I forgot I need to run something by L.B. Two minutes," he promised Ella, and loped off.

"So," Ella began, "are we okay?"

"We're okay. It's . . . strange, but we're okay. I guess you've told your son and daughter."

"Yes. My daughter's thrilled, which may be partially due to hormones as she's pregnant and that was just great news."

Another one? she thought. "Congratulations."

"Thanks. My son's . . . a little embarrassed right now, I think, at the distinct possibility Lucas and I do more than jigsaw puzzles and watch TV together."

"He shouldn't be embarrassed that you guys play gin rummy now and then."

Ella let out an appreciative laugh. "He'll get over it. I'd like to have you over for dinner, all the kids, when you can manage it. Nothing formal, just a family meal."

"Sounds good." Or manageable, she decided, which had the potential for good. "You should know, straight off, I don't need a mother."

"Oh, of course you do. Everyone does. A woman who'll listen, take your side, tell the truth—or not, as you need it. A woman you can count on, no matter what, and who'll love you no matter how much you screw up. But since you've already got that in Marg, I'm happy to settle for being your friend."

"We can see how that goes."

The siren shrilled.

"Hell. I'm up."

"Oh, God! You have to go. You have to— Can I watch? Lucas told me how this part works, but I'd like to see it."

"Fine with me. But you have to run." Without waiting, Rowan tore toward the ready room.

She breezed by Cards, so he kicked it to keep pace.

"What's the word?" she asked.

"Laborious. Got one up in Flathead, tearing down the canyon. That's all I know."

"Are you spotting?"

"Jumping."

They rushed into the controlled chaos of the ready room, grabbing gear out of lockers. Rowan pulled on her jumpsuit, checked pockets, zippers, snaps, secured her gloves, her letdown rope. She shoved her feet into her boots and caught sight of Matt doing the same.

"How'd you get back on the list?"

"Just my luck. I checked back in twenty minutes ago." He shook his head, then snagged his chute and reserve off the speed rack. "I guess the fire god decided I'd had enough time off."

Rowan secured her chutes, her PG bag. "See you on the ship," she told him, and tucked her helmet under her arm.

She shuffled toward the door, surprised to see Gull, already suited up, standing with her father and Ella.

"That was quick."

"I was in the loadmaster's room when the siren went off. Handy. Are you set?"

"Always." Rowan tapped her fingers to her forehead, flashed her father a grin. "See you later."

"See you later." He echoed the good-bye they'd given each other all her life.

"I asked if it was allowed, and since it is, I'm going to say stay safe."

Rowan nodded at Ella. "I plan on it. Let's roll, rook."

"I know you told me it all moves fast," Ella said as Rowan walked with Gull toward the waiting plane, "but I didn't realize just how fast. There's no time to think. The siren goes off, and they go from drinking coffee or packing boxes to flying to a fire, in minutes."

"It's a routine, like getting dressed in the morning. Only on fast forward. And they're always thinking. Kick some ass," he told Yangtree.

"Kicking ass, taking names. And counting the days. Catch you on the flip side, buddy."

He spoke to others as they waddled toward the plane, some he'd worked with, others who seemed as young as saplings to him. He slipped his hand in Ella's as the plane's door closed.

One of them might be a killer.

"They'll be fine." She squeezed his fingers. "And back soon."

"Yeah." Still, he felt the comfort of having her hand in his as he watched the plane taxi, rev, then rise.

AFTER THE BRIEFING IN FLIGHT, Rowan huddled with Yangtree and Trigger over maps and strategy.

Gull plugged his MP3 in, slid on his sunglasses. The music cut the engine noise, left his mind free to think. Behind the shaded glasses, he scanned the faces, the body language of the other jumpers.

Maybe it felt wrong, this suspicion, but he'd rather suffer a few pangs of guilt than suffer the consequences of more sabotage.

Cards and Dobie passed some time with liar's poker while Gibbons read a tattered paperback copy of *Cat's Cradle*. Libby huddled with Matt, patting his knee in one of her there-there gestures. The spotter got up from his seat behind the cockpit to pick his way through to confer with Yangtree.

When the call came out for buddy checks, Gull walked back himself to perform the ritual with Rowan.

"Yangtree's dumping us," Rowan told him.

Yangtree shook his head with a smile. "I'm going to work for Iron Man the first of the year. I'm going to take the fall off, buy myself a house, get my other knee fixed, do some fishing. I'll have a lot more fishing time without having to ride herd over the bunch of you every summer."

"You're giving up this life of travel, glamour and romance?" Gull asked him.

"I've had all the glamour I want, and might just find some romance when I'm not eating smoke."

"Maybe you should take up knitting while you're at it," Trigger suggested.

"I might just. I can knit you a real pretty sling since you like keeping your ass in one." He climbed over men and gear for another consult with the spotter and pilot.

"He's barely fifty." Trigger folded gum into his mouth. "Hell, I'm going to be fifty one of these days. What's he want to quit for?"

"I think he's just tired, and his knee's killing him." Rowan glanced forward. "He'll probably change his mind after he gets it fixed."

Once again, the spotter moved to the door. "Guard your reserves!"

Hot summer air, scorched with smoke, blasted in through the opening. Rowan repositioned to get a look out the window, at the blaze crowning through the tops of thick pines and firs. Red balls of ignited gases boomed up like antiaircraft fire.

"She's fast," Rowan said, "and getting a nice lift from the wind through the canyon. We're going to hit some serious crosswinds on the way down."

The first set of streamers confirmed her estimate.

"Do you see the jump spot?" she asked Gull. "There, that gap, at eight o'clock. You'll want to come in from the south, avoid doing a face-plant in the rock face. You're second man, third stick, so—"

"No. First man, second stick." He shrugged when she frowned at him, knowing Lucas had asked L.B. to switch him to her jump partner. "I guess L.B. shuffled things when he put Matt back on."

"Okay, I'll catch the drift behind you." She nodded out the window at the next set of streamers. "Looks like we've got three hundred yards."

He studied the streamers himself, and the towers of smoke, glinting silver at the fire's crown, mottled black at its base.

On final, Trigger snapped the chin strap of his helmet,

pulled down his mesh face mask before reaching for the over-head cable to waddle his way toward the door. Matt, second man, followed.

Rowan studied the fire, the ground, then the flight. Canopies billowed in the black and the blue as the plane came around for its second pass.

"We're ready," Gull answered at the spotter's call. With Rowan behind him, he got in the door, braced to the roar of wind and fire. The slap on his shoulder sent him out, diving through it, buffeted by it. He found the horizon, steadied himself as the drogue stabilized him, as the main put the brakes on to a glide.

He found Rowan, watched her canopy billow, watched the sun arrow through the smoke for an instant to illuminate her face.

Then he had a fight on his hands as the crosswinds tried to push him into a spin. A gust whipped up, blew him uncomfortably close to the cliff face. He compensated, then overcompensated as the wind yanked, tugged.

He drifted wide of the jump spot, adjusted, then let the wind take him, so he landed neat and soft on the edge of the gap.

He rolled, watched Rowan land three yards to his left.

"That was some fancy maneuvering up there," she called out to him.

"It worked."

Gathering their chutes, they joined Matt and Trigger at the edge of the jump spot. "Third stick's coming down," Trigger commented. "And shit, Cards is going into the trees. He can't buy luck this season."

Rowan clearly heard Cards curse as the wind flipped him into the pines.

"Come on, Matt, let's go make sure he ain't broke nothing important."

Since she could still hear Cards cursing, meaning he hadn't been knocked unconscious, she kept her eyes on the sky.

"Yangtree and Libby," she said as the plane positioned for the next pass. "Janis and Gibbons." She rattled off the remaining jumpers. "When they're all on the ground, I want you to take charge of the paracargo."

She put her hands on her hips, watching the next person hurtle out of the plane. Yangtree, she thought. He'd instruct, and he'd keep jumping out of planes. But doing free falls with sports groups and tourists was a far cry from . . .

"His drogue. His drogue hasn't opened." She ran forward, shouting for the others on the ground. "Drogue in tow! Jesus, Jesus, cut away! Cut away. Pull the reserve. Come on, Yangtree, for Christ's sake."

Gull's belly roiled, his heart hammered as he watched his friend, his family, tumble through the sky and smoke. Others shouted now, Trigger all but screaming into his radio.

The reserve opened with a jerky shudder, caught air—but too late, Gull realized. Yangtree's fall barely slowed as he crashed into the trees.

29

She ran, bursting through brush, leaping fallen logs, rocks, whatever lay in her path. Gull winged past her; her own fear raced with her. With her emotions in pandemonium, she ordered herself to think, to act.

His reserve had deployed at the last minute. There was a chance, always a chance. She slowed as she reached Cards, face bloody, shimmying down a lodgepole pine with his let-down rope.

"Are you hurt bad?"

"No. No. Go! Jesus, go."

Matt stumbled through the forest behind her, his cheeks gray, eyes dull. "Stay with Cards. Make sure he's okay."

She didn't wait for an answer, just kept running.

When she heard Gull's shout, she angled left, dry pine needles crunching under her feet like thin bones.

She caught sight of the reserve, a tattered mangle of white draped in the branches high overhead. And the blood, dripping like a leaky faucet, splatting on the forest floor.

Caught in the gnarled branches seventy feet above, Yangtree's limp body dangled. A two-foot spur jutted through his side, the point of it piercing through like a pin through a moth.

Gull, spurs snapped on, climbed. Rowan dumped her gear, snapped on her own and started up after him.

Broken, she could see he'd been broken—his leg, his arm and likely more. But broken didn't mean dead.

"Can you get to him? Is he alive?"

"I'll get to him." Gull climbed over, then used his rope to ease himself onto the branch, testing the weight as he went. He reached out to unsnap the helmet, laid his fingers on Yangtree's throat.

"He's got a pulse—weak, thready. Multiple fractures. Deep gash on his right thigh, but it missed the femur. The puncture wound—" He cursed as he moved closer. "This goddamn spur's holding him onto the branch like a railroad spike. I can't maneuver to stabilize him from here."

"We secure him with the ropes." Rowan leaned out as far as she could, trying to assess the situation for herself. "Cut the branch, bring him down with it."

"It's not going to take my weight and a saw." He crawled back. "It cracked some at the base. I don't know if it'll hold for you."

"Let's find out."

"Dobie or Libby. It would hold one of them."

"I'm up here, they're not. He's losing a lot of blood. Let me see what I can do. Get me more rope, a saw, a first-aid kit."

"How bad?" Trigger called up. "How bad is it?"

"He's breathing."

"Thank Christ. I've got a medevac team coming. Is he conscious?"

"No. Fill him in, okay?" She and Gull switched positions. "We need rope, first-aid kit, a chain saw. Gull's heading down."

Rowan leaned back in her harness, stripped off her shirt, cut strips and pads with her pocketknife. Tying herself off, she scooted out onto the branch. It would hold, she vowed, because she damn well needed it to.

"Yangtree, can you hear me?" She began to field-dress the jagged gash in his thigh. "You hold on, goddamn it. We'll get you out of this."

She used what rope she had, wrapped it around his waist, then shimmied back to secure it. Gull was there, handing her more.

"I'm going to secure it to the branch just above, get it under his arms." She watched Trigger and Matt scaling the neighboring tree, nodded as she saw the plan.

"Get another over to them, and we lower him down in a vee after I cut away the harness, saw off the branch."

Fear sweat dripped into her eyes as she worked, and, forced to shift the shattered leg, she prayed Yangtree stayed unconscious until they'd finished. She padded the wound around the spur as best she could, used her belt to strap him even more securely to the branch.

Then she hesitated. If it didn't work, she might kill him. But his pulse was growing weaker, and left no choice.

"I'm going to release his harness. Get ready."

Once she'd freed him from the ruined chute, she reached back for the saw. "It's going to work," she said to Gull.

"Medevac's no more than ten minutes out."

She planted her feet, yanked the starter cord. The buzz sent a tremor through her. She saw Trigger and Matt brace to take the weight, knew Gull and Dobie did the same behind her.

Trusting the rope, for him, for herself, she inched out onto the branch to set the blade into bark and wood as close to Yangtree's body as she dared.

"Hold him steady!" she shouted. "Don't let him drop."

She cut clean, felt the branch shimmy from the shock. Then Yangtree hung suspended, the spur and the lever of branch fixed in his side like a corkscrew. His body swayed as they lowered him slowly, hand over hand, to where Libby and Stovic waited to take his weight.

"We've got him! We've got him! Oh, Jesus." Stovic's voice trembled. "Jesus, he's a mess."

But breathing, Rowan thought, as she heard the clatter of the chopper. He just had to keep breathing.

IT CUT HER in two, standing on safe ground, watching as the copter lifted off with her friend. Shattered, she thought, as the wind from the blades whipped over her. His arms, his legs, and God knew what else—and there was nothing more she could do.

She shouted into her radio, updating base, realigning strategy while Cards, battered face in his hands, sat on the ground. Trigger watched the copter, then slowly turned to her. Everything she felt—the shock, the grief, the stupefying rage—was reflected on his face.

"Paracargo," she began, and Gull squeezed her arm.

"I've got that. I've got it," he repeated when she just stared at him. "Dobie, Matt, give me a hand?"

Pull it together, Rowan ordered herself. "Trig." She took a breath, then walked over to draw in the dirt. "She's moving northeast, gaining steam. I need you," she said quietly when he just stood, shaking his head.

"Give me a sec, okay? Just a goddamn fucking second."

Crouched, she laid a hand on his boot. "We've got to slay this dragon, then get back to Yangtree. The delay." Rowan had to stop, steady her voice. "The fire's taken advantage. She's burning hot, Trig. They've dumped some mud on her head, but she caught some wind, jumped this ridge line, and she's climbing fast."

"Okay." He swiped the back of his hand under his nose, crouched with her. "I can take the left flank, cut line with five, hold her in."

"Take seven. L.B.'s sending us another crew, and I'll pull from that. You got a water source here." She drew an X in the dirt. "So take pumper and hose. I'll get a crew heading up the right, and do some scouting."

When he reached for her hand, she linked fingers. "We're going to kill her," he said. "Then we're going to find out what the hell happened."

"Damn right we are."

They talked Cat lines, safe spots, two possible fire camps.

When he'd culled out his seven, gathered the gear, Rowan turned to the rest. "Cards, I need you to stay here and—"

"Fuck that, Swede." His snarl had blood leaking from his split lip. "I'm not hanging back."

"I'm not asking you to hang back. I need you to wait for the next load, take half and start up the left flank after Trigger. Send the rest to me. I need Gibbons on my crew, and Janis.

And make it clear they're going to bust their asses. I need you to take charge of this," she said before he could speak. "And Trigger's going to need you on the line."

She turned away when he nodded. "Gull, Dobie, Libby, Stovic. Tool up."

No time to waste. No time to think beyond the fire. Everything else had to stay locked outside.

They dug and cut, with every strike of Pulaski or buzz of blade echoing to Rowan like vengeance. And the fire reared and snapped.

"I need you to take charge here until Gibbons makes it in," she told Gull. "He just checked in. Everybody hit the jump spot safely. I'm going to work my way toward the head, get a better sense of her. If you tie in with the Cat line before I get back, let me know."

"Okay."

"You've got a water source about fifty yards up, this same course. You're going to end up with a crooked line, and Gibbons is going to be coming double time, but if you get there before he meets up, get Stovic and Libby on the hose. Any change in the wind or—"

"I've got it, Rowan. Go do what you need to do; we'll work it from here. Just stay in touch."

"Don't let them think about it. Keep them focused. I'll be back."

She set off fast, moving through the trees, up the rough incline, and vanished in smoke.

All she heard was the fire, the muttering glee of it. It crackled over the dry timber, lapped at molten pine resin, chewed through leaves, twigs littering the ground. She dodged a firebrand as she climbed, beat out the spot.

She thought of bodies charred to the bone.

When she crested the ridge she stopped to check her bearings. She could see the red-orange fury, gobbling up fuel. They'd given her a head start, she thought; they'd had no choice. The dragon ran strong and free.

She called in to request retardant drops, and received a brief, unsatisfying report on Yangtree.

They were working on him.

She felt the change in the wind, just a flutter, and saw the fire grab its tail to ride. A cut to the west now, still north of Trigger's crew, she noted, but moving toward them.

She circled around, contacting him by radio.

"She's shifting, curling back toward you."

"We've got a Cat line here, a good, wide one. I don't think she can jump it. Escape route due south."

"They're bringing mud. I just called to tell them to dump a load west, down your flank. Stay clear."

"Roger that. Cards just got here with reinforcements. We're going to hold this line, Swede."

"After the mud drops, I'm going to get an air report. I want to take four from your team, same from mine, get them up to the head. Squeeze it. But if she jumps the road, get gone."

"Bet your ass. And watch yours."

As she worked her way through the fire, she coordinated with Gibbons, with base, kept her ears and eyes peeled for the tankers. She cut east, eyes smarting with smoke, then jumped back, skidding onto her back as a burning limb thick as a man's thigh crashed to the ground in front of her.

It caught fresh fuel on the forest floor, ignited with a whoosh to claw at the soles of her boots before she scrambled clear.

"Widowmaker," she shouted to Gibbons. "I'm good, but I'm going to be busy for a minute."

She beat at the fresh flames, chopping at the ground to smother what she could with dirt. She heard the thunder of a tanker, muttered curses as she fought her small, personal war.

"I'm clear." Shoveling, stomping, she signaled Gibbons, then the tanker pilot. "I'm clear."

And ran.

The thick pink rain fell, smothering flame, billowing smoke, thudding onto the ground, the trees, with heavy splats. She sprinted for shelter as globs of it struck her helmet, her jacket. A volley of firebrands sent her on a zigzagging dash for higher, clearer ground.

She heard the telltale roar at her back, felt the ground shimmy under her feet. Following instinct, she leaped through the undulating curtain of fire, all but heard it slam shut behind her before the blowup burst. Rocks skidded under her feet as she pushed herself up an incline above the hungry, murderous blaze.

"I'm clear." She shouted it as her radio popped with voices. "Had a little detour."

She wheezed in a breath, wheezed one out. "Give me a minute to orient."

A wall of fire, solid as steel, cut off her route back to her team.

She pulled out her compass to confirm direction, accepted that her hand shook lightly.

Cut across to Trigger's line, she calculated, regroup, then circle down and around to her own.

She relayed her plan, then took a moment to hydrate and settle her nerves.

Back on the line, Gull looked straight into Gibbons's eyes. "Is she hurt?"

"She says no. She's playing it down, but I think she had a close one." He swiped at sweat. "She's cutting over to Trig, then she'll circle around back to us. The mud knocked it back some on their flank, and they're working the pumps up toward the head. They're in good position."

He shook his head. "We can't say the same. The wind's whipping her up this way. Elf, take Gull, Stovic and Dobie and get these pumps up there. Follow the Cat line. Start drowning her. I'll send you up four more as soon as we get the men."

"Spot!" Libby shouted, and two of the team leaped to action.

"We're getting hammered over here," Gibbons told Trigger over the radio. "Can you spare anybody?"

"Give you two. That'll be three when Swede gets around."

"Tell them to hump it!"

GULL MANNED the hose and swore the force of water only made the fire dance. The wind chose sides, blew flames into massive walls.

"L.B.'s sending in another load, and pulling in jumpers from Idaho," Janis told him.

"Did Rowan make it to Trigger?"

"Rowan changed tactics. She's doubling back to Gibbons. We've got to catch this thing here, catch her here, or fall back." She yanked out her radio. "Gibbons, we need help up here."

"I'm waiting on Matt and Cards from Trigger's line. And the Swede. Fresh jumpers coming. ETA's thirty."

"Thirty's no good. I need more hands or we're pulling back."

"Your call, Elf. I'll get locations and come back. If you've got to move, move."

"Goddamn it, goddamn it. Stovic, get those snags. If she crowns, we're screwed." As water arced and sizzled, she looked over at Gull. "We can't hold her for thirty without more hands."

Something stirred in his gut. "Rowan, Cards and Matt should've gotten through by now. Radio her, get her location."

"Gibbons is—"

"Radio her, Janis," he interrupted. "This has been going south since the jump."

And maybe it wasn't just nature they fought.

He listened to her try to raise Rowan once, twice, a third time. And with each nonresponse his blood ran colder.

She tried Matt, then Cards, then answered swiftly when Gibbons hailed her.

"I can't reach any of them on the radio," Gibbons told her. "I'm going to send somebody in to their last known location."

But Janis had her eye on Gull. "Negative. Gull's going. He's the fastest we've got. Send me somebody. We're going to try to hold it."

"Libby's heading up now. I'll get more mud, call in another Cat. If you have to retreat, head southwest."

"Copy that. Find her," she said to Gull.

"Count on it." He turned to Dobie. "Hold it as long as you can."

"As long as you need," Dobie vowed, and took the hose.

He ran, using his compass and the map in his head to gauge direction. She'd been forced west, then south before she'd angled toward the left flank. He tried to judge her speed, her most probable route before she'd reversed to head east again to assist the right flank.

She'd have met up with Matt and Cards if possible, he calculated, but she wouldn't have wasted time waiting for them or changing from the best route back, not when her team needed help.

A spot burst to his left, flames snaking from ground to tree. He ignored the instinct to deal with it, kept running.

But she wouldn't have, he thought. She'd have fought the fire as she went, and doing so shifted her direction at any time.

And if another enemy had crossed her path, she wouldn't have recognized him. She would see a fellow soldier, a friend. Someone trusted, even loved.

He jumped a narrow stream, pushing himself through the heat and smoke and growing fear.

She was smart, and strong, and canny. She'd fight, he reminded himself—maybe more fiercely when the enemy had disguised himself as friend.

He forced himself to stop, check his compass, reorient. And to listen, listen, for another under the growling voice of the fire.

North, he decided. Northeast from here, and prayed he was right. A tree crashed, spewing out a whirlwind of sparks that stung his exposed skin like bees.

The next sound he heard came sharper, more deadly. He raced toward the echo of the gunshot, even as his heart leaped as if struck by the bullet.

30

When she could, Rowan moved at a steady jog. She'd bruised her hip avoiding the widowmaker, but the pain barely registered—just a dull, distant ache.

They were losing the war, she thought, had been losing it since Yangtree's chute failed to open.

Everything felt off, felt wrong, felt out of balance.

The wind continued to rise, to shift and stir, adding to the fire's speed and potency. Here and there, small, sly dust devils danced on it. The air remained dry enough to crack like a twig.

She'd never made it to Trigger's crew to judge the progress or lack of it for herself, to check that flank, sense just what the fire was thinking, plotting. No, she thought now, not when she'd heard the urgency in Gibbons's voice. No choice but to reverse.

She'd cut north, through the fire, to carve off a little distance, and calculating her path might cross with Matt and Cards.

Spots sprang up so fast and often, she began to feel like she was playing a deadly game of Whac-A-Mole.

She gulped down water on the run, splashed more on her

sweaty face. And resisted the constant urge to call in to base, again, for a report on Yangtree.

Better to believe he was alive and fighting. To believe it and make it true.

Under that remained the nagging fear that it hadn't been an accident but sabotage.

How many others harbored that same fear? she wondered. How did they bear down and focus with that clawing at the mind? How could she when she kept going over every minute and move in the ready room, on the flight, on the jump sequence?

Had something been off even then? Should she have seen it?

Later, she ordered herself, relive it later. Right now, just live.

With her stamina flagging, she pulled an energy bar out of her bag, started to tear the wrapper.

She dropped it, ran, when she heard the scream.

Smoke blinded her, disoriented her. She forced herself to stop, close her eyes. Think.

Due north. Yes, north, she decided, and sprinted forward.

She spotted the radio smoldering and sparking on the ground, and the blood smeared on the ground at the base of a snag that burned like a candle. Nearby a full engulfed branch snaked fire over the ground.

Alarmed for her friends, she cupped her hands to her mouth, started to shout. Then dropped them again with sickness countering fear. She saw the blood trail, heading east, and followed it as she slowly drew her radio out of her belt.

Because she knew now, and somewhere inside her she wondered if she'd always known—or at least wondered. But loyalty hadn't allowed it, she admitted. It simply hadn't allowed her to cross the line—except in dreams.

Now with her heart heavy with grief, she prepared to cross the line.

Before she could flick on her radio, he was there, just there, a lit fusee in his hand, and his eyes full of misery. He heaved it when he saw her, setting off his tiny bomb. A black spruce went off like a Roman candle.

"I don't want to hurt you. Not you."

"Why would you hurt me?" She met those sad eyes. "We're friends."

"I don't want to." Matt pulled the gun out of his belt. "But I will. Throw away the radio."

"Matt—" She jolted a little when Gibbons spoke her name through the radio.

"If you answer it, I'll shoot you. I'll be sorry for it, but I'll do what has to be done. I'm doing what has to be done."

"Where's Cards?"

"Throw the radio away, Rowan. Throw it!" he snapped. "Or I'll use this. I'll put a bullet in your leg, then let the fire decide."

"Okay. All right." She opened her hand, let it drop, but he shook his head.

"Kick it away. Don't test me."

"I'm not. I won't." She heard Janis's voice now as she kicked it aside. "We've got to get out of here, Matt. The place is coming apart. It's not safe."

She struggled to keep her eyes level with his, but she'd seen the Pulaski hooked in his belt, and the blood gleaming on the pick.

Cards.

"I never wanted it to be you. It wasn't your fault. And you came to the funeral. You sat with my mother."

"What happened to Jim wasn't anyone's fault."

"Dolly got him worked up, got him all twisted around. Got us both all twisted around so the last things we said to each other were ugly things. And Cards was his spotter. He should've seen Jim wasn't right to jump. You *know* that's so."

"Where's Cards?"

"He got away from me. Maybe the fire's got him. It's about fate anyway. I should've shot him to be sure of it, but it's about fate and destiny. Luck, maybe. I don't decide. Dolly fell. I didn't kill her; she fell."

"I believe you, Matt. We need to head north, then we can talk when—"

"I gave her money, you know, for the baby. But she wanted more. I was just going to talk to her, have it out with her when I went by her house. And she was just driving off, without the baby. She was a bad mother."

"I know." Calm, agreeable, understanding. "Matt, who'd know better than me about that? About Shiloh being better off now? I'm on your side."

"She went to that motel. She was a tramp. I saw him, the preacher, come to the door to let her in. My brother's dead, and she's balling that preacher in a motel room. I wanted to go in, but I was afraid of what I might do. I waited, and she came out and drove away."

She heard another tree torch off. "Matt—"

"She got that flat tire. That was fate, wasn't it? She was surprised to see me—guilt all over her—when I pulled in behind her. I told her to pull off onto the service road. I was going to have it out with her. But the things she said . . . If she hadn't been screwing around, hadn't been a liar, a cheat, a selfish bitch, I wouldn't have pushed her that way. She was just going to up and leave that baby. Did you know? What kind of mother does that?"

"We have to move," she told him, keeping her tone calm but firm. "I want you to tell me everything, Matt. I want to listen, but we're going to be cut off if we don't move."

"Shiloh's . . . may be my baby."

He wiped his free hand over his mouth as Rowan stared at him. "It was just one time, when I was so lonely and missing Annie so much, and drinking a little. It was just one time."

"I understand." It made her sick inside, for all of them. "I get lonely, too."

"You *don't*! She told me it was mine, and she told Jim it was his. Then she said it was mine, maybe, because she *knew* he didn't want a baby, didn't want her. She *knew* I'd do what I had to do, and I'd have to tell Annie. And we fought about it right before the siren went off, me and Jim. He was on the list. I wasn't. He's dead. I'm not."

"It's not your fault."

"What do you know about it! I told him to go to hell, and he did. This is hell. I was just going to fix Cards so he couldn't jump because that's what he loves most. Like I loved my brother. Put something in his food, trip him up. And I was just going to get the baby from Dolly, have her for my ma. That was the right thing. But she fell, and I had to do something, didn't I?"

"Yes."

"I sent her to hell. That's when I knew I had to do what needed doing. I had to get the baby for my ma, so I had to get Leo out of the way. Make him pay, too. He was always giving Jim grief, never had a good thing to say."

"So you got his rifle out of his gun safe, and you shot at me. You shot at me and Gull."

"Not at you. I wasn't going to hurt you. Dolly told Jim the combination, and he told me. It was like he was showing me what to do. Leo had to pay, and he did. I got the baby for my ma. Jim would've wanted that."

"Okay." Firebrands flew like missiles. "You were getting justice for Jim, and doing what you could for your family. And I'll listen to you, do whatever you want, just tell me. But not here. The wind's changed. Matt, for God's sake, we're going to be trapped in this if we don't move."

Those sad eyes never wavered. "It's up to fate, like I said. Up to fate who got the bad pumps and saws, who got the bad chute."

"You played Russian roulette with our chutes?" She regretted it immediately, but the fury just bubbled out. "Yangtree never did anything to you. He might die."

"I could've gotten the doctored one just as easy as him. It was a fair deal. In the end, Ro, it was all of us killed Jim. All of us doing what we do, getting him to do it, too. And everybody had the same chance. I didn't want it to be you, even though I saw how you looked at me when I said how we'd get a lawyer over the baby, how my ma was going to raise her. I saw how everybody looked at me because I was alive, and Jim wasn't."

She couldn't outrun a bullet, Rowan thought as her heart kicked in her chest. Before much longer, she wouldn't be able to outrun the fire.

She could hear the whoosh and the roar as it built, as it rolled toward them.

"We need to go, so you can be there for the baby, Matt. She needs a father."

"She has my parents. They'll be good to her." Fire glowed red and gold on his sweat-sheened face. His eyes had gone from sad to mad. "I broke it off with Annie last night. I've got nothing for her. And I knew when I got in the door today, it had to be the last time. One way or the other. I thought it would be me, going like Jim did. The fire's all I got left."

"You have the baby."

"Jim's dead. I see him dead when I look at her. I see him burning. It's just the fire now. I liked it. Not the killing, but the fire, making it, watching it, seeing what it did. I liked making it more than I ever did fighting it. Maybe I'll like hell."

"I'm not ready to go there." She rolled to the balls of her feet.

A tree fell with a shrieking crash, shaking the ground when it landed less than a yard away. Rowan sprang to her right, dug in to run blind. She heard the crack of the gunshot, her spine snapping tight as she braced for a bullet in the back.

She heard a whine, like an angry hornet wing by her ear, then jagged left again as a firebrand burst at her feet.

If Matt didn't kill her, the fire would.

She preferred the fire, and like a moth, flew toward the flames.

For a moment, they wrapped around her, a fiery embrace that stole her breath. The scream shrieked inside her head, escaping in a wild call of fear and triumph as she burst free. Momentum pitched her forward, had her skidding onto the heels of her hands and her knees. Her pack weighed like lead as she struggled up again, hacking out smoke. Around her, the forest burned in a merry cavalcade with a deep, guttural roar as mad as the man who pursued her.

At the snap of another gunshot, she fled deeper into the belly of the beast.

She heard him coming, even over the bellow of the fire. The thud of his footsteps sounded closer than she wanted to believe. She scanned smoke and flame.

Fight or flight.

She was done with flight, finished letting him drive her like cattle to the slaughter. With the burn towering around her, she planted her feet, yanked out her Pulaski. Gripping it in both hands, she set for fight.

He might kill her. Hell, he probably would. But she'd damn well do some damage first.

For herself, for Yangtree. Even, she thought, for poor, pathetic Dolly.

"You'll bleed," she told herself. "You'll bleed before I'm done."

She saw the yellow shirt through the haze of smoke, then the silhouette coming fast.

Deliberately she panted air in and out, pumping adrenaline. She had an instant, maybe two, to decide whether to hurl her weapon, hope for a solid strike, or to charge swinging.

Charge. Better to keep the ax in her hands than risk a miss.

She sucked in more filthy air, cocked the Pulaski over her shoulder, gritting her teeth as she judged the timing.

Coming fast, she thought again—then her arms trembled.

Coming really fast. Oh, God.

"Gull." She choked out his name as he tore through the smoke.

She ran toward him, felt his hands close tight around her shoulders. Nothing, she realized, no caress, no embrace, had ever felt so glorious.

"Matt."

"I got that."

"He's got a gun."

"Yeah, I got that, too. Are you hurt?" He scanned her face when she shook her head, as if verifying for himself. "Can you run?"

"What do you take me for?"

"Then we run because Matt's not our only problem."

She started to agree, then stiffened. "Wait. Do you hear that?"

"You're the one with ears like a . . . Yeah. Now I do."

"He's coming. That way," she added, pointing. "It sounds like he's crying."

"I feel real bad for him. Best shot's south, I think."

"If we can reach the black. But if we can, so can he."

"I sure as hell hope so. That's where we'll take him down. Run now; talk later."

"Don't hold up for me," she began.

"Oh, bullshit." He grabbed her hand, yanked her into a run.

She bore down. She'd be damned if he held back because

she couldn't keep pace. It didn't matter if her lungs burned, if her legs ached, if the sweat ran into her eyes like acid.

She ran through a world gone mad with violence, stunning in its kaleidoscope lights of red and orange and molten blue. She flung herself through fetid smoke, leaping or dodging burning branches, hurdling burning spots that snapped over the ground like bear traps.

If they could get into the black, they'd fight. They'd find a way.

She risked a glance at Gull. Sweat poured down his soot-smeared face. Somewhere along the run he'd lost his helmet, and his hair was gray with ash.

But his eyes, she thought as she pushed, pushed, pushed herself on. Clear, focused, determined. Eyes that didn't lie, she thought. Eyes she could trust.

Did trust.

They'd make it.

Something exploded behind them.

Breath snagging, she looked back to see an orange column of smoke climb toward the sky. Even as she watched, it brightened.

"Gull."

He only nodded. He'd seen it as well.

No time to talk, to plan, even to think. The ground shook; the wind whipped. With its roaring breath, the fire blew brands, coals, burning pinecones that burst like grenades.

Blue-orange flames clawed up on their left, hissing like snakes. A snag burst in its coils, showered them with embers. The smoke thickened like cotton with the firefly swirl of sparks flooding through it.

A fountain of yellow flame spewed up in front of them, forcing them to angle away from the ferocious heat. Gull grunted when a burning branch hit his back, but didn't break stride as they flung themselves up an incline.

Rocks avalanched under their boots, and still the hellhound fire pursued. Came the roar, that long, throaty war cry, as the blowup thundered toward them.

A fire devil swirled out of the smoke to dance.

Nowhere to run.

"Shake and bake." Gull yanked the bandanna around Rowan's throat over her mouth, did the same with his own.

It screamed, Rowan thought as she tore the protective case off her fire shelter, shook it out. Or Matt screamed, but a madman with a gun had become the least of their problems.

She stepped on the bottom corners of the foil, grabbed the tops to stretch it over her back. Mirroring her moves, Gull sent her a last look and shot her a grin that seared straight into her heart.

"See you later," he said.

"See you later."

They flopped forward, cocooned.

Working quickly, Rowan dug a hole for her face, down to the cooler air. Eyes shut, she took short, shallow breaths into the bandanna. Even one breath of the super-heated gases that blew outside her shelter would scorch her lungs, poison her.

The fire hit, a freight train of sound, a tidal wave of heat. Wind tore at the shelter, tried to lift and launch it like a sail. Sparks shimmered around her, but she kept her eyes closed.

And saw her father, frying fish over a campfire, the flames dancing in his eyes as he laughed with her. Saw herself spreading her arms under his on her first tandem jump. Saw him open his as she ran to him after he'd come back from a fire.

Saw him, his face lit now by an inner flame as he told her about Ella.

See you later, she thought as the impossible heat built.

She saw Gull, cocky grin and swagger, pouring a helmet of water over her head. Saw him tip back a beer, cool as you please, then fight off a pack of bullies as ferocious as a fire devil.

Felt him yank her into his arms. Turn to her in the dark. Fight with her in the light. Run with her. Run to her.

He'd come through fire for her.

The fear speared into her belly. She'd been afraid before, but she realized most of it was because she damn well wasn't ready to die. Now she feared for him.

So close, she thought while the fire screamed, crashed, burst. And yet completely separate. Nothing to do for each other now but wait. Wait.

See you later.

She held on. Thought of Yangtree, of Jim. Of Matt.

Cards—God, Cards. Had Matt killed him, too?

She wanted to see him again, see all of them again. She wanted to tell her father she loved him, just one more time. To tell Ella she was glad her father had found someone to make him happy.

She wanted to joke with Trigger, rag on Cards, sit in the kitchen with Marg. To be with all of them, her family.

But more, she realized, even more, she wanted to look into Gull's eyes again, and watch that grin flash over his face.

She wanted to tell him . . . everything.

Why the hell hadn't she? Why had she been so stubborn or stupid or—face it—afraid?

If he didn't make it through this so she could, she'd kick his ass.

Dizzy, she realized, sick. Too much heat. Can't pass out. Won't pass out. As she regulated her breathing again, she realized something else.

Quiet.

She heard the fire, but the distant snarl and song. The ground held steady under her body, and the jet-plane thunder had passed.

She was alive. Still alive.

She reached out, laid a hand on her shelter. Still hot to the touch, she thought. But she could wait. She could be patient.

And if she lived, he'd damn well better live, too.

"Rowan."

Tears smarted her already stinging eyes at his voice, rough and ragged. "Still here."

"How's it going there?"

"Five-by-five. You?"

"The same. It's cooling down a little."

"Don't get out yet, rook."

"I know the drill. I'm calling base. Anything you want me to pass on?"

"Have L.B. tell my dad I'm A-OK. I don't know about Cards. There was blood. They need to look for him. And for Matt."

She closed her eyes again, let herself drift, passing the next hour thinking of swimming in a moonlit lagoon, drinking straight from a garden hose, making snow angels—naked snow angels, with Gull.

"Cards made it back," he called out. "They had to medevac him. He lost a lot of blood."

"He's alive."

Alone in her shelter, she allowed herself tears.

When her shelter cooled to the touch, she called to Gull. "Coming out."

She eased her head out into the smoky air, looked over at Gull. She imagined they both looked like a couple of sweaty, parboiled turtles climbing out of their shells.

"Hello, gorgeous."

She laughed. It hurt her throat, but she laughed. "Hey, handsome."

They crawled to each other over the blackened, ash-covered ground. She found his lips with hers, her belly quivering with a wrecked combination of laughter and tears.

"I was going to be so pissed off at you if you died."

"Glad we avoided that." He touched her face. "Heck of a ride."

"Oh, yeah." She lowered her forehead to his. "He might still be alive."

"I know. We'd better figure out where we are, then we'll worry about where he is."

She took out her compass, checking their bearings as she drank what water she had left in her bottle. "If we head east, we'll backtrack over some of the area, plus it's the best course for the camp. We need water."

"I'll call it in."

Though her legs still weren't steady, Rowan got to her feet to examine the shelters.

"Inner skin's melted," she told Gull. "We hit over sixteen hundred degrees. I'd say we topped a good one-eighty inside."

"My candy bar's melted, and that's a crying shame." He reached for her hand. "Want to take a walk in the woods?"

"Love to."

They walked through the black with ash still swirling.

Training outweighed exhaustion, and had them smothering smoldering spots.

"You came for me."

Gull glanced up. "Sure I did. You'd have done the same."

"I would have. But I thought I was dead—not going down easy, but dead all the same. And you came for me. It counts. A lot."

"Is there a scoreboard? Am I winning?"

"Gull." She didn't laugh this time, not when everything she felt rose up in her raw throat. "I need to tell you—" She broke off, grabbed his arm. "I heard something." She closed her eyes, concentrated. Pointed.

She looked in his eyes again. Toward or away? He nodded, and they moved toward the sound.

They found him, curled behind a huddle of rocks. They'd protected him a little. But not nearly enough.

His eyes, filled with blood, stared up from his ruined face. She thought of her dream of Jim, of his brother. The fire had turned them into mirror images.

He moaned again, tried to speak. His body shook violently as his breath came in rapid pants. Raw, blistered burns scored the left side of his body, the most exposed, where the fire had scorched the protective clothing away.

He'd nearly made it out, Rowan noted. Another fifty yards, and he might've been clear. Had he thought he could make it, left his life to fate rather than shake out his shelter?

Gull handed her the radio. "Call it in," he told her, then crouched. He took one of Matt's ruined hands carefully in his.

He had that in him, Rowan thought. He had that compassion for a man suffering toward death, even though the man was a murderer.

"Base, this is Swede. We found Matt."

His eyes tracked to hers when she said his name. Could he still think? she wondered. Could he still reason?

For an instant she saw sorrow in them. Then they fixed as the panting breaths cut off.

"He didn't make it," she said, steady as she handed the radio back to Gull.

Steady until she sat on the ground beside a man who'd been a friend, and wept for him.

SHE WANTED TO STAY and fight, termed it a matter of pride and honor to be in on the kill. She rehydrated, refueled, replaced lost and damaged equipment. Then complained all the way when ordered to copter out.

"We're not injured," she pointed out.

"You sound like a frog," Gull observed as he took his seat in the chopper. "A sexy one, but a frog."

"So we ate some smoke. So what?"

"You lost most of your eyebrows."

Stunned, she pressed her fingers above her eyes. "Shit! Why didn't you tell me?"

"It's a look. They've got it on the run," he added, scanning down as they lifted off.

"That's the *point*. That bitch tried to kill us. We should be in on the takedown."

"Don't worry, babe." He reached over to pat her knee. "There'll be other fires that try to kill us."

"Don't try to smooth it over. L.B.'s letting the cops push us around. What the hell difference does it make when we give them a statement? Matt's dead." She turned her face, stared out at the sky. "I guess most of him, the best of him, died last year when Jim did. You held his hand so he didn't die alone."

Though Gull said nothing, she clearly felt his discomfort so turned to him again. "That counts a lot, too. You're really racking them up today."

"People have a choice when life takes a slice out of them. He made the wrong one. A lot of wrong ones."

"You didn't. We didn't," Rowan corrected. "Good for us."

"Don't cry anymore. It kills me."

"My eyes are watering, that's all. From all the smoke."

He figured it couldn't hurt for both of them to pretend that was it. But he took her hand. "I want a beer. I want a giant, ice-cold bottle of beer. And shower sex."

The idea made her smile. "I want eyebrows."

"Well, you're not getting mine." He tipped his head back, closed his eyes.

She watched out the window, the roll of land, the rise of

mountain. Home—she was going home. But the meaning had changed, deepened. Time to man up and tell him.

"I need to say some things to you," she began. "I don't know how you're going to feel about it, but it is what it is. So . . ."

She shifted back, narrowed her eyes.

No point baring her soul to a man who was sound asleep.

It could wait, she decided, and watched the sun lower toward the western peaks.

SHE SAW HER FATHER running toward the pad, and L.B., and the flying tangle of Ella's hair as she rushed after them.

Marg sprinting out of the cookhouse. Lynn stopping to bury her face in her apron. Mechanics, jumpers not cleared for the list pouring out of hangars, the tower, the barracks.

The cop and the fed standing together in their snappy suits just outside Ops.

She gave Gull an elbow poke. "We've got a welcoming committee."

She climbed out the second the chopper touched ground, then ran hunched over under the blades to jump into her father's arms.

"There's my baby. There's my girl."

"A-OK." She breathed him in, squeezed hard. And, seeing Ella over his shoulder, seeing the roll of tears, held out a hand. "It's nice to see you."

Ella gripped her hand, pressed it to her cheek, then wrapped her arms as best she could around both Lucas and Rowan.

"Don't go anywhere," Lucas murmured, then, setting Rowan down, walked over to Gull. "You took care of our girl."

"That's the job. But mostly she took care of herself."

Lucas pulled him into a bear hug. "Keep it up."

They both looked over when Rowan let out a shout, broke from Marg and ran toward the man slowly walking toward the pad.

"I told that son of a bitch he could only check out of the hospital if he stayed in bed." L.B. shook his head at Cards.

"Yangtree?" Gull asked.

"Fifty-fifty. They didn't expect him to make it this far, so I'm putting my money on him. Got a cold one for you."

"Let's not keep it waiting."

"Do you want me to tell the cops to back off until you and Rowan settle in?"

"We might as well get it done and over. She needs it finished. I guess I do, too."

"He just started talking crazy," Cards told Rowan. "About me letting Jim die, about Dolly. And he said . . . he said Dolly called Vicki, and told her we'd been screwing around. Hinted to her the baby was mine, for God's sake. That it was his idea."

"You can fix it with her."

"I'm going to try. But . . . Ro, he came at me. Jesus." He touched his shoulder where the pick had dug in. "Matt came at me. I knocked him back, or down. I told the cops it's like this crazy reel inside my head. I ran. He was coming after me. I think he was, then he wasn't. I just kept running. Got all screwed around until I found the saw line. I followed it."

"Good thinking."

"I don't know how he could've done what he did, Ro. I worked right beside him. All of us did. Yangtree . . ." His eyes watered up. "Then to come after you, to die like he did. I can't get my head around it."

"You're worn out. Go on and lie down. I'll come in and see you later."

"I loved the fucker."

"We all did," Rowan said, as Cards walked back into the barracks.

Gull stepped up. "Unless you want to do it otherwise, we can talk with the cops now. Marg's throwing on some steaks."

"There is a God."

"We can get it done while we eat."

They took seats at one of the picnic tables.

"First, I want to say it's good to see both of you back here, safe." Quinniock folded his hands on the table. "It doesn't do much good, but you should know after some digging, a little pressure, Agent DiCicco learned earlier today that Matthew Brayner ended his engagement a short time ago, cut off communication with his fiancée. Also, that he quit his job."

"I also learned a few days ago that he has a number of

trophies and awards. Marksmanship. There are several people in your unit who have sharpshooter experience."

Rowan nodded at DiCicco. "You've been investigating all of us."

"That's my job. We arrived here to question him about the same time he assaulted your associate," DiCicco continued. "We were able to convince Mr. Little Bear to let us search Brayner's quarters. He kept a journal. It's all there. What he did, how, why."

"He was grieving," Rowan said.

"Yes."

She looked at Quinniock. "He blamed himself, at the bottom of it, for what happened to Jim. For being weak, sleeping with Dolly, for fighting with his brother before that jump. He couldn't live with that, so he had to blame Cards, Dolly, all of us."

"Very likely."

"But it was more." She looked at Gull now. "He fell in love with the fire. Found a kind of purpose in it, and that justified the rest. He said he left it up to fate, but he lied to himself. He gave it all to the fire, turning what he loved and had trained to do into a punishment. Maybe he thought he could burn away the guilt and the grief, but he never did. He died, grieving for everything he'd lost."

"It would help," DiCicco told her, "if you could tell us exactly what happened, what was said and done."

"Yeah, I can do that. Then I'm never talking about it again, because he paid for all of it. There's nothing more to wring out of him, and no changing anything that happened."

She went through it like a fire report. Precisely, briefly, pausing only to lean into Marg's side when the cook set down still sizzling steaks.

She ate while Gull did the same from his perspective.

"You knew it was Matt when you caught up with me," Rowan interrupted.

"Cards has had nothing but shit for luck all season. Card was Jim's spotter. You have to respect the streak, good or bad but when you break it down it seemed like maybe it wasn't matter of bad luck. Then Matt couldn't bring himself to loo at Yangtree once we got him down.

"You were too busy to notice," he added, "but Matt was the only one who couldn't. When Janis said none of the three of you answered the radio, it was point A to B."

He looked back over at DiCicco. "That's it. There's nothing more to tell you."

"I'll do whatever I can to close this without bothering you again," DiCicco said to Rowan. "And I'm pulling for your friend, for Yangtree."

"Thanks. What happens with Leo Brakeman?"

"He's cleared of the murders, and as Brayner detailed the shooting at the base in his journal, how he had the combination for the safe—from Jim through Dolly—he's clear of those charges. Regardless, he jumped bail, but given the circumstances, we're recommending leniency there."

"Matt didn't kill him," Rowan murmured, "but he shattered his life. He did it so he could get the baby for his mother."

Quinniock rose. "A smart man would head to Nebraska and work to put his life back together. That'll be up to Brakeman. Despite the circumstances, it was a pleasure meeting both of you. Thank you for your service."

"I'll say the same."

Rowan chewed over a bite of steak as they walked away. "That was kind of weird at the end."

"Just at the end?"

She laughed. "You know what I mean. I need to spend some time with my father. You could get in on that."

"Sure. Is that before or after shower sex?"

"After, for a variety of reasons. Right now, I need a walk. Moon's rising."

"So it is." He got up, reached for her hand.

It would probably be more appropriate, she thought, if they got cleaned up first, if she waited until the base slept and they were alone.

Then again, covered with soot, smelling of smoke and sweat? Wasn't that who they were?

"I did a lot of thinking in the shake and bake," she began as they strolled toward the training field.

"Not much else to do in there."

"I thought about my father. The two of us at little moments. About him and Ella. I'm only going to admit this once, but you were right about my first reaction to them, and the reasons for it. I'm done with that."

"You don't have to say it again, but maybe you could write it down, for my files."

"Shut up." She hip-bumped him. "I thought about Jim and Matt, about all the guys. Yangtree."

"He's going to make it. I'd put money on it."

"I believe that because he's a tough bastard, and because there's been enough loss this season. I thought about you."

"I hoped I was in there somewhere."

"Little moments. And when you narrow it, look at them really close, they can turn out to be key." She stopped, faced him. "So. I want to get married."

"To me?"

"No, to Timothy Olyphant, but I'm settling for you."

"Okay."

"That's it?"

"I'm still dealing with Timothy Olyphant, so give me a minute. I think I'm better-looking."

"You would."

"No, seriously. I've got better hair. But anyway." He swooped her in, right up to her toes. The kiss wasn't casual or lighthearted, but raw and deep and real. "I was going to take you on another picnic and ask you. This is better."

"I like picnics. We could—"

He laid his hands on either side of her face. "I love you. I love everything about you. Your voice, your laugh. Your eyebrows when they grow back. Your face, your body, your hard head and your cautious heart. I want to spend the rest of my life looking at you, listening to you, working with you, just being with you. Rowan of the purple lupines."

"Wow." He'd literally taken her breath away. "You're really good at this."

"I've been saving up."

"I didn't want to fall for anybody. It's so messy. I'm so happy it was you. I'm so happy to love you, Gulliver. So happy to know I'll have a life with you, a home, a family with you." She pressed her lips to his. "But I want a bigger bed."

"Big as you want."

"Where are we going to put it? After the season, I mean."

"I've been thinking about that."

Naturally, she thought. "Have you?"

"First, I think I should get my pilot's license. We'll be doing a lot of zipping between Montana and California."

He took her hand and, as she'd once seen her father do with Ella, gave their linked arms a playful swing.

"Maybe we'll find a place between, but I'm fine setting down here most of the year."

She cocked her head. "Because Missoula needs a family fun center?"

He grinned, kissing her knuckles as they walked again. "I've been doing some research on that."

"I really do love you," she told him. "It's kind of astonishing."

"I'm a hell of a catch. Really better than Olyphant. Where we dig in, that's just details. We'll work them out."

She stopped and, trusting them both, linked her arms around his neck. "We'll work them out," she repeated.

"Hey!" L.B. shouted across the field. "Thought you'd want to know, they've got her contained. They caught her, and they're taking her down."

"Go Zulies," Gull called back.

She grinned at him. More good news, she thought. They'd go in soon, give their own good news to her father, to their family.

But for now, she'd caught her own fire and wanted to walk awhile sharing the warmth of it, just with him, under the rising moon.

Keep reading for an excerpt from
the first novel in the Bride Quartet
by Nora Roberts

VISION IN WHITE

Now available from Berkley Books

PROLOGUE

By the time she was eight, Mackensie Elliot had been married fourteen times. She'd married each of her three best friends—as both bride and groom—her best friend's brother (under his protest), two dogs, three cats, and a rabbit.

She'd served at countless other weddings as maid of honor, bridesmaid, groomsman, best man, and officiant.

Though the dissolutions were invariably amicable, none of the marriages lasted beyond an afternoon. The transitory aspect of marriage came as no surprise to Mac, as her own parents boasted two each—so far.

Wedding Day wasn't her favorite game, but she kind of liked being the priest or the reverend or the justice of the peace. Or, after attending her father's second wife's nephew's bar mitzvah, the rabbi.

Plus, she enjoyed the cupcakes or fancy cookies and fizzy lemonade always served at the reception.

It was Parker's favorite game, and Wedding Day always took place on the Brown Estate, with its expansive gardens, pretty groves, and silvery pond. In the cold Connecticut winters, the ceremony might take place in front of one of the roaring fires inside the big house.

They had simple weddings and elaborate affairs. Royal weddings, star-crossed elopements, circus themes, and pirate ships. All ideas were seriously considered and voted upon, and no theme or costume too outrageous.

Still, with fourteen marriages under her belt, Mac grew a bit weary of Wedding Day.

Until she experienced her seminal moment.

For her eighth birthday Mackensie's charming and mostly absent father sent her a Nikon camera. She'd never expressed any interest in photography, and initially pushed it away with the other odd gifts he'd given or sent since the divorce. But Mac's mother told her mother, and Grandma muttered and complained about "feckless, useless Geoffrey Elliot" and the inappropriate gift of an adult camera for a young girl who'd be better off with a Barbie doll.

As she habitually disagreed with her grandmother on principle, Mac's interest in the camera piqued. To annoy Grandma—who was visiting for the summer instead of being in her retirement community in Scottsdale, where Mac strongly believed she belonged—Mac hauled the Nikon around with her. She toyed with it, experimented. She took pictures of her room, of her feet, of her friends. Shots that were blurry and dark, or fuzzy and washed out. With her lack of success, and her mother's impending divorce from her stepfather, Mac's interest in the Nikon began to wane. Even years later she couldn't say what prompted her to bring it along to Parker's that pretty summer afternoon for Wedding Day.

Every detail of the traditional garden wedding had been planned. Emmaline as the bride and Laurel as groom would exchange their vows beneath the rose arbor. Emma would wear the lace veil and train Parker's mother had made out of an old tablecloth, while Harold, Parker's aging and affable golden retriever, walked her down the garden path to give her away.

A selection of Barbies, Kens, and Cabbage Patch Kids, along with a variety of stuffed animals lined the path as guests.

"It's a very private ceremony," Parker relayed as she fussed with Emma's veil. "With a small patio reception to follow. Now, where's the best man?"

Laurel, her knee recently skinned, shoved through a trio of

hydrangeas. "He ran away, and went up a tree after a squirrel. I can't get him to come down."

Parker rolled her eyes. "I'll get him. You're not supposed to see the bride before the wedding. It's bad luck. Mac, you need to fix Emma's veil and get her bouquet. Laurel and I'll get Mr. Fish out of the tree."

"I'd rather go swimming," Mac said as she gave Emma's veil an absent tug.

"We can go after I get married."

"I guess. Aren't you tired of getting married?"

"Oh, I don't mind. And it smells so good out here. Everything's so pretty."

Mac gave Emma the clutch of dandelions and wild violets they were allowed to pick. "You look pretty."

It was invariably true. Emma's dark, shiny hair tumbled under the white lace. Her eyes sparkled a deep, deep brown as she sniffed the weed bouquet. She was tanned, sort of all golden, Mac thought, and scowled at her own milk white skin.

The curse of a redhead, her mother said, as she got her carroty hair from her father. At eight, Mac was tall for her age and skinny as a stick, with teeth already trapped in hated braces.

She thought that, beside her, Emmaline looked like a gypsy princess.

Parker and Laurel came back, giggling with the feline best man clutched in Parker's arms. "Everybody has to take their places." Parker poured the cat into Laurel's arms. "Mac, you need to get dressed! Emma—"

"I don't want to be maid of honor." Mac looked at the poofy Cinderella dress draped over a garden bench. "That thing's scratchy, and it's hot. Why can't Mr. Fish be maid of honor, and I'll be best man?"

"Because it's already planned. Everybody's nervous before a wedding." Parker flipped back her long brown pigtails, then picked up the dress to inspect it for tears or stains. Satisfied, she pushed it at Mac. "It's okay. It's going to be a beautiful ceremony, with true love and happy ever after."

"My mother says happy ever after's a bunch of bull."

There was a moment of silence after Mac's statement. The unspoken word *divorce* seemed to hang in the air.

"I don't think it has to be." Her eyes full of sympathy, Parker reached out, ran her hand along Mac's bare arm.

"I don't want to wear the dress. I don't want to be a brides-maid. I—"

"Okay. That's okay. We can have a pretend maid of honor. Maybe you could take pictures."

Mac looked down at the camera she'd forgotten hung around her neck. "They never come out right."

"Maybe they will this time. It'll be fun. You can be the official wedding photographer."

"Take one of me and Mr. Fish," Laurel insisted, and pushed her face and the cat's together. "Take one, Mac!"

With little enthusiasm, Mac lifted the camera, pressed the shutter.

"We should've thought of this before! You can take formal portraits of the bride and groom, and more pictures during the ceremony." Busy with the new idea, Parker hung the Cinder-ella costume on the hydrangea bush. "It'll be good, it'll be fun. You need to go down the path with the bride and Harold. Try to take some good ones. I'll wait, then start the music. Let's go!"

There would be cupcakes and lemonade, Mac reminded herself. And swimming later, and fun. It didn't matter if the pictures were stupid, didn't matter that her grandmother was right and she was too young for the camera.

It didn't matter that her mother was getting divorced again, or that her stepfather, who'd been okay, had already moved out.

It didn't matter that happy ever after was bull, because it was all pretend anyway.

She tried to take pictures of Emma and the obliging Har-old, imagined getting the film back and seeing the blurry fig-ures and smudges of her thumb, like always.

When the music started she felt bad that she hadn't put on the scratchy dress and given Emma a maid of honor, just because her mother and grandmother had put her in a bad mood. So she circled around to stand to the side and tried harder to take a nice picture of Harold walking Emma down the garden path.

It looked different through the lens, she thought, the way

she could focus on Emma's face—the way the veil lay over her hair. And the way the sun shined through the lace was pretty.

She took more pictures as Parker began the "Dearly Beloved" as the Reverend Whistledown, as Emma and Laurel took hands and Harold curled up to sleep and snore at their feet.

She noticed how bright Laurel's hair was, how the sun caught the edges of it beneath the tall black hat she wore as groom. How Mr. Fish's whiskers twitched as he yawned.

When it happened, it happened as much inside Mac as out. Her three friends were grouped under the lush white curve of the arbor, a triangle of pretty young girls. Some instinct had Mac shifting her position, just slightly, tilting the camera just a bit. She didn't know it as composition, only that it looked nicer through the lens.

And the blue butterfly fluttered across her range of vision to land on the head of a butter yellow dandelion in Emma's bouquet. The surprise and pleasure struck the three faces in that triangle under the white roses almost as one.

Mac pressed the shutter.

She knew, *knew*, the photograph wouldn't be blurry and dark or fuzzy and washed out. Her thumb wouldn't be blocking the lens. She knew exactly what the picture would look like, knew her grandmother had been wrong after all.

Maybe happy ever after was bull, but she knew she wanted to take more pictures of moments that *were* happy. Because then they were ever after.

1

On January first, Mac rolled over to smack her alarm clock, and ended up facedown on the floor of her studio.

"Shit. Happy New Year."

She lay, groggy and baffled, until she remembered she'd never made it upstairs into bed—and the alarm was from her computer, set to wake her at noon.

She pushed herself up to stagger to the kitchen and the coffeemaker.

Why did people want to get married on New Year's Eve? Why would they make a formal ritual out of a holiday designed for marathon drinking and probably inappropriate sex? And they just had to drag family and friends into it, not to mention wedding photographers.

Of course, when the reception had finally ended at two a.m., she could've gone to bed like a sane person instead of uploading the shots, reviewing them—spending nearly three more hours on the Hines-Myers wedding photos.

But, boy, she'd gotten some good ones. A few great ones.

Or they were all crap and she'd judged them in a euphoric blur.

No, they were good shots.

She added three spoons of sugar to the black coffee and drank it while standing at the window, looking out at the snow blanketing the gardens and lawns of the Brown Estate.

They'd done a good job on the wedding, she thought. And maybe Bob Hines and Vicky Myers would take a clue from that and do a good job on the marriage.

Either way, the memories of the day wouldn't fade. The moments, big and small, were captured. She'd refine them, finesse them, print them. Bob and Vicky could revisit the day through those images next week or sixty years from next week.

That, she thought, was as potent as sweet, black coffee on a cold winter day.

Opening a cupboard, she pulled out a box of Pop-Tarts and, eating one where she stood, went over her schedule for the day.

Clay-McFearson (Rod and Alison) wedding at six. Which meant the bride and her party would arrive by three, groom and his by four. That gave her until two for the pre-event summit meeting at the main house.

Time enough to shower, dress, go over her notes, check and recheck her equipment. Her last check of the day's weather called for sunny skies, high of thirty-two. She should be able to get some nice preparation shots using natural light and maybe talk Alison—if she was game—into a bridal portrait on the balcony with the snow in the background.

Mother of the bride, Mac remembered—Dorothy (call me Dottie)—was on the pushy and demanding side, but she'd be dealt with. If Mac couldn't handle her personally, God knew Parker would. Parker could and did handle anyone and anything.

Parker's drive and determination had turned Vows into one of the top wedding and event planning companies in the state in a five-year period. It had turned the tragedy of her parents' deaths into hope, and the gorgeous Victorian home and the stunning grounds of the Brown Estate into a thriving and unique business.

And, Mac thought as she swallowed the last of the Pop-Tart, she herself was one of the reasons.

She moved through the studio toward the stairs to her upstairs bed and bath, stopped at one of her favorite photos.

The glowing, ecstatic bride with her face lifted, her arms stretched, palms up, caught in a shower of pink rose petals.

Cover of *Today's Bride*, Mac thought. Because I'm just that good.

In her thick socks, flannel pants, and sweatshirt she climbed the stairs to transform herself from tired, pj-clad, Pop-Tart addict into sophisticated wedding photojournalist.

She ignored her unmade bed—why make it when you were just going to mess it up again?—and the bedroom clutter. The hot shower worked with the sugar and caffeine to clear out any remaining cobwebs so she could put her mind seriously to today's job.

She had a bride who was interested in trying the creative, a passive-aggressive MOB who thought she knew best, a groom so dazzling in love he'd do anything to make his bride happy. And both her B and G were seriously photogenic.

The last fact made the job both pleasure and challenge. Just how could she give her clients a photo journey of their day that was spectacular, and uniquely theirs?

Bride's colors, she thought, flipping through her mental files as she washed her short, shaggy crop of red hair. Silver and gold. Elegant, glamorous.

She'd had a look at the flowers and the cake—both getting their finishing touches today—the favors and linens, attendants' wardrobes, headdresses. She had a copy of the playlist from the band with the first dance, mother-son, father-daughter dances highlighted.

So, she thought, for the next several hours, her world would revolve around Rod and Alison.

She chose her suit, her jewelry, her makeup with nearly the same care as she chose her equipment. Loaded, she went out to make the short trek from the pool house that held her studio and little apartment to the main house.

The snow sparkled, crushed diamonds over ermine, and the air was cold and clean as mountain ice. She definitely had to get some outside shots, daylight and evening. Winter wedding, white wedding, snow on the ground, ice glistening on the trees, just dripping from the denuded willows over the pond. And there the fanciful old Victorian with its myriad rooflines, the arched and porthole windows, rising and spreading, soft blue against the hard shell of sky. Its terraces and generous portico heralded the season with their festoons of lights and greenery.

She studied it as she often did as she walked the shoveled paths. She loved the lines of it, the angles of it, with its subtle touches of pale yellow, creamy white picked out in that soft, subtle blue.

It had been as much home to her as her own growing up. Often more so, she admitted, as her own had run on her mother's capricious whims. Parker's parents had been warm, welcoming, loving and—Mac thought now—steady. They'd given her a calm port in the storm of her own childhood.

She'd grieved as much as her friend at their loss nearly seven years before.

Now the Brown Estate was her home. Her business. Her life. And a good one on every level. What could be better than doing something you loved, and doing it with the best friends you'd ever had?

She went in through the mudroom to hang up her outdoor gear, then circled around to peek into Laurel's domain.

Her friend and partner stood on a step stool, meticulously adding silver calla lilies to the five tiers of a wedding cake. Each flower bloomed at the base of a gold acanthus leaf to glimmering, elegant effect.

"That's a winner, McBane."

Laurel's hand was steady as a surgeon's as she added the next lily. Her sunny hair was twisted at the back of her head into a messy knot that somehow suited the angular triangle of her face. As she worked, her eyes, bright as bluebells, held narrowed concentration.

"I'm so glad she went for the lily centerpiece instead of the bride and groom topper. It makes this design. Wait until we get to the Ballroom and add it."

Mac pulled out a camera. "It's a good shot for the website. Okay?"

"Sure. Get any sleep?"

"Didn't hit until about five, but I stayed down till noon. You?"

"Down by two thirty. Up at seven to finish the groom's cake, the desserts—and this. I'm so damn glad we have two weeks before the next wedding." She glanced over. "Don't tell Parker I said that."

"She's up, I assume."

"She's been in here twice. She's probably been everywhere twice. I think I heard Emma come in. They may be up in the office by now."

"I'm heading up. Are you coming?"

"Ten minutes. I'll be on time."

"On time is late in Parker's world." Mac grinned. "I'll try to distract her."

"Just tell her some things can't be rushed. And that the MOB's going to get so many compliments on this cake she'll stay off our backs."

"That one could work."

Mac started out, winding through to check the entrance foyer and the massive Drawing Room where the ceremony itself would take place. Emmaline and her elves had already been at work, she noted, undressing from the last wedding, redressing for the new. Every bride had her own vision, and this one wanted lots of gold and silver ribbon and swag as opposed to the lavender and cream voile of New Year's Eve.

The fire was set in the drawing room and would be lit before the guests began to arrive. White-draped chairs sparkling with silver bows formed row after row. Emma had already dressed the mantel with gold candles in silver holders, and the bride's favorite white calla lilies massed in tall, thin glass vases.

Mac circled the room, considered angles, lighting, composition—and made more notes as she walked out and took the stairs to the third floor.

As she expected, she found Parker in the conference room of their office, surrounded by her laptop, BlackBerry, folders, cell phone, and headset. Her dense brown hair hung in a long tail—sleek and simple. It worked with the suit—a quiet dove gray—that would blend in and complement the bride's colors.

Parker missed no tricks.

She didn't look up but circled a finger in the air as she continued to work on the laptop. Knowing the signal, Mac crossed to the coffee counter and filled mugs for both of them. She sat, laid down her own file, opened her own notebook.

Parker sat back, smiled, and picked up her mug. "It's going to be a good one."

"No doubt."

"Roads are clear, weather's good. The bride's up, had breakfast and a massage. The groom's had a workout and a swim. Caterers are on schedule. All attendants are accounted for." She checked her watch. "Where are Emma and Laurel?"

"Laurel's putting the finishing touches on the cake, which is stupendous. I haven't seen Emma, but she's started dressing the event areas. Pretty. I want some outdoor shots. Before and after."

"Don't keep the bride outside for too long before. We don't want her red-nosed and sniffling."

"You may have to keep the MOB off my back."

"Already noted."

Emma rushed in, a Diet Coke in one hand, a file in the other. "Tink's hungover and a no-show, so I'm one short. Let's keep this brief, okay?" She dropped down at the table. Her curling black hair bounced over the shoulders of her sweatshirt. "The Bride's Suite and the Drawing Room are dressed. Foyer and stairway, nearly finished. The bouquets, corsages, and boutonnieres checked. We've started on the Grand Hall and the Ballroom. I need to get back to that."

"Flower girl?"

"White rose pomander, silver and gold ribbon. I have her halo—roses and baby's breath—ready for the hairdresser. It's adorable. Mac, I need some pictures of the arrangements if you can fit it in. If not, I'll get them."

"I'll take care of it."

"Thanks. The MOB—"

"I'm on it," Parker said.

"I need to—" Emma broke off as Laurel walked in.

"I'm not late," Laurel announced.

"Tink's a no-show," Parker told her. "Emma's short."

"I can fill in. I'll need to set the centerpiece of the cake and arrange the desserts, but I've got time now."

"Let's go over the timetable."

"Wait." Emma lifted her can of Diet Coke. "Toast first. Happy New Year to us, to four amazing, stupendous, and very hot women. Best pals ever."

"Also smart and kick-ass." Laurel raised her bottle of water. "To pals and partners."

"To us. Friendship and brains in four parts," Mac added, "and the sheer coolness of the whole we've made with Vows."

"And to 2009." Parker lifted her coffee mug. "The amazing, stupendous, hot, smart, kick-ass best pals are going to have their best year ever."

"Damn right." Mac clinked her mug to the rest. "To Wedding Day, then, now, and always."

"Then, now, and always," Parker repeated. "And now. Timetable?"

"I'm on the bride," Mac began, "from her arrival, switch to groom at his. Candids during dressing event, posed as applies. Formal portraits in and out. I'll get the shots of the cake, the arrangements now, do my setup. All family and wedding party shots separate prior to the ceremony. Post-ceremony I should only need forty-five minutes for the family shots, full wedding party, and the bride and groom."

"Floral dressing in bride and groom suites complete by three. Floral dressing in foyer, Parlor, staircase, Grand Hall, and Ballroom by five." Parker glanced at Emma.

"We'll be done."

"Videographer arrives at five thirty. Guest arrivals from five thirty to six. Wedding musicians—string quartet—to begin at five forty. The band will be set up in the Ballroom by six thirty. MOG, attended by son, escorted at five fifty, MOB, escorted by son-in-law, directly after. Groom and groomsmen in place at six." Parker read off the schedule. "FOB, bride, and party in place at six. Descent and procession. Ceremony duration twenty-three minutes, recession, family moments. Guests escorted to Grand Hall at six twenty-five."

"Bar opens," Laurel said, "music, passed food."

"Six twenty-five to seven ten, photographs. Announcement of family, wedding party, and the new Mr. and Mrs. seven fifteen."

"Dinner, toasts," Emma continued. "We've got it, Parks."

"I want to make sure we move to the Ballroom and have the first dance by eight fifteen," Parker continued. "The bride especially wants her grandmother there for the first dance, and after the father-daughter, mother-son dance, for her father and his mother to dance. She's ninety, and may fade early. If we can have the cake cutting at nine thirty, the grandmother should make that, too."

"She's a sweetheart," Mac put in. "I got some nice shots of her and Alison at the rehearsal. I've got it in my notes to get some of them today. Personally, I think she'll stay for the whole deal."

"I hope she does. Cake and desserts served while dancing continues. Bouquet toss at ten fifteen."

"Tossing bouquet is set," Emma added.

"Garter toss, dancing continues. Last dance at ten fifty, bubble blowing, bride and groom depart. Event end, eleven." Parker checked her watch again. "Let's get it done. Emma and Laurel need to change. Everyone remember their headsets."

Parker's phone vibrated, and she glanced at the readout. "MOB. Again. Fourth call this morning."

"Have fun with that," Mac said, and escaped.

She scouted room by room, staying out of the way of Emma and her crew as they swarmed over the house with flowers, ribbons, voile. She took shots of Laurel's cake, Emma's arrangements, framed others in her head.

It was a routine she never allowed to become routine. She knew once it became rote, she'd miss shots, opportunities, bog down on fresh angles and ideas. And whenever she felt herself dulling, she thought of a blue butterfly landing on a dandelion.

The air smelled of roses and lilies and rang with voices and footfalls. Light streamed through the tall windows in lovely beams and shafts, and glittered on the gold and silver ribbons.

"Headset, Mac!" Parker rushed down the main staircase. "The bride's arriving."

As Parker hurried down to meet the bride, Mac jogged up. She swung out on the front terrace, ignoring the cold as the white limo sailed down the drive. As it eased to a stop she shifted her angle, set, and waited.

Maid of honor, mother of the bride. "Move, move, just a little," she muttered. Alison stepped out. The bride wore jeans, Uggs, a battered suede jacket, and a bright red scarf. Mac zoomed in, changed stops. "Hey! Alison!"

The bride looked up. Surprise turned to amused delight,

and to Mac's pleasure, Alison threw up both arms, tossed back her head, and laughed.

And there, Mac thought as she caught the moment, was the beginning of the journey.

Within ten minutes, the Bride's Suite—once Parker's own bedroom—bustled with people and confusion. Two hairdressers plied their tools and talents, curling, straightening, styling, while others wielded paints and pots.

Utterly female, Mac thought as she moved through the room unobtrusively, the scents, the motions, the sounds. The bride remained the focus—no nerves on this one, Mac determined. Alison was confident, beaming, and currently chattering like a magpie.

The MOB, however, was a different story.

"But you have such beautiful hair! Don't you think you should leave it down? At least some of it. Maybe—"

"An updo suits the headdress better. Relax, Mom."

"It's too warm in here. I think it's too warm in here. And Mandy should take a quick nap. She's going to act up, I just know it."

"She'll be fine." Alison glanced toward the flower girl.

"I really think—"

"Ladies!" Parker wheeled in a cart of champagne, with a pretty fruit and cheese tray. "The men are on their way. Alison, your hair's gorgeous. Absolutely regal." She poured a flute, offered it to the bride.

"I really don't think she should drink before the ceremony. She barely ate today, and—"

"Oh, Mrs. McFearson, I'm so glad you're dressed and ready. You look fabulous. If I could just steal you for a few minutes? I'd love for you to take a look at the Drawing Room before the ceremony. We want to make sure it's perfect, don't we? I'll have her back in no time." Parker pushed champagne into the MOB's hand, and steered her out of the room.

Alison said, "Whew!" and laughed.

For the next hour, Mac split herself between the Bride's and Groom's suites. Between perfume and tulle, cuff links and cummerbunds. She eased back into the bride's domain, circled around the attendants as they dressed and helped one another dress. And found Alison alone, standing in front of her wedding dress.

It was all there, Mac thought as she quietly framed the shot. The wonder, the joy—with just that tiny tug of sorrow. She snapped the image as Alison reached out to brush her fingers over the sparkle of the bodice.

Decisive moment, Mac knew, when everything the woman felt reflected on her face.

Then it passed, and Alison glanced over.

"I didn't expect to feel this way. I'm so happy. I'm so in love with Rod, so ready to marry him. But there's this little clutch right here." She rubbed her fingers just above her heart. "It's not nerves."

"Sadness. Just a touch. One phase of your life ends today. You're allowed to be sad to say good-bye. I know what you need. Wait here."

A moment later, Mac led Alison's grandmother over. And once again stepped back.

Youth and age, she thought. Beginnings and endings, connections and constancy. And, love.

She snapped the embrace, but that wasn't it. She snapped the glitter of tears, and still, no. Then Alison lowered her forehead to her grandmother's, and even as her lips curved, a single tear slid down her cheek while the dress glowed and glittered behind them.

Perfect. The blue butterfly.

She took candids of the ritual while the bride dressed, then the formal portraits with exquisite natural light. As she'd expected, Alison was game to brave the cold on the terrace.

And Mac ignored Parker's voice through her headset as she rushed to the Groom's Suite to repeat the process with Rod.

She passed Parker in the hallway as she strode back to the bride. "I need the groom and party downstairs, Mac. We're running two minutes behind."

"Oh my God!" Mac said in mock horror and ducked into the Bride's Suite.

"Guests are seated," Parker announced in her ear moments later. "Groom and groomsmen taking position. Emma, gather the bridal party."

"On it."

Mac slipped out to take her stand at the bottom of the stairs as Emma organized the bridesmaids.

"Party ready. Cue the music."

"Cuing music," Parker said, "start the procession."

The flower girl would clearly be fine without the nap, Mac decided as the child nearly danced her way down the staircase. She paused like a vet at Laurel's signal, then continued at a dignified pace in her fairy dress across the foyer, into the enormous Parlor, and down the aisle formed by the chairs.

The attendants followed, shimmering silver, and at last, the maid of honor in gold.

Mac crouched to aim up as the bride and her father stood at the top of the stairs, holding hands. As the bride's music swelled, he lifted his daughter's hand to his lips, then to his cheek.

Even as she took the shot, Mac's eyes stung.

Where was her own father? she wondered. Jamaica? Switzerland? Cairo?

She pushed the thought and the ache that came with it aside, and did her job.

Using Emma's candlelight, she captured joy and tears. The memories. And stayed invisible and separate.

Penguin Group (USA) Inc. is proud to continue the fight against breast cancer by encouraging our readers to "Read Pink®."

read pink®

Penguin Group (USA) Inc. is proud to join the fight against breast cancer.

In support of **Breast Cancer Awareness** month, we are proud to offer eight of our bestselling mass-market paperback titles by some of our most beloved female authors.

Participating authors are Jodi Thomas, Carly Phillips, JoAnn Ross, Karen Rose, Catherine Anderson, Kate Jacobs, LuAnn McLane, and Nora Roberts. These special editions feature **Read Pink** seals on their covers conveying our support of this cause and urging our readers to become actively involved in supporting The Breast Cancer Research Foundation.

Penguin Group (USA) Inc. is proud to present a $25,000 donation (regardless of book sales) to the following nonprofit organization in support of its extraordinary progress in breast cancer research:

The Breast Cancer Research Foundation®

Join us in the fight against this deadly disease by making your own donation to this organization today.

∞

How to support breast cancer research:

To make a tax-deductible donation online to The Breast Cancer Research Foundation you can visit: www.bcrfcure.org

You can also call their toll-free number, **1-866-FIND-A-CURE (346-3228)**, anytime between 9 A.M. and 5 P.M. EST, Monday through Friday. To donate by check or a U.S. money order, make payable and mail to:

The Breast Cancer Research Foundation, 60 East 56th Street, 8th floor, New York, NY 10022

About The Breast Cancer Research Foundation®
www.bcrfcure.org

The Breast Cancer Research Foundation® (BCRF) was founded by Evelyn H. Lauder in 1993, to advance the most promising breast cancer research that will help lead to prevention and a cure in our lifetime. The Foundation supports scientists at top universities and academic medical centers worldwide. If not for BCRF, many facts about the genetic basis of breast cancer would not be known, the link between exercise, nutrition and breast cancer risk would not be established, and the rate of mortalities would not continue its downward curve. BCRF-funded scientists are responsible for these and many other critical achievements.

If you would like to learn more about risk factors, visit www.penguin.com/readpink.
Read Pink® today and help save lives!

Read Pink is a registered trademark and service mark of Penguin Group (USA) Inc.

M742JV0513

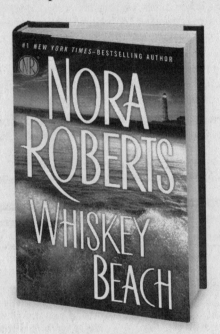